THE BLACK FLEMINGS

THE BLACK FLEMINGS

KATHLEEN NORRIS

WILDSIDE PRESS

Originally published in 1924.
Published by Wildside Press LLC.
wildsidpress.com

CHAPTER I

ONCE through the dark old iron gates, he seemed to have left the warm and friendly autumn day, the warm and friendly world, behind him.

David Fleming laughed half aloud at the fancy and stepped back into the rambling country road, where wheel tracks were so quickly obliterated in the loose-drifting sand, to contrast once more, for his own amusement, the peaceful dreaming landscape in the afternoon sunlight and the sinister shadows of Wastewater.

Five miles away along the rugged coast lay Crowchester, the little fishing village whose activities tinged the fresh salty air, even here, with the odour of salted fish. Between Crowchester and Wastewater, beside whose forbidding great gates he stood, ran the irregular road, rising through dunes, skirting wind-twisted groves of pine and fir, disappearing into ragged hollows to emerge again on turfy bluffs, and finally winding in here toward the old brick house that lay hidden behind these high walls.

On his right lay the shore, rocky, steep, rough, with pebbles complaining as the tide dragged them to and fro, surf hammering restlessly among the rocks or brimming and ebbing with tireless regularity over the scooped stone of the pools. No two inches of it, no two drops of its immensity ever the same; it held him now, as it had held him for so many hours in his very babyhood, in a sort of tranced contemplation.

The sun was setting in angry red beyond the forest behind him, but a hard and brilliant light still lay on the water, and the waves were sculptured harshly in silver-tipped steel. Where the old brick wall of Wastewater descended to the shore enough sand had been stored in the lee of the wall to form a triangular strip of beach, and here scurfy suds were eddying lazily, hemmed back from the tide by a great jammed log and only stirred now and then by a fringe of the surf, which formed new bubbles even while it pricked the old.

On the sharp irregular fall of the cliff, distorted, wind-blown pines and tight-woven mallows clung, with the hardy smaller growths of the seaside: blown blue lupin, coarse sedge and furzy grasses, yellow-topped odorous sage and dry fennel. About their exposed, tenaciously clinging roots was tangled all the litter of the sea: ropes, slender logs as white and bare as old bones, seaweeds, and cocoanut shells.

David breathed the salty, murmuring air, faintly scented with fish, looked back once more toward the shining roofs and the rising faint plumes of smoke above Crowchester, shrugged his shoulders with a philosophic laugh, and turned again toward Wastewater's gates.

These were four: two great wrought-iron wings in the centre, where carriages had once entered and departed, and, designed ingeniously in the same enormous framework, two smaller gates, one on each side, for foot passengers.

The carriage gates had been closed for years and were bedded deep in dry grass and fallen leaves, and the right-hand smaller gate had perhaps not been opened three times in its more than one hundred years' existence. But the left-hand gate stood slightly ajar, and beyond it ran a faintly outlined footpath into a deep old garden. The whole elaborate structure, met by the mossy brick wall on both sides, was thick with rust, its scrolls and twisted bars shone brickred in the last of the sunlight.

David had walked briskly from the village and his blood was moving rapidly, but he shivered as the familiar atmosphere once more enveloped him. Once again the dilapidated, stately old garden with its bottle-edged flower beds, where the ragged rose bushes were already showing red and yellow hips, where the pines were shedding their slippery needles, and where the maples and elms looked tattered and forlorn.

The place had been thickly planted almost two hundred years ago; it was densely overgrown now; the trees crowded each other, and the growth underneath them was sickly. The old path was spongy with wet leaves underfoot, and the air so pungent with their sharp odour as to be almost anæsthetic. Between the blackened trunks on the right David could again see the serenely moving, deeply breathing surface of the ocean, but now the garden and low cliffs shut off the shore.

On all other sides lay the garden and the thicket of the plantation through which presently, after some winding, he came upon Wastewater Hall itself, standing up boldly in the twilight gloom. The last dying fires of the sunset, burning through black tree trunks behind it, seemed only to make darker than ever the outlines of the great dark red brick house, three-storied and with a steep mansard as well, its uncompromising bulk enhanced rather than softened by a thickly wooded coat of black ivy.

It was an enormous old Georgian building, impressive for size if for nothing more. Wastewater's twenty acres stood on a sharply jutting point of cliff, and the house faced the sea on three sides; the garden was shut off from the road by the long western wall. Immediately back of the kitchen and stable yards there was a rear gate, buried in shrubbery and quite out of sight from the house, for delivery wagons and tradespeople.

The main entrance was on the eastern front, facing straight out to sea, but this presented now only rows of shuttered windows and stone steps deep in fallen leaves, and David stopped instead at the stone steps of the columned side door. Leaves had littered the paths and lay thick upon the struggling grass of the rose beds, but these three steps had been swept clean, their dried surfaces still showing the marks of a wet broom.

David, absorbing the details with the eye of one who perhaps is reluctant to see confirmed previous impressions or fears, shrugged again, made a little face between impatience, amusement, and misgiving, and gave the old-fashioned iron bell-pull a vigorous jerk.

Then came a long wait. But he did not ring again. The first fifteen of David's thirty-one years had been spent here, within these grave old walls, and he knew exactly what was happening now inside.

The jerk on the brass-handled wire would set into convulsive motion one of a row of precariously balanced bells far down in the enormous stone-floored kitchen. Most of these bells had not been rung for two generations at least. They were connected with the bedrooms and the study—it had been a long time since any resident of Wastewater had felt it necessary to summon a servant to bedrooms or study. In the row, David remembered, were also the front-door bell, dining-room bell, and the side-door bell. He began to wonder if the last were broken.

No, someone was coming. He could not possibly have heard steps behind that massive and impenetrable door, but he assuredly sensed a motion there, stirring, creaking, the distant bang of another door.

Then another wait, not so long. And at last the door was carefully opened by Hedda, who looked casually at him with squinting old white-lashed eyes, looked back in concern at her bars and bolts, closed the door behind him, and then said in a mild old voice in which traces of her Belgian origin lingered:

"Good. How is Mister David?"

"Splendid," David answered, with a heartiness that the chill of the dark old hall already tinged with a certain familiar depression. "Where's my aunt, Hedda?"

Hedda had been staring at him with a complacent, vacuous smile, like the slightly demented creature she really was. Now she roused herself just a shade and answered in a slightly reproachful voice:

"Where but upstairs shall she be?"

David remembered now that Gabrielle had long ago announced, with her precocious little-girl powers of observation, that "Hedda always tells us things the first time as if it were the twentieth, and her patience quite worn out with telling us!" An affectionate half smile twitched the corners of David's mouth as he thought of that old tawny-headed, rebellious little Gabrielle of ten years before, and he followed the smile with as sudden a sigh.

He mounted gloomy, wide old stairs through whose enormous western windows a dim light was struggling. The treads were covered with a dark carpet strapped in brass rods. Gabrielle, as a baby, had loved the top-shaped ends of these rods, had stolen them, been detected, restored them, how many, many times!

The thought of her more than the thought of his old little self, of Tom and Sylvia, who were the real Flemings, after all, always came to him strangely when he first returned to the old house after any absence. Gabrielle, shouting, roaring, weeping, laughing, had roused more echoes in Wastewater than all the rest of them put together; she roused more echoes now, poor little Gabrielle!

Poor Gabrielle, and poor Tom! mused David. Life had dealt oddly with both these long-ago, eager, happy children, as Life seemed to have a fashion of dealing with the children of so strange and silent, so haunted and mysterious an old house. The shadow of the house, as real upon his spirit as was the actual shadow of the autumn twilight upon these stained old walls, shut heavily upon David as he crossed the upper hallways and turned the knob of the sitting-room door.

His aunt, in the widow's black she had worn for some eighteen years, was sitting erect in an upholstered armchair by the fire. She turned to glance toward him as he came in and welcomed him with a lifeless cheek to kiss and with the warmest smile her face ever knew.

It was not very warm; Flora Fleming had the black colouring of the clan; her look was always heavy, almost forbidding. She was in the middle fifties now; there was a heavy threading of gray in her looped, oily dark hair. Her skin was dark and the rough heavy eyebrows almost met above her sharply watchful eyes. There were black hairs at the corners of her lips and against her ears below her temples; her eyes were set a shade too close together, her teeth were slightly yellowed, too prominent, and rested upon her bitten lower lip. She wore, as always, a decent handsome silk that seemed never old and never new; there was a heavy book in her knuckly, nervous hands, and David noted for the first time to-day a discoloured vein or two in her somewhat florid, long face.

"This is good of you, David," she said, dispassionately, putting her glasses into her book and laying it aside.

"Didn't wake you from a nap?" David said, glad to sit down after his brisk walk.

"A nap?" She dismissed it with a quiet, not quite pleased smile. "Since when have I had that weakness?" she asked. "No. On an afternoon like this, with the leaves falling, one hears the wind about Wastewater if it blows nowhere else, and the sea. I can never nap in the afternoons. I hear—voices," she finished, as if half to herself.

"Lord, one realizes how lonely the old place is, coming back to it!" David said, cheerfully.

"Not for me," his aunt again corrected him in her quiet voice that seemed full of autumnal reveries and the quiet falling of leaves itself. "Other places are lonely. Not this."

"Well, it's extremely nice to know that you feel so," David pursued, resolutely combating the creeping quiet, the something that was almost depression, always ready to come out of musty corners and capture one here. "But when the girls are home we'll have some young life at Wastewater, and then—when they marry, you'll have to move yourself into brighter quarters—into a city apartment, perhaps!"

"When they marry?" she repeated, slightly stressing the pronoun.

"As I suppose they will?" David elucidated, looking up.

"They?"

"Sylvia—and Gabrielle, too!" he reminded her.

"Oh, Gabrielle?" She repeated the name quietly. "To be sure, she will marry," she said, musingly. "But I can hardly feel that quite as much my affair as Sylvia's future, David," she finished, mildly.

"Daughter and niece!" David summarized it. "Sylvia rich and Gabrielle penniless, but both young and both our girls!"

"I can't see it quite that way," Mrs. Fleming said, thoughtfully, after a pause. "Gabrielle gets here to-night—you knew that?"

"That's what brings me," he answered. "I thought perhaps you would like me to meet her in Boston, bring her home?"

"I wired in answer to the Mother Superior's wire," Flora said, "that she was quite capable of making the journey herself. She should be here at about eight to-night. She is eighteen, David. There is no necessity of making a child of her!"

9

"No," he conceded, good-humouredly. "But it might seem a little warmer welcome. I'll go in to Crowchester for her, at least. After all, we've not seen her for years—for more than two years! When I was in Paris—when Jim Rucker and I were on our way to Spain—it was midsummer, and she and some of the other girls and nuns were in Normandy. I shall be glad to see her again."

"I wish," said Mrs. Fleming, slowly, "that I could say as much. But her return brings it all up again, David. I shall do all I can for her, try my best to place her well. But when I think of my delicate little sister," Flora rushed on, in a voice suddenly shaking, "and of her giving her life for this unwelcome child—the old bitterness rises up in me——!"

She stopped as if she were choking, and with set lips and inflated nostrils sat breathing quickly and looking into the fire, shaken by the painful agitation of a passion usually suppressed.

"I know. I know," David, who came nearer than any one else in the world to intimacy with this woman, said soothingly. "But it wasn't Gabrielle's fault that poor little Aunt Lily made a stupid marriage with a—what was he? A travelling agent? Surely—surely, if you loved Aunt Lily, you can make up all the sorrow and shame of it to Gabrielle! There was—there *was* a marriage there, Aunt Flora?" David added, with a keen look up from his own finely shaped hands, now linked and hanging between his knees as he sat forward in his low chair.

"Between Lily and Charpentier? Certainly!" she answered, sharply. And suspiciously she added: "What makes you ask that?"

"It has sometimes gone through my head that there might not have been—that that might account for her despair and her death," David suggested. "Not that it matters much," he added, more briskly. "What matters is that here we have Gabrielle, a young thing of eighteen, apparently all over her early frailness and delicateness—at least, I gather so?" he interrupted himself to ask, with another upward glance.

"The Superior writes that she is in perfect health."

"Good. So here we have Gabrielle," resumed David, "eighteen, finished off most satisfactorily by almost eight years with the good Sisters and with two post-graduate years in the Paris convent—discovered not to have a vocation——"

"Which I profoundly hoped she would have!" put in Flora, forcefully.

"Oh, come, Aunt Flora—the poor little thing! Why should she be a religious if she doesn't want to? After all, she's your sister's child and your own Sylvia's cousin—give her a chance!" David pleaded, good-naturedly.

Flora looked at him temperately, patiently.

"But of course I shall give her a chance, David!" she said, quietly. "She will unquestionably have some plan for herself. I shall see that it is helped, if it is reasonable. But in the old days," Flora added, "she was treated exactly as a child of the house. She must not expect that now. There have been changes since then, David. Poor Tom's loss, Roger's death—poor Mamma's death——"

She was silent. David, staring thoughtfully into the fire, was silent, too. The strangely repressive influence of the twilight, the old room, the cold, reminiscent voice that somehow rang of the tomb, the autumn winds beginning to whine softly about the old house, and beyond and above and through all sounds the quiet steady suck and rising rush of the sea, the scream of little pebbles beneath the shrill fine crying of gulls in the dusk, had taken possession of his spirit again. Something mysterious, unhappy about it all—something especially so about Flora—was oppressing him once more.

But why? David asked himself, angrily. Here was a widowed woman, living in an old house only a few miles from the very heart of civilization, contented with her solitude, yet counting the hours until her idolized daughter's return to Wastewater for the summer months; conscientious in the discharge of her duty where Gabrielle, her sister's motherless little girl, was concerned, spending her days peacefully among servants and flowers, books and memories.

Many and many another elderly woman lived so. What was there so strangely disturbing, so almost menacing about this one? He did not know. He told himself impatiently now that it was only because she was his kinswoman that she had power to make him so uneasy; this was, in short, the disadvantage of knowing her so well.

"The girls will brighten you up!" he remarked, hopefully.

"Perhaps," his aunt answered, forbiddingly. And again there was silence, and presently Mrs. Fleming went away, with some murmur of dinner.

Left alone, David glanced about the familiar room, whose every detail had been just as it was now in all the days he could remember. It was a large room with rep-curtained bays on two sides. The furniture was all dark and heavy, sixty, seventy years old. Carved walnut, oak, horsehair, heavy-fringed upholstery, stiffly laundered antimacassars, bookcases whose glass doors mirrored the room, gas jets on heavy black-and-gilt brass arms.

A hanging lamp was lowered over the centre table, where albums and gift books, shells and vases were neatly ranged upon a mat of Berlin wool. A coal fire was smoking sulkily in the steel-rodded grate; the mantelpiece was of brown marble flanked with columns of shining black; the mantelshelf bore another fringed specimen of Berlin wool work and was decorated by a solid black marble clock with gilt horses mounting it in a mad scramble; two beautiful great Sèvres vases of blue china wreathed with white roses and filled with dry teazels, some small photographs in tarnished metal frames, and several smaller articles: Turkish and Chinese boxes, Japanese lacquer ash trays, and a tiny Dresden couple.

There were what-nots in two corners, with their flights of graded and scalloped shelves similarly loaded; here were more photographs, more gift books, a row of lichen owls on a strip of stiff silvery lichen, small specimens of Swiss wood-carving and cloisonné, a china clock that had not moved its hands in all of David's lifetime, a teacup or two, a vial of sand from the banks of the Jordan, a bowl of Indian brass filled with coloured pebbles, bits of branched coral, goldstone, a chain of Indian beads, and some Aztec pottery in rich brick-brown and painted stripes.

On the walls were dark old paintings, engravings, and woodcuts in heavy frames, interspersed here and there with rubbishy later contributions: "A Yard of Roses" in a white-and-gilt mat and frame, and a coloured photograph of ladies and children, too sickeningly pretty, in high-belted empire gowns and curls, dancing to the music of a spinet.

The only notable thing among all these was a life-size study that hung above the mantel: the portrait in oil of a man of perhaps thirty or thirty-five. David ended his inspection with a long look at it, and his thoughts went to its subject.

CHAPTER II

THIS was Black Roger, who had been master here at Wastewater all the days of his stormy and brilliant life. The face at which David was staring now so thoughtfully had been one of the handsomest of its generation. When Roger Fleming, arrogant, young, rich, had posed for this picture, now a whole third of a century ago, the world had been at his feet.

What a different world it had been, mused David; a world without an electric light or bell or street car to disturb it—without a moving picture or an automobile! But Roger Fleming, this exquisite, negligently smiling gentleman pictured with the bay horse and the slim greyhound, had missed none of these things from his crowded life. He had had wealth and beauty, travel, books, he had inherited Wastewater, and women—women had always been but too kind to him!

His first wife, Janet Fleming, the widow of a distant relative, had come first to Wastewater about thirty years before. Janet was then twenty-two, weeping, helpless, alone—unless the four-weeks-old baby in her arms might be considered a companion. This baby had been David himself, fatherless since five months before his birth. Exactly seven weeks after her tearful and black-swathed arrival in the house of her kinsman, Janet, David's young mother, had married Black Roger Fleming of Wastewater.

There had been quite a houseful of relatives, all more or less distant, there to receive her, for in the comfortable fashion of a past day the rich young heir of Wastewater had felt himself responsible for his less fortunate kin, especially his women kin; and more than that, it had suited his somewhat feudal ideas of hospitality to gather the entire clan about his big dining table.

So David's mother had found Roger with a stately, withered little gray-headed second cousin—his uncle's widowed daughter-in-law—"Aunt John," keeping house for him, and assisting her a dark-eyed, vivacious daughter named Flora, and a smaller, more delicate, and timid daughter, Lily—third cousins, if relationships were to be traced. And besides these there was Roger's younger brother, Will, a sweet, idle, endearing ne'er-do-well, who was supposedly studying law with a Boston firm, and who was actually doing nothing at all except enjoy life as an irresponsible junior.

Roger's marriage made small difference in the others' lives; David, whose memory began a few years after this, indeed could remember them all, living along comfortably in the big house. He remembered his dark-eyed, animated mother, who shortly after marrying Roger had had another boy baby in her arms; he remembered "Aunt John," who managed the house and ruled the children and servants; Aunt Flora, watchful and jealous and sharp-tongued; Uncle Will, idle and laughing; Aunt Lily, small and delicate, reading Tennyson and singing "In Old Madrid" at the square piano; remembered his own splendid, rollicking baby half-brother Tom, and remembered above all Roger himself, still handsome, superb, riding his horses along the cliffs all about, driving splendid bays in an open barouche, carrying off the boys' mother to hear Irving's "Thomas à Becket" or Rostand's "L'Aiglon" in Boston.

A veritable horde of servants kept this big household comfortable—butlers, gardeners, a coachman, a stable boy, fat cooks in the kitchen, whispering maids in the upper halls, and almost always a comfortable middle-aged housekeeping person who conferred constantly with old "Aunt John" and haggled with fruit peddlers at the gate in the sandy back lane.

This staff of domestics was lessened now, although there were still a butler and half-a-dozen underlings. But there had been other changes more important at Wastewater.

First, when David was six and little Tom Fleming five years old, their mother had died. Afterward, the boys had been packed off to boarding school and had been there when they heard of another death at home, this time of old "Aunt John."

But Flora and Lily and Will continued to live there with Roger, and it was only a few months after their mother's death that Flora, between a frown and a smile, had told them that she was shortly to take that mother's place: she and Roger were to be married as soon as his year of mourning was over.

This had not deeply impressed the little boys; they cared little what their elders did, and had it not been that a new figure had immediately come upon the scene, David thought, long afterward, that he might easily have believed himself to have dreamed Flora's announcement.

But a new figure did come, among the many friends and relatives who were always drifting through Wastewater, the figure of a certain handsome, sensible blonde Mrs. Kent, from Montreal, merely visiting Roger on her way back home, and with her, her little daughter Cecily, fresh from a Baltimore school. Cecily had been seventeen then, dark, fragile, flower-like. She was merely a child, going home to her father and little brother and stopping to visit a friend of Mamma's on the way.

Roger was in the early forties at this time—actually older than Cecily's mother, whom he had known as a girl, in Boston. But six days after their arrival at Wastewater Cecily ran away with him and they were married.

David remembered all this well, the uproar in the house, Flora's loud voice, Lily crying loudly, Mrs. Kent fainting and sobbing. Lily and Flora came to their senses because they had no choice, and settled down to keeping house for the white-faced little bride, but Mrs. Kent never forgave her daughter or spoke to her again. It was at about this time that Flora quietly married Will Fleming; married him, David knew now, because she could not marry his brother.

Then came sad, sad years to Wastewater, years that sobered the dashing master of the house for the first time in his life. For it became evident from the first that the new Mrs. Fleming would not bear her title long. The city doctors, one after the other, gave her illness the name of a lingering and incurable malady, but Cecily herself knew, and perhaps Roger knew, that it was youth—youth forced too soon into the realities of loneliness, responsibility, passion, and fear—that was really killing her.

Placid, uncomplaining, sweet, Cecily lay on a couch for months and months, sometimes worse, sometimes so much better that she could walk slowly up and down the garden paths above the sea on Roger's arm. Aunt Flora, David remembered, had been living in Boston then, where Uncle Will had some temporary position, but Flora came back to Wastewater for the long vacation, bringing with her her own baby, the lovely black-eyed girl that was Sylvia; "even then the little thing was as proud as Lucifer himself!" thought David, reaching this point in his recollections with a smile.

Flora and her tearful little sister Lily and the baby did not go back to Boston in the winter; they would join Will "later on after Cecily's operation," they said. And even David knew that "later on" might be only when Cecily was dead. He and Tom went back to school in September, and neither ever saw Cecily again; he and Tom had played late in the clear twilight, along the shore, their new school suits had been laid neatly upon their beds when they came into the close, stuffy house, and their valises packed capably by Aunt Flora.

Cecily had been lying on a big couch by the fire; David sat on a low tuffet beside her and held her hand with all the heartache of an inarticulate fifteen-year-old before a tragedy he may not share. Lily, who had been strangely pretty and gay of late, was at the piano, sometimes singing, sometimes murmuring with Roger, who was leaning above her. Sylvia, three years old, was running back and forth in the pleasant soft light that shimmered with the reflected motion of the sunset on the sea.

That was the last of domestic peace and happiness at Wastewater for a long time. For it was only a week after that that young Tom ran away from school, and Roger was dragged from the bedside of his wife, just facing another operation, to go in search of his boy.

Tom, a sturdy, self-confident boy, now past fourteen, had indeed often threatened this; he was no student; his only books were sea tales; his one thought was of the open sea. He had picked up enough sea talk in Keyport, the straggling village of fishermen's huts halfway between Crowchester and Wastewater, to pass for a sailor anywhere; he left for his father a smudged and misspelt but unmistakably gay letter, assuring him that he would be back by Christmas, anyway, and love to everybody, and tell Sylvia that he would bring her a doll, maybe from China, and not to worry about him, because——!

Eighteen long years ago now, but they had never seen Tom since. That had been the beginning of Roger's long cruises, always seeking his son, always returning to Wastewater with the hope of word from him. He had come back that same winter from the first search to find Cecily dying, sinking under heavy narcotics, but knowing that he was there, they thought, and happier when he was beside her. And twice there had been word, a scratched letter from Tom in Pernambuco three years after he went away, and another several years later from Guam. Both contained love, casual greeting; Tom was on an interesting trip now, but immediately after it he was coming home.

So Roger travelled, hoped, came and went untiringly, and Flora kept Wastewater open, ready for the runaway's return, and meanwhile a home, a headquarters for all the other members of the family. Here David himself came for all his vacations, here Lily crept back, crushed, almost vacant-minded, deserted by her "travelling agent," and with a tawny-headed baby girl something a little worse than fatherless.

Will Fleming, who had protested for cheerful idle years that office work would kill him, had proved his words when Sylvia was only four by quite simply dying of pneumonia during a long absence in the West, and so Flora and Lily were alone again at Waste-water, but with the two little girls to take their places as the children of the old place. Flora's child, Sylvia, was a superbly proud little creature, tall, imperious, with scarlet cheeks, the white Fleming skin, the black Fleming eyes, indeed as absolute a "black Fleming" as ever had been born. Lily's Gabrielle, three years younger, was a thin, nervous, tawny-headed little creature, full of impish excitements and imaginings. Roger would find the two little girls, when he came back weary-hearted and sick, playing "flower ladies" with much whispering and subdued laughter in the old garden, or penning crabs and small sea creatures in pebbly prisons on the shore.

One day, only a few weeks before his death, Roger had a long talk with David, walking back and forth along the garden paths that were sweating and panting under the breath of an untimely summer day in mid-May. There was no sun; a sort of milky mist lay over the sea; the warm plants dripped, and smelled of hothouses. David remembered watching the slow silky heaving of the obscured ocean as his stepfather talked.

"I made my will when you were only a baby, Dave—when Tom was born. That's—my God, that's twenty years ago. But I put a codicil in a week or two back, giving Will's child—Sylvia here—the whole of it in case—he may have got mixed up in this sea warfare, you know—in case the boy never comes home. But he will! I gave Will's widow—poor Flora—all that my own mother left, when Will died; that'll take care of her and of Sylvia; Tom'll see that they stay here at Wastewater if they want to. And Flora'll care for poor Lily's child. Your father fixed you pretty well—I've left you the Boston houses to remember your stepfather by. You've been like my own son to me, David. I've had a long run for my money," Roger said somewhat sadly that same evening, looking up at his own portrait over the mantel, when the men were alone in the sitting room. "But a better man would have made a better job of it! Tom'll come home, though, and there'll be Flemings here again, boys and girls, David, to keep the old place warm."

"I hope you'll keep it warm yourself," David had answered, cheerfully. "You're not fifty-three yet!"

"No, Dave—I've lived too hard. I've broken the machinery," Roger said; and it was true. "I remember my twenty-first birthday," he went on, musingly, "when Oates turned the estate over to me. He was a nice fellow—forty, I suppose, making perhaps six thousand a year, and with half-a-dozen children. Homely little sandy fellow—he doesn't look a day older to-day. I remember his watching me, I'd a hatful of florists' and tailors' bills to pay—watching me scribble off checks for twice his year's income, right there in his office. I bought my dog, 'Maggie'—that was 'Queen Vic's' mother—that day. They were great years, David; young men don't know anything like them to-day—but a better man might have made a better job of them! I didn't want a wife—I wanted all the women in the world, until the day your mother walked in here with you in her arms, and that was a dozen years later. I wish we'd had a houseful like you, David—I wish Tom had had sisters and brothers—might have held the boy! Well," the master of Wastewater had ended, "if Tom's not here, turn it all over to Flora's girl when she's twenty-one. Women manage these things better. Sylvia'll have her fun and build for the future, too. Or maybe she and the boy may make a match of it—they're both Flemings, Dave. And more than that—your Aunt Flora has a score to settle with me—there's a sort of poetic justice in her daughter's getting it all. She—she cared, in her way—she's not a woman to care easily, either. And she forgave my marrying your mother—she stood by your mother. But when it came to Cecily—Flora and I were to have been married then, you know—she won't mention her name to this day! I've treated a good many women badly," Roger had confessed, with a twitch of his handsome mouth, "but I never treated any one as badly as poor Flora."

David had been pleased, and secretly amused, to see that the old incorrigible smile was lighting his stepfather's magnificent eyes. Upon whatever episodes in the past Roger's mind was moving, he found them sweet. David liked to fancy the bustled and chignonned ladies of the 'Eighties thrilling over "Papagontier" roses from the irresistible Roger Fleming of Wastewater, the two-button kid gloves that agitated the clicking fans in the opera house when this winner of hearts sauntered in.

And after all, Death had come kindly, as Life had, to Black Roger Fleming. There had been one more hope about Tom; Roger had been eagerly and confidently flinging clothes into his well-worn trunk, telephoning, shouting directions, exulting in the need for action, all through a sweet June morning. Sylvia, nine years old, and Gabrielle, six, had been running at full speed along the upper hall, and they saw him come to his door—saw him fall, with one hand clutching his heart.

Aunt Lily's periodic melancholia had developed into a more serious condition now, and she was away on one of her long absences in a sanitarium. But David was there. Flora was there, the old ser-

18

vants were there to fly to Roger's side—already far too late. He had been warned of his heart; this was not utterly unexpected.

Three days later David wrote a letter to Tom, launched it out into the great world with little hope that he would ever read it. He was the heir, there was a large estate, he must come home.

But Tom had never come home.

CHAPTER III

So THERE was the story, thought David, rousing himself from his favourite position of leaning forward in his low chair, with his linked hands between his knees, and looking upward at the superb and smiling portrait once more—there was the story to the present day. Flora had guarded her forlorn little sister to the end, ten years ago; had educated Lily's child, Gabrielle, that same Gabrielle who was to return from years of schooling to-day. Flora's own splendid child, the beautiful Sylvia, would also be coming home from college one of these days to claim her great inheritance, to be owner and mistress of Wastewater. David himself, finishing college, had had some rather unhappy dull years in business in New York, had gone from the handling of pictures to the painting of pictures, and was now happy in the knowledge that his day as a painter of this same murmuring sea was coming, if not quite come.

In his thirty-first year, he kept a small studio in New York; his friends, his fellow workers, were there, the galleries and exhibitions were there. But he did much of his painting near Wastewater and had a sort of studio-barn at Keyport, where canvases were stored, and into which he sometimes disappeared for days at a time. Flora regarded him, however coolly and suspiciously, as a son; he was Sylvia's guardian, he was Roger's trustee, he advised and counselled the mother and daughter in everything they did. And then—he added this fact with a rather rueful smile to all the other facts of his life—he had always loved Sylvia, from the days of her imperious babyhood. He had gone from a big-brotherly adoration to a more definite thing; she knew it—trust Sylvia!—although he had never told her.

Aunt Flora knew it, too, or at least suspected it, but then it was natural to Aunt Flora to suppose all the world in love with her splendid child. Sylvia was just twenty; give her another year or two, David would muse, let her feel her wings. And then perhaps—perhaps they two would bring the Fleming line back to Wastewater.

The clock on the mantel struck an uncertain, silvery six. David looked at his watch in surprise: six o'clock. Gabrielle would be here in another two hours. Heavens, he said half aloud, stirring the fire and glancing over his shoulder at the deepened shadows of the ug-

20

ly old room, how the wind howled about Wastewater in the autumn evenings, and how clearly one heard the gulls and the slash-slash of the sea!

Flora came in with a lamp; usually Hedda's burden, but Hedda had gone downstairs, she explained; David rose. They were setting its familiar pink china globe carefully upon the crowded table when there was a stir outside in the upper hall, and the door opened, and a tall girl came quickly in, with a little nervous laughter in her greeting.

David had last seen Gabrielle at sixteen, when her teeth were strapped in a gold band and her young boyish figure still had a sort of gawky overgrownness about it. She had been convalescent after a fever when she had sailed for France, then, and wearing big dark glasses on her bright eyes for fear of the glare of the sea, and had been plainly dressed in a heavy black coat and a school-girlish hat. She had been crying, too, emotional little Gabrielle; she had not altogether been a prepossessing little person, although David had always liked her and had given her a genuinely affectionate brotherly kiss for good-bye.

But that memory had not prepared him for this girl's appearance; tired she undoubtedly was, train-rumpled, cold, and wind-blown, but she was oddly impressive for all that.

She enveloped Flora, who had stood wiping her oily hands on a barred tea towel, with a quick embrace and a kiss; then her eyes found David, and she held out both her hands.

"David! But how exactly as you were! And how like Uncle Roger!"

David had forgotten the husky voice, with a delicious touch of contralto roughness in it; he had forgotten nothing else, for this eager, graceful woman had about her little of the awkward, tear-stained child of more than two years before.

She was tall, perhaps not quite so tall as Sylvia, but very much more so than he had remembered her. Her hair, tawny, thick, spraying into fine tendrils on her forehead in the old way, hardly showed at all under her traveller's hat, but her mouth had gained in sweetness and power, and in the creamy pallor of her face—so different, as it had always been different, from Sylvia's rose-and-whiteness!—her eyes were astonishing. Even as a child she had had memorable eyes.

They were beautifully shaped, deep-set eyes, of the living grayness of star sapphires. In odd contrast to the warm brunette skin and the fair hair, they were black-fringed, and the brows above them were black and straight. This had made the child look odd, pixy-like, years ago, with her flying fair hair and nervous little forehead, but it made this serene girl superb.

Best of all, David thought, covertly studying her, as she sat upon the stiff-backed little chair Flora indicated, between Flora's own armchair and David's; best of all were her contours, the making of her. Child of little cry-baby Aunt Lily and the peripatetic agent she might be, but she was splendidly fine in her outlines and textures for all that. Her hands were fine, white, not too small, beautifully shaped. Her ankles were fine, her head nicely set and nicely poised when she moved it quickly to look at him or at her aunt. The shape of her face was fine, the cheek-bones a thought too high, the upper lip a shade too short, but the modelling of the mouth and temples and the clean cut of the chin were perfect. Her big teeth were white and glistening, her fair hair controlled to neatness in spite of its rebel tendrils, and brushed to a goldeny lustre. Her voice, husky and sweet, and lower than that of most women, was most distinctive of all. David wished that Aunt Flora would show something a little more motherly, a little more hospitable in her welcome—would at least ask Gabrielle to take off her hat.

But Flora, for her, was not ungracious.

"You are early, Gabrielle," she said, kindly. "David had said something of meeting you in Crowchester if you came down on the two o'clock train."

"I came on a special train this morning. We stopped at Worcester, with some girls who live there."

"You're not tired?"

"Well." The white teeth flashed. "Rumpled and train-dusty and a little confused. We got into Montreal—what is to-day?—day before yesterday. Yesterday we were on the train, last night in the Boston convent."

"You hardly know where you are?" David, speaking for the first time, suggested.

"Ah, I know I'm at Wastewater!" she answered, eagerly. "Every inch of the way I've been getting more and more excited. The sea—you can't know what it meant to me! I could just see it, in the dusk. I can't believe that to-morrow it will be there, right outside the windows, right below the garden!"

"Yet you've been on the sea all the way from France," Flora said, repressively. Flora disliked enthusiasm.

"But not our sea, as we know it here at Wastewater," Gabrielle answered, more quietly. "To-morrow I'll walk along our shore and out the little gate on to the cliffs toward Tinsalls—do you ever walk that way now, David? And Keyport! I must go to Keyport, too."

Her voice faltered on the last phrases a little uncertainly, and David interpreted aright her quick flush and the glance she sent her aunt. Tom's name was indissolubly linked with that of Keyport, for his father had first sought him, and had always suspected that his escape had been planned there. And since Uncle Roger's death, Flora, whose own daughter's fortune hinged upon Tom's return or non-return, had not encouraged much hopeful speculation about him among the younger members of the family. But Flora had been rooted securely for many placid years now, and she only commented mildly:

"Keyport. That's where your uncle first hunted for poor Tom. Dear me, how many years ago!"

"No word—never any word," David said, shaking his head in answer to Gabrielle's quick questioning glance. "We won't hear, now. The war split up the whole world; there must have been hundreds of lives lost upon the sea, and upon the land, too, for that matter, with no record left anywhere."

"Think of it—Tom!" Gabrielle said, under her breath. And for a long moment they were all silent. Then Flora asked the newcomer if she would like to go upstairs.

"You'll hardly have time to change, now," said Flora. "One of the girls has made the old blue room ready for you. Call Maria if you need anything."

"Maria! Then she didn't marry her sailor!" Gabrielle said, laughing as she rose. "And Margret's not here any longer?"

"She comes and goes; she's pretty old now," David said, as Flora merely seemed to be waiting patiently for Gabrielle to go.

"She'll come over to see me, or I'll go into Keyport and find her," Gabrielle promised. "Ah," she said, on a long sigh, departing, "it's so good to be home!"

The door shut behind her; there was utter silence in the room. Flora, who usually had her knitting at this time, sat back with leaden, closed eyes; David glanced at her, looked back at the fire.

"Is she like what you expected?" David asked.

"She's like nothing—*nobody*," Flora answered, in a low tone.

"She's handsome!" David offered. "Poor child!"

Flora made no answer. She opened her eyes, and began to knit, flinging the granite-gray yarn free with little flying jerks. David was mending the fire when Hedda came stolidly in to announce dinner.

Gabrielle joined them on the way downstairs; David smiled at

23

her.

"Seems strange to be home?"

"It seems," she said, "as if I had never been away! The old rooms, the old things, this old good feeling of the first autumn cold in the house—and that loud sound of the sea——"

Meals at Wastewater nowadays were tedious and formal affairs. The dining room was large and draughty, and the candles lighted on the side tables wavered in the cool autumn evening. There were great bay windows on the north and east walls; the latter sometimes caught the clean sweet light of sunrise, but almost all the year through it was a dreary room even in the daytime. These bays were now shut off in heavy rep curtains, with tassels and ropes; the walls were covered with a heavy old pressed paper in chocolate and gold; the floor, outside the "body-Brussels" rug, shone slippery and dark. In one corner, cunningly concealed in paper and wainscoting, was the door into the enormous, inconvenient pantry; the kitchen and storerooms were downstairs, and in pauses in the meal the diners could hear the creaking of the dumb-waiter ropes and the maids' anxious voices echoing in the shaft.

There was a great rubber plant in one corner, heavy walnut sideboards, and a great mirror over the black-and-white marble mantel that seemed to make the room darker and more gloomy. On the mantel was another heavy bronze-and-marble clock, this one under a clear tall bubble of glass ringed by a chenille cord. On each side of the clock stood heavy bronze statues of Grecian women holding aloft four-branched candlesticks that were never lighted.

There was never a fire nowadays in this fireplace, which was indeed a good twenty-five feet from the table, and must have burned for half a day in winter weather to make any impression upon the diners. Sometimes in January Flora would have an oil stove lighted in here during meals; usually she ate shuddering and rubbing her cold fingers dryly upon each other between courses, and escaped as soon as possible to the heavy warmth of the upstairs sitting room again.

Over the square walnut table hung a heavy lamp upon adjustable tarnished chains. Upon a walnut table in a corner stood the large birdcage, empty now, but where once Roger had kept the two green talkative parrots that had been one of the joys of David's childhood and Tom's.

"Here, open that cage, Katy—Addie—one of you!" David could remember his stepfather saying, when it was time for dessert. "Come here, Cassie-girl—come here, old Sultan!" And out would come the chuckling and murmuring birds, with the unearthly green of their feathers turned upside down or swept sideways as they sidled and climbed their way to their master's shoulders. How often had David seen his stepfather, whom he so passionately admired, composedly eating his fruit and his cheese, with one small jade body mincing on his shoulder and the other weaving its way down his busy arm!

Gabrielle asked an occasional question or two to-night as the meal progressed; David—never an easy talker—did his best to keep the conversation moving. But Flora's heavy silences were too much for both, and in the end it was a quiet meal. The wind outside whined and whispered at the closed shutters, shutters that, Gabrielle knew, gave upon a very jungle of heavy shrubbery on the northern and eastern fronts of the lower floor. Now and then an unused door, in some distant unused room, banged sullenly and was still.

Afterward they went back to their places beside the fire again, but in pure charity David presently suggested that the traveller be sent to bed. The warmth, the food, the quiet, and her fatigue were causing her an absolute torture of sleepiness; she held her eyes open with an effort, and answered her aunt's questions with sudden stares and starts, smiling nervously as she roused herself to a full realization of where she was and what she was saying.

"Yes, go to bed," said Flora, knitting. "And—sleep late if you like," she added, as the slender young figure moved wearily to the door.

"Thank you," Gabrielle answered, very low. "Good-night!" And it was only with his last glance at her that David realized with sudden compunction that she was on the verge of tears.

Tears, however, that she did not shed. She went resolutely up through the cold dark hallways and stairs to the third flight, where was the big room that had been assigned to her. The halls were pitchy dark, and the room, when she got to it, was impenetrably black.

Gabrielle groped for the matches, found them, struck a light, and drew toward her the hinged arm of the gaslight at the bureau. There was a bare brown marble top on the bureau, with a limp fringed towel laid across it; the bureau and the great table, desk, and bookcases were all enormous, heavy, and as impersonally bare as those in some old hotel. There was no closet, but there were two great wardrobes flanking a door that led to a sort of dressing passage or hallway, where there was a stationary washstand of wide, bare brown marble.

There were four high windows, reaching to the floor, with iron balconies outside; these were curtained in old-rose brocade, all silvery scrolls and cyclamen, tassels and cords. The bed was walnut, decorated with dots and ripples in mill-work, flat and bare. There were antimacassars on all the chairs, the neat green blotter on the desk had seen much use, Gabrielle's trunk and suitcase had been set down in the centre of everything, and in her hurried scramble for a brush and a handkerchief before dinner she had tumbled the contents of the latter dishearteningly upon a sort of lounge set "cater-cornered" toward the empty fireplace.

Tumbled linen, the book she had been reading, her writing materials, a dozen disorderly trifles—Gabrielle quailed before the awful thought of having somehow to segregate them, to empty the suitcase and the trunk to-morrow. She was so dirty, too, and so cold, and the bathroom was across that formidable dark hall! She opened the bed with vigorous tugging—the sheets felt icily damp and lifeless.

Suddenly, as she struggled about forlornly in the dim light, a tap on the door made her heart leap. The old house was sufficiently full of ghosts without any such tangible horrors as this! But it was only good-natured, pock-marked Maria, with a kettle of hot water and a sympathetic look.

"Mr. David," it appeared, had just slipped down to the kitchen, by whose sociable tea table Maria had been seated, to send someone up to Miss Gabrielle. Maria moved about the big chamber capably and not too silently, and Gabrielle felt her fears dissipate under the wholesome companionship. She managed a sort of sponge bath in the dressing room when Maria went downstairs for more hot water, this time in a rubber bag.

"Tell me about Margret, Maria. She's not here any more?" Gabrielle questioned, when the maid came back. The girl was seated on her bed now, in her nightgown, brushing the long thick masses of her bright hair.

"She lives with her daughter in Keyport, mostly: she's here nearly every day, though," said Maria, folding and straightening capably. "She's 'most eighty, Margret is."

"She was my first nurse, when I came here as a baby with my mother," Gabrielle said. "Such an old darling! My mother was—delicate, you know. She was Mrs. Fleming's sister."

"Sure, but that was before I come here," Maria reminded her, with her pitted, plain face full of interest. "You don't look like Miss Sylvia," she added, mildly.

"Oh, no! She's like all the Flemings—dark. Is she pretty?" Gabrielle demanded.

"They say she's what you call a beauty," Maria stated, dispassionately. Gabrielle felt a little thrill of interest, perhaps of more, the beginning of a jealous stir at her heart. When Maria had gone she sat on, cross-legged on her bed, in her shabby old convent wrapper, absent-mindedly brushing her hair, with her wide-awake eyes staring into the shadows of the stately old chamber.

Sylvia was "what you call a beauty." Sylvia would have this whole place some day—would own Wastewater. Wastewater, the house that Gabrielle naturally thought the most interesting and important place in the world.

What did David think about Sylvia? Gabrielle wondered. He had sat there by the fire, with his handsome head bent a little to one side, and his hands linked, and a half smile upon his handsome face. He had glanced up at Gabrielle now and then, and always with a kindly smile. Was Sylvia to have David, too, with everything else?

But Gabrielle would not think about David. She dismissed him with a fervent, "I hope I won't like him as well to-morrow! I hope he's really horrid and disappointing!" and knelt down to say her prayers. Prayers had always been in the chapel at St. Susanna's, and the girls had worn their black veils. But she dared not think of that, either—not to-night, when she was so alone.

She crossed the big room and opened a French window, pushed resolutely on the heavy shutters beyond, and hinged them back. The night was moonless, starless, and dark, and filled with the troubled creaking and rushing of branches and the steady crashing of the sea. The girl could not distinguish where the garden ended and the wide surface of the moving waters began, but these had been her loved and familiar companions from babyhood, and she felt nothing but a restful sense of being home again when she heard their voices.

A current of cool moving air stirred the room, the bureau gas-jet wavered and went out, and Gabrielle, used to electric lighting, laughed nervously and aloud as she turned back to grope once more for matches.

But turning on the narrow iron balcony her eyes were arrested by the great eastern façade of Wastewater, of which her windows were a part. It loomed in the night a shadow just a little blacker than the prevailing dark; her own room was in a corner, next came a deep angle, like the three sides of a court, and then the northern wing, where seamstresses and house servants and coachmen, ladies' maids and valets, agents delayed overnight, all sorts of odd and inconsiderable gentry had been lodged in Wastewater's days of glory, years before.

Gabrielle stared oddly at this wing for a few moments, looked back into her own room. There was no light behind her to be caught in a distant window and reflect itself like another light.

Her heart began to beat strong and fast. In the opposite wing, across the wide blackness of the court, in another corner room at the level of her own room—there was certainly a light. Gabrielle felt a sense of utter and unreasoning terror, she did not know why. She stared in a sort of horrified fascination at the yellow glints of light behind the shutter, her breath coming hard, one hand clutching her heart.

"David!" she whispered. Then frightened by her own voice she stumbled madly back in the dark, groping for gas fixtures, for matches, lighting her bedside lamp with shaking fingers, and springing in under the blankets with a long shudder of fear.

Safe—of course! But for a long time her heart did not resume its normal beat. There was something utterly unnerving about the sight of that quietly lighted apartment, mysteriously hung between the dark mysterious sky and wind and night and sea. Gabrielle did not fall asleep until she heard Aunt Flora and David come upstairs.

CHAPTER IV

GABRIELLE was wandering along an overgrown path before breakfast the next morning when David came after her and sauntered at her side. The sun was shining brilliantly after a clearing storm, the air aromatic with delicious leaf-scent, and the sea dancing and blue. Everything was singing and shining in a warm bath of sweet clear light, there were a few late birds hopping about, and gulls walked on the sunken brick paths as boldly as the pigeons did. Under the thick growth of the cedars and conifers golden shafts penetrated; the paths and garden beds were deep in sodden and drifted leaves.

"Oh, what a morning!" sang Gabrielle, as David joined her.

"What a morning!" he echoed. And he added, "I needn't ask if you slept well?"

For indeed she was glowing from a bath, from a night's deep rest, glowing with all the morning beauty of healthy eighteen. The sun shone upon her warm brown hair, rousing golden lights in it, and her gray-sapphire eyes were shining. David noted that she walked with a little spring, as if in mere walking there were not quite enough action to free the bubbling vitality within her.

"I didn't dare go far," she said, "for I suppose breakfast is still at half-past eight? But presently—when I've unpacked and gotten things straightened out—I'm going to explore!"

"I like this Quaker costume," David said, glancing at the plain gray dress.

"This? It's the Sunday uniform," Gabrielle told him. "Black on week-days, and black always for the street—sometimes we went to the Madeleine or Notre Dame on Sundays, you know, and twice to organ concerts. But these we always wore indoors at St. Susanna's."

"All very well for the smaller girls," David smiled, "but didn't you others rebel?"

"Ah, but I have other clothes," said Gabrielle, interestedly. "There's a lovely countess in Paris, a widow, who is one of the old children——"

"One of the——?"

"Old children. One of the alumnæ of St. Susanna's," she elucidated, laughing at his bewildered look. "That's what the nuns call

29

them, 'the old children.' And every year this countess takes the graduates and goes with them to buy suitable clothes—that is, if there aren't fathers and mothers to do it for them," added Gabrielle. "So she took me, the darling! We all know her quite well, and the last year one may go to her Sunday afternoon teas four or five times," explained the girl, seriously. "That is, if you've no *devoirs*."

"*Devoirs?*"

"Penances. Punishments to write for breaking rules," she said.

"I feel dense. *Devoirs*, of course," said David, diverted. "Tell me more of this. If you had no *devoirs* you might go to tea with the countess?"

"So that we might comport ourselves becomingly in society," agreed Gabrielle. "And then, two weeks before we left for Cherbourg, she took me into the city, and bought me—oh, lovely things! A velvet dress; I wore that once on the boat. And a lovely brown lace dress, and a hat, and a suit, and three blouses. But we had to travel in our uniforms, of course. 'Religious in habit. Students in uniform.' That's the rule."

David was finding this extremely amusing and interesting. Through the medium of such engaging youth and freshness, such simplicity and eagerness, almost anything would have been somewhat so. But this glimpse of girlhood managed so decorously by rule was new to him, and it contrasted oddly with—well, for example, with Sylvia's breezy independence and that of all the other young women he knew.

"Did you—did any of the girls really like it, Gabrielle?"

"Did——?" The wonderful eyes widened and were more wonderful than ever. "But we all loved it!" she exclaimed. "We had—*fun*. The gardens were perfectly beautiful, and on Sundays there was always a sweet, and often on Thursdays! Or some girl's father would send her a great box of chocolates."

"You were in Normandy when I was in Paris," David said, wondering if he would have thought to send a box of chocolates to St. Susanna's if she had been there.

"Normandy! Isn't it—but you don't know it!" she said. "It's heavenly. We have such a cunning little place there; it was a sort of gate-lodge once, and of course we had the sea!—it used to remind me of Wastewater, only of course the sun seemed to set in the wrong direction!——David," Gabrielle broke off to ask earnestly, "didn't you find Paris very disappointing?"

"Rucker and I were only there ten days, on our way to Spain, to paint," David reminded her. "No, I don't remember that it was exactly—disappointing," he added, in a tone that made her laugh.

"To me," the girl said, "Paris was all Dumas and Victor Hugo and Stanley Weyman. I like their Paris the best. Sedans, masked riders, horses waiting in the angles of the walls——It made me almost glad not to see London," she added, gravely. "Imagine losing Dickens's London, and Thackeray's, and Trollope's! Oh, look," she said, in a tone rich with affectionate recollection, as they stopped by the old sundial set in a mouldy circle of emerald grass.

"You still like adventure stories?" David suggested, remembering that she always had liked them.

"Not always," Gabrielle answered. And with a suddenly warming enthusiasm, she recounted to him a story she had read on the boat, one of a collection of short stories.

It was so simple that it hardly engaged his attention at first: the story of two rich little girls, with a marvellous doll's house, and two poor little girls socially debarred from being asked in to inspect it. Gabrielle described the minute perfections of the doll's house, the tiny beds and curtains, the marvel of a microscopic glass lamp, and the wistful wonder of the little pariahs, one bold and eager, the other shy, her little head hanging, her little hand always grasping a corner of her big sister's apron. By chance the poor little girls were offered an opportunity to creep in, and they were rapturously inspecting the wonder when the rich little girls' mother indignantly discovered them, sent them forth with insulting scorn, sent them shamed and bewildered on their homeward road. And the older child sat by the roadside, heaving with hurt and fury and heat and fatigue, with the little sister close beside her. And the simple story ended quite simply with the little sister's murmured words of courage and comfort:

"Never mind. I seen the little tiny glass lamp!"

David was an artist, he adored beauty in youth, in words, in voices. Here he found them all combined in this eager creature who ended her tale with tears in her glorious eyes and a smile that asked for his sympathy twitching her splendid mouth. Told so plainly, under the dreaming autumn sky, in the thinning soft autumn sunlight of the old garden, the whole thing had a quite memorable pathos and charm, and when he thought of Gabrielle—as David did often in the days to come—he always thought of her standing by the sundial in the morning freshness, telling him the story of the doll's house.

She had brushed the face of the dial free of leaves and pine needles and was scraping the deep incisions with a stick.

"Twenty minutes past eight," she said, tipping her head to read the time. And afterward she read the inscription in her sweet husky voice:

"Turn, Flemynge, spin agayne;

  The crossit line's the kenter skein.

"One of my first recollections," said Gabrielle, "is being down here with Uncle Roger and Sylvia—I must have been about six, for it was just before he died. He set us both up on the sundial, and told us it was older than the Stars and Stripes, that it had come from England for his grandfather, and what it meant. It meant that the Flemings were always bringing home wives from overseas and crossing the line. I remember it," she added, as they strolled back toward the house, "because I said—looking out to sea—'Will Tom have a wife when he comes home?' and that pleased Uncle Roger, as anything did, I suppose," Gabrielle ended, sighing, "that made Tom's coming back at all seem likely!"

"Poor Tom! It would have been a nice inheritance," David mused. "It has increased, even since Uncle Roger's time, you know."

"Is Sylvia apt to make her home here, David?" Gabrielle asked. "She sounds rather worldly—that's a great convent word! But tell me, what is she like?"

"She is very beautiful, extremely clever, enormously admired," David answered, with a little flush. "She has the white Fleming skin, high colour, shining black hair."

"A girl off a handkerchief box?" Gabrielle suggested.

"Exactly."

"And are there admirers?"

"A great many."

The girl looked a quick question, half smiling, and he answered it pleasantly:

"Myself among them, of course! But Sylvia can look much higher than a painter of mediocre pictures."

"I don't believe they're mediocre!" Gabrielle said, stoutly.

"I've some at Keyport, most of them are in New York, some on their way now to an exhibition in Washington," David said. "When I come back you must see them, Gay!"

"When you come back——?" Her walk halted.

"I'm off for New York and then Washington this morning."

"Oh." It was not a question, not an exclamation. She pronounced the little monosyllable quietly, resumed her walking. "I like my little old name!" she presently said, with a glancing smile. And then, with sudden interest, as they came closer to the house: "David, tell me—who lives in that wing—up there, on the third floor?"

"Nobody, now. Those are old servants' rooms; but the servants are on the other side now—Aunt Flora has only five or six. Hedda's cousin is the cook, an old Belgian woman who's been here—well, she must have been here several years before you went abroad?"

"Trude?"

"Yes, Trude. Then there's Maria, the pock-marked one, and a couple of new ones from Crowchester, sisters named Daisy and Sarah, who live with John and Etta at the tenant house, out near the stables, and seem mainly interested in going into Crowchester. John occasionally employs others to assist him in the garden, his wife helps, I believe, with the laundry-work, and old Margret comes over from Keyport to lend a hand now and then. That's the staff."

"But look here, David," said Gabrielle. "You see my open window up there, with the curtain blowing—and then all those blank windows—then turn the corner of the court and come out again in the north wing—up there—there was some light up there last night! I saw it when my own gaslight blew out. It was unmistakable, coming through the chinks of shutters! It gave me the creeps for a moment."

"Reflection!" David said, smiling. "Reflection in glass."

"No, for my light was out."

"Reflection of some other window, then."

"Yes, but whose?"

"I don't know," he told her, amused. "You'll have ample opportunity to find out, my dear. I'm wondering what you'll do with yourself, here all alone with Aunt Flora!"

"I'll work," she said, stoutly. But he could see that she herself felt a little daunted by the prospect. "I'll practise, and keep up my French, and take walks into Keyport and Crowchester, and perhaps"—and she gave him a laughing look—"design all the little rooms and hallways of houses in beans when it rains!"

"Good Lord!" David said, with a great laugh. "Do you remember my houses designed in white beans to amuse you and Sylvia on wet holidays? But you have no special plans for yourself, Gay?" he asked, more soberly. "Nothing you especially want to do?"

"I talked it over with Sister Borromeo and Sister Alcantara——" she was beginning, with a faintly worried look, when David laughed again.

"Are these Pullman cars?"

"No!" said Gabrielle, shocked yet laughing, as they mounted the three steps to the side door. "They are wonderful nuns. And they both feel that, under the circumstances, I had better wait and see if

33

Aunt Flora has any plans or any use for me here!"

"And I think that, too," David said, heartily, delighted to find her so reasonable. "You are not yet nineteen, after all, and we'll find the happiest solution for you one of these days. I'll be coming and going all winter, and Sylvia'll be home, with a degree, in June. So keep up your spirits!"

"Ah, don't worry about me!" she answered, courageously, going in to breakfast.

CHAPTER V

THREE hours later she said good-bye to him composedly at Aunt Flora's side. He carried away a pleasant recollection of her, standing there tall and smiling, with her gray eyes shining. She was a more than usually interesting type of girl, David mused, going upon his way, and as the man of the family it behooved him to think out some constructive line of guidance in her direction. What about an allowance? Just what would Gabrielle's status be a year from now, when Sylvia reached her majority and Aunt Flora no longer controlled both girls as if their position were equal? Sylvia might graciously provide for this less fortunate cousin if Sylvia were properly influenced.

This was October; Sylvia was going with the Montallen girls to Quebec for a simple family Thanksgiving week-end, but she would be home for almost three weeks at Christmas time. David must manage a talk with her then. Perhaps the peculiar embarrassments and deprivations of Gabrielle's position had never occurred to Sylvia, as indeed they never had presented themselves so forcibly to David before. "She is certainly a stunning creature—character, too," David thought. "God help the child, shut up there with Aunt Flora and the servants, and with Aunt Flora always so curiously hostile to her, at that! I'll try to get down there before Christmas—see how it goes!"

And he put the thought of Wastewater behind him, as he usually did at about this point in his journey toward Boston or New York.

But Gabrielle had found nothing at Wastewater to make her forget David, and the thought of him lingered with her for many, many days.

They were hard days, these first after her return. Flora was not visibly unfriendly toward her, and the servants were always responsive and interested. But Gabrielle was left almost entirely to her own resources, and after the regular rule of the convent life, the orderly waxed halls in which the sunshine lay in shining pools, the low, kindly voices, the chip-chipping of girls' feet, the cheerful chatter in the long refectory, the sheltered fragrance of the walled garden, the girl felt lonely and at a loss for employment.

She aired her bed and ordered her room before breakfast; descended promptly, commented with Aunt Flora upon the weather.

"What a wind this morning, Aunt Flora!"

"Yes, indeed, and in the night."

"It didn't keep you awake, Aunt Flora?"

"Not the wind, no. I am not a good sleeper."

Then silence; and Daisy or Sarah with the rolls and coffee, to ask in a low tone:

"Will you have an egg, Mrs. Fleming?"

"I think not, this morning. Perhaps Miss Gabrielle——"

For Gabrielle was not "Miss Fleming" really, although she was used to the name. Sylvia was that, always. Perhaps Miss Gabrielle would have an egg; oftener not. There was no deep golden corn bread to be anticipated here, as a regular Friday morning treat; but sometimes special muffins or a little omelette came up, and then Gabrielle always smiled affectionately and said to herself: "Margret's here!"

After breakfast every morning she mounted through the large, gloomy halls to her room, wrote in her diary, went resolutely at her French or Italian. Then she went down to the square piano and began with scales, études and nocturnes, sonatinas. When the half-hour after eleven sounded, usually she went out, down to the shore, scrambling among the big rocks she remembered so well, watching this favourite pool or that, as it slowly and solemnly brimmed, overflowed, drained again.

This side of the shore was in shade now, for Wastewater stood on its own little jutting point of cliff and forest, and the sun, at autumn midday, had moved behind the trees. Gabrielle would fall to dreaming, as she stared across the softly heaving, shining expanse of the water, her back against a great boulder, her feet, in their rough little shoes, braced against a smaller one.

Going in to lunch blinking and hungry, the instant effect of closeness, odorous age, and quiet darkness would envelop her. She would look with secret curiosity at her aunt's mottled, dark face. Aunt Flora had been quietly reading and writing all morning, she would read and write all afternoon.

Immediately after luncheon came Mrs. Fleming's one outing of the day. Sometimes she walked about the borders with John, discussing changes, her silk skirt turned up over her decent alpaca petticoat, efficient-looking overshoes covering her congress gaiters if the paths were damp. Sometimes John brought the surrey, and Aunt Flora and Gabrielle went into Crowchester to shop. Flora kept a small car, but she did not like it; she did not even like the cars of others,

Gabrielle discovered, when they honked behind the stout old bay horse on the roads.

Aunt Flora had acquaintances in Crowchester, but no friends. She never made calls, or entertained at luncheon or dinner. She bowed and talked to the minister's wife when she met her in a shop, she knew the librarian and the school superintendent, and she belonged, at least nominally, to the Woman's Improvement Club. Once, in December, there was a lecture at the club on the modern British poets and Flora took Gabrielle, who wore her velvet dress, and was much flushed and excited and youthfully friendly in the dim, women-crowded rooms, and who carried away a delightful impression of Hodgson and Helen Eden and Louise Guiney and tea and cake.

But a week later, when the president of the club sent Gay a card for a dance to be given by the choicest of Crowchester's youth that winter, Flora shook her head. Much better for Gay not to associate with the village people; Sylvia despised them. It was too easy to become involved in things that had never been acceptable to Wastewater. Gabrielle wrote a charming little note of regret.

Flora wrote to Sylvia every three or four days and received delightful letters from her daughter at least once a week. Sylvia wrote interestedly of a hundred activities, and Gay's word for her cousin came to be, in her own heart, "superior." Sylvia was assuredly "superior." She was still playing golf, for the snows were late, and basket ball, and squash; she was working for mid-term examinations in history, philosophy, and economics. She would have sounded almost formidable if the Thanksgiving letter had not struck a warmer note: Sylvia was ski-ing, tobogganing, dancing; she had been to a little home fancy-dress party as "Night"; her letter was full of delightful allusions to young men, "Bart Montallen, who is in diplomacy," a charming Gregory Masters, and a "dear idiotic cousin of Gwen's, Arthur Tipping, who will be Lord Crancastle some day, in all probability—but all such simple people and not rich!" Some of these might come down to Wastewater for a few days before Christmas. Gabrielle's heart leaped at the mere thought.

Gabrielle sometimes wondered what Flora wrote to Sylvia in those long, closely lined letters that went so regularly from Wastewater. Flora would sit scratching at her desk in the upstairs sitting room, look away thoughtfully, begin to scratch again. Sometimes Gabrielle saw her copying long excerpts from books; indeed, Flora not infrequently read these aloud to her niece, a thought from some bishops' letters from the Soudan, lines from "Aurora Leigh" or "Lady Clare."

These were almost all gift books, bound in tooled leather and gilded, with gilded tops. The old house was full of gift books. Gabrielle imagined the last generation as giving its friends large, heavy, badly bound, or at least insecurely bound, books on all occasions, "The Culprit Fay," "Evangeline," and "Hiawatha," Flaxman's gracious illustrations for Schiller's "Bell," Dante with the plates of Doré.

Idly she dipped into them all, idly closed them. Sometimes in the long wintry afternoons she opened the lower drawers of the bookshelves and looked at all the stereoscope pictures of Niagara, and Japan with wistaria falling over arbours, and Aunt Flora and Lily, Gabrielle's own slender mother, in riding habits, with long veils flowing from their black silk hats. The tiny figures stood out in bold relief, the flowers seemed to move in the breezes of so many years ago; there was a Swiss mountain scene that Gabrielle had loved all her life, with a rough slab of drift almost in the very act of coasting upon the road where men and Newfoundland dogs were grouped.

Her hardest time was when the decorous afternoon excursion or walk was over, at perhaps four o'clock. Dinner was at seven; the winter dusk began to close down two and a half hours before dinner. The girl could not with propriety walk far from the house in the dark, even if she had cared to traverse the cliff roads at night. The servants were far downstairs, all elderly in any case. Aunt Flora hated young servants.

Sometimes she went to the piano and would find herself meandering through an old opera score, "Traviata" or "Faust." Sometimes, if the afternoon was clear, she walked rapidly to Keyport and rapidly back. Many an afternoon, as long as the light lasted, she prowled about within the confines of Wastewater itself, for besides the always fascinating half-mile of shore there were the cliffs, the woods back of the house, and all the stable yards, cow yards, chicken yards, all the sheds and fences, the paddocks and lanes, the gates and walls that almost two hundred years of homekeeping had accumulated. The big stables were empty now except for one or two dray horses, the sturdy bay that dragged the old surrey, and a lighter horse that Sylvia—Gabrielle learned—sometimes used for riding. There was perhaps one tenth of the hay stored that the big hay barn would accommodate, one tenth of the grain. There were two cows, chickens, pigeons; there were intersecting catacombs of empty rooms and lofts and sheds where apples were left to ripen, or where feathers fluffed at the opening of a door, or where cats fled like shadows.

Towering above all, among towering pear trees, there was the windmill, still creaking, splashing, leaking.

John the gardener had a substantial brick house, a nice wife, and a stolid little girl of fourteen who walked the three miles every day to the Union High School between Tinsalls and Crowchester. Gabrielle presently gathered that young Etta was taking two fifty-cent music lessons every week in Crowchester, and that she was going to be a school teacher. Her "grammer" lived in Crowchester, and when the weather got very bad Etta and her mother sometimes stayed with "grammer," and Uncle Dick drove her to school, and she and her cousin Ethel went to the movies every night.

Wastewater itself might have filled many a lonely afternoon, for there were plenty of unused rooms worthy of exploring. But Gabrielle had small heart for that. There was something wholesome and open about the garden and the stable yards and the sea, but the big closed rooms inside filled her with a vague uneasiness.

The girl would look up at them from outside when the winter sunsets were flaming angrily behind the black etched branches of the bare trees; look up at blank rows of shuttered windows, identify her own, Aunt Flora's, the upstairs sitting room with gaslight showing pink through the shutters when the cold clear dusk fell; the dining room, with Daisy pulling the rep curtains together.

These were human, used, normal, but there were so many others! Two thirds of the entire lower floor was always sealed and dark, showing from outside only solemn bays, and flat surfaces screened heavily in shrubs and bushes. In the western wing, with hooded windows rising only two or three feet above the old walk, were the kitchen windows; but the older servants, Hedda and Maria and the cook, Trude, had rooms obscurely situated somewhere far back of Aunt Flora's rooms and Sylvia's room and the upstairs sitting room on the second floor. Gabrielle's room was on the third floor, and David's, and the rooms still kept ready for Tom; these were all that were used of some score of rooms on that level, and Wastewater rose to a mansard as well, to say nothing of the cupola that rose for two floors, and was finished off with columns and a small circular room of glass, high above the tops of the highest trees. Gabrielle remembered when she and Sylvia used to think it a great adventure to creep up there and look down upon a curiously twisted landscape, with all the familiar barns and fences in the wrong places, and so little land, cut by such insignificant ribbons of roads, and so much sea, broken by nothing at all!

"You could put a hundred people in here!" Gabrielle used to

think. In the days of its glory, Uncle Roger had told them more than once, there had often been half that number at Wastewater.

All the sadder to find it so empty now, the girl would muse, wandering through the quiet halls. If the winter sun were shining bright, sometimes she opened the great double doors that shut off the end of the dining-room hall, and penetrated, with a fast thumping heart and nervously moving eyes, into what had been the boasted ballroom, billiard room, library, drawing rooms of the house.

In this section was the unused front stairway; curved, enormous, wheeling up from a great square hall. There were doors on all sides, decorous heavy doors, all closed. Beyond them, Gabrielle's peeping eyes found great silent rooms, whose crystal-hung chandeliers tinkled faintly and reminiscently when the door was opened; swathed hideous satin furniture, rose-wreathed Moquette carpets in faint pinks and blues, looped brocaded curtains creased and cracked with the years, tables topped with marble and mosaic, great mirrors rising up to the high ceilings; everything that could rot, rotting, everything that could bear dust covered with a deep plush of dust.

Sometimes, on a winter noon, chinks of bright light penetrated the closed shutters and spun with motes. Sometimes an old chest or chair gave forth a pistol shot of sound, and for a few hideous seconds Gabrielle's heart would stand still with utter terror. Once the busy scratching of some small animal behind a wainscot brought her heart into her mouth.

In one room—it had been the "cherry-and-silver parlour" a hundred years ago—there was a cabinet of odds and ends: Dresden statues, broken fans, collapsed ivory boxes and cloisonné. In other rooms there were odd bits, some good, but almost all very bad: majolica, onyx, ormolu, terra cotta. There were one or two good pictures, forty bad ones: seascapes with boats, still-life studies of dead fish, English nobility of the First Empire days, breakfasting in gardens, peasants doing everything ever done by peasants, old woodcuts of Queen Victoria and "Yes or No?", "Dignity and Impudence," and Mrs. Siddons, curling and water-stained in their heavy frames.

The books that filled the handsome glass-doored shelves in the dimly lighted, mouldy library, where light crept as into a cave, and where the air was always damp and heavily scented with decay, were almost all ruined after some especially wet winter. Their backs were loosened, their badly printed pages clung together with black stains: Lever and Scott, Shakespeare, The Iliad, Somebody's History of the World in Twenty Volumes, Somebody Else's Classic Literature in Forty. Sometimes Gabrielle selected one or two, and carried them upstairs with her. She read voraciously anything and everything: "Innocents Abroad," "Forty-one Years in India," "The Household Book of English Verse," Strickland's "Mary of Scotland."

But even with reading, wandering, tramping, exploring, music, languages, the time passed slowly. Gabrielle became, and laughed to find herself becoming, deeply interested in Aunt Flora's evening game of solitaire. Perhaps the two women never came quite so close to each other as then, when Gay bent her bright head interestedly above the cards, and Flora, with a card suspended, listened to advice. Affectionate, and hungry for affection, Gabrielle was oddly touched when she realized that Flora really liked her companionship at this time, if at no other. Gay had been perhaps a week at Wastewater when one evening, Flora, shuffling her packs, said mildly:

"Don't tire your eyes, Gabrielle, with that book!"

Gabrielle looked up, saw that the game was about to be commenced. She had turned back to "Stratton" again, with a grateful smile, when Flora said again:

"Was it last night when five aces came out in the first row?"

This was enough. The girl closed her book, leaned forward. Presently she took a lighter chair, on the other side of the little card table, and after that she always did.

On one of these evenings, when the wind was crying and they two seemed alone, not only in the house, but in the world, Gay asked suddenly:

"Aunt Flora, does anybody live in that north wing, opposite where I am but on the same floor?"

"I don't understand you. How could—how do you mean?" said Mrs. Fleming. Gay saw that she had turned a deathly colour, and was breathing badly, and she told herself remorsefully that such a query, hurled unexpectedly into the silence, might well terrify any nervous elderly woman, living alone.

Eager to simplify matters, she recounted her odd experience on the very first night after her return. She had often looked over in that direction since, she went on, but had seen nothing. But, weary and confused that first night, she might never have gotten to sleep but for the reassuring knowledge that David was so near!

"You may have seen a reflection of some light in the trunk room, up above where you are," Flora suggested. "Perhaps Maria or Hedda went up there with John and your trunk."

"No, for they didn't take my trunk until next day! But they might have gone up there to make room," Gabrielle conceded, cheerfully, distressed at the continued pallor of her aunt's face.

41

"I'll have Hedda and Maria go all over everything," Flora said. "I'll tell them to lock everything and look over everything to-morrow." And with a mottled hand that shook badly, she resumed her manipulation of the cards, and Gabrielle for a time thought no more about the matter.

The two lonely women had a turkey on Thanksgiving Day, and Flora a telegram from Sylvia. And not long after that it was time to prepare for Sylvia's homecoming at Christmas.

This, Gabrielle perceived, was to be an event quite unparalleled by any of the sober festivities at Wastewater since Uncle Roger's day. Last Christmas Flora had gone to Sylvia, shut in the college infirmary with a sharp touch of influenza, and last summer Sylvia had taken a six weeks' extension course, and had spent only odd weeks and week-ends at Wastewater; she had not been enough at home to alter in any way the quiet routine of the household.

But this was different. The Christmas holidays, beginning with a little Christmas house party, would be almost like a housewarming—a sort of forerunner of Sylvia's attaining her majority and becoming the real owner and the mistress of Wastewater. Sylvia would be twenty-one in late June, when David and her mother would end their long guardianship and surrender to her her inheritance from Black Roger Fleming. Tom was legally, technically, dead; the family felt now that he was truly dead, and every passing year had helped to entrench Flora in her feeling of security. If she had ever expected his return, she did so no longer. The courts had confirmed Sylvia's expectations. David and Flora had administered her affairs carefully—Flora felt that to her Wastewater would always be home, and that her beautiful child would be rich.

Gabrielle, speculating upon Sylvia's prospects, had long ago satisfied herself that whatever they were, David would share them. It was the logical, the probable thing; Gabrielle had indeed taken it half for granted, for years. Now, when she heard the quiet little note of admiration in his voice when he spoke of Sylvia, when she studied Sylvia's pictures and found them beautiful, when she realized how pledged he was to the service of Sylvia's interests, anxious to do everything that Sylvia would approve, she appreciated that forces as strong as love bound them together, and she fancied—and not without a little wistful pain—that love might easily—easily!—be there too. Everything, everything for Sylvia.

The scale upon which the preparations for the Christmas house party were commenced was astonishing to Gabrielle. She had not supposed her aunt capable of even thinking in such terms. Aunt Flora had always been the last person in the world to associate with thoughts of lavish hospitality, generous and splendid entertaining.

But Aunt Flora went about this business of getting ready with a sure and steady hand that astonished Gabrielle, who could remember nothing of the old days of Wastewater's splendour.

By mid-December some of the big downstairs rooms were opened, and Margret, aged, gray, wrinkled like a rosy apple, and always with a kindly word for Gabrielle, was directing the other servants in the disposition of the furniture. Linen covers came off, mirrors were rubbed, and fires crackled in the unused fireplaces. The chairs were pushed to sociable angles, and whenever there was sunlight the windows were opened wide to receive it.

Upstairs Flora counted out the beautiful heavy linen sheets, aired the blankets, hung fringed towels upon the balcony railings to lose their scent of camphor. From the dining-room mantel projected a new and ugly but eminently satisfactory airtight stove, and the crackle of wood within it and the delicious corresponding softness in the cool heavy air of the room gave Gay one of the pleasantest sensations she had had at Wastewater. In the big square pantry the maids washed and piled china and glass; some of it Gabrielle had never seen before: pink Doulton, green and pink Canton, fine Old Blue.

Downstairs in the kitchen region was pleasantest of all, for Trude had a free hand at last, and she and Hedda often broke into their own ecstatic tongue under the novelty and excitement of it, remembering old days in Bruges, when they had made Christmas cakes and had stuffed fat geese for the oven. Trude chopped mincemeat, made her famous damp, dark, deliciously spiced dried-apple cake "by the yard," Gabrielle said, prepared great jars of sauces and mayonnaise and stored them in the vault-like regions of the cellar, ready for the onslaught of young appetites and unexpected meals between meals. The grocer's boy from Crowchester delivered whole crates of cereals and vegetables, and from Boston came hams and bacon, raisins and nuts, meats and oysters in boxes and kegs that dripped with ice.

Yet it was not to be so very large a party, after all. There would be Laura and Gwen Montallen, the nice Canadian girls from Quebec; Bart Montallen, their cousin from England; Arthur Tipping, "who will be Lord Crancastle some day"; and Bart Montallen's chum, a man named Frank du Spain, from Harvard. All three of the men were in college together, and the three girls had been classmates for years. David would of course join them, making seven, and "Gay eight," wrote Sylvia, kindly, "and we may have an extra man for good measure, if I find just the right one, so that we'll be just ten, with you, Mamma dear. And that's just right. Now please don't go to making too elaborate preparations, these are all the simplest and least exacting of people, as you'll instantly see. They want to walk, talk, have some music perhaps—ask Gay to be ready, for Mr. Tipping sings—have good meals, and in five days it will all be over, and then you and I can have some real talks and make up for lost time. Of course, if we could dance, one of the nights, that would be wonderful, in the old parlour where the Neapolitan boy is, for the ballroom's much too big for so few. But I confess the thought of the music daunts me——"

The thought of it, however, did not daunt Flora. There was even a triumphant little smile on her face when she came to this line. A four-piece orchestra should of course come down from Boston; the square piano was wheeled into the ballroom, and two days before Sylvia's expected arrival two men with mud and ice on their boots, and mittens crusted with ice, and red, frost-bitten faces, came out from Crowchester with a whole truckload of potted palms and shining-leafed shrubs, all boxed and sacked, tagged and crated carefully for their return trip to Boston when the festivities should be over.

Gabrielle caught the joyous excitement of it, or perhaps created it to a large extent, and in a shabby linen uniform and an old sweater of David's rushed about with dusters and buckets, nails and strings, climbed ladders, rubbed silver, and flung herself into the preparations generally with an enthusiasm that warmed even Aunt Flora. Flora had loitered, coming out from church on the Sunday previous, and had quite composedly asked a score of the nicest young persons in Crowchester to the dance; invitations that, to Gabrielle's surprise, were pleasantly and informally worded and invariably accepted by mothers and aunts with much appreciation. One day, when they were filling a great jar with the spreading branches that bore polished fine leaves of wild huckleberry, Flora said suddenly:

"What frocks have you, Gabrielle?"

"Well, I have my uniforms, and my new suit that I wear to church," Gabrielle responded, readily, "and my velvet for afternoons, and my brown lace, and my three blouses."

Flora said nothing at the time; she struggled with the branches silently, removed the rough gloves that had covered her hands, and called Daisy to sweep up the pantry floor. But later in the day she showed Gabrielle one of the wardrobes that held Sylvia's clothes.

"It will be a small dance, of course," she said, "and your lace dress is just from Paris, after all. But it's possible that you might

wear one of these—some of them Sylvia hasn't had on this year."
And she drew out a limp skirt or two, a pink satin, a white net with
pink roses flouncing it, a brocaded scarlet and gold.

"All the rose colours!" Gabrielle said, smiling.

"She's dark," the mother said, in a quiet voice that swelled in
spite of her. And she glanced at the picture of Sylvia on Sylvia's bureau—a stunning Sylvia in a big fur collar and a small fur hat.

It was for Gabrielle to scour the woods for beautiful shrubs and
winter colours, and she did it enthusiastically, well rewarded when
Flora smiled, in spite of herself, at the sight of berry-studded bri-
ars and glossy pointed holly interspersed with scarlet beads. There
were no loneliness and no idleness for Gabrielle now; she was
off, well wrapped and in heavy overshoes, immediately after lunch,
sometimes laughing aloud when she found herself in the sunlighted
snowy sweetness of the woods, trampling the first light fall of virgin
snow, breathing the spicy, tingling air with great eager respirations,
and calling out a holiday greeting to other holly- and mistletoe-hunt-
ing folk.

CHAPTER VI

ON THE day that Sylvia and her guests were coming from the north, and David probably from the south, there was no sunshine. There was a cold, unsteady, wind, and a cold, hard, low-hung mackerel sky, under which the sea moved rough and restless, topped with racing caps of white. All the world was gray and forlorn; distances were shortened, the little houses in Crowchester and Keyport were closed against the weather and showed no sign of life except the varying plumes of smoke that rose from their frosted roofs. From them occasionally emerged muffled and mittened figures, with tippets blowing behind them or bellying giddily before; Gabrielle, who had gone into town with John on some last errands, thought she had never seen so many shabby hungry gulls, so many lean cats investigating snow-topped garbage barrels, such dreary-looking raiment hung snow-laden upon such sagging clotheslines.

"A heavy storm on the way," John said. And Gabrielle, beside him on the front seat of the little car, with a crate of eggs steadied at her feet and two quarts of whipping cream held firmly in two bottles in her lap, looked up at the scudding sky and thought with exhilaration that it was probably true, and that all the company, and David, would be here in a few hours, to make merry in Wastewater and defy it.

She picked and seeded raisins for an hour in the kitchen before luncheon, and came to the meal with her cheeks red and her head hot, and after luncheon went out into the woods, where a genuine colour presently stung the warm brunette skin to glowing, and where wrestling and tugging with obdurate saplings made her tingle from head to foot and push her hat back from her damp forehead, laughing and panting with the tussle. Aunt Flora had said, with one of her rare touches of companionship, "I would just like that empty corner of the hall filled up—some sort of branchy thing——" and Gabrielle had been only too glad to make it her business to fill it. She had left her aunt "resting," as unusual an employment for Flora as were the flush on her face and the wire curlers in her hair.

Everyone in the big house had been wrought, now, to a pitch of expectation bordering upon fever. The last plate was washed, the last spoon polished; the shelves of long-unused pantries downstairs were loaded with cakes and pies and cold meats and bread and sauces and trembling jellies; the big rooms upstairs were aired and warmed; there were fat comforters folded invitingly across the foot of the big, freshly made beds; there were open fires and stove fires everywhere. Floors shone with wax; palms moved green fronds gently in well-dusted corners; lamps were filled, clocks were ticking busily. Gabrielle felt in her veins the excitement that is a part of physical strain. She, like everyone else, was tired, but it was a happy sort of fatigue, after all.

On this last afternoon she had gone a little deeper into the woods than was necessary, or than she had planned to go for the last greens, as a glance at her wrist watch showed her. It was already half-past three o'clock when, with her arms full of fragrant boughs, she started back toward the house, perhaps a mile away. The day had grown a little colder, the wind had steadied to something like a gale, and the sea—for she never was quite out of sight of the sea—was in an uproar, running high and wild, breaking furiously upon the rocks, and flinging itself twenty feet into the air when these stood fast, as they had stood for a thousand years.

Suddenly, creeping through bare boughs like little silent fairies shod in down, came drifting the first snowflakes. They came timidly, irresolutely at first, clinging here to a fir and there to a bare maple twig, moving restlessly and gently in all directions, fluttering, changing places, like the breast-feathers of a white baby swan, from which perhaps, thought Gay whimsically, Mother Nature, who loves to repeat her forms, had copied them.

"Oh, this is glorious!" she said aloud to the sweet, empty forest. And she began to walk briskly with that dancing step of hers that meant utter happiness and felicity.

When she came within sight of Wastewater's walls the storm was upon them; the snow was falling rapidly and steadily now, and with a denseness that made a sort of twilight in the world. It fell dry, close, only slightly at an angle; Wastewater's outbuildings were already furred deep, and John's wife Etta was laughing as she backed the little car into the shed for shelter.

"This is a terror, Miss Gabrielle!" she shouted. "It'll be a white Christmas, all right! I only hope that Miss Fleming and her company don't get held up somewheres! I declare, you can't see twenty feet in it!"

Gabrielle shouted back, fled upon her way about the big north wing, through a sort of tunnel of dry branches above an arbour already heavily powdered with white.

Her thoughts were all on the house, all intent upon reaching the side door, all upon the necessary stamping, shaking, disburdening herself of outer garments and her branches of snow; it was after four now, she must be ready in the velvet dress when Sylvia came at six——

Suddenly she stopped short in the lonely side garden, where the snow was falling so fast, recoiled, and heard her own choking exclamation of dismay. Something was moving in the snow, something bent and whitened with flakes—but human! Gabrielle's heart almost suffocated her, and she felt her throat constrict with pure terror.

It was a child—it was a little old woman, doubled up with years, with wisps of white hair showing about a pallid old face that was scarcely a wholesomer colour than they, or than the falling snowflakes. She had her back half turned to Gabrielle, and was creeping along against a sort of hedge of tightly set firs, her old black cape or shawl topped with white, her thick shoes furred with it. She was muttering to herself as she went, and Gabrielle could hear her, now that the wind had died out and the silent, twisting curtains of snow muffled all other sounds.

Pity and concern for the forlorn old creature almost immediately routed the girl's first wild, vague fears, and she dropped her branches and followed the wavering footsteps, laying a timid hand upon the woman's shoulder. Instantly a yellowish ivory face and two wild eyes were turned upon her, and the stranger shrieked with a sound that was all the more horrible because so helpless and so weak. It was almost like the cry of a wind-blown gull, and here in the unearthly solitude and quiet of the storm it frightened Gabrielle with a sense of forlornness and horror. The house, only a few feet away, with fires and voices, seemed unattainable.

"Come in—come in!" cried Gabrielle, guiding her with a strong young arm. "You'll die out here—it's a terrible night! And you know it will be dark in ten minutes," she added, half pushing and half dragging the old form, which was astonishingly light and made but a feeble resistance. "Daisy—Margret!" called Gabrielle, at last flinging open the side door upon the blessed security and warmth of the hall. "Call Mrs. Fleming, will you! This poor old woman's gotten lost in the garden——"

"*My God—what is this!*" It was Flora's voice, but not one that Gabrielle had ever heard before. The hallway was instantly filled with concerned and frightened women, unduly frightened, Gabrielle thought, for the last of her own terrors had disappeared under the first ray of lamplight. "It's nothing, Gabrielle," said Flora, choking, and with her face strangely livid, as she stood slightly above the level of the others, on the stairs, clutching her dressing gown together. "It's some poor woman from Crowchester, Margret!" she stammered. "Come upstairs and dress, Gabrielle. Take her—take her to the kitchen, Hedda, and give her some tea, and I'll be right down!"

"Imagine!" Gabrielle said, eagerly. "She might have died in the storm, the poor old thing!"

The old woman had been turning herself uneasily, looking with rapidly blinking eyes from one to the other. Now the servants were gently urging her toward the doorway that led to the warm kitchen regions, and to Gabrielle's amazement she seemed to be displaying a weak disinclination to go.

"Who's this girl, Flora?" she said now, in a cracked, querulous voice. "You stop pushing me, Margret!" she added, fretfully.

It was Gabrielle's turn to show amazement and consternation. She looked from one stricken, conscious face to another, and her own bright, frost-glowing cheeks faded a little. This trembling bit of human wreckage, dragged in from the storm, was not quite a stranger, at all events.

Flora's face was ghastly; Hedda looked more than ordinarily idiotic. But Margret, eighty years old, spoke hearteningly.

"It's old Mrs. Smith, Mrs. Fleming, from Keyport. She's——" Margret had one stout old arm about the cowering stranger, and now she gave the other women a significant glance and tapped her own forehead with her free hand. "We'll give her some tea and dry her out a bit, and then maybe John'll take her home," said Margret, "when he takes the sleigh in for Miss Fleming!"

Gabrielle, perfectly satisfied with the explanation and the arrangement, went upstairs beside her aunt.

"Oh, will John have the big sleigh out?" she asked, enthusiastically. Flora did not answer; she looked ill. She parted from Gabrielle without a word and went downstairs. But half an hour later, when the girl had had a hot bath and was busy with the bright masses of her hair before her mirror, she started suddenly to find that her aunt had come quietly into the room.

By this time Gabrielle had had time to think over her little adventure, and even in all the day's excitement and expectation she had felt an uncomfortable reaction from it. She shuddered whenever she remembered herself hurrying so innocently along the snowy lanes in the twilight, and the hideous fright of that first sight of something moving—something human, shadowy gray and white against the gray and white shadows of the hedge.

"That was a horrid experience with that poor old woman, Aunt Flora," she said now, distressed at her own emotion.

"You must think no more about it," Flora, giving no reason for her visit to Gabrielle's room, said firmly. "The girls have taken good care of her, and John is to drive her back when he goes. She's perfectly harmless—poor soul. I would rather you didn't mention it to Sylvia, Gabrielle, by the way."

Gabrielle, after a bewildered upward glance, of course agreed never to mention the circumstance to Sylvia—indeed, never to think of the poor old soul again. She went cheerfully on toward the pleasant moment of assuming the velvet gown, when Aunt Flora was gone, brushing her rich hair simply back, pleased in spite of herself with her unusual colour, and satisfied with the brown silk stockings and the brown pumps.

Suddenly there was a sound of laughter and voices and sleigh bells under her window, and for a moment she thought, with a sense of panic, that the company had come. She ran to her window and peeped down.

Below was darkness, through which the snow was falling—falling. But a great shaft of light shone out from the side door, and in it she could see the old red sleigh, filled with furry robes, and John on the front seat, already looking like a snow man. Daisy and Sarah and Maria and Etta were teasing John; it was evident that he and the two big horses were about to start off into the storm, and the maids were amused.

But there was no little old woman being bundled into the sleigh. No, though Maria shook out all the rugs and Etta put a great waterproof cover over them, Gabrielle saw nothing of her.

Where was she, then? Had Margret decided to keep her at Wastewater overnight? Odd!——

Odd, mused Gabrielle, slowly finishing her dressing. Odder still to have Margret herself, coming upstairs to take a last look at the waiting rooms, affirm that the poor old lady had gotten off in a great bustle with John, and surely her family was already wild with fright over her disappearance on such a night.

But again things of more vital interest to herself put these little mysteries out of Gabrielle's head. For when she had gone downstairs, come up again, gone the rounds of the rooms, touching a new cake of soap here, and putting a small log into a stove there; when she had feared that this hall was too warm, and that passage too cold, and when she had stolen at least a hundred glances at her pretty flushed face in various mirrors and admired a hundred times the simple perfection of the velvet gown, Gabrielle really did hear sleigh bells again in the night, voices, laughter again. Then there was a sort of flurry downstairs, and the big front doors opened to a wild rush of wind and night and snow and storm that made the curtains balloon wildly even upstairs, and the lamps plunge convulsedly. Gabrielle heard "Mamma!" in what was of course Sylvia's voice; then eager greetings and introductions and a perfect babel of voices.

She had been upstairs in the front hall; now, by simply descending, she could follow the company into the downstairs sitting room, which had been made warm and ready for this moment of arrival. Gabrielle in the darkness above stretched a hand for the smooth guidance of the wide balustrade and went down in light flight, like a skimming bird.

She had almost reached the lower level, which was but dimly lighted, when she saw that two persons were lingering in the hall, and stopped short, instinctively fearful that she had disturbed them. One was a woman, dark, furred, slender, and wearing a small, snow-powdered hat. The other was David.

Gabrielle was eighteen in years, but older in many ways than her years. She looked down and saw David, smiling that attentive smile of his, tall, broad, yet leanly built, belted into a brown coat that was not new, saying nothing that she could hear—just looking at this girl—just himself—David——

And that instant changed the whole world. Gabrielle did not analyze the strange sweet weakness that flowed over her like a river, from head to foot. She did not say even to herself, "He is handsome. He is good. He is kind." No need for that—too late for that. Her heart went to him simply, completely. She had been one woman a moment ago, she was another now. Much of what she had heard and read of love had been a sealed book to her; it was all clear now. Reason, logic, convention had always influenced her; these were all so many words now.

She heard Sylvia, turning her head to look over her shoulder and so bring a beautiful face close to his, say affectionately: "So many thousands of things to tell you, David!" and although she did not hear the brief words, or perhaps the single word of his reply, she heard the tone, and she heard Sylvia's low laugh.

Gabrielle sat down on the stairs in the semi-darkness. Her heart was hammering, and her mouth dry. The world—youth—beauty, jealousy—love—marriage—all these things moved before her consciousness like maskers coming into the light. She stood up, on the halfway landing, and the woman in velvet with the tawny hair stood up, too. Gay walked slowly to the mirror, studied her own face. She was breathing hard, she was confused, half frightened.

She heard Maria calling her. Her aunt was asking for her.

"Say I'm coming!" Gabrielle said, clearing her throat.

David was down there, she would meet him—have to talk to him—before all their eyes——

She went slowly downstairs.

CHAPTER VII

FLORA's little Christmas house party for her daughter was a small affair, after all, but to Gabrielle's confused eyes there seemed to be eighteen laughing and talking persons rather than eight in the sitting room when she came in. The girls had flung off their big coats, but still wore hats, and were apparently only warming their hands and finishing their greetings before being distributed in bedrooms upstairs.

From the group, however, Sylvia instantly separated, and Gabrielle forgot everything else in the pleasure of seeing her cousin again. Sylvia gave her a warm, laughing kiss and stood talking to her with one arm still about her, holding the younger girl off while she studied her face.

"Well, Gay! How you've grown up—and with the hair up, too! Mamma wrote me all about you, but I had quite a different sort of person in mind! How dare you be fair among all us black Flemings!"

And with her arm still about Gay, she turned to the others for the introductions. Last of all came David's greeting with his kindly smile and keen-eyed inspection, and when his hand touched hers Gabrielle was conscious of that same suffocating flutter at her heart again and dared scarcely raise her eyes.

"Mamma, you're simply a miracle worker!" Sylvia was saying, gratefully. "I knew there'd be fires, and I knew you'd realize how weary and cold we are, but upon my word, I hardly know Wastewater! This room is actually civilized. I promise you nothing for the halls," Sylvia said to her guests, "but we can run through them at full speed. And as long as the *rooms* are warm——"

She was beautiful, no question of it. Dark, vivid, and glowing, yet with something queenly and superb about her, too. Instantly it seemed to Gay that she had never been parted from Sylvia, that all these separated school years had been a dream. Years ago, as a bony, pallid, big-toothed little girl, it had been decided that a balmier climate than Wastewater would be wise for Gay, and she had been bundled off to the Southern branch of the Boston convent quite contentedly and had been happy there. But now she remembered how close she and Sylvia had been in the days of sand castles and flower ladies, and that Sylvia even then had had this same bright, sweet, responsive manner that was yet impressive and fine, with something of conscious high integrity in it; something principled and constructive even in her gayest moods. Sylvia was really—Gay came back to the word with another little prick of envy—really "superior." She was poised where Gay was simple; she was definite, where Gay was vague; her voice had pleasant affectations, she broadened her a's in the Boston manner.

And Sylvia's youth and her fresh, glowing beauty kept these things from being in the least displeasing. She was happy, now, delighted with the unwonted warmth and brightness of the old house, delighted to be home, and perhaps delighted, too, to find herself already the most important person here, with these friends of hers seeing this big, imposing old mansion as some day to be all her own.

"Not tea, Maria!" she said, eagerly, to the old servant. "Mamma, I congratulate you upon introducing anything like tea into Wastewater!"

For Maria, followed by Daisy, one of the newer maids, was indeed beaming behind a loaded tray.

"I thought we'd dine about seven, dear," said Flora, crimped, rustling, flushed with excitement. "And that you might like the hot drink after your trip. It's not six yet."

"I assure you, girls," Sylvia laughingly said, "my mother's treating you like royalty! I've been telling them all the way down," resumed Sylvia, now dispensing the tea with quick murmurs and dextrous quiet movements that Gay secretly admired, "that we are absolutely Victorian here, and rather uncomfortable into the bargain."

"Tea's Victorian," Gabrielle said, as she paused. "It's just plain bread and butter," she added, smiling at the elder Miss Montallen hospitably.

"Tea's Victorian, of course, and I daresay coal fires and lamps and comfort are Victorian, too, and I like them both too much to find any fault with terminology, Gay!" Sylvia said, cheerfully.

"We live in just such a country house outside of Quebec; we're quite accustomed to country winters," murmured the charming voice of the older Miss Montallen. The travellers drank their tea standing, exclaimed over the delicious home-made bread. The young men were rather silent, exchanging little friendly murmurs and grins, except that the one named Frank du Spain attached himself instantly to Gabrielle; Flora chatted, Sylvia made the right comments, David stood by the mantel, tall, pleased, smiling at them all. Gay hardly identified the other men until dinner-time, so entirely monopolized was her attention by the one.

Meanwhile, Sylvia was delighted again, upstairs. Nothing could make Wastewater anything but old-fashioned, clumsy, draughty. But the old rooms did look hospitable and comfortable, the beds were heaped with covers, and there were two more airtight stoves roaring here. Daisy and Sarah were rushing about with great pitchers of hot water; the girls scattered their effects from room to room, and went to and fro in wrappers, laughing and running.

Sylvia's usual room was on the second floor, next her mother's. But for this occasion Flora had grouped all the young persons on the third floor, where the rooms were smaller, better lighted in winter, and connecting.

Outside the snow fell—fell. The world was wrapped in winding sheets, muffled and disguised, and the snow fell softly on the surface of the running, white-capped waves, and was devoured by them. Whenever a window was opened, a rush of pure cold snowy air rushed in and the bare-armed girls who had wanted a breath of it had to shut it out, laughing and gasping, once more.

But inside Wastewater's old walls there were noise and merriment, songs about the old piano, laughing groups about the fires, and the delicious odours, the clatter and tinkle of china and silver around the solemnly wavering candles on the dining-room table.

Gabrielle could not talk much, for Sylvia and these particular friends had shared several holidays, and their chatter was of other times and places. But her cheeks glowed with excitement, and she moved her star-sapphire eyes from one face to another eagerly, as if unwilling to lose a word of their talk. And again, Sylvia was always "superior."

She was evidently a girl who took her college life seriously; studied and excelled, and enjoyed studying and excelling. She was prominent in various undergraduate organizations; interested in the "best" developments of this and that element in school life, the "best" way to handle problems of all sorts. Laura and Gwen Montallen immensely admired her, Gabrielle could see, and were continually referring to her in little affectionate phrases: "Ah, yes, but you see you can do that sort of thing, Sylvia, for they'll all listen to *you!*" or "Sylvia here, with her famous diplomacy, went straight to the Dean——"

The men, Gabrielle thought, were unusually nice types, too. They were all in the early twenties, none was rich, and all seemed serious and ambitious. Bart Montallen was to have a small diplomatic berth when he graduated in June; Arthur Tipping was already well started toward a junior membership in his uncle's law firm and spoke concernedly of "making a home" for his mother and little sisters as soon as he could; and Frank du Spain was a joyous, talkative youth, who confessed, when he sat next to Gay at dinner, that his people were not especially pleased with his college record, and that, unless he wanted trouble with his parents, he had to "make good, by gum." He told Gay that his father had a ranch near Pasadena, and Gay widened her eyes and said wistfully, "It sounds delicious!" David, looking approvingly at her from the head of the table, thought the velvet gown with the embroidery collar and cuffs a great success.

Altogether the young guests were simple, unspoiled, enthusiastic about the delicious triumph of a meal, and over the pleasantness of being free from studies and together. Gay, impressed by this and anxious to establish cousinlike relations with Sylvia, said something of it rather shyly when Sylvia came in for a few friendly moments of chat alone, late that night.

The evening had been delightful, Gay thought; for a while they had all played a hilarious card game for the prize David offered, the prize being a large conch shell which David himself had selected upon a hilarious and candlelighted search through the freezing wilderness of some of the downstairs rooms. And then they had stood talking about the fire, and finally had grouped themselves about it; the girls packed into chairs in twos, the men on the floor, for five more minutes—and five more!—of pleasant, weary, desultory conversation. David had held his favourite position, during this talk, standing, with one arm on the mantel and his charming smile turned to the room, and Gabrielle noticed, or thought she did, that he rarely moved his eyes from Sylvia's face.

But when he did, it was almost always to give her, Gay, a specially kind look; every moment—she could not help it!—made him seem more wonderful, and every one of his rare words deepened the mysterious tie that drew her, strangely confused, strangely happy, and strangely sad, nearer and nearer to him.

There was another portrait of Roger here, this one painted in about his fortieth year; handsomer than ever, still smiling, a book open before him on a table, a beautiful ringed hand dropped on a collie's lovely feathered ruff.

"That was your father, Mr. Fleming?" Gwen Montallen had asked, looking up at Roger's likeness.

"Stepfather. My father died before I was born," David said, with his ready, attentive interest. "My mother married Mr. Fleming when

56

I was only a baby."

"And where does Gabrielle come in?" asked Gwen, who had taken a fancy to the younger girl and was showing it in the kindly modern fashion.

"Well, let's see. Gay's mother was Aunt Flora's sister," David elucidated. "They were Flemings, too. It's complicated," admitted David, smilingly. "To get us Flemings straightened out you really have to go back thirty years, to the time I was a baby. My mother was a young widow then, who had married a David Fleming, who was a sort of cousin of Uncle Roger. He doesn't come into the story at all——"

"And that's Uncle Roger?" Laura Montallen asked, looking up at the picture.

"That's Uncle Roger," David nodded. "I was only a baby when my mother married him, and he was the only father I remember. A year after she married him, my mother had another boy baby, so there were two of us growing up here together."

"Ah, you've a half-brother?" Laura asked.

"I think I have," David answered, with a grave smile. "But Tom ran away to sea when he was about fourteen—fifteen years ago now, and we've not heard of him since!"

"Is it fifteen years?" they heard Flora say, in a low tone, as if to herself.

"But how romantic!" Gwen said, with round eyes. "Wouldn't you know a wonderful old place like this," the girl added, as in the little silence they heard the winter wind whine softly about the sealed shutters of Wastewater, "wouldn't you know that an old place like this would have a story! So there's a runaway son?"

"We did hear from him once, from Pernambuco, and once from Guam, David!" Gay reminded him, animatedly.

"Do get it in order," Laura begged. "I've not yet fitted Sylvia in, much less Gabrielle!"

"Well," David said, returning to his story. "So there was my mother—she was pretty, wasn't she, Aunt Flora?"

"Beautiful!" Flora said, briefly.

"There was my mother, Uncle Roger her husband, and Tom and me," resumed David. "Then—this was an old-fashioned household, you know—there was a sort of cousin of his"—David nodded at the picture—"whom we called Aunt John. That was my Aunt Flora's mother, and she kept house for us all, and Aunt Flora and Aunt Lily were her daughters. Oh, yes, and then there was Uncle Roger's younger brother Will, who used to play the banjo and sing—what

57

was that song about the boy 'and his sister Sue!' The boy that ate the green apples, Aunt Flora, and 'A short time ago, boys, an Irishman named Daugherty, was elected to the Senate by a very large majority'——"

"Oh, wonderful!" said Laura Montallen, and Gay said eagerly, "Oh, David, go on!"

"I wish I could remember it all," David said, regretfully. "And there was another about the Prodigal Son, and one about 'the blow almost killed Father'——"

"Oh, David, David!" said Aunt Flora, between a laugh and a sob.

"Well, anyway, Tom and I used to think Uncle Will's songs the most delightful things we ever heard," David went on. "So that was the family when I was very small: Mother, Dad, as we both called Uncle Roger, Aunt Flora, Aunt Lily—who was very delicate and romantic—Uncle Will and his banjo, and of course Aunt John, who was a little wisp of a gray woman—— What is it, Gay?"

For Gay had made a sudden exclamation.

"Nothing," the girl said, quickly, clearing her throat. She looked very pale in the warm firelight.

"Then they sent Tom and me off to school in Connecticut. And then," and David's voice lowered suddenly, and he looked straight ahead of him into the coals, "then our mother died very suddenly—do you remember that you drove the buckboard into Crowchester to meet us, Aunt Flora, when we came home?"

"Ah, yes!" Flora said, from a deep reverie.

David, fitting it all together in his memory, remembered now that in here, chronologically, came Flora's engagement to Roger Fleming. But he looked up at the picture above the mantel, and then at her face, absent-eyed and stern now, and cupped in her hand, as if to promise that that secret at least should not be betrayed.

"Less than a year after my mother's death," he went on, "Uncle Roger married again, a very young girl—Cecily—Kent, was it, Aunt Flora?"

"Cecily Kent," Flora echoed, briefly.

"Who was very delicate, and who was in fact dying for years," David went on. "Anyway, that same year Aunt Flora married Uncle Will and—well, that's where Sylvia comes in, and little Aunt Lily married a man named Charpentier, and that's where Gabrielle comes in. And a few years later Tom ran away. That broke my stepfather's heart, and I suppose his wife's health didn't cheer him up exactly. And then my stepfather's little second wife died, and then Uncle Will died," David summarized it all rapidly, "and after he had hunted my half-brother, Tom, for years, *he* died!" And David finished with a final nod toward Roger's picture.

"And you've never found Tom? Not even when his father died?"

"We don't know that he knows it, even. It was just before all the confusion and change of the big war."

"Yes, but if your Aunt Lily was only a third cousin of your step-father, and married a man named Charpentier, he—your stepfather, I mean—wasn't really any relation to Gabrielle, then?" Gwen persisted, with another puzzled look from the portrait to Gay's glowing face.

"A sort of distant cousin, but that goes pretty far back," Flora said, unexpectedly, breaking through another conversation that she had been having on the other side of the fireplace. "My sister and I were cousins of Roger Fleming, third cousins, and my mother lived here, kept house for him, for years. My husband was William Fleming, Roger's brother. But Gabrielle is my sister's child—a sister named Lily, who died many years ago."

"It's hopelessly tangled!" Gay said, with a laugh.

"No, but look—look here!" Gwen Montallen had persisted. Gently catching Gay by the shoulder, for they were all standing at the moment, she wheeled her about so that the company could encompass with one look the painted likeness of the man of forty and the eighteen-year-old girl. "Do you see it, Laura?" she said, eagerly. "The mouth and the shape of the eyes—I saw it the instant she came into the room!"

"I see it," young Bart Montallen agreed, with a nod. "For a while I couldn't think who Miss Gabrielle looked like, and then I knew it was the picture."

"Nonsense!" Sylvia said, looking from one to the other. "Uncle Roger had such black hair and such a white skin——"

"Really your colouring, Sylvia," David suggested. "But apart from the colouring," he added. "I see the likeness. Look at Gay's mouth—look, Aunt Flora——"

"No, you may see it in the picture," Flora said, with her voice plunging in her throat like a candle flame in the wind. "But they—they are not alike. Lily—my sister—Gabrielle's mother—was dark, with rosy cheeks, something like Roger. But Roger—Roger never looked much like that picture—he hated it—always said it made him look fat——"

She was battling so obviously for calm that Sylvia remembered, with sudden compunction, that Mamma was the last of her generation, after all, and that—it was no secret!—she had certainly once, if not twice, been engaged to marry Roger Fleming. Sylvia exchanged a significant warning look with David, and they immediately guided the conversation into safer channels. But David was shocked and astonished to notice a few minutes later that his aunt's forehead, under the festive crimping of the gray hair, was wet.

That was all of that. Nobody apparently paid any more attention to the trivial episode, unless Gay felt an odd and indefinable satisfaction in being thought like Uncle Roger, in being thus included in the Fleming ranks.

She was trying to see this likeness at her own mirror an hour later, when Sylvia, brushing her hair and in a red wrapper infinitely becoming, came in.

"The girls are asleep," reported Sylvia, "and I don't like to light my lamp because Gwen is in with me. I stayed downstairs a few minutes to talk to David—I see him so little nowadays."

A sharp stiletto twisted in Gay's heart. She could see them lingering in the darkened room, by the dying fire: Sylvia so beautiful, with her glossy black coils of hair drooping, and her face glowing with firelight and winter roses, and David looking down at her with that kindly, half-amused, half-admiring look. Just a few moments' intimate talk, perhaps only of Sylvia's affairs, perhaps only of her mother's health, but binding these two together in that old friendship, kinship, utter ease and understanding, mutual liking and admiration.

Despair came suddenly upon Gabrielle, and she wanted to get away—away from Sylvia's superiorities and advantages, away from Sylvia's long outdistancing upon the road to David's friendship. Gay thought, braiding and brushing her own long hair, that she did not want Sylvia's money, she did not want anything that Sylvia had, she only wanted to be where she need not hear about it!

"They all say such kind things of you, Gay," Sylvia told her, with that pleasantness that was quite unconsciously, and only faintly, tinged with patronage.

It was then that Gay, aware of little pin-pricks of hurt pride, said something of the delightful quality of the guests.

"The Sisters had the idea that all college girls are either terrible bobbed-haired flappers who smoke cigarettes," Gay said, laughing, "or blue-stockings who think science can disprove all that religion has ever claimed!"

Sylvia smiled at her through the mirror.

"And what made you think I could make such girls my friends?" she asked, lightly reproachful, with an air of quietly posing her cousin, and even in this pleasant little phrase Gay detected the pretty pride in herself, her line, her blood, her code and intelligence and judgment that indeed actuated all that Sylvia did. "No, the Montallens are—unusual," Sylvia added, half to herself. "And so," she said, smiling, as she dextrously pinned up her rich black braid, "so it was all the nicer that they should like my cousin Gabrielle! Tell me," she went on, "how do things go here? Are you happy—getting nicely rested? Not too lonely?"

"Rested?" Gay echoed, at a loss.

"Between school," Sylvia explained, "and—and what?"

She said the last word with a really winning and interested smile, and sat looking expectantly at Gay, with an air almost motherly.

"Or have you plans?" she elucidated, as Gay looked puzzled. "Is there something you tremendously want to do? If you are like me," Sylvia added, now with just a hint of academic enlightenment in her voice, "you have forty, instead of one! I almost wish sometimes that I had to choose what I would do. I adore teaching! I love languages. I'd love anything to do with books—old books, reviewing books, library work, even bindings. My professor of economics wants me to go after a doctor's degree and my English man wants me to write books. So there you are! And here is David telling me that I must learn to manage my own estate."

Gay flushed, and hated herself for flushing. She had often enough, in the last quiet weeks, thought that she would like to work, to do anything rather than dream through all her quiet days at Wastewater; she had thought vaguely of little tea shops with blue cotton runners, and the companionship of some little girl of fourteen who would adore her—of offices—schools——

But embarrassed and taken by surprise, with her thoughts in no sort of order, she stammered, half laughingly, she knew not why, that she had thought she might like to be an actress. Sylvia's look of astonishment was so perfectly what it should have been that Gay felt even less comfortable than before.

"But, my dear child," she said, amusedly, "I don't believe that would be practical! We have—absolutely—no connections in that line, you know. And you're quite too young. I don't mean," Sylvia went on, kindly, as Gay, hot-cheeked, was silent, very busy with night ribbons, "I don't mean that it isn't a splendid profession for some women. But it takes character, it takes experience, associations. What makes you feel that you are fitted for it? Have you—you can't have!—seen more than a dozen plays in your life?"

"I just thought of it!" Gay said, with an uncomfortable laugh.

"Then I think I should just stop thinking of it!" Sylvia said. And with an affectionate arm about Gay's waist, she nodded toward the thick rope of tawny braided hair. "Such pretty hair. Gay!"

"Yours is gorgeous, Sylvia," the younger girl returned. "I noticed to-night that it is so black that it actually made David's dinner coat look gray when you stood beside him."

"I like my black wig," Sylvia returned, contentedly, "because it's—*Fleming*. I don't think I should feel quite right with anything but the family hair! But when all's said and done this colour of yours is the hair of the poets, Gay."

She said it charmingly, and she meant it, too. For like many women of unchallenged beauty, Sylvia was very simple and unself-conscious about her appearance, and seemed to take no more personal credit for the milk-white skin, rose cheeks, and midnight hair than for her perfect digestion or the possession of her senses.

"You're the one who looks like Uncle Roger, Sylvia!"

"In colouring, perhaps. How much do you remember him, Gay?"

"Oh, clearly. I was nearly seven when he died, you know."

"I really loved him," Sylvia said, dreamily. "And I hope I can keep up all the old traditions and customs he loved so here at Waste-water. I inherit a love for him," she added, with a significant look and smile. "There's no question that my mother loved him dearly for years. Oh, she loved my father, too, later on, and perhaps in a finer way," went on Sylvia, who could fit such meaningless phrases together with all the suavity of college-bred twenty. "But her first love was for Uncle Roger."

"Do you think he——?" Gay began, and paused.

"He——? Go on, Gay. Do you mean did he break the engagement? No," Sylvia stated, definitely. "I imagine he did not. He was a gentleman, after all! But probably there was a quarrel—Mamma was much admired and a beauty—and she's a perfect Lucifer for pride, you know, and neither one would give way."

Gay accepted this with all the pathetic faith of her years. She could not possibly imagine Aunt Flora as a beauty; but every middle-aged woman who talked of her own youth had been one, and Gay was perfectly willing to believe the last a beautiful generation. She thought of a picture she had seen of Aunt Flora as a bride, in a plumed hat, enormous puffed sleeves, a five-gored skirt sweeping the ground, a wasp-waist with a chatelaine bag dangling from the belt, and a long-handle parasol held out like Bo-Peep's crook, and lost the thread of Sylvia's conversation.

There was not much more. Sylvia expressed for the twentieth

time her entire delight and gratitude for all that had been done to start the house party successfully and parted from Gay with a final kiss and a few warm words about the pleasantness of having a nice little cousin in the house. It was only when the room was dark, that Gay, snuggling resolutely down against icy pillows to sleep, began to review the whole long day with that wearisome thoroughness that is a special attribute of tired, excited eighteen on a winter night.

The flowers, the dusting, the beds, the tramp in the woods, the funny old woman bunching herself along in the snow, the arrival and the tea, and the warm rooms and icy halls, and the splendid dinner and the talk——

Gay ached all over. With her eyelids actually shutting she said to herself in a panic that she was too tired to sleep.

Her big room was dark, cool, full of dim shapes; but a fan of friendly light came through the hall transom, and she could hear men's voices somewhere, laughing and talking gruffly; David and the boys, there was nothing to fear. Outside the snow fell, whispering, tickling, piling up solemnly and steadily in the dark.

After all, it was the little old woman who had Gay's last conscious thought. The girl started wide-awake from her first drowsing slipping into unconsciousness, with her heart hammering again, and her wild eyes roving the room for a whole frightened minute, before its familiar peace lulled her into calm again.

That writhing, shadowy white-and-gray thing, in the white-and-gray shadow of the hedge, and in the muffling softness of the curtaining snow. Horse—big dog—child—no, it was a terrible yellow-faced old woman! What a whining cry she had given! And how astonishing later had been her recognition of Flora and Margret!

Well, whether she had walked home in the blizzard or gone up the chimney on a broomstick was, after all, not Gay's affair. But she had most assuredly not been driven in to Keyport or Crowchester by John! Gay thought that she was meeting this old forlorn, half-witted thing again in the snowy lane—but this time David was with her....

CHAPTER VIII

THE rest of the house party was to her a thrilling, but too rapidly flying, dream. The young people walked, rosy and whirled and beaten and shouting with laughter, in the formidable ending of the storm the next day; they ate ravenously, laughed a great deal, and formed a whole new series of those special jokes and phrases that come into being in every successful house party. A dozen small incidents a day sent them into gales of mirth, and the recollection and recounting of these same incidents rendered everyone incoherent and hysterical at meals.

On the third day of the five the sun came out resplendent and dazzling, if not very warm, and the sea turned a clear sapphire, with jade-green lights where the chastened waves broke over the rocks. The sky was pale, high, clear, and bright as enamel, and the snow frozen hard underfoot. Skating was attempted in the old tennis-court; there was snowballing, faces grew hot, and deluges of the soft and silent cotton fell from low branches and spattered the girls' coats and the men's shoulders. Maids were always sweeping the mud- and snow-strewn side entry now, and hurrying away with wet wraps.

On the last night came the Christmas dance, when everybody knew everybody else, and the mere hasty dinner beforehand and the ecstasy of dressing after dinner were—Gabrielle thought—delight enough. They had trimmed the house yesterday with holly and greens, and even the Montallens had pushed chairs about with hearty good-will and climbed on ladders to try out chandeliers. Gabrielle told herself a hundred times that she must refuse to dance—she did not really know how to dance well—she was the youngest, anyway, and must make herself Sylvia's right hand, as hostess.

But in the end, studying herself in the *café-au-lait* lace gown, which came up almost to the round creamy column of her throat and down almost to her ankles, and which had long, delicately fluted sleeves to her very wrists and was altogether demure to the point of affectation, Gay hoped that she would be asked to dance. Frank du Spain would surely be kind if she did not dance very well.

"There will be a dozen prettier dresses to-night than this one!" she told herself, going slowly downstairs and wishing in a panic that the others had waited for her. Suppose they laughed at this dress—nuns and graduate pupils as old as the Countess might not be supposed to know much about clothes.

However, only a few guests had arrived, shy charming girls and boys from the old mansions in and about Crowchester; the musicians were tuning up deliciously, and the big floor shone inviting and bare. Sylvia, being introduced and introducing with her mother's and David's help, had time to say generously, "It's charming! It's just right for you, Gay, absolutely suitable!" and Gay's heart soared and her cheeks warmed; she became the pleasantest and most efficient of hostesses: piloting mothers and guardians to chairs, chatting simply and merrily, and too absorbed in the delightful scene to know or care what was happening to herself.

Aunt Flora was quite magnificent in plum colour; her nearest approach in many years to clothing that was not mourning. The Montallen girls were pretty in pink-and-silver and blue-and-silver gauze. Sylvia was superb in a simple white brocade with a thread of gold—her gold slippers made her look unusually tall—and there was a gold spray of something that looked like thistledown in her hair. Gabrielle was near enough to her sometimes to hear the pleasant sweetness of her replies to neighbourly greetings.

"Indeed I remember the Robinsons! I shall be coming home very soon now, you know, Doctor, and I certainly mean my good neighbours to be part of the new life! Mrs. George, and this is never Betty! Well, Betty——! No, but I shall really be home in June, and then we'll make some changes here, and see if we can't make Wastewater a little more comfortable!"

And now and then she turned to David, in a fashion that was sisterly, yet not quite sisterly either, and with her lovely smile.

"David, I wonder if you'd call Maria's or Daisy's attention to those candles? They'll be dripping directly." Or, "David, will you send Mrs. Wilkinson's coat upstairs? She doesn't want to go up——"

Gabrielle was talking to a nice old couple, established expectantly at one of the two card tables that had been provided, when the first dance started. Sylvia was still in the receiving line beside her mother, but David came up to the card table with another bridge-playing elderly couple, and when the four had settled themselves and cut the new pack, he stood smiling before Gay, with his tall, sleek black head a little bent, and his smiling eyes on her, and his arms open.

"Come on, Gay!"

"Oh, but, David," she said, flurried, "I don't dance! At least, I know I dance badly, for it's been mostly with girls! Really—really I'd rather not——"

David altered neither his position nor his expression.

"Come on!" he said. And Gay, with her face flushing exquisitely under the warm, colourless skin, put herself into his arms. And this was for her the wonderful moment of a wonderful evening; she liked to remember that happy second, when the lights and music and flowers and voices were all shining and flashing together in the shabby old ballroom, and David had made her dance with him.

They moved off smoothly. There were a few other couples already dancing, and presently David said: "I got the book, Miss Mansfield's book, with your dolls'-house story in it, and it is truly remarkable."

"Oh, I'm so glad you read it for yourself!" Gay exclaimed.

"You gave it to me quite as effectively," David commented, and was still again. But after a few moments, while they were walking before the first encore, he said: "You dance delightfully. Don't have the slightest hesitation about dancing!" And later, when they came up to Sylvia and Aunt Flora, he repeated to them: "She dances perfectly, of course. I've been trying her out. I hope we'll hear no more of this not-being-able-to-dance!"

Gay had a second's uncomfortable impression that Sylvia was not quite pleased; but as David immediately carried Sylvia off for the second dance, there was no time to wonder at it. Gay dutifully took Sylvia's place beside her aunt, but almost all the guests had arrived now; the girls and Aunt Flora had counted them, forty-three, a hundred times, but now Flora whispered with a sort of agitated pride that there were fifty-one, and, with the household, sixty-one. It was many years since Wastewater had had a party of this size!

"Sylvia says that we must have a furnace put in," sighed Flora, "and that means tearing up floors—goodness knows what——"

Gay now plunged into the delights of her first real dance with all the ecstasy of eighteen. She danced with any one and everyone, she scarcely knew or cared with whom, but she was always conscious of David, who, in his character as host, was obviously taking upon himself the responsibility for whatever girl looked momentarily like a wallflower, or whatever elderly woman needed an escort across the room.

The glorious, crowded hours flew by, with laughter and compliments and music, with icy brief drinks, and the exchanges of congratulations.

"Isn't it all wonderful! We're having the most wonderful time!"

"Isn't it! I'm so glad you're liking it!"

Then presently there was an old-fashioned and lavish supper, with bonbons and laughter, and Sylvia in a red-white-and-blue tissue cap that made her look like a beautiful, proud young Liberty, and Gay mischievous and delicious under a pomponned black-and-white Pierrette hat. It was long after midnight, and the first good-byes were being said, when Gay found herself sitting on the first step above the dim landing with David.

"I discovered this place," said David, panting, and wiping his forehead frankly. "You can look down on them and they can't see you. Glory——! It's warm."

Gay sat sweetly cool and radiant beside him; her little slippers were planted neatly in front of her, not a hair of the bright waves was disordered, her skin had the cool dewy freshness of a child's skin.

"Having a good time, Gay?"

"Oh, David!"

"What did you want to speak about?" he asked. For she had begged him for a quiet word.

"It's this," Gay began. She was still talking rapidly and earnestly, five minutes later, when Sylvia came tripping down behind them from the dimly lighted upper hall, with some well-wrapped women following.

"Sorry to disturb you! David, I think perhaps you'd better come down," said Sylvia. "People are going."

Gay and David stood up, and Gay realized then for the first time that she had had her fingers gripped tightly on David's arm, and for some obscure reason felt a little self-conscious about it.

They all went downstairs, and there were no more confidences that night. To Gay, who was tired out with felicity, the rest was all a blur. She managed to hang up the lace gown carefully, but left her other clothing and her slippers where they fell, and tumbled into bed with her massed hair untouched, nearer sleep already than waking.

And the next day was confusing, too. Even the girls looked weary, and the packing went on between yawning and laughing reminiscences, and congratulations upon what had really been a great success.

Outside were a low unfriendly sky and a strong wind across the snow. The sea was rough and wild, bare branches bent and whipped noisily about in the garden, and windows rattled. The house seemed big and blank this morning, with fallen leaves and oddly disposed furniture standing in the forlornly empty rooms that had looked so bright and gay last night. John was in the house, with dry sacking bagged over his boots as he moved palms about. But there was a roaring fire in the airtight stove in the dining room, and another in the downstairs sitting room, and the young persons, waiting for the sleigh to take them to their train, gathered there.

David kept rather close to Gay, in an unobtrusive big-brotherly manner, during the good-byes, and once he nodded to her and said briefly: "All fixed. Don't worry," but if Sylvia saw these cryptic indications she had no explanation of them until the following day. She did note, she remembered afterward, that Frank du Spain's farewells to them all, and especially to David and Gay, were rather odd; not quite pugnacious, not quite defiant, but with an odd touch of some such quality. David enlightened her on the next afternoon, when the family was alone again.

This was Christmas Day, and they had all gone in the sleigh to Crowchester to church in the morning, and, although Wastewater had hardly even now recovered from its unwonted festivities, there had been the usual great turkey, icy red cranberry jelly, crackling celery, and bubbling mince pies that indicated a fresh celebration. This meal, served in the warm dining room at half-past two, after the cold drive and wait, had reduced all the family to a state bordering upon comfortable coma. Sylvia, sleepily declaring that she meant to take a brisk walk, collapsed into an armchair before the fire immediately after the mid-afternoon dinner. David, determining from moment to moment to go upstairs and get into tramping clothes, took a chair on the other side; Flora went up to her room, where she indulged in the unheard-of relaxations of her wrapper and a nap on the top of her stiff, cold bed, with a comforter over her; and Gay, whose skin felt prickly and whose head heavy, and who had enjoyed the mince pies and the chestnut dressing and the walnuts only too well, wrapped herself up warmly, left a message with Maria, and slipped quietly out of the side door.

John was going into Keyport at five to take Margret home after the last of the Christmas dinner had been discussed in the kitchen; Gabrielle would walk the three miles in the roaring wind, and he could bring her home.

The gale tore at her gaily, whistled in her ears, stung her flushed face into chilly bloom again; rushes of spray blew across the dune road, and the sea boiled and tumbled beside her. Gulls were blown overhead, balanced yet tipped sidewise in the wild airs. The wind sang high above her.

Other pedestrians, similarly affected by Christmas cheer, were walking bundled and blown and bent forward, along the roads, and these and Gay exchanged joyous shouts of "Merry Christmas!" It was good—it was good—the girl exulted, to be out on such a day!

* * * *

Meanwhile Sylvia and David, left alone by the sitting-room fire, with only the occasional dropping of a coal or the onslaught of wind against the shutters to interrupt them, could have the first real talk they had had since their arrival at Wastewater. David, stretched luxuriously in his chair, was free to study her, as she sat erect and beautiful in the pleasant mingling of gray afternoon light and warm firelight. He had always had a definite feeling of admiration, loyalty, affection for and confidence in Sylvia, and he felt it still. But for the first time, in this past week, she had seemed oddly to take her place down on the comfortable level of other human beings. She no longer seemed—as she so long had seemed—a creature unique and apart, a little more beautiful, more fortunate, more clever than the rest. Her mother and he had watched her grow up—a bright little conscientious girl with dark braids, a splendid twelve-year-old, fifteen-year-old, meeting all the problems and the increasing responsibilities of life so willingly, so conscientiously; prettier every year, more responsive and satisfactory every year.

And then presently she had been recognized as Uncle Roger's heiress, and she was to own Wastewater one of these days, and the very substantial properties that went with Wastewater. David had initiated her, responsive and serious, into the secrets of her first allowance, her checkbook, her accounts. Did she know that she would be rich some day?

She had answered in Victoria's grave little phrase: "I had not known I was so near the throne!" And since that time, now several years ago, David had more than once thought that the proud beautiful young creature had really felt herself, in a certain sense, a queen, had really been a queen in her own little circle. Quite without realizing it, he had always seen a little halo, a little aura, about Sylvia.

Always—until now. David had always told himself that he dare not ask Sylvia to be his wife, although she was the woman he knew best and admired most in the world. It was an old habit of his to think of her as the person he would have wished to marry had it been possible to unite her youth and beauty and wealth to the small income, the uncertain profession, and the ten years' seniority of a man who was to her a sort of older brother.

But he knew to-day that he could ask her. She had oddly seemed

69

to come into his zone during this holiday week; it was not that she was less beautiful, less rich, less admirable. But she was—different, or he was. She was just an extremely charming and fortunate girl of twenty, who might love him as well as, perhaps better than, any other man. She was splendidly high-principled and intelligent, but even these qualities, at self-confident twenty, were not the surest guides in the world. Oddly and unexpectedly enough, he had once or twice experienced, just lately, a queer little pang of something like pity for Sylvia. She impressed him as someone who had little to learn, but much to experience.

Gay, on the other hand, was engagingly diffident and teachable. She had a well-balanced little head, she had excellent judgment, she played the piano nicely, spoke French perfectly, the Montallen girls had said, and danced even better than she knew. But one felt that there were no falls ahead of Gay, no humiliating descents from any heights, simply because she had never scaled any heights. David was not analytical enough to know that it was the sisterly little Gay who had quite innocently and unconsciously shifted his attitude toward Sylvia. Gay had told him of a delightful book that Sylvia called "pretty thin." Gay had said fervently, "Oh, thank you, David, you've saved me!" when he had done her a small service yesterday. Gay had quoted him, followed him with her eyes, consulted him, paid him a score of compliments in her charming little-girl way; and Gay was an exceptionally lovely young woman. Whatever her antecedents, she was delightful, eager, receptive, unaffected, and like a nice child, with her willing flying feet, her big eyes, her softly tumbled tawny hair, and her husky, protestant, velvety little voice.

To-day, while he was idly thinking of what life would be when Sylvia had taken possession of her inheritance, and had had her year or two of independence, and then had agreed to be his wife, Sylvia suddenly spoke of Gay.

"Have you any idea what she wants to do with herself, David?"

"Gay?"

Sylvia nodded.

"Mamma seems to feel nothing definite about it, and I couldn't get anything out of her. She said something vague about being an actress! I suppose she's at that age."

And Sylvia smiled good-naturedly as she looked into the fire.

"She's not happy here?" David asked, slowly.

"Yes, in a way I think she is. She's young, of course, to try her wings, and Mamma says she is really very conscientious about her practising and languages. But of course this isn't the place for her."

"Isn't?" David asked, looking up.

"No. In the first place, it's too dull. In the second——"

"Why, there are some nice kids over at Crowchester," David suggested, "and she seems happy here. Then you'll be home at midsummer——"

"Yes, I know, David," Sylvia said, with a sudden colour in her face. "But at the same time I don't feel that just idling here is quite the right solution for Gay. And I think it my duty, in a way, to think out, for her, what is the right solution," added Sylvia, with a smile. "She's handsome—she has her mother's most unfortunate experience back of her, and—if she should marry even six or eight years from now, it would surely be better to launch her first into some interesting and absorbing line of work."

"She may marry before that!" David said, with a significant half smile. "She had her first offer, it appears, on the night of the dance, and she was quite upset about it."

"Her first offer!" Sylvia echoed, in stupefaction. "One of the Crowchester boys?"

"No, I don't think she knows any of them well. Aunt Flora doesn't encourage any neighbourliness exactly. No, it was young Du Spain," David said.

"Frank du Spain!"

"It would appear that it was love at first sight with him."

Sylvia stared a moment; hot colour in her face.

"I don't believe it!" she said, finally.

"Oh, it was honest and above-board enough. That was the very point of her speaking to me as she did," David assured her, half amused and half serious. "It seems he spoke to her at the dance——"

"He must be twenty!" Sylvia broke in, impatiently.

"Twenty-four, he says. I don't imagine," David said, leniently, "that he had any immediate hopes, or indeed plans. But he assured her that he was free, and that his father was only too anxious to have him settle down; he said that his mother would ask her to visit them—at Lake Forest, I believe, this summer. He wanted a promise of some sort—he was in an absolute fever of excitement and eagerness when he left—almost wrenched my hand off!"

"David, you didn't——But it's all too absurd! You didn't encourage them in this sort of nonsense?"

"Them? My dear Sylvia, you couldn't have disposed of an unwelcome suitor more calmly yourself than Gay did!" said David. "She told him, it appears, that she was very much honoured, and she really liked him, but he please wasn't to say anything more about it for months, until after midsummer, in short. She only told me because he insisted that somebody—anybody—be informed that he never would change, and was in earnest, and all that. And he wants to correspond, and she felt that she ought to speak to Aunt Flora about that."

"One wonders why she didn't speak to Mamma in the first place," Sylvia said, slowly, remembering the farewells, and perhaps unreasonably resenting a little Gay's secret and Gay's handling of it.

"She seems to want to dismiss the whole thing," David explained. "I only mention it as a suggestion that she may solve her own problems in her own way one of these days."

"And you really think she ought to live along here calmly, doing nothing, and dependent upon other people?" Sylvia asked, with an anxious and appealing little frown.

"Who, Gay?" said Flora Fleming, who had come downstairs and was now being settled by David in her usual chair. "But there is no talk about her going away, is there?" she asked, blinking through her glasses from one face to another.

"Not immediately, Mamma dear," Sylvia answered, with just a faint hint of impatience in her voice that amused David with the realization that he had never before seen Sylvia so human, and incidentally so approachable. "But I suppose she will not stay here always. That wouldn't be fair to her or to you!"

"Oh, but what would you have her do, Sylvia?" demanded her mother in alarm.

"Nothing definite, and don't you two dear good people talk as if I were an ogre!" Sylvia said, with a laugh. "What I had vaguely in mind was some nice place—there are hundreds near the college—where she could have some young life and at the same time, by courses or special instruction, be fitting herself for her life work, whatever it's to be! That was my entire idea, I assure you."

David took refuge in his usual thoughtful study of the fire; Aunt Flora flung her yarn free with nervous fingers. Winter twilight was turning the windowpanes opaque, and the room was warm and close.

"You mean that we should make her an allowance, Sylvia?" her mother asked.

"Well—until she is on her own feet, of course. Pay her board, see that she has the right clothes, and pocket money. But the quickest way to be sure that she will take life seriously," Sylvia said, "is not to make it too easy for her!"

"But would you want her really to—to work, Sylvia?" demanded her mother, as David, staring into the embers, with his locked hands dropped between his knees, was still silent.

"Well, but, Mamma, wouldn't you?" Sylvia countered. "With her antecedents, perhaps inheriting that unfortunate nature of poor Aunt Lily's——"

"You never saw Aunt Lily!" David was upon the point of saying, good-naturedly. But although Sylvia had indeed been only three or four years old when frail, melancholy Aunt Lily had made the final disappearance into a sanitarium that ended much later with her death, he realized that Aunt Flora had talked frequently about her and held his peace.

"Inheriting that unhappy nature from Aunt Lily," pursued Sylvia, "and inheriting goodness knows what from that casual father of hers—who might, I suppose, turn up here any day and make trouble for all of us—it does seem to me wisest to lay the basis of a normal, useful life of her——"

"Her father's dead!" Flora interrupted, with a sort of pain in her voice, as Sylvia paused.

"You don't *know* that, Mamma."

"No, but if he isn't," David said, "he's dead to us. He has built up a new life somewhere that he is only too anxious to keep from our knowledge. If he had been in trouble he would have appeared fast enough!"

"Still, Sylvia," said Flora, trembling, "I should wish—and I know David would—that Gay should have some sort of allowance made for her, always. I know your uncle—I know Roger would want her not to have to worry about money—say, a hundred and fifty a month! Or two hundred——"

"Do you mean just paid out of the estate?" Sylvia demanded, in honest astonishment, and with a natural little resentment that her plans for Gay should be so outdistanced by the others' ideas. "But, David—don't you think that would be too ridiculous?" she asked, anxiously turning toward him, after a surprised study of her mother's flushed face.

"I think we can arrange it very nicely, somehow," David said, soothingly. "No need to go into it now, for she will certainly stay here with Aunt Flora until you come home, at midsummer. And in the meantime she may either form her own plans, or perhaps," he added more lightly, "perhaps another Frank du Spain will come on the scene, with better success!"

Flora, diverted, asked him his meaning, and Sylvia thought she took a surprising amount of interest in the immature affair. Young Du Spain had told her he would inherit something, Flora said, and he seemed a nice, cheerful young fellow. It seemed a great pity that they were not older—that something definite might not come of it!

"Even now," Flora argued, knitting fast, "if he really got a position, through his father—Gay will have *something*—I would certainly not let her go to him entirely empty-handed," she went on, half aloud, as if reasoning with herself. David remembered suddenly that, after all, he and she were administrators of the estate until mid-June; they would solve Gay's problem somehow before that; he hardly imagined Sylvia afterward disputing or changing any arrangement that they made about Gay.

Perhaps Sylvia remembered this, too, and decided that her only policy was a waiting one, until her full inheritance and liberty should be put into her hands. She fell into kindly desultory talk about Gay, how pretty the girl had grown, and how nicely mannered she was.

But when Flora, who seemed nervous and disturbed, presently got up and went out of the room, Sylvia said to David:

"What I really have in the back of my head is that Mamma and I shall have a long holiday in Europe next winter. I've never been, and it would be wonderful to see England in the fall, and Paris, with all the chestnuts turning red, and then settle down somewhere for two or three months, perhaps, on the Riviera. It would do her a world of good, and she seems upset of late. I think Gay's being here," Sylvia added, thoughtfully, looking straight up into David's eyes now, as they stood together before the hearth, "has roused old, sad memories, and I feel that I—well, I owe Mamma this holiday, after these years when I've seen so little of her! I'll get all my new responsibilities here straightened out as soon as I can, graduate, perhaps get paperers and furnace men working here, under Hedda and Trude, before we go, and then have a real vacation before we come back," she finished, smiling, "to be the Flemings of Wastewater for the next forty or fifty years!"

"And of course there's one more responsibility I hope you'll decide to assume, Sylvia," David said, significantly, quite unexpectedly to himself, but with his pleasant even voice and smile unchanged.

She understood him instantly and flushed rosily.

"Perhaps I will!" she answered, bravely.

"Be thinking it over?" he pursued.

Sylvia looked down at the pretty foot she had rested on the bright brass and iron fire rods.

"It's rather formidable," she said, appealingly, looking up, "all the business, the insurance and taxes and signatures—and my graduation—and Wastewater, and the servants coming to me! I feel—feel a little bit overwhelmed."

"Of course you do!" David conceded, sympathetically.

"But I think," Sylvia said, now with one hand on his shoulder and her dark eyes raised seriously to his, "I think I've always had you in mind, David—is that a very unwomanly thing to say? Give me a little time to get my bearings."

"All the time you want, dear!" David said, tenderly, as she paused.

For answer Sylvia raised her flushed and lovely face, and he kissed her solemnly. Then the girl laughed a little excitedly and held him off with both her hands linked in his, as she said:

"There, then! Is it 'an understanding'?"

"It's just what you wish, Sylvia."

"Then that's what I wish!" Sylvia answered, gaily. "Now let's get our coats on and race once or twice about the garden before it's quite dusk. Otherwise we sha'n't be able to eat any of that cold turkey and peach preserve dinner that Mamma's probably fussing about now."

But it was quite dark in the garden, and bitterly cold and windy, and they had made only one turn when John rattled up to the side door with the little car, from which Gay descended, weary, blown, but in high spirits, hungry, comfortably weary, glad to be at home again. David thought their all coming into the house together very homelike and pleasant; the company was gone, but the family was gathered together to discuss the remains of the big turkey and the memories of the house party. He thought it would be charming to have this old house home for them all, always; Gay was all the more attractive, after all, because of the clouds and mists that hung over her birth and parentage, and Sylvia would quickly get her bearings; she was too sane and fine to be upset long even by her new importance.

Then the two girls, one so dark and the other so oddly fair, would always be great friends, and even with Uncle Roger gone, and poor old Tom gone, and so many other voices and faces gone for ever, Wastewater would be a home for new Toms and Rogers, and again a hospitable and imposing landmark in the countryside.

So musing, David thought with deep satisfaction of the future. Only a few weeks before he had felt it would be an injustice to speak to Sylvia, Sylvia the beauty, the heiress, barely of age. But Sylvia had been brought into his own zone, in some strange manner, during these Christmas holidays; for the first time in her life David had seen her as perhaps needing affectionate guidance, sympathetic advice, as indeed the young girl she really was, for all her superiorities. College was all very well, thought David, for the nice, ordinary sort of girl like Gwen or Laura Montallen; it helped them to form character, a sense of balance and proportion, to make them into real women. But Sylvia was different, she had been born balanced and conscientious and intelligent and industrious, she needed softening now, and the interruption of her own serene and unquestioned will. There was beginning to be just a hint of the pedant, just a suggestion of the rut, about her.

It was sweet to him to think that with his love for her, his knowledge of her affairs, his happy familiarity here at Wastewater, he might actually give to a marriage with Sylvia more than any other man was apt to give. That confident, straightforward decisiveness of hers was exactly what led so many fine women into ridiculous marriages. He could imagine Sylvia seriously telling him that she was about to marry some engaging penniless idler: "He's a count, you know, David—one of the finest families in Europe!" Or perhaps she would not marry at all; she had said laughingly of some young admirer months ago, "Possibly he heard of Uncle Roger's money, David!"

That wouldn't do, either. Sylvia, pretty and spectacled, and entertaining other nice unmarried college women here twenty years from now was a dreadful thought.

For the world's opinion of the proverbial guardian wedding with the heiress David cared nothing at all. He was largely indifferent to money; the little that he had sufficed him comfortably; his chief expenses were for canvases and oils, and Wastewater and Keyport supplied him with subjects the year round. Less than a dozen close friends, a city club, an occasional dress rehearsal or first night, and a seat alone five times a season at the opera were enough for David, and for the rest he liked his comfortable old painting clothes, the panorama of the seasons steadily moving onward—and always, behind and through and above the leisurely tenor of his ways, Wastewater.

He roused from his reverie after supper to see Gay smiling at him from the opposite chair.

"What are you thinking about, David? You looked so serious."

"I was thinking very happy things about the future," David answered, exchanging just the fleeting shadow of a half smile with Sylvia. "Look, Sylvia, I see a likeness to Uncle Roger in Gay now!" he added, interestedly. "It's stronger in this picture than in the one downstairs!"

They all three looked up at the large portrait of Roger Fleming that was above the mantel in Flora's upstairs sitting room. Gay was just below it, and she twisted her tawny head to look upward, too.

"I don't see it!" Sylvia said, narrowing her eyes to scrutinize the painted face and the living one. "But yes, I do, the mouths are exactly alike!" she added, animatedly. "David, is mine like that?"

Flora was not in the room; they all glanced with instinctive caution at the door now, as it rattled in a rising wind, perfectly aware that to her nervous self-consciousness where all family discussions were concerned even this much would be unwelcome.

But nobody came in, and Gay ended the debate about likenesses by reminding them cheerfully:

"Turn, Flemynge, spin agayne;
  The crossit line's the kenter skein."

CHAPTER IX

THE next morning David was surprised, and a little touched, to have his aunt come up to him in the shadowy upper hall and embrace him warmly. It was a long time since he had had such a kiss from Aunt Flora.

"Sylvia's just hinted it to me—I'm so glad, my dear, dear boy!" said Flora. "She doesn't want anything said of it—I understand! She wants it just as if nothing had happened, until June—I understand! But I must let you know that I am so delighted, David."

And pressing his hands with a display of emotion very rare in her she hurried on. But for this David might almost believe that he had dreamed that little conversation with Sylvia in the firelight last night. Sylvia really showed less feeling than her mother; Aunt Flora was quite visibly beaming over the thought.

Yet Sylvia did show some; she was demure and sweet with David, and on New Year's Eve they had a few moments' grave conversation about the future.

"Perhaps there'll be a young Mrs. Fleming here next year, Sylvia?"

"Oh, not quite so soon, I think. Promise me, promise me you won't hurry matters! But some day——" And she let her smooth, warm hand rest in his until they were interrupted by her mother's entrance into the room.

Sylvia went back to college early on the day after New Year's Day, and David took her in to Boston, promising his aunt, however, that he would return to Wastewater that night. And late in the afternoon, before Sylvia went, she found an opportunity to give Gay a hint of the state of affairs.

The two girls had managed to establish a real friendliness and were merry and confidential and full of chatter together. Now Gay had asked curiously, as in an ice-cold bedroom she watched Sylvia packing her things:

"Sylvia, do you hate to go back?"

"Well, yes and no," Sylvia said, thoughtfully. "In a way, I wish June would hurry, and in another way I want to get every scrap of sweetness out of my last college days. I shall be tremendously busy when I get home, of course, for weeks and weeks, and then it's possible—I won't say definitely, but it's possible that Mamma and I may go abroad for a few months, after that. I feel as if, in a way, I owed Mamma a holiday."

Gay's face was radiant with sympathy.

"Oh, you will love it!" she said, enthusiastically, as she wrapped the big comforter tightly about her and curled her feet up in the big armchair. Sylvia, shuddering, blew upon her own fingers as she gave a last look about the room.

"There, everything's in!" she said. "Do let's get downstairs and have some tea as a celebration!" And to herself Sylvia added, "I wonder if she realizes that I don't plan to take her with us?"

But Gay was thinking: "She can't care for David or she wouldn't be making plans to go away!" and in the queer, indefinable happiness that came with this conviction, she could well afford to be indifferent to her own plans for the summer.

When they were downstairs again and shuddering with cold, as the heavenly warmth of the sitting room enveloped them Sylvia said:

"I should love to give Mamma a really happy time, because—next winter—there may be changes——"

Gay, kneeling by the hearth and hammering a great smoking lump of coal with a poker, felt salt in her mouth, and her heart sank like a leaden weight. Sylvia's serious yet happy tone was unmistakable. The younger girl did not turn.

"You mean—you and David——?" she said, thickly, putting one arm across her eyes as if the smoke had blinded her.

"I think so," Sylvia answered, smiling quietly and mysteriously.

Gay took her chair. "I always thought so!" she said, bravely. "Has it been settled—long?"

"It isn't settled now!" Sylvia responded, in a little tone of merry warning and alarm. "But I have promised"—and her smile was that of the consciously beloved and courted woman—"I have promised to think about it!"

When David came down with the suitcases a few minutes later Sylvia was alone. Gay did not come in until just before dinner, and then she seemed quiet and grave. David suspected that Sylvia's departure and the ending of the happy holidays were depressing her, but two or three times, catching her serious glance fixed upon himself during the evening, he was puzzled by something more serious than this, something almost reproachful, almost accusing.

However, he forgot it in the confusion of the early start the next morning, and when he returned to Wastewater late that evening, Gay seemed quite herself. David stayed on comfortably from day to day, and the three settled to a pleasant, if monotonous and quiet, life.

Gay worked busily at her music and with her books all morning and now and then had the additional interest of a postcard from one of the Montallens, or one of Frank du Spain's singularly undeveloped and youthful letters to answer. David was painting a study of the old sheds and fences on the western side of the house, buried in a heavy snow, with snow-laden trees bowed about them, and as a fresh blizzard came along early in the year, and the first study was extremely successful, he delayed to make a second.

In the cold afternoons he and Gay usually went for long walks, talking hard all the way, and David found it as often astonishingly stimulating to get her views of men and affairs and books as it was pleasant to guide her or influence her. Sometimes, bundled to the ears, she would rush out to the old cow yard to stand behind him as he painted, and what she said of his work, he thought, was always worth hearing. He was to have an exhibition in New York for a week in the early spring, and it was at Gay's suggestion that he did some small water colours for it.

"There!" she said. "Now those things that you call 'notes'—those are perfectly delightful! And many a person who couldn't—or wouldn't—spend several hundred dollars for a picture would love one of those."

"Lots of fellows either throw them out as rubbish or give them away," David protested.

"Yes, but yours are so lovely, David! I can't think that most men would make such nice ones. This little one—I'll tell you what it's like," said Gay, with a brightening face, "It's like a little Diziani in the Louvre!"

These little touches of familiarity with the field so infinitely interesting to him were delightful to David. He would spend whole winter afternoons going over his European catalogues with her and identifying picture after picture. Gay made him mark the "notes" at a hundred dollars each.

"Catalogue them separately under 'notes,'" she suggested one morning, "and then let's give each one of them a name." And following some line of thought she presently added dreamily, "David, does the money part matter so tremendously to you?"

"Does—God bless the child!" answered David, with a glance toward the sketches he was assorting in the big upstairs room in which he worked at Wastewater. "Of course it does!"

Gay, who had been making some little sketches herself on a large bare block with a very sharp pencil, laughed at his tone. Outside a January rain was sleeting roughly against the windows, the casements rattled. A small oil stove was burning in the cool gray daylight of the room, the air was faintly scented with the odour of kerosene and hot metal.

"Why, what would you do if you had more money?" Gay asked.

"Oh, Lord——!" David began. "Well, I'd take a studio near Rucker's," he began. "At least, I might. And probably about once in every three years I'd go across and study in Europe. I'd buy one of Neil Boone's pictures to-morrow," went on David, warming suddenly, "and I'd buy one every three months, to keep the poor fellow from committing suicide before people begin to find out what a marvel he is."

"Is he so clever, David?"

"Oh——" David said, briefly, almost impatiently. "The uses of adversity are sweet, Gay," he added, working busily with an eraser on a smudged pencil sketch, "but Boone has had a little too much of a good thing! He idolized his wife, and she died, and I think he feels that it might have been different if she'd had less want and care. He's mad about his kid, and a well-to-do sister has him in Washington. Boone can't afford to keep him."

"I must say that you don't seem to want money so much for yourself," said Gay, laughing. "You *might* get a studio, and you *might* go abroad. I'll tell you what I think," finished Gay, "you'd like money principally because, when a man's pictures sell, it's proof that he is succeeding in his profession!"

"Well, I shouldn't wonder if you're right, Gay," David said, surprised at the shrewdness of the analysis.

"Because, if you and Sylvia——" the girl was beginning, animatedly. She stopped. Her face was crimson. "Perhaps I wasn't supposed to know that," she stammered, smiling.

"Not much to know," David said, also a little red. "It—it's indefinite until Sylvia chooses to have it definite," he added. And then, with what was suddenly a rough, almost an angry manner, for David, he went on: "But what were you going to say, Gay? Did you mean that if Sylvia and I were married I *would* be rich?"

"Nothing quite so crude, David!" she answered, readily, with an apologetic smile. "I was contrasting the pleasure you would get from a—well, from a really sensational success with your exhibition," Gay went on, feeling for words, "to the pleasure any amount of money just put into your hand would give you! You and Sylvia can do anything you like, I suppose, but I know it won't make you feel like working any less!"

It was said with her innocent, sisterly smile, and with her usual unspoiled earnest interest, but David felt oddly uncomfortable whenever he thought of it throughout the day. A dozen times he wondered exactly what the situation would be if Sylvia were in—well, in Gay's position, looking to her husband for everything.

He could not be more fond of her, he was glad to think. Indeed, David thought, Sylvia's character would probably come out in far finer colours under these circumstances than it was apt to do as it was. To receive all that Sylvia was to receive upon coming of age, to be so clever, so beautiful, and so admired, was sure to prove more or less upsetting. As for the rest, he wished heartily that it had been his good fortune to fall in love with a woman who had not a penny!

Not that Sylvia would be anything but charming in her attitude to his income and her own. She would glide over any conceivable awkwardness with her own native fineness. She would ask—he knew exactly how prettily—"David, should I buy a new fur coat, do you think? David, would another maid be an awful extravagance?" There would never be a word or a hint to remind him that after all the safety-deposit box, and the check books, and indeed the very roof over their heads, were hers.

It was not that that he feared. But he did fear her quite natural opinion that money was extremely important. It was important to her. It was important to almost everyone. But it was not important to David.

If their friends would think him fortunate in winning so clever and beautiful and charming a wife, well and good. But he knew that they would go on to the consideration of her wealth, if indeed many of them did not actually commence there. "Pretty comfortable for him, she has scads of money!" the world would say, and Sylvia—unfortunately!—could hardly help having her own convictions upon that score, too.

Of course dear old David would love to be rich! Sylvia would think. Here he had been struggling along on a few thousands a year, making no complaints, happy in his work, travelling, with a keenly anxious eye on his checkbook, spending nothing on clothes, giving one odd and curious little presents that yet were so pitifully inexpensive, anxious about those exhibitions of canvases that as yet did not sell very fast—what could be more delightful than sudden riches to David? To buy him a big car, a big fur coat, to entertain their friends at the finest hotels, to travel, to pick up odd books and canvases, to have smart luggage, a beautiful home—who wouldn't like such a change?

Well, David knew himself that he would not. He realized perfectly that one of the difficulties of his early married life would be to persuade his rich young wife that he really preferred his old corduroys to paint in, that he really liked little restaurants, that he hated big hotels.

Far happier for him if Gay, for example, had been the heiress. Then he and Sylvia would have been the poor relations, would have had the tramping, the little studio in Keyport, the frugal trips abroad so full of adventures and excitements, and always the beloved old family homestead to turn to for holidays and special occasions. That would be a realler sort of living than he was apt to experience with all Sylvia's charming responsibilities and exaction upon his shoulders. There would be a distinct loss of something free and personal, something far higher and purer and more wonderful than even old Uncle Roger's money, in David's marriage. And he knew now that he could never expect Sylvia to see that loss. To Sylvia any one who could be rich, and who saw even the tiniest scrap of advantage anywhere in remaining poor, was stupid to the point of annoyance.

Well, it would all work out somehow, David thought philosophically, thinking these things seriously upon a certain bitter night late in January. A heavy storm was brewing again, for the winter was unusually severe, but he had resolved to turn his back upon it; he must get down into the city and arrange matters for the April exhibition. He would leave Wastewater the next day, after almost six weeks in which the days had seemed to fly by.

It was almost midnight now; Gay, who had seemed out of spirits to-night, had gone upstairs early, and Aunt Flora had followed her an hour ago. But David sat on by the fire, not so much reading the book he held in his hand, as musing, and occasionally leaning forward to stir the last of the coals. The passage to bed was a long and chilly one, the halls were cold, his room would be cold; he felt a deep, lazy disinclination to stir.

* * * *

Suddenly and hideously in the darkness and night he heard a wild scream, followed by other screams, all piercing, high—the shrieks of a woman in mortal terror. David, with a quick exclamation, started to his feet, ran to the door, opened it and shouted into the blackness of the hall, snatched the lamp from the centre table, and, always shouting, ran up toward the evident source of the confusion; which was in the direction of his room and Gay's, on the floor above.

It had all taken place so quickly and was so unspeakably horrifying and alarming that David had no time to think of his own emotions until he reached the upper hall and rushed into Gay's room. He set the light on a table, and caught the girl, who was blundering blindly about the doorway, in his arms.

"Gay—for God's sake—what is it!" he said, drawing her into the hall, holding her tight, and looking beyond her into the dimness of the room.

"Oh, David—David!" she sobbed, clinging to him. "Oh, David, it's that old woman again! She's in my room—I saw her! She had a candle in her hand—I tell you I saw her!"

"You had a dream, dear!" David said, tenderly. "She must have had a bad dream!" David explained to Flora, who came upstairs carrying a candle, and with a ghastly face, and to Hedda and Trude, who appeared from another direction, frightened and pale.

"Oh, no—no—no! I didn't dream it!" Gabrielle said, still gasping and clinging tight to David, but in a somewhat quieter tone. "No, I didn't dream it! She—I had just put out the light and she—she came into my room——"

"Now, don't get excited, dear," David interrupted the rising tone reassuringly. "We're all here, and she can't hurt you! What did you think you saw?"

"She came to my door," Gabrielle whispered, with a heaving breast and a dry throat. "She was—she was——" Her voice rose on a shrill note of terror in spite of herself, and she looked into David's eyes with a pathetic childish effort to control herself. "She was—smiling at me!" Gabrielle whispered.

David felt his own flesh creep; it was Flora's voice that said somewhat harshly:

"Come down to Sylvia's room for the rest of the night, Gabrielle."

They were all in the doorway of Gabrielle's room; the lamp that David had carried upstairs he had placed just within it, in a sort of alcove. Now he picked up the light and said reassuringly:

"Look here, dear, nobody's gone out of the hall! We'll go all over your room, and open the wardrobes, and look under the bed——"

He had gotten so far, turning courageously into the apartment, when he stopped, and Gabrielle screamed again. For the light now shone upon the girl's tumbled bed, her desk, her bureau, her bookshelves. And standing close to the latter, with bright mad eyes fixed

84

upon them all, and something of the hunted look of a cornered yet unfrightened animal, was a small, bent old woman, with gray hair straggling out upon the gray shawl she wore over her shoulders, and an extinguished candle in the stick she carried in her hands.

David's heart came into his mouth with shock; there was an uncanny and fearful quality about such an apparition in the quiet winter night and in the shadowy old house. Flora, behind him, made a sound of despair, and Hedda and Trude moaned together. Afterward, it seemed to him odd that it was Gabrielle who spoke.

The girl was still shaken badly, but the lights and the voices had instantly dissipated the horrifying mystery and fear, and although Gay was pale and spoke with a somewhat dry throat, it was steadily enough, it was even with a pathetic sort of reassurance in her voice, and a trembling eagerness to quiet the strange visitor, to restore the fantastic unnaturalness of the scene to something like the normal.

"You—you frightened me so!" she said to the little old woman, gently, touching her on the arm, even trying to draw about the shaking little old figure the big slipping gray shawl. "You—she didn't mean any harm, David," Gay said, with her breath coming easier every second. "She—I think she's a little——" A significant lifting of Gay's eyebrows finished the sentence. "Margret knows her—Aunt Flora knows who she is!" she added, appealingly.

"I wanted to see you, dear, and Flora wouldn't let me!" the old woman said, tearfully and childishly, catching Gay's hands and beginning to mumble kisses over them.

David made a sudden exclamation.

"Is it—I've not seen her for twenty years!" he said, with a puzzled look at his aunt, about whose shaking form he immediately put a bracing arm. "Isn't it your mother, Aunt Flora? Is it Aunt John? I thought she was dead."

"Yes—just help me take her to her room, David," Flora said, feverishly and blindly. "Just—take her arm, Hedda. We'll get her all comfortable, and then I'll explain. I'll explain to you and Gabrielle—you   needn't   be   afraid   of   this   happening again—I'll—I'll—— Let Trude take her, Gabrielle."

"But she doesn't want to go, do you, dear?" Gay asked, pitifully. And David thought her youth and beauty, the hanging rope of glorious tawny hair, the slim figure outlined in her plain little embroidered nightgown, and the kimono she had caught up, contrasted to that shaking old creature's feebleness and wildness, were the most extraordinary things he had ever seen in his life. But then the whole thing was like a crazy dream.

"But she must go," Flora reiterated, firmly, her voice shaking and raw, her face streaked with green lines across its pallor.

"Aunt John," David pleaded, gently, taking an elbow that controlled a thin old yellow hand like a hanging bird's claw. For he remembered the days when "Aunt John" had kept house for them all, when Flora was a brisk young woman, and Lily only a timid, romantic girl, when his own mother was mistress of Wastewater, and poor Tom and himself the idolized small boys of the family.

"What are you calling me 'Aunt John' for, David Fleming?" said the old woman, shrilly and suddenly. "Mamma died years and years ago, didn't she, Flora? I'm your Aunt Lily, and I came down to see my girl!"

Hedda and Trude exclaimed together; but David sensed instantly that they were not surprised. Flora choked, caught blindly at the back of a chair, and stood staring; David, in his quick glance, saw that her lips were moving. But she made no sound.

Then it was at Gabrielle that they all looked; Gabrielle, who stood tall and young and ashen in the uncertain lamplight, with her magnificent, pathetically widened eyes, like shadowy gray star sapphires, moving first to Flora's face, and then to David's, and then back to the little woman beside her, whose hand, or claw, she still held in her own.

David saw her breast rise and fall suddenly, but there was in her bearing no sign that she was conscious of his presence, or that of the maids or Flora. She bent down toward the forlorn little mowing and mumbling creature, looking into the wandering eyes.

"I'm sorry they wouldn't let you see me!" Gay said, gently, in just the essence of her own beautiful voice. To David every syllable seemed to throb and flower like a falling star in the unearthly silence of the room. Outside a winter wind whined, branches creaked, the ivy at Gay's window crackled as a load of snow slipped from its dry twigs; they could hear the distant muffled sound of the cold sea, tumbling and booming among the rocks.

The lamp flared up in a sudden draught, burned steadily again. Great shadows marched and wheeled on the ceiling. The two maids stared with dilated eyes. Flora caught at David with fierce fingers.

"Don't—don't let her talk! She's not responsible, David! I tell you it's all a mistake—no harm done—I won't have Gabrielle worried——"

"Don't worry about me, Aunt Flora!" Gay's voice said. And again it sounded strange to David; it had a sad and poignant sweetness that seemed to have more in common with the icy night, and the streaming winter moonlight, and the cold sea, than with this troubled little human group. "I'm glad to know. I never would have been afraid of you if I had known," Gay said, to the little bent old woman. "I won't be frightened again. You can—you can see me as much as you like. If you're Lily, I'm—I'm your little girl, you know—Mother."

CHAPTER X

THE night that followed was one of the strange, abnormal times that seemed—David thought more than once—so peculiarly appropriate, so peculiarly in tone with the atmosphere of Wastewater; with the empty, dusky, decaying rooms, with the shadowy mirrors clouded with mould, with the memories, the tragedies, the ghosts and echoes that on a bitter winter night seemed to throng the old place.

Outside there was a sharp frost, and when the massed silent snow slipped from the branches of the old elms, an occasional crack like a pistol shot sounded through the night. A cold bright moon moved over the packed snow, and the sea swelled with booming, sullen rushes over the rocks. Clocks seemed, to David, to stand still; to mark strange hours.

When Gabrielle had put her young arm about the shrinking, withered form of the harmless old feeble-minded woman that David did now indeed recognize as Aunt Lily, for some reason he had felt his throat thick, and his eyes blind with tears. The girl was so young, she had been so full of hope and gaiety and high spirits during the happy holidays and the weeks that followed; she had tramped beside him chattering like a sturdy little sister, belted into a big coat, her eager feet stamping and dancing on the snow, her cheeks glowing with the tingle of the pure cold air. They had had some contented rainy mornings together, in the bare upstairs room he called his studio, and they had sometimes played a sort of double solitaire in the evenings, Gay as anxiously excited as a child, and saying "Oh, fudge!" when the cards fell wrong, in a little baffled, furious tone that always made him laugh. He and she had thought the weak little mother and the worthless, wandering father long ago vanished from her problem; the child had quite a sufficient problem left, as it was! And she had faced it so bravely, faced it cheerfully even with the constant reminder of Sylvia's contrasted good fortune, Sylvia's wealth, Sylvia's impeccable parentage, right before her vision.

Now, suddenly, while her heart was thumping with the shock and terror of awakening from sleep to find this dreadful apparition in her room, she had had to accept this same mowing, gibbering, weeping old woman as her mother. And David loved her that she had not hesitated, where for sheer bewilderment he knew he might have hesitated.

She had not glanced at Aunt Flora, who was leaning sick and silent against a chair, nor at the cowed and white-faced old Belgian servants, nor at him. Quite simply she had put her arm about poor Aunt Lily, touched her young lips to the yellowed old forehead where the forlorn wisps of grayish hair hung down, and then turned, steady-eyed and ashen-cheeked but quite composed, to say quietly:

"Where does she sleep, Aunt Flora? In that room where I saw the light? I'll go up with her—she's shuddering with cold, she'll be ill. I'll—you'll go with me, won't you, Margret? We'll get her to bed."

For Margret, also pale, in a gray wrapper, and looking anxiously from one to the other as if to read in their faces what had occurred, had joined the group from some rear doorway.

"No, that was partly it, Gabrielle," Flora forced herself to say, with chattering teeth. "She hasn't been so bad until lately. And after you met her, that day, we moved her into the back of the house—someone was always supposed to be near her. You shouldn't have gotten out of bed and come through the halls in your bare feet, Lily!" Flora mildly reproached her sister. Lily clung stubbornly to Gabrielle's arm, but they were all moving slowly in the direction of the rooms Flora had mentioned now, through the bitter darkness of the halls. The lamp, carried by David, sent their shadows wheeling about the angles and corners ahead of them, doors banged, shutters creaked, and when Lily's chattering whisper of complacency and exulting triumph was silent, they could hear Hedda and Trude telling Margret that the sick lady had wandered into Miss Gabrielle's rooms in the night and frightened her.

Lily was really almost sick by the time they reached the homely, comfortable rooms, which, Gabrielle noted, were well furnished, and warmed by a still-glowing stove. David built up the fire while they put the poor little chattering creature to bed, and Gabrielle, without seeming to be even now conscious of anybody's presence but that of her mother, caught up an old ivory-backed brush and massed the straying gray hair into order, pinning it, David noted pitifully, with the pins that had held back from her face her own thick, rich braids. There was a tenderness, an absorbed, gentle, and childish pity about her whole attitude the while she did so that made his throat thicken again.

Meanwhile Margret and Hedda, evidently well used to this ministry and moving about the room with an air of being entirely at home there, had supplied Lily with hot-water bottles and some sort of milky hot drink which Lily fretfully complained was bitter.

"It has her sleeping stuff in it," Margret explained, in an aside. Lily smiled knowingly at Gabrielle.

"They wouldn't mind poisoning me a bit, dearie," she said, in a loud whisper. "At Crosswicks they used always be trying to poison us."

However, she took the drink, when Gabrielle held the glass, in short sips, meanwhile patting the girl's hand, beaming, and occasionally, with increasing drowsiness, recalling old memories.

"Gabrielle had a little gray coat and a hat with gray fur on it—beaver, it was real beaver—it looked so good with her golden curls!" she said once, complacently. "Roger said she looked like a squirrel. Where is Roger, Flora? Why don't he come up some night, so's we could all play euchre, like we use' to?"

And at another time, some moments later, she added, in a sweet and natural voice: "I was looking all over the place for Tom. He gets my nasturtium seeds and eats them! But I don't know where all this snow's come from. It was real sunny yesterday when I put them out, and Roger and Will were in swimming!"

All this time Flora had sat in an armchair by the stove, with one hard, veiny hand tight over her eyes. Margret lessened the lights, Lily began to sink into sleep, and Gabrielle sat timidly down near her, still holding her hand. The servants slipped away, but still Flora did not stir.

When Lily was so soundly off that their voices did not disturb her, David touched Gabrielle's arm, and stiff, and looking a little bewildered, she rose noiselessly to her feet. Flora started up, pale, and with a bitten under lip and a look of some deep fright in her eyes, and they quietly left the room, David carrying the lamp as before.

"And now," he said, cheerfully, when they were back in the hall outside of Gabrielle's room, "there's no good worrying ourselves about all this to-night! You look exhausted, Aunt Flora, and Gay here has had enough. Jump into bed, Gay, it's after two, and get off to sleep. I'll leave my door open and you leave yours—or if you like I'll wheel this couch up against your door and sleep on it myself."

"No, David, thank you; I'm not afraid now," the girl said, quietly and seriously, and David knew that there were more than vague unnamed terrors to occupy her thoughts now. "I'll do splendidly, and to-morrow we'll talk. I only hope," she added slowly, "my mother will not be ill, although"—and there was infinite sadness in her voice—"perhaps I shouldn't even hope that, for her! Good-night, Aunt Flora."

And with a sudden impulse that seemed to David infinitely fine and sweet, she stooped and kissed her aunt's cheek before she turned to her own door.

"Good-night, Gay dear, don't worry!" David said, tenderly. And with a quick emotion as natural as hers had been, he kissed her forehead as a brother might have done. Flora had already gone, and Gay smiled at him pathetically as she shut her door.

She would not think to-night, the girl told herself restlessly. But there was nothing for it but thought. She was bitterly cold, and shuddered as she snuggled into the covers, and stared out with persistently wakeful eyes at the blackness of the big room. Gay heard creaks, crackling, the lisp of falling blots of snow, the detonations of contracting furniture in distant closed rooms, the reports of breaking branches outside. And always there was the cold, regular pulse of the sea.

The girl looked at her watch; twenty minutes of three, and she seemed to have been tossing here for hours. Her brain seethed; faces, voices, came and went, problems for the future, speculations as to the past. She was deathly cold; she wondered if there were any fuel at her cold fireplace, lighted the candle, and investigated. None.

"Well, these windows at least can be closed!" Gay decided, with chattering teeth. The night struck through her thin nightgown like a wall of ice as she struggled with the heavy blinds. Gabrielle experienced a weary and desperate sensation of discouragement; the horrible night would never end, her thoughts would never straighten themselves out into peace and quiet again, there would never be sunlight, warmth, safety in the world!

Looking down, however, toward the kitchen wing, she saw that a heartening red light was striking through the shutters, and immediately she caught up her wrapper and went slippered and shuddering down the long stairs and passages that led to the kitchen.

She opened the door upon heartening lamplight and firelight; Margret, Trude, and Hedda were in comfortable talk beside the stove, and a boiling coffee-pot sent a delicious fragrance into the dark old room.

"Margret," Gay began, piteously, with a suddenly childish feeling of tears in her voice. "I can't sleep—I've been lying awake——"

And immediately she was on her knees beside Margret, and had her bright head buried in the old servant's lap, and Margret's hand was stroking her hair.

Gay, after the first tears, did not cry. But as the blessed heat and light seemed to penetrate to the centre of her chilled being, and as the old servant's hands gently stroked her hair, she felt as if she could kneel here for ever, not facing anything, not thinking, just warm again and among human voices once more.

Margret's words, if they were words, were indistinguishable; neither Hedda nor Trude spoke at all. The Belgian women looked on with their faded old eyes red with sympathy. Trude put a smoking cup of coffee, mixed in the French fashion, as Gay liked it, on the table, and Hedda turned a fresh piece of graham toast on the range, and Margret coaxed the girl to dispose of the hot drink before there was any talk.

Afterward, when Gay had dried her eyes upon a towel brought by the sympathetic Hedda, and rolled herself tight in her wrapper, and had her feet comfortably extended toward the range, Margret said:

"You mustn't feel angry at us, Miss Gabrielle. It was to spare you, I'm sure, that Miss Flora has kept this secret all these years."

"I'm not angry——" Gabrielle began, and stopped abruptly, biting her lip, and turned her eyes, brimming again, toward the glow of the range.

"I know, it seems awful hard, but this has always been a bitter thing to Miss Flora, and she has taken her own way about it," Margret said, kindly, and there was silence again. "You know your mamma," the old woman began again, presently, and Gay's eyes, startled, fixed themselves for a moment upon Margret's face, as if the girl found the term strange. "Your mamma made a silly marriage, dear," Margret went on, "and Miss Flora felt very badly about it. Your mother was such a pretty, gentle girl, too," she added. "I'd see her gathering flowers, or maybe hear her singing at the piano, when I'd come up here to Wastewater to help them out with sickness, or company, or whatever it was. Very pretty, Miss Lily was. There was quite a family then. Miss Flora had married Mr. Will Fleming, and Sylvia was just a little thing, as dark as a gipsy. And of course that was just the time that poor Mr. Roger's wife was dying of some miserable growth she'd had for years, and it was when Tom run away. Mrs. Roger Fleming had a big couch on the porch in summer, and she'd be laying there, and perhaps Mr. Roger reading to her, or talking about some cure; they were for ever trying new cures and new doctors! And Miss Flora would have Sylvia out there, with her big rag doll—Sylvia's father was never much of a success, they used to say, he was usually away somewhere getting a new job of some sort," Margret added, reminiscently.

"Somehow I never think of Aunt Flora as having a husband,"

Gay said, in a sombre, tear-thickened voice. "Her being Sylvia's mother, and all that, seems natural enough. But to think of her as Mrs. Will Fleming always is so queer."

"I don't know that she ever loved Mr. Will," Margret said, with a glance behind her at Hedda, who was straightening the kitchen as composedly and indifferently as if the hour had been four o'clock in the afternoon instead of the morning. Hedda was paying no attention and Margret went on, with all an old servant's significance: "It was well known that Miss Flora loved Roger Fleming all her life, and she was engaged to him after his first wife, that was David's and Tom's mother, died."

"Yes, I know," Gabrielle said, with a long sigh. She had heard all this before.

"When Roger Fleming married the second time, she took his brother Will," Margret resumed, "and for a while they had a little apartment in Boston, and he was in a bank there, but he died when Miss Sylvia was only three and Miss Flora was here more than she ever was there, anyway; Miss Lily stayed here all the time. And then, that terrible summer when little Tom ran away, if Miss Lily didn't fall in love with a man nobody knew anything about——"

There was an old-fashioned little peasant bench beside the stove, brought from across the seas when Hedda and Trude had come to America twenty-five years before, and Gabrielle was on this low seat now, with her arms across Margret's knees. She looked up into Margret's face wistfully as she said:

"But there was nothing against my father? Wasn't he just a young man who was staying in Crowchester for a while?"

"He had some sort of agency," Margret said. "No, dear, for all we ever knew he was a good enough man. But he was no husband for Miss Lily, who was Mr. Roger Fleming's cousin, and had lived here at Wastewater all her life. And more than that, she married him secretly, and that's always a bad thing!" the old woman added, impressively.

"Yes, I know!" Gabrielle murmured, with impatience and pain in her voice. "But I don't see anything so terrible in it!" she finished, looking back at the fire again and half to herself.

"Well, it was such a bad time, when they were all so upset," Margret argued. "Miss Flora felt something terrible," she added, simply, "when she knew that Miss Lily—her sister that she'd always guarded and loved so dearly—was secretly married and going to have a baby. I don't know that she told Mrs. Roger Fleming, who was so little and so delicate, anything about it, but I know she talked it over with Mr. Roger, for he came to me—so kindly! he was a wonderful man for being kind-hearted—and told me that Miss Lily was going into Boston to live in Miss Flora's little apartment for a little while, while they tried to find this man, Charpentier——"

"That was my father," Gay interpolated.

"That was your father, dear. I went to Boston with your mother and got her nicely settled," Margret resumed. "She was very quiet then, and pleased with the little things she was making for the baby, but it was only a few months later—when Mr. Roger was off hunting little Tom, and Mrs. Roger dying, with this doctor or that quack or dear knows what always in the house here—that poor Miss Lily got typhoid fever."

"Before I was born!" Gay had heard of the typhoid fever, but had never quite placed it in the succession of events before.

"Just after you were born. Poor Miss Flora was pulled every which way," said Margret. "She'd rush into Boston to see Miss Lily, and she'd rush back here, afraid Mrs. Roger had died while she was gone. She didn't dare risk the infection for Miss Sylvia, and so she sent for me, and I took Miss Sylvia into the rooms where poor Miss Lily is now, and Miss Sylvia hardly saw her mother for weeks. Miss Flora went up to see her sister—that was your mother—every week, and while she did that she'd never risk infection for little Sylvia.

"Well, then poor little Mrs. Roger died—very sudden, at the end. Miss Lily was convalescent then, but weak as a rag, and she and you came down here to Wastewater—and you were the most beautiful child I ever laid my eyes on!" Margret broke off to say, seriously.

Gabrielle, red-eyed and serious, laughed briefly.

"Well, you were a beautiful child," Margret persisted. "Miss Flora let Miss Sylvia and me go on and take a peep at you, in a blanket, the day you came. Miss Lily was very sick after the trip, and she didn't get out of bed for a week, and Hedda and I had you, and didn't we make Miss Sylvia jealous with the fuss we made over the new baby!

"I remember one day—they were all in black then for poor Mrs. Roger, and Mr. Roger came home suddenly from one of his trips, poor man! We'd not seen him since the day of the funeral——"

"He got here too late to see her again?" Gabrielle asked, knowing the answer.

"He'd gotten here the very day of the funeral," Margret nodded. "And he'd just stood looking at her as she lay there dead—she'd been more than five years his wife, and she was only twenty-two as she lay there with the flowers all around her! And he said to poor

Miss Flora, 'I killed her, Flora!' And out of the house he walked, and we never saw him again until this day I'm talking about, six months after the funeral.

"By this time Miss Lily, your mother, was all over her illness, but the typhoid had left her very weak and light-headed, and sometimes she'd talk very queer, or cry, or whatever it was," Margret went on. "In fact, that was the beginning of her trouble—she never again was—quite right—here," interpolated Margret, significantly, touching her forehead. "Well, this day she was all in white, and she had an innocent sort of childish look, and Mr. David was home from school, and Miss Sylvia was running about, and you were just getting to the cunning age—my goodness, but you were a beautiful baby!" the old woman said again, affectionately. "Well, Mr. Will Fleming was home, he was out of a job again, and they were all out on the lawn—Mr. David was a fine little fellow of about thirteen then, and he saw Mr. Roger first, and he went running over. And Roger Fleming came up to them and asked, as he always did: 'Any news of Tom? Any letter from my boy?' and they told him, No. And then Miss Lily held you out to him so gently, and her face flushed up and she said: 'Roger, you've hardly seen my pretty baby!' and I remember his taking you in his arms and saying, 'Well, hello, here's a yellow-headed Fleming at last!'"

"Nobody seemed to make much of my Charpentier blood, or my name," Gabrielle observed, drily.

"I remember," Margret resumed, without answering, perhaps unhearing, "that after a while Mr. Roger said to Miss Flora, so sadly, 'Look at them, David and Sylvia and this baby! But my own boy will never be master of Wastewater!' and she said to him, 'Roger, he'll come home, dear!'

"But indeed he didn't ever come home," Margret finished, sighing, "and Miss Sylvia's father died a year or two later and never left a son behind him. And after a while poor Mr. Roger died—he died a broken man. And then we had to send Miss Lily to Crosswicks, for she got worse and worse. She was there for fifteen years. But Crosswicks broke up last year, and Miss Flora didn't quite know what to do with her," Margret added, "and it was only while she was finding some other good place where she'd be happy that we thought of keeping her here. Poor, gentle little soul, she'd never hurt you or any one."

Her voice died away into silence, and Gabrielle sat staring darkly into the fire, with a clouded face.

For a long time the two sat together, the girl with her young strong hands locked in Margret's, and her eyes absently fixed on the dying fire, and gradually the old woman's soothing voice had its effect. Margret gently begged her not to worry, there was no harm done, and perhaps it would be better, after all, to have her see her mother daily and naturally, as the poor little mental and physical wreck she was, and get over the fright and mystery once and for all. And now Gabrielle must take a bottle of hot water upstairs and get to sleep, for it was long after four, and they mustn't keep poor Hedda up all night.

Hedda was quite frankly snoring in the rocker, back in the gloom, but Gabrielle obediently roused herself from deep study, and kissed Margret, and retraced her way up through the cold halls. Her room looked tumbled and was cold; she opened the window. Still night, night, night, black and cold and unbroken—there was no end to this winter night! But Gabrielle was young and cruelly wearied in mind and body, and after three minutes in the cool sheets a heavenly warmth began to envelop her, and she fell deeply asleep.

CHAPTER XI

WINTER sunlight was slanting into the room when she awakened, and for a while she lay still, trying to reconcile these beams from the southwest with any possible hour on a January morning. Her watch had stopped at half-past three. Or had it stopped?

She sat up, bewildered, the ticking watch at her ear. Sunshine from the southwest, and her watch briskly ticking at half-past three!

"It can't be!" Gabrielle said aloud, beginning heavily the business of dressing. "Why, where are they all?" she murmured, gradually fitting together in her mind the events of the past night. "Why didn't someone——"

Flooding sunlight and cold pure air from the southwest! The day seemed turned around as, fifteen minutes later, she went slowly downstairs. Nobody anywhere—sitting room, dining room, halls, pantry; but Hedda and Margret were quietly talking over some busy chopping and peeling in the spotless kitchen, and Margret started a wood fire in the dining-room stove, and Hedda brought Gabrielle a delicious breakfast luncheon and placed it on a small table near the blaze.

Gabrielle was there alone, thoughtful over her meal, when David came cheerfully in. He looked just his pleasant self as he sat down, his dark hair a little tumbled, and his old corduroy jacket spotted about the cuffs with paint, but Gabrielle thought he gave her an unusually sharp keen look, and felt tears prick behind her eyes as she smiled in answer.

"Well," he said, "you got some sleep!"

"Eleven hours," said Gay.

"I'm glad. You looked all in last night. And Margret said you came down to the kitchen, late as it was, and talked things over——"

"For an hour." Gay pushed away her table, almost untouched. "Feel like a walk?"

"Oh, no, thank you, David." She smiled gratefully, but he heard the sharp sigh that followed the words. "I feel—broken," she said, with suddenly wet eyes.

"I don't blame you," he answered, gently. "But you mustn't take all this too hard, Gay. There's nothing—disgraceful about it, after all. Your mother had typhoid fever, and it left her—like this. She doesn't suffer—indeed, poor Aunt Flora suffers much, much more than she does! Aunt Flora's just been telling me that Aunt Lily is usually perfectly serene and happy, wanders in the garden, loves the flowers——"

Balm was creeping into the girl's heart with every word he said, and David saw, with a deep relief in his heart, that he was making an impression.

"Finish your chocolate," he pleaded. And smiling over the brink of her cup with wearied eyes, Gay obediently picked it up and drank it to the dregs.

"It seems that Aunt Lily has been restless since you came home," David added. "They never really know how much she understands or how she learns things. But she knew that you were here and she has been wild to see you. Being winter, she had been indoors most of the time, and since Christmas, Aunt Flora says, she has been un-usually restless. That's really the whole explanation—and that isn't so terrible, is it?" he finished, with a smile.

Gabrielle looked at him soberly.

"I would like to see her again," she said, slowly.

"Well, by all means!" he answered, cheerfully. "I hear from Mar-gret that she seems to have a heavy cold and she's in bed. But you can go up there—talk to her——"

"My mother, David——" the girl faltered. And the eyes she turned from his were brimming again. "It's so different—from what most girls think—when they say 'Mother!'" she managed to say.

"I know," David said, quickly, with infinite pity in his voice, "I know, Gay. It's very hard, dear."

"What I realize now," Gay began again, after a brief silence, and in a voice she resolutely held steady, "what has come to me—sud-denly!—is that my name really is Fleming, that there was never any marriage at all—between my mother and Charpentier."

It was quite true that the thought had come to her suddenly, for at the actual commencement of the sentence she had had no distinct suspicion in the matter. Forlornly, she had been instinctively search-ing for some phrase that should win David's sympathy, that should help him to realize how lonely and sad she felt.

But now the vague sorrow in her heart, the indefinable weight upon her spirit, seemed to crystallize into these words, and almost frightened of herself when she had said them, she ended on a note of interrogation, and turned toward David for his denial.

There was a revulsion almost nauseating in its violence upon her when David only looked at her with infinite pity and concern, and asked:

"Gay, my dear, dear Gay, why do you say that?"

"Oh, my God, my God, my God!" Gay exclaimed, suffocating. And she got to her feet and walked to the embrasure of the big eastern bay window, where she stood staring blindly out at the paths white with shabby snow and the trees' bare wet branches twinkling in the sunlight. A passionate childish wish that she had never voiced this horrible thought and so made it concrete in his consciousness and hers shook her from head to foot. It was said—it was said—and now they must say more!

The fire in the stove had burned itself out; a chill was beginning to pervade the gloomy great spaces of the dining room. The ugliest hour of a cold, glaring winter afternoon lay upon the bare garden; through the denuded shrubs they could see the steely ripple of the sea.

"You see that explains it all, David," Gay said, hurriedly and briefly. "Aunt Flora's anger against my mother, and her anxiety to keep the knowledge of her marriage from everyone. There *was* no marriage——"

"That is a thing you could easily find out, Gay," David reminded her, watching her anxiously.

"Could find out?" There was a glint of hope in her voice, and in the heavy, beautiful eyes she raised to his. "Do you mean that you don't know?"

"I think of course your mother was married!" David said, stoutly. "But how can I convince you? I never gave it a moment's thought before. Or if I did," he added, conscientiously, remembering vaguely some talk before the fire with Aunt Flora, on the day that Gay had come home last fall, "I must have been entirely reassured, for I never understand that there was anything irregular about it at all."

"I can ask," Gay mused, sombrely.

"I *would* ask, if I were you!" David answered, with a quick nod. "Only remembering," he added, "that if it should be what you fear, it does not really touch *you*, Gay. You are not yet nineteen, and you are sure to win friends, and your own place, and create your own life and your own happiness, in these years that are ahead. Don't feel anything but pity, if this should be the case."

She glanced at him gravely over her shoulder. Then he saw the blood creep up under her clear, warmly colourless skin.

"I would like to have something—one thing!—in my life," she said, slowly, "of which I might be proud!"

David watched her as she walked slowly, and with her head held high in a sort of weary dignity, from the room.

Flora, before the sitting-room fire later, told him that the girl had been upstairs with poor Lily, who was in the drowsy state that followed fatigue and the rather strong astringent medicine that Margret had given her for a heavy cold. Gabrielle had sat beside her mother's fire, peacefully reading, Flora reported. Flora herself seemed oddly relieved and at ease about the matter.

Gabrielle came into the room just before dinner, with her eyes still clouded and heavy, but wearing the prettiest of her plain black uniforms, with the white collar and cuffs that enhanced the delicate beauty of her wrists and throat. She seemed composed but subdued, and was so extraordinarily lovely, sitting silent in her chair after dinner, raising her long curved lashes to look seriously at whoever addressed her, that David thought that if anything could make Gay more beautiful than before, this touch of tragedy and sorrow had done so. To-night she seemed to have no heart for cards, and David dared not suggest them; once, when Aunt Flora had left the room, she told him in a hurried phrase, and with the hot colour burning in her cheeks, that at the first opportunity she meant to question her aunt and clear up the whole matter.

"I think you're wise!" David said, warmly. "And meanwhile, would it do any good to have me stay at Wastewater? Are you in the least nervous about being left here?"

"Left here? With Margret and Daisy and Sarah and Hedda and Trude and Aunt Flora?" she queried, looking up with the shadow of a sad smile. "My dear David," she added, as if half to herself, staring back at the fire again, "what I have to fear is nothing from which you can save me!"

"Sad times come into every life, Gay," the man said, trying to comfort her. "I remember," he blundered on, "I remember the day Tom and I were brought home from school—when our mother died. That was before you were born, or Sylvia was born. Aunt Flora wasn't even married, if I remember rightly—no, of course she wasn't. For she was engaged to Uncle Roger after that——"

"Ah, losing your mother is different!" Gay said, in a voice of pain. "But with me, Davy, it would be better if I had lost her. If I had never had her!"

Nothing more was said until Aunt Flora returned, and then David felt a thrill of genuine admiration for the girl who could forget her own heartache to watch the elderly woman's card game, prompting her, correcting her, discussing plays. Watching them both, he told himself that he would remain at Wastewater, whatever the inconvenience to himself, at least until he could make sure that Gabrielle had settled the wretchedly upsetting question of her own legitimacy.

But the next day was bright, and the sunshine almost warm. Gay seemed over the stormiest pain of her new shock and new suspicions, and David saw that she did not intend to hurry any further investigations. Moreover, his closest friend and associate, the lazy, happy-go-lucky Jim Rucker, in whose city studio David occasionally set up an easel, wired him distressedly concerning a question of some frames. Billings wanted to know if the snowscapes were to have the same frames as the picture called "White's Barn, Keyport." And if those three pictures came back from the Washington Exhibition, where did David want them left?

David was needed. He departed, carrying the comforting last memory of Gay, gloved and muffled, walking briskly in the winter garden, and promising him that if there were any really sensational weather developments in the next few weeks, she would send him word.

"If there's a blizzard," she promised, with almost her old smile, "you shall come back and paint it. Or one of those ice storms that coat all the branches with glass! And be sure to let me know if the 'notes'—those little scrappy sketches I love so—sell, and which ones."

"Lord, she is beautiful. *Beautiful*," David said aloud, in the taxi. "I guess she'll be sensible. She's all right now!"

He did not know that she watched him out of sight with a heart like lead. With him the winter sunlight seemed to go, too, leaving only gray skies, gray sea, bare trees and frozen earth, leaving only shadows and damp odours of plaster and dust and kerosene in Wastewater's big walls, leaving loneliness and fear and shame to Gabrielle.

Almost three weeks later she wrote him. David saw the Crowchester postmark and instantly knew whose pretty, square handwriting that must be. She wrote closely, evenly, yet there were a dash and a finish about the blocked letters that gave the sheet the effect of a rather unusual copper-plate engraving:

> I had a long talk with Aunt Flora about ten days ago. And she told me the truth. It was what I suspected. There was never a marriage, and that was what broke her heart, and incidentally my poor mother's heart. The disgrace of it, and the fever, coming all at once, were too much for her soul and mind, and can you wonder? I

think I had braced myself to hear it, David, and expected it, and I am trying to meet it as well as I can, trying to work hard, and to keep busy, and to believe that it is only fair that I should pay for what was not my fault. That is the reason, of course—I mean the fact that it was all secret and wrong—that Uncle Roger never made any search for Charpentier, my father. My mother had no claim on him.

Aunt Flora was kindness itself about all this, and I think she feels bitterly sorry for me. She talked to me so kindly about Sylvia and herself always wanting me here, and indeed I could hardly be anywhere else now, for my mother has been pretty sick, and likes to have me about her. It seems that she fears any doctor we call in may be from one of those sanitariums she so hates, so we have not called one. She lies very peaceful and still, and, oddly enough, likes best to have me play and sing to her. One kind thing that Aunt Flora did was to have the old square piano upon which Sylvia and I used to practise years ago, brought up to my mother's room, and often we spend our evenings there now.

And the letter went on, in a composed and courageous tone that David found astonishing in any girl so young:

While she lives, which will not be long, for she seems more like eighty than fifty now, and is so frail we hardly know whether she will ever get up again—while she lives I must stay here, since Sylvia and Aunt Flora will let me, whether my pride likes it or not, of course. Afterward, I look to *work*—[she had underscored it twice]—any sort of work, to help me get my balance back, to help me feel that life is just in the long run, and that there is good somewhere under all this.

David read the thin sheets more than once, and mused far more steadily than he realized upon the situation of the lovely and loving young creature to whom life had been so strangely harsh. There was not, truly, as she had said, one thing of which she might be proud. Her father was nothing to her, her mother was poor little weak-minded Aunt Lily, the bread she ate, the roof that covered her, were Sylvia's. Nameless, penniless, at eighteen she faced the world with bare hands.

One day he stopped at a fancier's, in the East Thirties, and sent up to Wastewater a coffee-coloured airedale, seven weeks old. The creature had somewhat the shape and feeling of a little muff, but was stocky, warm, and wriggling, with a little eager red tongue coming and going, and an entreating whine for whosoever stopped to finger his soft little head. If Aunt Flora objected, David scribbled on his card, Gay was to ask John please to keep Benbay, who was alas somewhat lacking in points, but whose father was Champion Benbay Westclox II, until David could take him away.

David, however, hoped that Aunt Flora would not object to Benbay. His lack of "points" would not prevent the woolly little affectionate creature from being a real companion and comfort to the lonely girl at Wastewater. Studying, practising, brooding, walking alone in the snow, eating meals alone with Aunt Flora in the dreary dining room, singing her little songs to her forlorn and dying mother in the winter evenings—David would shut his eyes and shake his head at the mere thought of such a life for such a girl!

His exhibition was early in April, and was followed by another in Chicago, where he would show pictures, and must be, if possible. David planned to go to Wastewater immediately afterward and establish himself there for the summer. Sylvia would be coming home in June, and there would be all sorts of questions to settle. Sylvia would have plans—she brimmed with plans. And of late David, musing over the problem of Gay and her youth and her beauty and her future, had been entertaining a new plan of his own.

It had come to him suddenly, this thought of a new solution for Gay, and it had a strangely thrilling and heart-warming quality about it, for all its undoubted whimsicality and unexpectedness. David had first found himself thinking of it on the day when he and Jim Rucker were bound for Chicago. David had been thinking idly, in his comfortable big Pullman chair, and staring through the wide window at a landscape that, although still bleak and bare, was already so different from what it had been even a few weeks before.

Clouds so heavily packed then were flying wildly now across a sky that seemed nearer, more accessible. Trees, leafless, yet had a faintly moist and expectant air, as they whipped madly about. There were thawing, and the taste of rain, and a great softening in the air; there was ploughing under way, and children's coats and winter hats were already shabby and ready to be shed. Shadows lay longer, and daylight lingered in the car almost until the dinner hour. David watched school children stamping and running by the big roadside pools that were ruffled by the wind; he saw mired cars in the muddy roads that were hard as steel a few weeks before, and except on the northeastern sides of fences and barns there was no more snow.

He was thinking of Gay, in a desultory fashion that had been customary of late, just of Gay at Wastewater, coming and going in her plain frocks, with her beautiful hand set off by the thin lawn cuff, and her beautiful creamy throat rising from the broad, transparent organdy collar, with that husky sweetness in her voice, and the fashion of raising her up-curled lashes to look at him. Gay, opening doors, walking by the sea——

And suddenly, full-grown in his mind, was the idea of marrying Gay. He did not know whence it had come; it seemed complete, it was finished to the last detail.

David was oddly shaken by this extraordinary inspiration. He did not think of it as an idea: it was an obsession. Once in his mind, he could think of nothing else, nor did he wish to think of anything else. Under his desultory rambling conversations with Jim Rucker, during their dinner, and while he was trying to read afterward, the insidious sweetness of this astonishing vision persisted. David abandoned himself to it over and over, as he might have done to some subtle and dream-provoking drug.

He always imagined his homecoming to Wastewater, to find Gay in the sitting room, sitting alone by the fire. He would come in to her, and she would raise to his those beautiful, serious eyes, and he would hear that husky, sweet voice in greeting. Sometimes the mere pleasure of this much so intrigued David that he was obliged to go back to the beginning and picture it all over again: the upstairs sitting room, the drowsy coal fire in the steel-rodded grate; Uncle Roger's smiling picture, with the favourite horse and the greyhound, looking down from above the mantel.

Then they would talk a little about her mother and Aunt Flora and Sylvia, and then David would say unexpectedly: "I've thought of a wonderful solution for you and all your troubles, dear old Gay. I want you to marry me." And when David reached this point in his dream, he had to stop short. An odd, happy sort of suffocation would envelop him, something that had nothing to do with love, but that seemed sheer emotion, by a realization of the poignant dramatic beauty of the scene.

To be sure, David had said almost these very words to Sylvia only a few months before. But strangely, strangely!—they had not seemed to have anything in common with the same phrases when addressed to Gay. In the first place, for ten years he had been steadily and admiringly moving toward the day of his marriage to Sylvia. He had administered her fortune with that in view, and being at this moment under a flexible sort of promise to marry Sylvia, an "understanding" that was to be made more definite presently, only if she so decreed, he had given some concerned thought a few months before to his future status as the husband of a rich young wife, as a money-hating, society-hating, display-hating painter married to a girl of twenty-one who might quite naturally be expected to enjoy her money and the social advantages it would give her.

David even now thought of himself as loving Sylvia and of being the proper mate for her. But Sylvia did not love him, or if she did, she also loved the thought of her independence, of travel with her mother. They had always thought they loved each other, and, there being no change now in his feeling toward her, David quite honestly believed that he loved her still.

But part of his plan for Gay included an explanation to Sylvia of the complications of the situation. Oddly enough, David did not dwell, in his thoughts, upon this explanation. There was no thrill in imagining that. He thought of it hurriedly; Sylvia beautiful and understanding, of course; Sylvia saying, "Why, certainly, David. It does solve everything for poor little Gay, and is much the wisest arrangement all round!"

That would be gotten through as briefly as possible; probably by letter, or perhaps David could see her for a moment at college. And immediately this was over, he would be free for that strangely thrilling scene with Gay—a scene of which he did not think as connected with love-making in any way. He had "loved" Sylvia for years, and there was none of that feeling here. No, this was just an inspired solution of poor little Gay's affairs.

For however wise and charming, she was not the type of girl who battles, or who wishes to battle, successfully with the world. She was alone, poor, nameless, and beautiful, and David shuddered as he thought what life might add to her present load of troubles and wrongs.

On the other hand, it would be excruciating to her to live along indefinitely at Wastewater. She would be dependent upon Sylvia, she would have no real place in the family, and on every side would be constant reminders of her mother's unhappy life and of her own illegitimacy.

But—married to him, established in the sunshiny little farmhouse in Keyport where he kept a sort of studio—Mrs. David Fleming——!

"What a wonderful thing marriage is!" David thought, shutting the book he could not read and lapsing contentedly into his golden dream again. He pictured Gay as his happy, simple, busy young wife, pictured them breakfasting on the shabby little east porch of the Keyport house on some summer morning when the peaceful ocean swelled and shone like a stretch of blue Chinese silk. "What a wonderful thing it is to take a woman right out of her own house like that!" David said, with a strange plunging at his heart. "I don't know that I ever realized just what an extraordinary thing it is, before!"

He began to imagine himself as introducing her to the simple household arrangements there: the little wood stove, the saucepans in which he and Rucker had sometimes scrambled eggs, the odd sketches and "notes" on the walls, the whole slipshod, comfortable little bachelor establishment. And his heart sang at the thought.

He was only Uncle Roger's stepson, whose income was something like four thousand a year. Gay was—nothing. What they did, where they went, how they spent the little money they had, would be nobody's business. They would go to Spain, if a few pictures sold at some sale, next year, or the year after—and if they had a child some day, David added in his thoughts, with a little unconscious squaring of his shoulders, and a grin, they would take him with them—drag him along and toughen him, and let Aunt Flora and Sylvia say what they would!

The relief of not having to think of Wastewater, Aunt Flora, and—and, yes, of Sylvia, too, made him feel a sort of shamed joy. In that arrangement he would always have been self-conscious, fighting against nameless and subtle and cramping opposition for his identity and his freedom. If he wanted a studio in Wastewater, he knew just how Sylvia would cushion it and beautify it. If he wanted old Rucker to come up and paint for a while, he knew just how Aunt Flora, abetted by Sylvia, would ask innocently: "How long will Mr. Rucker be with us, David?" He knew—because he had indeed experienced it, when rendering her accounts—exactly how conscientiously and incessantly Sylvia would discuss money matters with him.

"If you are in that neighbourhood, David," he could imagine her saying pleasantly, "do get those bonds from Crocker and put them in the safety-deposit boxes. I do think it was just a little irregular to leave them there since they aren't needed." And, "Will you go over that once again, David? You say they are reorganizing the company and want me to accept these securities for the old—I don't understand."

"You only have to sign that certificate, dear; all the other stockholders in the old company are doing it," he imagined himself responding, for the tenth time.

"Yes, but David, suppose this is so much worthless paper?" Sylvia would ask, intelligently. And Aunt Flora would nod in grave approval and admiration. No cheating Sylvia! "I don't believe in scribbling my signature anywhere and everywhere," Sylvia would go on, reinforced. "Please let's go over it again and again, until it's all quite clear!"

But with Gay, how simple and easy it would all be! Just their own happy daily plans to discuss, and their own microscopic income to administer. They would go up to Wastewater for Sunday dinner with Sylvia and Aunt Flora, and Gay would really be a Fleming then, and all her old unhappiness forgotten. Who would know—or care!—that beautiful young Mrs. David Fleming had been born outside of Mrs. Grundy's garden walls? Gay would come in to her husband's exhibitions, wearing that little velvet gown, or another like it, so vitally eager, so interested, so familiar with every stroke of the brush——

And at this point in his musing David would go back to the beginning again, and think of Wastewater in an April twilight, a week or two from now, and himself arriving there, to find Gay dreaming alone before the fire in the upstairs sitting room. She would raise those star-sapphire eyes and give him that radiant smile, and they would talk about Aunt Lily, and Aunt Flora, and Sylvia, and then he would say suddenly:

"I've thought out a real plan for you, Gay! It involves my having a talk with Sylvia, and it involves a little green-and-white farmhouse and barn in Keyport, for which I pay a hundred dollars rent a year, and a plain gold ring——!"

How bewildered she would look; he could see that faintly smiling, maternally indulgent look——!

His dream took complete possession of David, and made everything he did and said in these days seem unreal. The exhibition was under-run by a strong current of it: "It involves you and me, Gay, and my having a talk with Sylvia," David was saying to himself over and over, and the sale of a picture only made him think suddenly that he would like to give her a little present. Oh, and he had his mother's beautiful old-fashioned diamond engagement ring, and also some almost valueless but pretty topazes that had been hers, a ring and earrings and a chain, and an oval onyx pin with a pearl in it. These would be charming with Gay's warm golden colouring—especially if she wore those plain little velvet frocks——

Life took on quite a new meaning for David, and he said to himself that it must be because he was moving in this matter with Gay's safety and comfort and future rather than his own predominant in his mind, that this odd fluttering happiness, this poignant interest in the tiniest things in his day—because oddly they all seemed connected with his dream—this new delightful sense of values in anything and everything, had come to him.

Spring was always late at Wastewater, but spring was surely here, he thought, when he reached the old place late in an afternoon early in May.

He had hoped to get to Wastewater in the middle of, or at least by the third week in April, but upon returning to New York he found business matters of Sylvia's there which could not wait. It was with a grim little twitch in the corner of his mouth that David devoted himself to them. Sylvia would pay her next administrator; and it would not be her affectionate cousin David!

Now he would not get to Wastewater until May, and the twenty-third of April was Gay's birthday! David felt quite disproportionately provoked by the delay. Poor little Gay, she would not have much fun on her nineteenth anniversary. And because it seemed so newly and delightfully his business to think of Gay's pleasure now before his own, he sent her a birthday letter.

David wrote, with something less than the truth:

> I've been thinking a lot about you, and hoping that, between us all this summer, we can lighten that sad heart of yours. Or no, I won't say "us," for I hope to do something toward it all by myself. I've got a most attractive plan to propose to you, and you must make up your mind to agree to it. I'm writing Sylvia about it, for she comes into it a little—but not much. It is almost entirely dependent upon you, and somewhat upon yours ever faithfully and affectionately,
>
> DAVID.

She would get nothing from that, David assured himself as he mailed the letter. Having done so he tried to think just why the thrilling excitement that possessed him had seemed to exact that he relieve his overcharged emotions with just so much of a hint. It would only puzzle her——

CHAPTER XII

GABRIELLE, however, was more affronted than puzzled by it. It made her definitely uneasy. She suspected at once what was in his mind, and in the utter despair that engulfed her she felt that this would be the crowning trial, the crowning indignity, in a life that was filled with both.

The days since her discovery regarding her mother had seemed endless to her. They were the cold dark days that follow the coming in of the new year, there was nothing of the holidays' snap and exhilaration about them. Rain, clouds, winds, heavy snows, rushing storms had thundered and banged about Wastewater; Gay felt that every out-of-door garment she had was twisted and soaked and half dried; she was sick with loneliness and discouragement.

In vain she made herself practise, made herself walk and study. There was no life in it; everything she did come up against a blank wall, a dreary "What's the use?" What was the use of living, to find that so much that was weak and stupid and wrong was blended into one's blood?

If there had been a sweet, interested mother to put her arm about one, or a big father to advise and adore, if there had been normal friendships, neighbours, all the cheerful life of the average American girl—ah, that would have been so different! But Gabrielle was alone, yet curiously imprisoned in this dreary old silent place, tied to the poor little invalid who rarely identified her, and to dismal, quiet Aunt Flora, and to all the ghosts and echoes of Wastewater.

Tied, too, to an unceasing contemplation of Sylvia's perfections, Sylvia's good fortune, Sylvia's charms. Sylvia would be home in June as the daughter of the house, and the heiress; already some papering and painting was being done in preparation for her return; she herself had selected papers and hangings in Boston weeks ago.

Gabrielle had borne bravely the initial shock of discovering her mother but she weakened as the slow, cold weeks went by, let her music go, neglected her books, wept and brooded a great deal. David's birthday letter brought the first smile of many days to her face, and she opened it with the old brightness he always brought to her shining in her eyes.

The cryptic phrases made her bite her lip thoughtfully; look off into space for a little while. And presently she went for a lonely walk by the sea, and half-a-mile away from the house, seated upon a rock above the ebbing teeth of the cold tide, she read the letter again.

Then she tore it to scraps and buried it under a stone. Her cheeks blazed with colour and a nervous hammering commenced in her heart. He could not mean—but he *could* not mean that he meant to ask her to marry him?

This would be preposterous; it certainly was not that. Yet as Gabrielle remembered the phrases of the short letter the horrible conviction came to her that her suspicion was justified. He was engaged to Sylvia, or at least there was between them an understanding more or less definite; that was what he meant by Sylvia's part, Sylvia's "coming into it a little." And the rest was between him and Gabrielle.

Oh, he could not intend to hurt her so terribly, to add this insufferably humiliating thing to all that she was enduring now!

"I don't believe it!" Gabrielle said aloud to the gulls and the sea. "David wouldn't do it. It wouldn't be honest, and he would know how mortally—how mortally hurt I would be!"

But the uncomfortable fear persisted. David always entered into Sylvia's and Aunt Flora's plans with all the affectionate interest of a devoted son. He knew they were troubled about Gay. He would step into the breach and solve the Gay problem once and for all.

"Oh, my God, I cannot bear it, if he begins to say something like that to me!" Gay said, passionately, getting to her feet and beginning to walk along the rough shore blindly, hardly conscious of what she was doing. "How cruel—how cruel they are! They don't know, you see," she added, to herself, more quietly. "They don't know how hard it is! Aunt Flora will think it over and decide that David would be a most wonderful match for me——"

Her heart began to beat fast again, and her face burned.

"If he comes here next week," she said, hurriedly and feverishly, "I will not be here! Where can I go? I won't—I can't have him tell me about it, that Sylvia thinks it wise, and Aunt Flora thinks it wise. No, my dear David," Gay said, stumbling on, and crying bitterly as she went, "you are the one man in the world who cannot solve my problems by marrying me! You would do it, to have them happy, and to make me happy, but that would be more than I can bear! I've borne a great deal—I wish I had never been born!" And blinded by tears, she sat down upon a rock, and buried her head in her arms, and sobbed aloud.

But when she got home she was quite herself again, and had the puppy in the sitting room before dinner, playing with him charmingly in her low chair; standing him up on his indeterminate little hind legs, in a dancing position, doubling him up with little bites and woofs of affection, to which the struggling puppy made little woofing and biting replies.

Gabrielle had by this time quite convinced herself that it was idiotic to suspect sensible David of anything so fantastic as disposing of Sylvia, whom he so heartily admired, and offering himself to her, whom he had not seen for twelve long weeks. She put the suspicion resolutely from her.

Aunt Flora had softened so much to Ben, as the puppy was called, that he was a regular third in the evening group, and had even been up to Lily's room. Flora often pretended that Ben could not be comfortable curled up in a ball in an armchair and sound asleep, and would drag him into her lap with an impatient "Here, if you won't be quiet anywhere else!" To-night Gay forestalled this by surrendering him to Aunt Flora as soon as dinner was over. Neither played cards to-night, Flora thoughtfully pulled the little dog's soft ears, Gabrielle sat opposite, with Emerson's Essays open in her lap.

"Poor Lily isn't going to last much longer, Gabrielle," Flora said, presently, with a sigh. The relief of sharing her secret had quite visibly softened Flora, and she often discussed Gay's mother with the girl as with a confidante and an equal. "I think we must have a doctor, now. I know, of course, what he will say; she had constant care from a doctor while she was at Crosswicks. But, afterward, it is as well to have had some advice."

Gabrielle, listening soberly, nodded with a sigh. She could not pretend to grieve. More, she could not pretend that it would not be a great lightening of her load when that frail little babbling personality was no more. She thirsted to get away from Wastewater, away from ghosts and shadows and echoes, into the world again! Away from David, with his kind eyes and his interested smile, away from Sylvia, who was so cruelly armed at all points with beauty and intelligence, with friends and money and position and power!

Presently Flora spoke of Sylvia; David would be home in a few days now, and Sylvia in less than five weeks. It would be so wonderful to have Sylvia home for always.

"Do you know, Gabrielle," said Flora, jerking her yarn composedly over Ben's little sleeping head, "I would not be intensely surprised if nothing came of the understanding between David and Sylvia. From something she wrote me, I rather suspect that there is somebody—— No, I can't say that. Perhaps it is only that she does not want to think of anything so serious so soon. She's not yet twenty-one, after all. But she wrote me as if she might be thinking it wiser for David——"

Gabrielle heard no more. Her throat constricted again, and her hands grew cold. All the fears of the afternoon returned in full force. But surely—surely they couldn't all be so simple as to think that she would placidly and gratefully accept this solution of her problem, her poverty, her namelessness, her superfluousness!

David would not, anyway, she told herself a hundred times in the days to come. David was understanding, David was everything that was kind and good. He would help her find her independence, he would always be her friend, and Gay knew, in her own secret heart, that her universe would always revolve about him, that there would always be a mysterious potency in the mere sound of his voice, or touch of his hand, where she was concerned.

But discuss her with Sylvia and Aunt Flora, and kindly and with big-brotherly superiority offer her a "plan," a plan to accept his name and his protection, simply because she was so apparently incapable of taking care of herself! Gabrielle suffocated at the thought. No, David couldn't be David and do that.

In the ten days that elapsed before his arrival at Wastewater she alternated between such violent extremes of feeling, and lay awake pondering, imagining, and analyzing the situation so constantly at night that she was genuinely exhausted when the afternoon of his coming came at last.

There were moments when she felt she could not see him, dared not face him. There were times when she longed for his arrival, and to assure herself with a first glance that all this nervous anticipation was her own ridiculous imagining, and that no thought of it had ever crossed his mind!

When he finally came Gay was in the garden. For spring had come to Wastewater, and David's fancy of finding her before a fire in the sitting room had been outdated by two full weeks of sunshine. There was fresh green grass sprouting about the old wall, there were daisy-starred stretches of it under the massed blossoms of the fruit trees; gracious shadows lay long and sweet everywhere over new green leaves; the willows were jade fountains of foliage, the maples uncurling moist little red and gold tendrils, and the lilacs were rustling columns of clean new leafage and plumy blossom. The last of the frost had melted from the newly turned sods; gulls were walking about, pulling at worms, and spring sunset lay over the broad, gently heaving surface of an opal sea.

David had taken his bags upstairs, greeted his aunt, who was knitting in the sitting room, but without the fire, and had spent perhaps ten restless and excited minutes in outward conversation and in inner excitement. Where was Gay? When would the door handle turn and the plainly gowned girl come in, with the smile flashing into her star-sapphire eyes when she saw him, and the beautiful hand she extended so quaintly, so demurely enhanced by the transparent white cuff? David was so shaken by a strange emotion at the thought that every moment was bringing their meeting closer, so confused by the undercurrent of his thoughts—the undercurrent that would dwell upon her greeting, and his introduction of all he had to say to her—that he could hardly hear what his aunt was saying. When he did finally escape to search for Gay, and when Hedda told him that she was in the garden, he found himself standing quite still in the side passage, with his heart thundering, and his senses swimming, and an actual unwillingness upon him, after all these waiting days and weeks, to make real the dream that he had cherished so long.

There she was, about the western turn of the house, half walking and half running, with the puppy sometimes keeping his feet and sometimes swung dizzily in the air on the rope that Gabrielle was carrying and the little dog biting in a frenzy of joy. There was warm sweet light in the garden at five o'clock, the day had been balmy enough to make cooler airs at its close almost a relief.

Pleasant domestic sounds in the barnyard were all about: clucks and moos, John whistling, and the stamping of big horses' feet on distant floors. The scent of violets and syringa, of lilacs and new grass, of damply turned, sun-warmed earth was like a delicious sharp and heady ether in the air.

David joined the girl just as she and the dog were turning down a rambling sort of back road that led toward the sea; Gabrielle turned, and although indeed she smiled, he saw that she was an older and a soberer Gabrielle than the little schoolgirl of the Christmas holidays. They walked the quarter mile to the shore deep in a conversation he had not anticipated; she talked of her mother, whose life was a question only of days now, and made one allusion to the deeper cause of pain to herself.

"My finding out about myself—about my mother's never having been married, David—has made a sort of change in everything to me," she said, unemotionally. "I seem to feel now that I must do something—that it is more than ever my duty to do something to make my own place in life and stand upon my own feet. That's the only way that I can ever be happy, and I will be happy so, believe me!" she added, nervously intercepting an interruption from him. "Doctor Ensicoe, from Crowchester, says that my mother will not outlive the month. And then I mean to write to the nuns in Boston and stay with them until I find something that I can do. I know Aunt Flora will help me, for indeed she offered to most generously, and, while I must—I will let her. She was very kind about it all," Gabrielle added, reaching safer waters now, and so speaking more quietly. "We have never spoken of it except at that one time. I said to her quite suddenly, one night when we were going up to my mother's room—I'd had it terribly on my mind, of course, 'Aunt Flora, answer me one question. There would be no use in my attempting to trace Charpentier, my father, would there? There is no record of that marriage, is there? That is the real reason for all the mystery and secrecy, isn't it?' And she turned very pale," went on Gay, "and answered, 'Yes.' We never alluded to it again, although many times since she has told me that Sylvia would always take care of me—that I must not worry!" And catching a sudden look of determination and interest in David's face Gay went on hurriedly, "But indeed I don't worry, I shall get along splendidly and make you all proud of me!"

A sensation of pity so sudden and acute as to dry his mouth and press like a pain behind his eyes silenced David for a moment. Then he said:

"But you are very young, Gay, and inexperienced, to face all the ugliness and coldness of the world. Suppose," David added, conscious suddenly of the quickened beat of his heart, "there was some other plan that eased, or helped to ease, all those worries of yours——?"

"Oh, my God," Gay prayed, in a very panic of fear. "Oh, David," she cried, in the deeps of her being, "spare me! Oh, God, don't let him mean that he is going to ask me to marry him. Oh, no—no—no!"

Aloud she said nothing. They were on the sweet, grassy cliffs above the sea, now, and Gay was looking out across the level stretches of the peaceful water, over which shone the last of the long day's light.

She was so beautiful, as she stood there, that for a moment David was content to look at her and tell himself that he had not remembered how lovely she was. Loose delicate tendrils of her tawny hair were blowing about her white temples; there was a delicate creamy glow on her warm, colourless skin, her great eyes seemed to give forth a starry shimmer of their own. In the fine hands, encircled at the wrists, as David had anticipated they would be, by transparent white cuffs, she held the restless puppy against the young curve of her breast; in the old garden and the spring sunset she looked like a slender, serious impersonation of Memory or Poetry, or of some mythical young goddess, wandering under the great trees.

But it was not only the physical beauty that he saw. He saw in her too the dearly companionable girl of the past mid-winter, whose husky, sweet laughter had rung out over the card table, whose eager helpful interest had made bright so many a dark sleety morning in the upstairs studio, when the oil stove slowly warmed the air and scented it with hot metal and kerosene vapours. He saw her buttoning on the big coat, tramping through snowy woods at his side, with her hands deep in her pockets, and her bright face glowing like a rose. And a first little chilling fear crept over his bright dream; suppose—suppose she was not for him, after all?

"Gabrielle," he said, suddenly, his face reddening and his voice shaking a little, "will you let me tell you what I planned for you and for me?"

She gave him an agonized half glance, nodded, and said some indistinguishable word of assent as she turned away.

"I was wondering——" David began. And suddenly it seemed all to go flat and dull. He felt himself to have no business to be putting it to her this way, this half-laughing, half-sympathetic, wholly kind and comfortable way. The smooth phrases of his imaginings vanished in air, he was merely a rather stupid man of thirty-one, bungling the most delicate thing in all the world. It was too late to stop. The girl's face was crimson, but she had turned toward him gravely and expectantly, and was looking at him steadily and bravely.

"This was my idea," David began again, miserably. "I—I felt—I knew that you were most unhappy, and that you felt lonely and as if you were wasting time here, and yet doubtful about making a start elsewhere. And it occurred to me——" He tried his best at this point to recapture the affectionate whimsically practical note that these words had always had in anticipation, but do what he would they sounded stupidly patronizing and heavy. "It occurred to me," he said again, "that you and I are somewhat in the same boat. We're Flemings, yet we don't truly belong at Wastewater—that belongs to Sylvia now! And wouldn't it be a very delightful thing for you and me to give them all a surprise and just take ourselves out of their way, once and for all?"

She heard him so far. Then she stopped him with a sudden backward movement of her head, and answered quietly, with a downward glance at the puppy's little snuggled form:

"Thank you, David. But you must see that I can't—I can't do that! But thank you very much."

David was honestly taken aback. Not that he had expected her to fall into his arms—he did not know just what he had expected her to do. But certainly not this! He had perhaps imagined her beautiful and irradiating smile turned toward him, heard a rich cadence half of reproach and half of pleasure in her voice as she said, something like, "David Fleming! Are you asking me to marry you?"

This actuality was all confusing and different from the plan, and his own feelings were disconcertingly different, too. The girl looked unmistakably hurt and humiliated by what he had said, which was astonishing enough. But even more astonishing was his own sudden conviction that she had reason to seem so. What was he saying to her, anyway? After all, her love affair was the most important thing in all a girl's life! It was not something to be flung at her unexpectedly, between one's arrival after weeks—after months of absence—and a family dinner!

A half-analyzed consciousness of being wrong, combined with a general confusion of mind and senses, was strong upon David as he blundered on:

"I may be surprising you, Gay. You see, I've been thinking about all this for a long time! You can certainly say, 'This is so sudden,' in the good old-fashioned manner, if you want to," added David, nervously, hoping to win back his humorous, comprehending little companion of January with his anxious and appealing laugh.

But Gay did not laugh.

"I do appreciate your taking my problems so much to heart, David," she said, turning to pace staidly back through the twilight greenness and sweetness toward the house. "But I really blame myself a good deal for being such a baby! I've been selfishly dwelling upon my troubles, and acting as if no girl ever had them to face before, and of course it has worried you and Aunt Flora and Sylvia. But that's over now, and I want you to know that I do appreciate your sympathy, and your having thought out this way of escape for me, and having planned it all with Sylvia."

"As a matter of fact," David interposed, eagerly, hoping that matters might yet adjust themselves, "Sylvia's letter to me, asking to be set entirely free of any real or imaginary understanding between us, crossed my letter to her saying that I—had other plans in mind."

He looked at Gabrielle hopefully with the words; perhaps when she knew how completely above-board and deliberated the step had been she would begin to see it in his light. But Gay merely reddened the more deeply, if that were possible, and said hastily and uncomfortably:

"I see. And I do thank you! And I ask you—I *beg* you—for the little time I am at Wastewater," she added, feverishly, as the vertigo of shame and confusion that had been almost nauseating her threatened to engulf her in a humiliating burst of tears, "please never to say anything like this to me again! *Please*——! There are reasons——" Gay fought on desperately, feeling with terror that tears might end in his arms, and that utter capitulation on his own kindly humorous terms must follow such a break-down, "there are reasons why it *kills* me to have you talk so! I beg you, David, to consider it all settled—all over——"

"Why, of course I will!" David said, in a cold, quiet voice that braced her like a plunge into icy waters. "I'm only sorry to distress you," he added, formally. "I had been thinking about it with a great deal of pleasure, and I thought you might. I'm sorry. We'll never speak of it again."

Then they were at the side door, and Gay escaped into the gloomy dark hallway, and fled red-cheeked and panting to her room, where she could cry, rage, shake herself, walk the floor, and analyse the whole situation unobserved.

"Oh, you fool!" she said, scornfully, to her panting image in the mirror. "You hysterical schoolgirl! Oh, how I hate him and his plans for me!" she gritted, through shut teeth. "And I hate Sylvia worse! I hate them all. He thought I would die of joy—he knows better now. Oh, insulting! He wouldn't have done that to Sylvia or one of the Montallen girls! But it didn't matter with me—Aunt Lily's daughter, with no father to stand up for me. And it isn't my fault I haven't a father," Gay said, pitifully, half aloud, leaning her elbows on the bureau, and beginning to cry into her hands; "it isn't my fault that I'm all alone in the world!"

And again she flung herself on the bed, and her whole form was racked and shaken by the violence of her weeping.

"He'll see my red eyes at dinner and think it's for him," she broke off, savagely, sitting up in the early dark and reaching for the scrambling and mystified puppy, who was going upon a whimpering tour of investigation among the pillows. Gay dried her eyes upon his downy little back, lighted her lamp, and soused her eyes with cold water. Half an hour later she went down to dinner, quite restored to calm and ready to take a cheerful part in the conversation. But she would not share the sitting room with her aunt and David after dinner.

She said, with that touch of new maturity and decision that David found so touching and so amusing in little Gabrielle, that she would go up and sit with her mother, thus releasing Margret for an hour or two below stairs.

The room seemed to become blank, however, when she had gone quietly away, and David was surprised to find that the thought of her had become so habitual with him in the last few weeks that he was thinking of her still, as steadily as if that strange hour in the garden were the dream, and the Gay of his plan, the gracious Gay who had so many, many times promised him, in his thoughts, to marry him, were the reality.

He found himself restlessly making excuses to follow her upstairs. Was Aunt Flora going up to see Aunt Lily to-night? Later, Flora said, sombrely. Was it quite safe for Gabrielle up there alone with the invalid? Oh, quite. Poor Lily had not the strength of a baby, now.

After an endless time they went upstairs, to find that Margret had just come up, and Gay was ready to plead fatigue and slip away to bed. Aunt Lily was a mere colourless slip of flesh and blood, quiet upon smooth pillows now, with her gray hair brushed and pinned up neatly. Gay was kneeling beside her in the orderly, lamp-lighted room when David went in, with one of her beautiful hands clasping the yellowed old lifeless fingers. She got to her feet with no sign of embarrassment, and in another two minutes had disappeared for the night.

David saw a light in her transom, half an hour later, when he went to his room. She was probably quietly reading, he thought; discomfited, preferring the society of books to his own, after what had transpired this afternoon.

He felt disappointed and humiliated, he missed the thrilling dream that had kept him company for so long, and for a day or two he managed to persuade himself that it was because Gay had failed him. She had proved very much less satisfying than his thoughts of her; he had unconsciously been idealizing her all this time. He had thought of her as gracious, merry, provocative, responsive, and she had proved to be merely embarrassed and awkward.

"Well!" he said, going off to sleep, "That's over—no harm done!" But he could not dismiss it. Again he said, almost aloud; "That's over. No harm done!"

CHAPTER XIII

HE PLUNGED, the next morning, into work, going off to Keyport immediately after breakfast and returning late in the afternoon. The day was exquisite beyond words, the sea satiny blue, and there was real summer warmth in the sweet spring stillness of the air. David saw Gabrielle in the garden when he came back, and took his painting gear upstairs, determined not to make himself ridiculous in her eyes again. But a power stronger than himself immediately took him downstairs again. He walked, with an air of strolling, to the hollies, where she had been. But she was gone.

David now felt irrationally and without analysis that he must see her, and at once. He had nothing to say to her, and if he had, he might have waited until dinner-time brought them together. But he felt like a lost child, not seeing that figure in blue gingham—his eyes searched for it hungrily, swept each new vista; he felt actually sick with disappointment when moment after moment went by and there was no sign of her down the lane, on the cliff road, or among the rocks. He thought of nothing but the finding of her; Gabrielle in her blue gingham seated by a pool, running along with Ben—just to find her——

She came into the sitting room just before dinner, and David, who was actually exhausted from the monotonous hammering of thoughts about only her, dared not trust himself to look up as she slipped into her chair. He was glancing over a new *Atlantic*; he pretended that he had not heard Gay enter.

"It was young Doctor Ensicoe, the son," said Gabrielle's voice, suddenly, quietly in the silence, to Aunt Flora. "I took him upstairs. He says to watch, and let his father know if there seems to be any pain or restlessness."

If the words had been so many bombs they could scarcely have had a more extraordinary effect upon David. He felt as if his heart had given a great plunge, stopped short, raced on again madly; he felt as if his mouth and throat were dry, a sort of weakness and vertigo that were yet exquisitely pleasant seized him.

It was impossible for him to speak to this girl, or to look up, while this state of affairs lasted. If she saw that he was nervous and unlike himself, she must think what she would——! David could only try to get a grip upon soul and body, and betray himself as little as possible.

This moment was the end of all peace for him. For although he did indeed presently hand his aunt the magazine with some brief comment, and although dinner and the evening proceeded as usual, he was beginning to suspect that his whole life had been changed now, mysteriously changed—partly perhaps his own doing, through that long-cherished dream of an imaginary scene with an imaginary Gabrielle.

But no matter how it had come about. The blazing and inescapable truth was that there was nothing else in the world for him but this quiet, slender, serious, tawny-headed girl. He did not know what he felt toward her, or whether the wild confusion of his senses might be called anything so reasonable as feeling; she was simply in the world, she was sitting in chairs, opening doors, speaking in that incredibly thrilling voice, raising those extraordinary eyes—that was enough.

David had never before been really in love. But he had thought he loved Sylvia, and he did not put in that same category his feeling for Gabrielle. This was nothing that could be classified or regulated; regulate it, indeed, David thought, with an almost audible groan when he came to this word in his thoughts; as well regulate raging flames or rushing waters!

It devoured him with fever. He was unable to eat for excitement, never happy one instant out of Gabrielle's company, acutely miserable when in it. He lay awake in the warm spring nights thinking of what he had said to her during the past day, and as her looks and words in reply—such quiet words, such rare looks!—came back before his vision, he would feel his heart stop, and his breath would fail him with sheer fear and terror and hope and agony of doubt.

He sat at breakfast, pushing about the toast that was so much chalk and plaster to his palate, scalding himself with his coffee one morning, forgetting it entirely the next. His eyes never left Gabrielle. She would glance up, passing him perhaps the omelette that he would not even see, much less taste, and at his awkward laugh, muttered words, and hastily averted look she would perhaps colour confusedly. If she directed a simple question to him, he found it maddeningly difficult to answer.

"I beg pardon——?" He had to leave the sentence hanging rawly. He could not say her name.

"I asked you: did Margret say anything about medicines?"

"I—I—you mean on Sunday——?"

"No," Gay would say, astonished at his manner. "I mean this morning, five minutes ago."

"Oh, I see—I see! Did—who? What?"

"Never mind. I'll ask her," Gay would finish, deciding that David must be absolutely absorbed in the picture he was painting. David would watch her go from the room, gracious, sweet, beautiful in her cotton gown. All the spring seemed only a setting for her love-liness, the lilacs and the blue sky, the sunshine and the drifting snow of fruit blossoms.

It was this wonderful, this incomparable woman, he would re-mind himself scathingly, that he had affronted with his insultingly casual offer of marriage a week ago. No wonder the girl had put a definite distance between them since! But he knew he would ask her again, simply because there was no other conceivable thing for him to do.

His dream of the little farmhouse in Keyport returned now, but it was a dream infinitely enhanced, and haloed by all the colours of the rainbow. David could hardly bear the poignant sweetness of the thought of Gay as his wife; Gay perhaps chatting over a late breakfast on the porch with him; Gay travelling with him, and look-ing over a steamer rail as the blue mountains of Sicily or the green shores of the Isle of Wight slowly formed themselves on the horizon. Once, when he was quietly painting, the thought of Gay with a child in her arms came to him suddenly, and David felt his eyes sting and the palms of his hands suddenly moist.

She was leagues away from him now, never with him when she could avoid it, never alone with him at all. She was apparently liv-ing a life of her own, coming and going gently and pleasantly, an-swering, listening, but no longer the Gabrielle he had known a few months ago.

And ten days after his return she was still further removed by her mother's death. Lily died quite peacefully one sweet May evening, after an afternoon when she had seemed more normal than for years. She had had for some days the idea that Gabrielle was her old nurse, Miss Rosecrans, and made all her few demands of the girl under that name. But at the very end, when Gabrielle was kneeling beside her, with sorrowful, tear-brimmed eyes fixed upon the yellowed lit-tle sunken face, Lily opened her eyes, fixed them affectionately up-on Flora, and asked feebly:

"Is this big girl my baby, Flo?"

"This is Gabrielle, Lily," Flora said, clearing her throat.

Lily smiled with ineffable satisfaction at Gabrielle, and said contentedly:

"Gabrielle. Isn't it a pretty name? Do you like it? Did Roger like it?"

"I am going to say some prayers, Mother," Gabrielle said, smiling with wet cheeks, and with the salt taste of her own tears in her mouth. Lily opened her eyes briefly, for the last time.

"Ah, I wish you would!" she said, with a smile and a deep sigh. And she never moved or spoke again.

Two days later she was buried in the little plot within Wastewater's wide walls; the doctor, Flora weeping on David's arm, Gay standing straight and alone, and the awestruck maids were all her little funeral train. It was Flora who seemed to feel the loss most, and with surprising force; she seemed broken and aged, and it was for Gabrielle to comfort her.

"I never supposed it would be so," Flora repeated, over and over. "That I would be the last—that Will and Roger and Lily would all be gone before me!"

She would not stay in bed; Flora did not belong to the generation that can eat and read and idle comfortably under covers. She was up at her usual hour upon every one of the sweet, warm fragrant mornings, when dawn crept in across the sea and the wet garden sent up a very bouquet of perfumes through the open upstairs windows. But she was silent and sad, and when Sylvia's long-awaited happy Commencement came, Flora was really too ill to go, although she refused to concede to herself the luxury even of one hour upon a couch, or the satisfaction of a single visit from the doctor. David went up alone to the Commencement, and brought Sylvia back with him. It was on that last day of her college life, a day of flowers and white gowns, crowds, music, laughter, and tears, that Sylvia found time to say to him pleadingly:

"David dear, my letter didn't hurt you terribly?"

"I'd had something of the same feeling myself, you know," he reminded her. "Our letters crossed. You remember I said just what you did, that it must either be an engagement or nothing, and that I knew you would prefer it to be nothing just at this time."

"Oh, yes!" responded Sylvia, narrowing her eyes, and speaking a little vaguely. And David saw that while her letter, a letter written in a charmingly frank fashion, and asking please—please to be free from any engagement to him for a little while, had made a romantic sort of impression upon her mind, his had scarcely registered upon her consciousness at all. In other words, Sylvia was her own whole world just at the moment, and the only things that mattered were her own moods, her own ideas, her own individual desires.

The highly distinguished and honourable conclusion of her school days, her youth, her beauty, her sense of closely impending power could not but be deliciously stimulating to a nature like Sylvia's. She and David stopped two nights in Boston, Sylvia with a schoolmate, David at a hotel, met on the languid, warm spring mornings to explore the quiet shops and to discuss various plans for Wastewater: electric lighting for Wastewater, a furnace for Wastewater, a hot-water system for Wastewater. There was a delightful new, red, slim checkbook; there was an imposing balance at the bank. Sylvia bought herself one or two charming frocks as a sort of promissory note of the financial independence that was so soon to be, and she did not forget a broad lacy black hat for dear little Gabrielle, who had had such a sad year, and a lacy thin black afternoon gown to match it.

Gabrielle, when they reached Wastewater, met them all in white, and Sylvia gave her a warm kiss and murmured just the right phrase of sympathy as they went upstairs to find her mother. The gardens were exquisite in early June bloom; the whole house smelled of roses and summer weather; birds were flashing in and out of the cherry trees; John was on his knees beside the strawberry bed.

But Flora sat upstairs before the cold grate, with the windows shut, and her first words to Sylvia were broken by tears. Sylvia comforted her with a sort of loving impatience in her voice.

"Mamma, darling! Is this reasonable! Isn't it after all a blessed solution for poor little Aunt Lily?"

"But I never thought it would be so!" Flora faltered, blowing her nose, sniffling, straightening her glasses with all the unlovely awkwardness of hard-fought grief. And immediately she regained her composure, almost with a sort of shame, and David could say truthfully to Sylvia a little later, when the three young persons were wandering through the garden, that Sylvia had done her mother good already.

Sylvia indeed did them all good; she was delighted with everything, appreciative and pleasant with the maids, and sisterly in her manner toward Gabrielle. David found her sensible and clever in the business conferences they had on the dreamy summer mornings in the little office downstairs, where perhaps the first mistress of Wastewater had transacted her business also, more than a hundred years before—the business of superintending stores and soap-making, weaving and dyeing, bartering in cocks and geese and the sell-ing of lambs. Sylvia waived all unnecessary matters, was brightly receptive, and in every way businesslike and yet confident in David's judgment. Later she would debate with John about fruit, with Trude about preserving, with Daisy about tablecloths, all in her own pleasantly unhesitating yet considerate manner. It was evident that she would assume her responsibilities thoroughly, yet with no jarring and disrupting of the accustomed course of things.

In one of the late evenings when Sylvia came into Gay's room to brush her hair and to gossip, Gay broached her plan of going to a Boston convent as soon as the hot weather should be over, to look about her and find some sort of work. Sylvia listened thoughtfully and looked up with a kindly smile.

"You'd be happier so, Gabrielle?"

"I think so," Gay answered.

"What is it?" Sylvia questioned, kindly. "Wastewater too lonely?"

Gabrielle did not answer immediately, except by a quick shake of her head. Presently she said, a little thickly:

"No, I love Wastewater more than any other place in the world."

"Well," said Sylvia, musing, "if you must try your wings, by all means try them! Be sure we'll all be interested in making it a success, Gay. Mamma and I may go abroad in the fall—it isn't definite, of course, but I think she would like it, if all my various anchors here can be managed without me."

Gabrielle had been burning, fearing, hating to ask it; she found herself saying now, with a little unconquerable incoherence:

"Then you and David——?"

"David and I," answered Sylvia, with a quick, mysterious smile, "are quite the best friends in the world!"

Did she know? David, in asking her to free him, had told her how much? Gay looked at her cousin through the mirror, and her face blazed. But Sylvia, curling the end of her long braid thoughtfully about her finger, was unsuspicious. Gay wondered if she could be acting.

"I don't mind telling you, dear," said Sylvia, presently, "that I wrote David in the spring, feeling that our understanding was an injustice to us both, and asked him to be just my good friend—my best friend," Sylvia interrupted herself to say, with a little emotion, "for to me he is the finest man in the world!—for a little while longer. And as he has been my obedient knight ever since I was a little curly-headed despot in short frocks, of course he obeyed me," she ended, with a little whimsical glance and smile. And now, having gotten to her feet, and come over to the mirror, she laid one arm affectionately about Gabrielle's shoulder. "I love that bright thick hair of yours," Sylvia said.

Suddenly Gabrielle felt young, crude, hateful because she did not adore Sylvia, contemptible because she suffered in seeing that this other girl's position and happy destiny it was to be always admired, always superb. Why couldn't she—why couldn't she school herself to think of Sylvia as rich and beautiful and adored, and married to David, and mistress of Wastewater? Weren't there other men, other fortunes, other friends to be won? Gay laid Sylvia's smooth hand against her cheek, and said like a penitent child:

"You're awfully good! I *am* grateful to you."

"That's right!" Sylvia said, laughing. And she went upon her serene way, to brush her teeth and open her windows and jump into bed with her book of essays, always adequate and always sweet.

Gabrielle determined, as she usually determined at night, to begin again to-morrow, to force herself to meet Sylvia's friendship and affection, David's friendship and affection, with what was only, after all, a normal, natural response. Why must she tremble, suspect, watch, turn red and turn white in this maddening and idiotic manner, when these two older and infinitely superior persons only wanted her to be pleasant, natural, friendly, as they were? The younger girl felt as if she were living over a powder magazine; at David's most casual word her throat would thicken, and her words become either incredibly foolish or stupidly heavy; and when he and Sylvia were together and out of her hearing, her soul and mind were in a tumult beside which actual bodily pain would have been a relief.

When they cheerfully asked her to join them on their way down for an afternoon of idling or reading on the shore, Gay put herself—as she furiously felt—in a ridiculous position by gruffly refusing. The two, and Aunt Flora, spectacled and armed with a book, would look at her in astonishment.

"Oh, if Aunt Flora's going——" Gay might stammer, in her embarrassment using the very phrase she meant not to use. And Sylvia's pretty mouth would twitch at the corners, and she would exchange a demure look with David, as if to say—Gabrielle fancied—"Isn't she a deliciously gauche little creature? She is trying to clear the tracks for our affair!"

If, on the other hand, Gabrielle came innocently from half an hour among the sweet warmth and flying colour and the buzzing of bees about the sweet-pea vines, to meet David and Sylvia in the path, she might hear Sylvia say lightly and good-temperedly—and might lie awake in the nights remembering it with a thumping heart and cheeks hot with shame!—"Not now, David. We can discuss this later!"

On a certain burning July day, several weeks after Sylvia's homecoming, all four Flemings had planned to drive into Crowchester in the new car, for some shopping. Sylvia's birthday was but a week ahead, and she was to have a house party for the event. To-day she had a neat list: gimp, enamel, candles, glue, lemonade glasses, Japanese lanterns? (with a question mark) and charcoal? (with another). For there were to be a beach picnic and a garden fête next week.

Just before they started, however, Gay begged to be excused. She was feeling the heat of the day, she said, and wanted to spend the afternoon quietly down on the shore with her Italian grammar. Instantly, without premeditation, David felt himself growing excited again—here was his chance at last for a talk alone with her; a chance that the last few weeks had not afforded him before. The sudden hope of it put him almost into a betraying confusion of excuses; but Sylvia, dismissing him amiably, fancied she knew the cause—and an entirely different cause—of his defection.

For David was in no mood to dance attendance upon his pretty elder cousin this particular afternoon. He had driven the new car down from Boston the week before with real enjoyment; it was a beautiful car, and David, who was not after all an experienced driver, was rather proud of his safe handling of it. But since it had been at Wastewater Sylvia had shown a strong preference for Walker's driving. Walker was a nice young fellow of perhaps nineteen, a newcomer, who was to act as chauffeur and to help John with errands, and perhaps in September, when the road was less used, to teach Sylvia to drive.

For some obscure reason it angered David to have to sit idle beside the pleasantly youthful and amiable Walker and hear Sylvia's clear-cut directions. He would rather, he thought ungraciously, he would far rather walk.

And to-day, when Gabrielle was graciously excused by Sylvia, he determined to stay at home, too. Of course this might mean that Aunt Flora would also stay, David reflected, to walk up and down above the sea, leaning upon his arm in her new feebleness and sadness.

But for once Aunt Flora made no sign of abandoning the trip, and although Sylvia looked at him steadily, she also offered no objections. David could hardly believe that he was actually free, after these crowded weeks, to walk after Gabrielle through the garden, with no prospect of an immediate interruption.

His heart beat with a quite disproportionate emotion. If any one had told David Fleming a few weeks ago that the chance to follow his lonely little cousin down to the shore and to have a few minutes of talk alone with her would have made his temples hammer and his breath come quick with sheer emotion, he might have laughed.

But he was shaking to-day, and there was a drumming in his ears. Since Sylvia's return he had had no such opportunity for a talk. Gabrielle was down in a favourite cranny of the great rocks; the blue tides swelling at her feet. David saw her black hat first, flung down on the strip of beach, then the slender white-shod feet, braced against a boulder, and then the white figure, with the tawny head bent over a book.

It was shady here, for this particular group of gray water-worn stones faced east, and the cliff was at her back. But there was a soft shimmer of light even in the shadow, and across the rocks above and behind her head the reflected sunshine on the sea ran in little unceasing ripples of brightness. She started as David came across the strand, and put her hand to her heart with a quite simple gesture of surprise.

"David, I thought you went with Sylvia!"

"Too hot," he answered, briefly, flinging himself down at her feet and falling into contemplation of a weed-fringed pool that was patiently awaiting the tide. The water brimmed it, and grasses opened and moved mysteriously, showing exquisite colours as they spread. The ebb emptied it again, and the ribbons of grass lay lifeless against the wet and twinkling mosaic of life that coated the rocks. A steamer going by like a toy boat on the blue water ten miles away sent out a mild little plume of sound.

"'*Mia sorella ha una casa*,'" David stated, with a careless glance at the book. "I had three Italian lessons once, and I know that!"

Gabrielle laughed, a little fluttered laugh, and extended to him a white hand and a stout volume, held title out.

"'Anna Karenina,'" David read aloud, with a reproachful look. "Oh, you Gay deceiver!"

He had sometimes called her that in her babyhood, years ago, and he fancied there was a little softening shine, like a flurry of wind on gray water, in her eyes when she heard it now. But she gave no other sign.

"Is it the first time you have read it?" David asked, conventionally, wondering where his dear, confident companion of the January days had gone, and whether this new dignity and aloofness in Gabrielle were only a passing effect of sorrow, and of the displeasure his most ill-chosen words had given her, or whether he had dreamed that once she was ready to flash, to respond, to be affectionate with him.

"Oh, no!" she answered. "But I have to read it over now and then like 'Cranford' and 'Adam Bede' and 'The Ring and the Book.'"

"A lot you get out of 'The Ring and the Book!'" David teased, with a brotherly smile.

"I get what I can," she answered, demurely, unprotesting, and with just a hint of her old easy fun with him. It was enough to turn his heart to water, and he formed within his confused mind a solemn resolution not to fail her again, not to offend, to watch this timid little seedling of returning confidence and friendship reverently and tenderly; to keep that at least, if he might have no more.

"But Anna's is a sad story," he said, looking at the book.

"Yes, but I like sad stories," Gabrielle answered, thoughtfully.

"Love stories. Don't all girls like love stories?"

"I don't call this love," Gabrielle objected, after a brief silence, when she had looked at the two words on the cover of the book until they spun and quivered before her eyes.

"Come now," David offered, mildly, actually trembling lest some misstep on his part shatter the exquisite pleasure of this blue hour of summer, and the ripple and quiver of the sea against the big shady rocks, and the quiet beauty of the girl's voice. "Don't say that you think 'Anna Karenina' isn't a love story!"

"It isn't my idea of love," Gabrielle persisted, with a faint stress on the personal pronoun.

"What would you call it?" David asked.

"Passion, egotism, selfishness," the girl answered, unexpectedly and quietly, not raising her eyes, and as if she were thinking aloud.

"Oh——? And do you get this out of books?"

"Get what?" Gabrielle asked, after a pause.

"Your knowledge of love, Gay."

Again a silence. Her eyes did not meet his, but she did not seem discomposed or agitated. She had gathered up a handful of white sand, and now she let it sift slowly through her fingers into the hemmed waters of the tide pool.

"Not entirely," she answered, presently. And again the notes of her husky sweet voice seemed to David to fall slowly through the air like falling stars.

"I feel as if I had just begun to learn about it lately," David said, clearing his throat and beginning to tremble. And as she did not answer, he told himself despairingly that he had again taken with her the very tone of all tones that must be avoided. "You've never been in love, Gabrielle?" he went on, desperately trying to lighten the tone of the conversation, make it seem like an ordinary casual talk.

"Why do you say that?" she asked, quickly. And now he had a flash of the star-sapphire eyes.

"But, Gay——" protested David, with the world falling to pieces about him. "Already?"

"Enough," she answered, in a low voice, her beautiful hands busily straightening the little rocky, sandy frame of the pool, "to know that it is not vanity, and passion, and selfishness!" And she glanced at "Anna Karenina" again, as if their words were only of the book.

What she said was nothing. But there was a note of confession, of proud acknowledgment, in her tone that struck David to a numbed astonishment. Gay! This explained her silences—her depressions, her attitude toward his kindly brotherly offer of protection! The child was a woman.

"Gay, tell me," he said, turning the knife in his heart. "Is it—a man?" he was going to ask. But as the absurd tenor of these words occurred to him, he slightly altered the question: "Is it a man I know, dear? Is it Frank du Spain?"

She gave him a quick level glance, flushed scarlet, and looked out across the shining sea. Cloud shadows were marking it with purple and brown, and there was a jade-green reef in the blue. Far off thunder rumbled; but in the hot still air about them there was no movement.

"No, it isn't Frank. I don't think you know him," she answered, quietly, with her little-sisterly smile.

David was too thoroughly shaken and dazed to answer. He sat, in a sort of sickness, trying to assimilate this new and amazing and most disquieting truth. Here was a new element to fit in among all the others—the child, the little tawny-headed girl of the family, cared for some unknown man. An unreasoning hate for this man stirred in David; he visualized a small and bowing Frenchman, titled perhaps, captivating to these innocent, convent-bred eyes.

"And will there be a happy ending?" he asked.

The girl seemed suddenly to have gained self-possession and her old serene spirit. She was smiling as she said:

"No. I think he likes another woman better than he likes me."

"I can see that you don't mean that," David said, hurt and confused. Gabrielle caring———! Gabrielle keeping this away from them all———! He could not adjust himself to the thought of it easily, nor change all his ideas to meet it. "Some day will you tell me?" he said, a little uncertainly and clumsily, looking out upon what seemed suddenly a brazen glare of sea and sky.

"Some day!" she answered, quietly. And there was a silence.

* * * *

It was broken by a calling voice from above them, first like the pipe of a gull, then resolving itself into a summons from Sarah. Gabrielle and David got to their feet with disturbed glances; it was perhaps only a caller, but Sarah sounded, as Gay said, scrambling briskly up the cliff at his side, "important."

Sarah looked important, too, and her face had the deep flush on one side and the shiny paleness on the other that indicated an interrupted nap. If they pleased, it was a man for Mr. Fleming.

"From Boston?" David said, as they accompanied the maid through the garden.

"He didn't say, sir."

"It may be the electric-light man," Gabrielle suggested, yet with an odd impending sense of something grave. Sarah quite obviously felt this, too, for she added curiously, flutteringly: "He's a queer, rough sort of feller."

"Where did you put him, Sarah?"

"He didn't go in, Miss Gabrielle. He says he'd walk up and down outside. There he is."

And Sarah indicated a tall, lean young man who was indeed walking up and down among the roses with long strides, and who now turned and came toward them.

Gay saw a burned, dark, sick-looking face, deep black eyes, a good suit that was somehow a little clumsy, on a tall figure that seemed a little clumsy, too. The man lifted his hat as he came toward them, and smiled under a curly thatch of very black, thick hair.

"Hello!" he said, in an oddly repressed sort of voice, holding out his hand. Gay could only smile bewilderedly, but David sprang forward with a sort of shout.

"Tom!" he said. "Tom Fleming! My God, you've come home!"

CHAPTER XIV

SO THERE was this new fact with which to deal: Tom Fleming had come home. Tom, thirty, lean, burned a leathery brown by a thousand tropic suns, had apparently determined to return with infinitely less deliberation than he had exercised over his running away, almost twenty years before.

He made no particular explanation of his old reasons for departure; on the other hand, there was no mystery about it. The sea, and ships, adventure, danger, exploration, storms, had always been more real to Tom than his name and family and Wastewater. He had found them all, drunk deep of them all, between fourteen and thirty; he meant, of course, to go back to them some day.

Meanwhile, he had been ill, was still weak and shaken and unable to face even the serenest cruise. And so he had come home, "to see the folks," he explained, with a grin on his brown face, which wore smooth deep folds about cheek-bones and chin, for all his leanness, that made him look older than he was.

In actual features he was as handsome as his handsome father. But Tom, garrulous, boastful, simply shrewd and childishly ignorant, was in no other way like Black Roger. Roger had been an exquisite, loving fine linen, fine music and books, the turn of a phrase, or the turn of a woman's wrist. All these were an unknown world to Tom, and Tom seemed to know it, and to be actuated in his youthful, shallow bombast by the fear that these others—these re-discovered relatives—might fancy him ashamed of it.

Tom never was ashamed of anything, he instantly gave them to understand. No, sir, he had knocked men down, he had run risks, he had been smarter than the others, he had "foxed" them! In Archangel or Tahiti, Barbadoes or Yokohama, Tom's adventures had terminated triumphantly. Women had always been his friends, scores of women. Mysterious Russian women who were really the political power behind international movements, beautiful Hawaiian girls, stunning Spanish señoritas in Buenos Aires, he held them all in the hollow of his lean, brown-hided hand.

He was a hero in his own eyes; he wanted to be a hero in the eyes of his relatives, as well. It was perhaps only Gabrielle, who had wistfully longed to be claimed and admired, too, so short a time ago, who appreciated, upon that strange first evening, that there was something intensely pathetic in Tom's boasting.

What were this old brick house, and these women with their fuss about vases of flowers and clean sheets, to him? he seemed to ask, scornfully. Let 'em think he was a rough-neck if they wanted to, he didn't care! Everyone looking at him so solemnly, everyone implying that this money of his father's was so important—let 'em find out it didn't mean so much to Tom Fleming!

Yet Tom was impressed, deeply and fundamentally stirred by this homecoming, in a sense that all his adventures had never stirred him. Old memories wrenched at his heart; his wonderful father had been here at Wastewater when Tom had last been here, and his father's frail little second wife, the delicate Cecily, who had been the object of a sort of boyish admiration from Tom. Perhaps the lean, long, sun-browned sailor, whose actual adventures had taken the place of that little boy's dreams of the sea, felt deep within himself that he had not gained everything by the change. Slowly all the fibres of soul and body had been hardening, coarsening; Tom had not been conscious of the slow degrees of the change. But he was vaguely conscious of it now.

The old house had seemed to capture and preserve the traditions, the dignified customs of his race; the very rooms seemed full of reproaches and of questions.

His aunt he found only older, grimmer, more silent than he had remembered her; Sylvia had grown from a tiny girl into a beautiful woman, and Gabrielle's birth had not been until after his departure. But David and he had spent all their little-boy days together, and David immediately assumed the attitude of his guide, wandering about the old place with him in a flood of reminiscences, and taking him down to the housekeeping regions, where old Hedda and Trude and Margret, who remembered him as a child, wept and laughed over him excitedly.

Tom enjoyed this, but when the first flush of greetings to the family and the first shock of stunned surprise were over, a curious restraint seemed to fall upon their relationship, and the return of the heir made more troublesome than ever the separate problems of the group.

Sylvia, from the first half-incredulous instant, had borne the blow with all her characteristic dignity and courage. It was hard for her to realize, as she immediately realized, that even in her loss she was comparatively unimportant, and that whoso surrendered the fortune was infinitely of less moment than whoso received it. But she gave no sign.

She welcomed Tom with charming simplicity, with a spontaneous phrase or two of eagerness and astonishment, and no word was said of material considerations until much later. Yet it was an exquisitely painful situation for Sylvia, the more because she had been so absolute a tool in the hands of the fate that had first made her rich and now made her poor in a breath.

She had not wanted Uncle Roger's money; she had indeed been a child when the will was made; Tom might easily have been supposed to return, the second Mrs. Fleming might have had children, and her own mother, although she had indeed married Will Fleming rather late in life, might have given Sylvia younger sisters and brothers.

But gradually the path had cleared before Sylvia. Tom had not come home, Sylvia's father had died, leaving her still the only child, Cecily had died childless, and Uncle Roger had died.

For years Sylvia's mother and David, watching her grow from a beautiful childhood to a fine and conscientious girlhood, had prefaced all talk of her fortune with "unless Tom comes home." But gradually that had stopped; gradually they, and her circle, and the girl herself, had come to think of her as the rightful heiress.

Now, between luncheon and dinner upon a burning summer afternoon, all this had been snatched from her; instantly taken, beyond all doubt or question. Here was Tom, indisputably reëstablished as sole legatee, as owner of everything here at Wastewater. Yesterday, a rather carelessly dressed brown-faced sailor, with a harsh blue-black jaw, unnoticed among a hundred others in a crowded harbour city, to-night he was their host.

Sylvia asked no sympathy and made no complaint. But the very foundations of her life were shaken; all the ambitions of her busy college years were laid waste, and from being admired and envied, she must descend to pity and obscurity. She and her mother would have Flora's few thousand a year; plenty, of course, much more than the majority of persons had, Sylvia knew that. But she must readjust everything now to this level, abandon the little red checkbook, and learn to live without the respectfully congratulatory and envious glances. It was bitterly hard. Wherever her thoughts went she was met by that new and baffling consideration of ways and means. Europe? But could they afford it? Escape from the whole tangle? Yes, but how? They could not leave Gabrielle here with Tom, even if Sylvia were not indeed needed while all the matter of the inheritance was being adjusted. Sylvia had said a hundred times that she would really have liked to be among the women who must make their own fortune and their own place in the world; now she found it only infinitely humiliating and wearisome to contemplate.

She did not know whether to be resentful or relieved at the general tendency now to overlook her; Tom naturally had the centre of the stage. But it was all uncomfortable and unnatural, and the girl felt superfluous, unhappy, restless, and unsettled for the first time in her well-ordered life.

Flora had borne the news with the look of one touched by death. She had not in fact been made ill, nor had her usual course of life been altered in any way, unless her stony reserve grew more stony and her stern gray face more stern. But David thought more than once that her nephew's reappearance seemed to affect Aunt Flora with a sort of horror, as if he had come back from the dead.

She had presented him with her lifeless cheek to kiss when he arrived, and there had been a deep ring, harsh and almost frightening, in the voice with which she had welcomed him. Flora was not mercenary; Gabrielle and David both appreciated clearly that it was not her daughter's loss of a fortune that had affected her. But from the very hour of Tom's return she seemed like a woman afraid, nervous, apprehensive, anxious at one moment to get away from Wastewater, desolated at another at the thought of leaving the place where she had spent almost all her life.

Oddly, seeing this fear, David and Gay saw too that it was not of Tom, or of any possible secret or revelation connected with Tom. It was as if Flora saw in his reappearance the reappearance too of some old fear or hate, or perhaps of a general fear and hate that had once controlled all her life, and that had seemed to be returning with his person.

"There is a curse on this place, I think!" Gabrielle heard her whisper once, many times over and over. But it was not to Gabrielle she spoke. And one night she fainted.

Tom had been telling them a particularly hair-raising tale at table, and because he really felt the horrible thrill of it himself, he did not, as was usual with him, embroider it with all sorts of flat and stupid inventions of his own. It was the story of a man, stranded on a small island, conscious of a hidden crime, and attempting to act the part of innocence.

"Of all things," Gabrielle had said, impressed, "it seems to me the most terrible would be to have a secret to hide! I mean it," the girl had added, seriously, turning her sapphire eyes from one to another, as they smiled at her earnestness, "I would rather be a beggar—or in prison—or sick—or banished—anything but to be afraid!"

Flora, at the words, had risen slowly to her feet, staring blindly ahead of her, and with a hurried and suffocated word had turned from her place at the table. And before David could get to her, or Sylvia make anything but a horrified exclamation, she had fainted.

This had been on Tom's third evening at home, a close summer night that had afforded Flora ample excuse for feeling oppressed. Yet Gay, looking about the circle as the days went by—David as always thoughtful and sympathetic, if he was more than usually silent, Sylvia beautiful and serene, if also strangely subdued, Tom seeming to belong so much less to Wastewater, with his strange manners and his leathery skin, than any of the others, Aunt Flora severe and terrible—felt arising in her again all the fearful apprehensions of her first weeks there, almost a year ago.

What was going to happen? her heart hammered incessantly. What was going to happen?

What *could* happen? These were not the days of mysterious murders and secret passages, dark deeds in dark nights! Why did Wastewater suddenly seem a dreadful place again, a place that was indeed allied to the measureless ocean, with its relentless advance and retreat, and to the dark woods, behind which red sunsets smouldered so angrily, but that had nothing in common with the sweet village life of Crowchester and Keyport, where happy children played through vacation days and little boats danced in and out.

"I am afraid!" Gabrielle whispered to herself, more than once, as the blazing blue days of August went by, and the moon walked across the sea in the silent, frightening nights. David and Tom were there, seven or eight maids, gardener, chauffeur, stableman—yet she was afraid. "If we are only all out of here before winter comes!" she would think, staring at the high, merciless sky, where distant wisps of cloud drifted against the merciless bright distances of the summer sea. She could not face another winter at Wastewater!

David was quiet in these days, spending long hours with Tom, painting, taking solitary walks before breakfast, Gabrielle knew. The girl would look at him wistfully; ah, why couldn't they all seem as young as they were! Why weren't they all walking, talking, picnicking together as other families did! David was always kind, always most intelligently sympathetic in any problem; but he seemed so far away! She could not break through the wall that seemed to have grown between them. It made her quiet, unresponsive, in her turn.

135

David, watching her, thought what a mad dream his had been, of Gabrielle as his wife! and felt himself, bitterly, to be a failure. Had he taken his place years ago in the world of business and professional men, had he risen to a reputation and an income, he might have had the right to speak now! As it was, she was as inaccessible, from the standpoint of his poverty, his stupid silences and inexperience, as a star. She had no thought of him, except as a useful older brother, and talking business with Tom. He was an idling fool of an unsuccessful painter in a world full of conversational, pleasant failures. He hated himself, his canvases and palettes, his paltry four thousand a year, his old sickening complacencies over a second-hand book or a volume of etchings. Life had become insufferable to him, and David told himself that if it had not been for Tom's needs he would have disappeared for another long year of painting in Europe—or in China!

As it was, he had to see her every day, the woman who filled all the world with exquisite pain for him, and with an agonizing joy. She came downstairs, pale and starry-eyed, in her thin white gown and shady hat, on these hot days, she asked him a simple question, she pleaded without words for his old friendship and understanding.

He could not give it. And one day Sylvia asked him if he had noticed that Tom was falling in love with Gay.

David stood perfectly still. For a few seconds he had a strange brassy taste in his mouth, a feeling that the world had simply stopped. Everything was over. Hope was dead within him.

"Haven't you noticed it?" Sylvia said. "Ah, I do hope it's true!"

They were in the downstairs sitting room, which had been darkened against the blazing heat of the day. All four of the young Flemings had been down on the rocks, by the sea, on a favourite bit of beach. But even there the day had been too hot for them, and now, at five, they had idled slowly toward the house, through a garden in which the sunlight lay in angry, blazing pools of brightness, between the unstirring thick leafage of the trees. There was no life in the air to-day, no life in the slow lip and rock of the sea. The girls had talked of a sea bath at twilight when the night might be shutting down with something like a break in the heat, but even that necessitated more effort than they cared to make. Dressing again, Gabrielle had protested, would reduce them to their former state of limp and sticky discomfort.

The sitting room was hot, and smelt of dust and upholstery and old books. Through the old-fashioned wooden blinds the sun sent dazzling slits of light, swimming with motes. There was a warm gloom here, like the gloom in a tropic cave.

Sylvia, whose rich dark beauty was enhanced by summer, and who was glowing like a rose despite tumbled hair and thin crumpled gown, came to stand at the window and look over David's shoulder. Gabrielle and Tom, with the dog, had just walked down the drive, and disappeared in the direction of the stable. It had been Gabrielle's extraordinary voice, heard outside, that had brought David to the window.

"You speak with feeling, Tom!" she had been saying.

The words had drifted in at the window, and David seemed still to hear them lingering, sweet and husky and amusedly maternal, in the air.

Of course, that was it. She would marry Tom.

The thought had never crossed his mind before; he seemed to know the fact now, and his heart and mind shrank away from it with utter unwillingness to believe. A month ago, poor as he was, he might have done anything——!

Now it was too late.

"I see him just as you see him, David," Sylvia was saying. "A big, lax, good-natured sort of boastful boy, that's what he is. But I don't believe she sees him that way! And—if she could like him, it would be a wonderful marriage for her, wouldn't it? Fancy that youngster as mistress here. And isn't he exactly the sort of rather—well, what shall I say?—rather coarse, adoring man who would spoil a young and pretty wife?"

"She likes him?" David managed to say, slowly.

"I think she's beginning to. She has a nice sort of friendly way with him," Sylvia said. "He doesn't seem to bore her as he does me! He wearies me almost to tears."

"I thought—it seemed to me it was just—her way," David reasoned. And the darkest shadow that he had ever known at Wastewater fell upon his heart then, and he felt that he could not support it. Of course; she would be the rich and beloved, the furred and jewelled little Mrs. Fleming of Wastewater—he must not stand in her way——

A few days later he went off for a fortnight's tramp, with Rucker, he said, somewhere in Canada. He left no address, promising to send them a line now and then. And Gabrielle, bewildered with the pain of his composed and quiet parting, watching his old belted suit and the sturdy, shabby knickers out of sight, said to herself again, "I am afraid."

Tom had made her his special ally and confidante of late, and only Gabrielle knew how far her friendship had been influential in keeping him at home at all. He disliked his Aunt Flora, and felt that Sylvia looked down upon him, as indeed she did. David, affectionately interested as he was, was a forceful, almost a formidable element, wherever he might be, and nobody knew it better than Tom. David might be, comparatively speaking, poor, he might wear his old paint-daubed jacket, he might deprecatingly shrug when a discussion was under way, he might listen smilingly without comment when Tom was noisily emphatic, yet Tom knew, and they all recognized, that there was a silent power behind David. He was a gentleman; books, art galleries, languages, political and social movements, David was quietly in touch with them all. He was what Tom would never be, that strange creature, a personality. Even while he nodded and applauded and praised, he had an uncomfortable effect of making Tom feel awkward and even humble, making him see how absurd were his pretence and his shallow vanity, after all.

But Gay was inexacting, friendly, impressionable, and she combined a most winning and motherly concern for Tom's physical welfare with a childish appetite for his tales. She felt intensely sorry for Tom, chained here in the unsympathetic environment he had always disliked, and she assumed an attitude that was somewhat that of a mother, somewhat that of a sister, and devoted herself to him.

She liked him best when he talked of the sea, as they sat on the rocks facing the northeast, sheltered by the rise of the garden cliff from the afternoon sea. Dots of boats would be moving far out upon the silky surface of the waters; now and then a big liner went slowly by, writing a languid signature in smoke scarcely deeper in tone than the summer sky. Tom talked of boats: little freighters fussing their way up and down strange coasts, nosing into strange and odorous tropic harbours; Palermo, with the tasselled donkeys jerking their blue and red headdresses upon the sun-soaked piers; Nictheroy in its frame of four hundred islands; Batavia, Barbadoes, Singapore—Tom knew them all. Sometimes the listening girl was fascinated by real glimpses of the great nations, seen through their shipping, saw England in her grim colliers, fighting through mists and cold and rolling seas, saw the white-clad cattle kings of the pampas watching the lading of the meat boats from under broad-brimmed white hats.

And it seemed to Gabrielle, and to them all, that as the days went by Tom lost some of his surface boastfulness and became simpler and more true. He was not stupid, and he must see himself how differently they received his inconsequential, honest talk from the fantastic and elaborate structures he so often raised to impress them. "I'm beginning to like him!" she said. And she wondered why Aunt Flora and Sylvia looked at her so oddly.

CHAPTER XV

ONE afternoon, when he had been at home for several weeks, he and Gay were alone on the rocks. It was again a burning afternoon, but Tom liked heat, and Gabrielle's dewy skin still had the child's quality of only glowing the more exquisitely for the day's warmth. Sylvia and her mother had gone into Crowchester. David was still away.

Tom had taken a rather personal tone of late with Gabrielle, a tone that the girl found vaguely disquieting. Now he was asking her, half smiling, and half earnest, if she had ever been in love. And as he asked it, he put his lean brown hand over hers, as it lay on the rocks beside him. Gay did not look down at their hands, but her heart rose in her breast, and she wriggled her own warm fingers slightly, as a hint to be set free.

"Have I ever been in love? Yes, I think so, Tom."

"Oh, you think so? As bad as that! A lot you know about it," Tom jeered, good-naturedly. "If you'd ever been in love, you'd know it," he added.

"I suppose so," Gabrielle agreed, amiably.

"Well, who is it?" asked Tom, curiously. "David, huh?"

Gabrielle felt as if touched by a galvanic shock. There was a choking confusion in all her senses and a scarlet colour in her face as she said:

"David? David is—Sylvia's."

"Oh, zat so?" Tom asked, interestedly. "I thought so!" he added, in satisfaction. And with a long half whistle and pursed lips, after a moment of profound thought, when his half-closed eyes were off across the wide seas, he repeated thoughtfully, "Is—*that*—so? Say, my coming home must have made some difference to them," he added, suddenly, as Gay did not speak.

"Only in this way," the girl said, quickly, with one hand quite unconsciously pressed against the pain that was like a physical cut in her heart. "Only in that now he will feel free to ask her, Tom!"

"Sa-a-ay—!" Tom drawled, with a crafty and cunning look of incredulity and sagacity. "He'd hate her with a lot of money tied to her—I don't think," he added, good-naturedly. But a moment later a different look, new to him lately, came into his face, and he said more quietly and with conviction: "I don't know, though. I'll bet you're right!"

Immediately afterward he fell into a sort of study, in a fashion not unusual with him. He freed Gabrielle's hand, crossed his arms, and sat staring absently out across the ocean, with his lean body sprawled comfortably into the angles of the rocks, and his Panama tilted over his face.

"I wish to God I knew if I was going to get well and back to sea again!" he said, presently, in a fretful sort of voice.

Gabrielle, who had relievedly availed herself of this interval to shift by almost imperceptible degrees to a seat a trifle more distant, was now so placed that she could meet his eyes when he looked up. She had intended to say to him, as they had all been saying, some comforting vague thing about the doctor's hopeful diagnosis of his illness, and about patience and rest. But when she saw the big, pathetically childish dark eyes staring up wistfully, a sudden little pang of pity made her say instead, gently:

"I don't know, Tom. But you're so young and strong; they all say you will!"

"I'm in no condition to ask a girl to marry me!" Tom said, moodily.

"Oh, Tom," Gabrielle said, interested at once, "have you a girl?"

He looked at her, as she sat at an angle of the great shaded boulders, with a sort of sea-shine trembling like quicksilver over her. She was in thin, almost transparent white, with a wide white hat pushed down over her richly shining tawny hair and shadowing her flushed earnest face. The hot day had deepened the umber shadows about her beautiful eyes; tiny gold feathers of her hair lay like a baby's curls against her warm forehead. Her crossed white ankles, her fine, locked white hands, the whole slender, fragrant, youthful body might have been made for a study of ideal girlhood and innocence, and sweetness and summer-time.

"Lemme tell you something," the man began, in his abrupt way. And he took from his pocket a slim, flat leather wallet, brown once, but now worn black and oily, and containing only a few papers.

One of these was an unmounted camera print of a woman's picture. She was a slim, dark woman, looking like a native of some tropic country, wearing a single white garment, barefooted, and with flowers about her shoulders and head. The setting was of palms and sea; indeed the woman's feet were in the waves. She was smiling, but the face was clumsily featured, the mouth large and full, and the expression, though brightly happy, was stupid. The picture was dirty, curled by much handling.

"She's—sweet," Gay said, hesitatingly, at a loss.

"Sweet, huh?" Tom echoed, taking back the picture, nursing it in both cupped hands, and studying it hungrily, as if he had never seen it before. "That's Tana," he said, softly.

"Tana?"

"My wife," Tom added, briefly. And there was no bragging in his tone now. "She was the sweetest woman God ever made!" he said, sombrely.

"Your—Tom, your *wife*?"

"Certainly," Tom answered, shortly. "Now go tell that to them all!" he added, almost angrily. "Tell them I married a girl who was part nigger if you want to!"

His tone was the truest Gabrielle had ever heard from him; the pain in it went to her heart.

"Tom, I'm so sorry," she said, timidly. "Is she dead?"

"Yep," he said, like a pistol shot, and was still.

"Lately, Tom?"

"Two years. Just before I was ill."

Gabrielle was silent a long time, but it was her hand now that crept toward his, and tightened on it softly. And so they sat for many minutes, without speaking.

Then the girl said, "Tell me about her."

Tom put the picture away reverently, carefully. For a few dubious minutes she felt that she had hurt him, but suddenly he began with the whole story.

He had met Tana when she was only fourteen, just before the entrance of the United States into the war. Her father was a native trader, but the girl had some white blood. Tom had remembered her, and when he was wounded and imprisoned, had escaped to make his way back, by the devious back roads of the seas, to the tropical island, and the group of huts, and Tana. And Tana had nursed him, and married him solemnly, according to all the customs of her tribe, and they had lived there in a little corner of Paradise, loving, eating, swimming, sleeping, for happy years. And then there had been Toam, little, soft, round, and brown, never dressed in all his short three years, never bathed except in the green warm fringes of the ocean, never fed except at his mother's tender, soft brown breast until he was big enough to sit on his father's knee and eat his meat and bananas like a man. There were plenty of other brown babies in the settlement, but it was Toam's staggering little footprints in the wet sand that Tom remembered, Toam standing in a sun-flooded open reed doorway, with an aureole about his curly little head.

Tom had presently drifted into the service of a small freighting line again, but never for long trips, never absent for more than a few days or a week from Tana and Toam. And so the wonderful months had become years, and Tom was content, and Tana was more than that; until the fever came.

Tom had survived them both, laid the tiny brown body straight and bare beside the straightly drawn white linen that covered Tana. And then his own illness had mercifully shut down upon him, and he had known nothing for long months of native nursing. Months afterward he had found himself in a spare cabin upon a little freighter, bound eventually for the harbour of New York. Tana's family, her village indeed, had been wiped out, the captain had told him. The ship had delayed only to superintend some burials before carrying him upon its somewhat desultory course. They had put into a score of harbours, and Tom was convalescent, before the grim, smoke-wrapped outlines of New York, burning in midsummer glare and heat, had risen before him. And Tom, then, sick and weary and weak and heartbroken, had thought he must come home to die.

But now, after these weeks at home, a subtle change had come over him, and he did not want to die. He told Gabrielle, and she began indeed to understand it, how strangely rigid and unlovely and lifeless domestic ideals according to the New England standards had seemed to him at first, how gloomy the rooms at Wastewater, how empty and unsatisfying the life.

But he was getting used to it all now. He thought Sylvia was a "beautiful young lady, but kinder proud." Aunt Flora also was "O. K." And David was of course a prince.

"He's painting a I-don't-know-what-you-call-it up in my room," Tom said, unaffectedly. He had furnished one of the big mansard rooms at the top of the house with odd couches, rugs, and chairs, and sometimes spent the hot mornings there, with David painting beside him. If there was air moving, it might be felt here, and Tom liked the lazy and desultory talk as David worked. "Can he paint good at all? They don't look much like the pictures in books."

"They are beginning to say—at least some of them do—that he is a genius, Tom. No, it's not like the pictures that one knows. But there are other men who paint that way—in his school."

"He has a school, huh?"

"No, I mean his type of work."

"I get you," Tom said, good-naturedly. "I'm glad about him and

Sylvia," he added, after thought. "Engaged, are they?"

"Well, I suppose they will be. There was an understanding between them—he has something, you know, and Aunt Flora has an income, too. Your father settled something on her when Uncle Will died."

"Do you suppose it's money that's holding them back?"

"I don't imagine so. I think perhaps it's all the change and confusion, and the business end of things."

"I could fix 'em up!" Tom suggested, magnificently. "I wish to God," he added, uneasily, under his breath, and without irreverence, "that *something* would happen! The place makes me feel creepy, somehow. It's—voodoo. I wish David would marry and take that death's head of an old woman off with him—Aunt Flora. And then I'd like to beat it somewhere—Boston or New York—see some life! Theatres—restaurants—that sort of thing!"

Gabrielle did not ask what disposition he would make of herself under this arrangement. She knew.

* * * *

She was down among the flowering border shrubs of the garden on the quiet September day when David unexpectedly came home. The whole world was shrouded in a warm, soft mist; the waves crept in lifelessly, little gulls rocked on the swells. Trees about Gabrielle were dripping softly, not a leaf stirred, and birds hopped like shadows, like paler shadows, and vanished against the quiet, opaque walls that shut her in.

She and Sylvia had been spending the afternoon upstairs in Tom's "study," as his mansard sitting room was called. The old piano upon which all these young men and women had practised, years ago, as children, had been moved up there now; there was a card table, magazines, books. The electric installation would be begun downstairs in a few weeks, and the whole place wore an unusually dismantled and desolate air; the girls were glad to take their sewing up to the cool and quiet of Tom's study. Flora had been wretched with malaria of late, and spent whole days in bed, lying without a book or even her knitting, staring darkly and silently into space.

This afternoon Gabrielle had escaped, to scramble for half an hour along the shore, her busy eyes upon the twinkling low-tide life among the rocks, her thoughts a jumble of strange apprehensions and fears. Now she was lingering in the garden, reluctant to surrender herself once more to all the shadows and unnamed menaces of the house, picking a few of the brave bronze zinnias and the velvet wallflowers; the floating pale disks of cosmos, on their feathery leafage, were almost as high as her tawny head.

She started as David's figure loomed suddenly through the soft veils of the autumn fog, close beside her, and laid her hand with a quite simple gesture of fright against her heart. The colour, brought by her scrambling walk into her cheeks, ebbed slowly from beneath the warm cream of her skin. Her eyes looked large and childish in their delicate umber shadows. David saw the fine, frail linen over her beautiful young breast rise and fall with the quickened beat of her heart; the soft moist weather had curled her tawny hair into little damp feathers of gold, against her temples.

An ache of sheer pain, the pain of the artist for beauty beyond sensing, shook him. She was youth, sweetness, loveliness incarnate, here against a curtain of flowers and gray mist, with wallflowers in her hand, and the toneless pink and white stars of the cosmos floating all about her head. David gave her his hand, and she clung to it as if she would never let it go, as if she were a frightened child, found at last.

"David—thank God you're home!" she said. "But you've tired yourself," she added, instantly concerned. "You look thinner, and you look pale."

"I'm fine," he said, with his good smile. "But why did you want me back?" he asked, a little anxiously, in reference to her emotion at seeing him.

"Oh, I don't know. Things"—she said, vaguely, with a glance toward the looming black shape of Wastewater, netted in its blackened vines—"things have—made me nervous. I'm not sleeping well."

"Aunt Flora looks like a ghost, too," the man said, and Gay gave a nervous little protesting laugh.

"Don't talk about ghosts! But it's only her old malaria, David," she added, frowning faintly.

"I don't know. Her colour looks ghastly. And Sylvia seems twitchy, too. What's the matter with us all?"

"Us all?" She caught up the phrase accusingly. "Then you feel it, too?"

"I think I have always felt—something—of it, here!"

"It?" Gabrielle repeated the monosyllable thoughtfully, and as they turned slowly toward the house, "*Horror*——" she said, under her breath. "David, David, can't we all get away?"

"We must get away," he amended. "It isn't a good atmosphere

for any one! Perhaps next summer——"

He stopped. Sylvia had given him another significant hint a few minutes ago. But he dared not ask Gabrielle to confirm it. No, he was only a sort of big brother to her—she did not need him much now; presently she would not need him at all.

"David," she said, quickly and distressedly, when in their slow and fog-enshrouded walk they had reached the little alley under the grapevines where Gay had seen her mother almost a year ago, "will you advise me?"

His face was instantly attentive; of the sudden plunge of his heart there was no sign.

"Gladly, dear."

"Tom has asked me to marry him, David," Gabrielle said.

Their eyes met seriously; David did not speak.

"I have known for some time that he would," Gabrielle added, with the pleading look of a child in trouble who comes to an omnipotent elder.

"You told him——?"

"I—didn't say no."

There was a long pause while neither moved. A bird, unseen in the mist, croaked steadily, on a raucous note.

"You have promised him, Gabrielle?"

"No. I couldn't do that. But—I couldn't say no. I tried," Gabrielle went on, in a sort of burst, and quite unconsciously clinging to David's hands, "I did try to prevent it, David. You don't know how I tried! He has been talking about it—oh, since before you went away! He told me he liked a girl, and he would tell me all about her, pretending that she was not I. I—prayed," Gabrielle went on, passionately, "that it was not I!"

"Gabrielle, I would have spoken to him, saved you all this!"

"No, no, no, I know you would!" she said, feverishly. "Aunt Flora would have told him. But, David, we couldn't have that! Why, it would have broken his heart! You see, he's proud, and he feels—feels that there is—a difference between us and himself. He has been like a child about this, a child with a wonderful 'surprise' for me. I am to have jewels and travel and cars—everything."

"If you marry him?" David asked, slowly.

"If I marry him. And I like him, David—ah, truly I do! I feel so badly for him. I feel as if it would be a real—a real *life*, for me," persisted little Gabrielle, gallantly, feeling for words, "to fill Wastewater with guests and hospitality and happiness again. I can't bear to have him feel that, poor as I am, and—and nameless—and he knows I am nameless!—still, I couldn't love him. It will make him bitter, and ugly, and he'll go off again, and perhaps die. I've *had* to be kind, to put anything definite off, and so I've said nothing to anybody—not even Sylvia. I've had to—to—fight it out alone," finished Gabrielle, with a trembling lip and swimming eyes, "and it has made me—nervous!"

"My dear girl," David said, slowly, heavily, "you're sure you wouldn't be happy? You would be very rich, Gabrielle, and you could teach him to make the most of his money. I think it would make Aunt Flora and Sylvia very happy."

Gabrielle was moving slowly ahead of him toward the house now. She half turned to look at him over her shoulder.

"David, do you think I should say yes?" she whispered.

"I think perhaps you should consider it gravely, Gay. You say you like him, and what other woman is he ever apt to find that would understand him, or even like him, so well? Imagine what harm his money is going to do to him, once he is better, mixing in the world again!? All sorts of social thieves will be upon him——"

"That's what I think of!" she responded, eagerly, so childishly, so earnestly concerned that David felt his heart wrung afresh with a longing to put his arms about her, comfort her, kneel at her feet and put his lips to her beautiful young hands. "If—if only we can get out of here!" she whispered, with another strangely fearful glance at the old house, "his affairs straightened out, Sylvia and Aunt Flora and I—going somewhere!—anywhere! David, we mustn't spend another winter here. And yet now, now," she began again, with fresh agitation, "I don't know what Tom thinks! He may think—indeed, I know he does think, that everything will be as he wishes! What could I do? I couldn't help—and indeed, I didn't say anything untrue! I only told him he must not think of such things until he was much, much better, but he seems to have taken that as a sort of—as a sort of—consent—in a way——"

"Shall I talk to him, dear? Tell him that you need more time?"

"Oh, no, please, David! Leave it to me!"

"Sometimes, I've been given to understand," he said, with his quiet smile, "that a girl feels this way when she really is sure, or when, at all events, it develops that the doubt and hesitation were all natural enough, and part of—of really caring. Take time about it, Gabrielle. Money and position do count for something, after all, and he is a Fleming, and he knew your mother. It isn't," added David, with a little conscious change in his own tone, "it isn't the other man of whom you spoke to me last June?"

For a moment Gay did not answer. Then she said, in a peculiar voice:

"I've often wondered what you meant by that conversation, David. Whether you remembered it? What was it? Had you consulted Aunt Flora and Sylvia as to my destiny—as to the problem of what was to become of me?"

"I—yes, I had written Sylvia, or no—not exactly that," David stammered, taken unawares, and turning red. "I—it was just an idea of mine, it came into my head suddenly," he added, with a most unwonted confusion in his manner, as he remembered that old bright dream of a porch on the seaward side of the Keyport farmhouse, and himself and poor little unwanted, illegitimate Gay breakfasting there. "I wrote Sylvia about setting her free of a sort of understanding between us," David went on, with a baffled feeling that his words were not saying what he wanted them to say. "As a matter of fact, a letter from her, saying the same thing, crossed mine," he finished, again feeling that this statement was utterly flat and meaningless and not in the least relevant to the talk.

"You didn't say you—cared," Gabrielle said, very low. "You simply put it to me as a sort of—solution."

"I see now that it was an affront to you, Gay," David answered, sorely. "I have regretted it a thousand times! I wanted to offer you—what I had. But God knows," he added, bitterly, "I have nothing to offer!"

"So that you—would not—do it again?" Gabrielle said, hardly above a breath, and breathing quickly, yet with an effort to appear careless.

"I would never offer any woman less than—love, again," David answered. "If I had not been a bungling fool in such matters, you should never have been distressed by it!"

"You see, you did not care for me, David," the girl reminded him, in a low, strained voice, and not meeting his eyes, when they were at the gloomy side door. The mist was thickening with twilight, and a fitful, warm wind was stirring its fold visibly.

"I had been thinking about it for days," he said, "it had—I don't know how to express it!—it had taken possession of me."

Gabrielle, her shoulder turned toward him, flung up her head with a proud little motion.

"Tom—loves me," she said, steadily. Yet David saw the hand that held the flowers shake and the beautiful mouth tremble.

"Tom," his half-brother said, still unable to shake off the wretched feeling that they were talking at cross-purposes, "would make you a devoted and generous husband, Gabrielle."

Neither spoke again. They went into the dark hallway, and up-stairs, and the gloom of Wastewater sucked them in and wrapped them about with all its oppressive silences, its misunderstandings, and its memories.

CHAPTER XVI

THE weeks that followed seemed to Gabrielle Fleming, even at the time when they were actually passing, strangely and darkly unnatural, and afterward they remained a fearful memory in her life. Long before the tragedy in which they culminated she was quite definitely conscious of some brooding cloud, some horror impending over the household, she felt herself bound by a strange interior inhibition, or by a hundred inherited and instinctive inhibitions, from speaking freely, from throwing off, or attempting to throw off, the fears that possessed her.

Outwardly, as the serene autumn darkened and shortened into winter, the household seemed merely what the return of the heir had made it; Tom invalided, restless, in love with his cousin Gabrielle; Sylvia beautiful and confident, as she faced the changed future; Aunt Flora silent, coughing with her usual autumn bronchitis, moving about the house as the very personification of its sinister history; David grave and kindly, managing, advising, affectionate with them all; and the staff of kindly old servants duly drawing shades, lighting fires, serving meals.

Actually, Gabrielle felt sometimes that they were all madmen in a madhouse, and vague disturbing thoughts of her own unfortunate little mother would flit through her mind, and she would wonder if her own reason would sustain much of this sort of suspense.

For suspense it was. The girl knew not why or what she feared, and they all feared. But she knew that their most resolute attempts at laughter and chatter somehow fell flat, that they glanced nervously over their shoulders when a door slammed, and that the shadows and gloom of the half-used old place seemed, of an autumn evening, when the winds were crying, to be creeping from the corners and lurking in the halls, ready to capture whatever was young and happy in dark old Wastewater and destroy it as so much youth and happiness years ago had been destroyed.

Nowadays, she fancied, the very voices of the maids, as they talked over trays or brooms in the hall, took on wailing notes, the clocks ticked patient warnings, a shattered coal on the fire would make them all jump. Gabrielle, with her heart beginning a quick and unreasoning beat, would turn off her bath water lest its roaring drown some warning sound, would stand poised, in her wrapper, as if for flight from she knew not what, listening—listening——

But it was only the October winds, sweeping the trees bare of their last tattered banners, only the fresh, harsh rush of the sea against the rocks, and the scream of a blown gull!

"Sylvia, does it make you feel as if you would like to scream, sometimes?" Gay asked one day, in the bare sunlight of the garden.

"Does what?" But in Sylvia's dark eyes there was perfect comprehension. "It is almost," she added, in a low tone, "as if people did really stay about a place to haunt it. That poor little shadowy Cecily—the second Mrs. Fleming—who died, and your mother, and my father, and Uncle Roger——"

"And all their passions and all their hates!" Gabrielle said, in a fearful whisper, glancing up at the grim outlines of the enormous pile, "and all those dusty, empty halls and locked rooms! To me," she went on, speaking with her eyes still on the black-brick, black-vine-covered house, "it is all coloured by that horrifying experience, here in the side lane, almost a year ago—when I first saw my mother——"

The mere memory of it frightened her. She seemed to see again the gray whirls of snow in the shadowy lane, the writhing, huddled gray figure among the writhing ropes and curtains of white.

"Gabrielle, don't!" Sylvia said quickly, with a nervous laugh.

"No, but Sylvia, you feel it, too?"

"Ah, of course I do! Mamma so ill and silent, Tom so strange, David not——" Sylvia's lip trembled, as much to her own surprise as Gay's—"David is not himself," she said, hurriedly. "He came back from this trip—changed! Whether it is Tom's return, with all the memories and changes, I don't know. Only," added Sylvia, quite frankly blinking wet eyes, "only I have noticed a change in him, just lately, and it has—worried me! Perhaps it's only a passing phase for us all," she interrupted herself hastily, "one of those wretched times that all families go through! Partly weather, and partly nerves, and partly changes and sickness——"

"And largely Wastewater," Gay said, hugging her great coat about her, as the girls rapidly walked about the garden. "There seems to be an atmosphere about the place stronger than us all. We're all nervous, jumpy. Last night, just as I was about to turn out the light in the sitting room, it seemed to me the picture of Uncle Roger was—I don't know! breathing, looking at me—alive! I almost screamed. And the night after David came back, I picked up his letters, he had

151

dropped them in the hall, and when I knocked on his door with them he fairly shouted 'What's that!' and frightened me, and himself, too, he told me, almost out of our senses!"

"I don't sleep well," Sylvia confessed. "I don't believe any of us do. I don't think we should stay here. If Tom has to go away——"

She stopped. It was impossible not to assume now that Tom's plans depended upon Gabrielle. Yet there was about the younger girl none of the happiness that comes with a flattering and welcome affair. Gabrielle instead was quite obviously experiencing a deepening depression and uneasiness. Every day showed her more clearly that Tom considered her bound to marry him, interpreting everything she said and did according to his own cheerfully complacent self-confidence.

Her kindness had carried her too far, now, for honourable retreat. She could not even get away from Wastewater, to think in peace, for Tom would not hear of separation, they had known each other long enough, they had "considered" enough, he said; when Aunt Flora and Sylvia took the apartment of which they were always speaking for the winter, Tom and Gabrielle would be married and go south together—go anywhere she wanted to go, but together. Bermuda or Florida or San Diego were all equally indifferent to Tom, as long as he had his wife with him.

The very words made Gabrielle's blood run cold. It was in vain that she tried to imagine herself married, rich, going about the world as Mrs. Tom Fleming. Every fibre of body and soul revolted; she liked Tom, she would have done almost anything to please him, but somehow the thought of him as her husband made her feel a little faint.

Yet how, after all this kindly talk, after these hours of listening, of companionship, suddenly break free? Gabrielle dared ask no help; Sylvia or Aunt Flora would only hurt him a thousand times more than she would, even David's touch could not be trusted here. Besides, she did not feel herself deserving of help or extrication; she had brought this most uncomfortable state of affairs upon herself, she *had* been too kind to Tom, she *had* let him drift happily into the idea that they cared for each other.

The girl began to feel with a sort of feverish terror that she must be free—free if she had to run away into the world alone. From a distance she could write them, she could explain! But she could not go on in this fashion, with every hour deepening the misunderstanding between herself and Tom, tightening the net.

November came in bare and cold, with a faint powdering of

snow upon the frozen ground. Suddenly summer-time, and shining seas, and sunshine seemed but dreams, life had become all winter, there would never be warmth and flowers again. Wastewater was bleakly cold; oil stoves burned coldly, like lifeless red-eyed stage fires in mica and coloured glass, the halls were frigid, the family huddled about fires.

Tools sounded metallically all day upon the new radiators, that, still unconnected, stood about wet and cold and forlorn against the walls. Tom spent most of his days upstairs in his "study," where a roaring airtight stove, connected with the old flue, made the air warm. He must start southward soon, they all said, and yet there was no definite plan of a departure.

David was still immersed in the business of the estate; Flora was wretched with rheumatism and malaria; Gabrielle, of them all, was the least anxious to suggest a change, and so precipitate a settlement with Tom.

On the fourth day of the month came the Great Wind. Keyport and Crowchester, and indeed all the towns along the coast for miles, would long talk of it, would date domestic events from it. The night of the third was cold and deathly clear, with a fiery unwarming sunset behind sombre black tree trunks, and a steely brightness over the sea. Gabrielle saw milk-white frost in the upturned clods in the garden; the light was hardly gone when a harsh moonlight lay upon the bare black world.

There was a good deal of air stirring in the night, and toward morning it grew so cold that the girls, chattering and shaking, met in the halls, seeking blankets and hot bottles. Gay and Sylvia knocked on David's door; he must take extra covering to Tom; David's teeth clicked and his laughter had a ghoulish sound as he obeyed.

The day broke gray and cold in a hurricane that racked and bowed the trees and bushes, laid the chrysanthemums flat, rattled dry frozen leaves and broken branches on the porches. Whitecaps raced on the gray, rough sea, doors slammed, casements rattled, and at regular intervals the wind seemed to curl about the house like a visible thing, and whined and chuckled and sobbed in the chimneys. Fires were kept burning, and Sylvia and Gabrielle, in their thickest sweaters, stuffed the sitting-room window ledges with paper to keep out the straight icy current of the air.

The family was at breakfast, with the lights lighted, when one of the oldest maples came down, with a long splintering crash that was like a slow scream. During the morning two other smaller trees fell, and whosoever opened an outside door was immediately spun about, and in a general uproar and rattle and flutter of everything inside, was obliged to beg help in closing it. After luncheon, John came in to say that his wife and little girl were so nervous that he was going to take them in to Crowchester. He could get the papers——

"No," David said, "I may walk into Keyport later!"

"You'll never keep your feet on the roads, sir. I never seen such a blow in my life. There was great gouts of foam blown as far back as the cow barn," John said, respectfully. "I tied up the mill."

David only smiled and shrugged, and at three o'clock went down to the side door, belted into his thick old coat. Sylvia and Gabrielle he had seen a few minutes before established with Tom and Aunt Flora in the comfortable study far upstairs, where there was a good fire burning.

As he slipped out, and dragged the door shut behind him, the wind snatched at him, and for a moment he really doubted his ability to make even Keyport, less than three miles away. There was a whirlwind loose in the yard; everything that could bang or blow or rattle or shriek was in motion, and the roar of the sea was deafening. The sun shone fitfully, between onslaughts from clouds that swept across a low iron sky; there had been a cold rush of hail an hour or two before; ledges and north fronts were still heaped white with it. There was not a boat upon the running high waters of the sea; David, letting himself out at the narrow back gate, saw the waves crashing up against the Keyport piers and flinging themselves high into the gray cold air.

Wastewater stood upon a point, and there was less uproar on the highway than upon their own cliffs. The wind faced him steadily here, stinging tears into his eyes, and pressing a weight like a moving wall against his breast. There was no escaping it, there was no dodging; David bent his head into it, knowing only that the road was hard and yellow beneath his staggering feet.

He jumped and shouted as a hand touched his arm, and he saw at his elbow Gabrielle's blown and laughing and yet somewhat frightened face. Unsure of her welcome, she caught her arm tightly in his and pushed along gallantly at his shoulder.

"I couldn't stand it!" she shouted, above the shriek of the wind, "I had to get out!"

"What did Aunt Flora say?" he shouted back, moving ahead simply because it was impossible to stand still.

"She doesn't know! I only told Hedda—when I came downstairs!" Gay screamed.

"Well—hang tight!" And together they breasted the wall of air.

"Gay, you were mad to do this!" David shouted, after a hard mile.

"Oh, I'm loving it!" answered her exulting voice, close at his ear.

"I'm loving it, too!" he said. And suddenly they were both human, free of the shadows, able to laugh and struggle, to catch hands and shout again.

On their left the sea raged and bubbled, above them swept the wild airs; clouds and cold sunshine raced over the world, and the wind sailed with foam and mad leaves. But perhaps to both the man and the woman the physical struggle after these weeks of mental strain was actually refreshing; at all events, they reached Keyport, after an hour's battling, in wild spirits.

The little town was made weather-tight against the storm, and presented only closed shutters and fastened storm doors to the visitors. Gabrielle and David made their way along the main street, catching at knobs and corners, and were blown into the bleak little post office, whose floors were strewn with torn papers and tracked with dried mud. The old postmaster eyed them over his goggles with mild surprise as he gave them letters from a mittened hand. The place smelled warmly of coal oil and hot metal; its quiet dazed them after the buffet of the storm.

The piers were deserted, except for a few anxious gulls that were blown crying above lashing waves; a group of tippeted boys exclaimed and shouted over the tide that had caught the end of River Street. David guided his companion into Keyport's one forlorn little restaurant, and they sat at a narrow table spread with steel cutlery and a lamp, spotted cloth, drinking what Gabrielle said was the best coffee she had ever tasted.

"You crazy woman!" David said, affectionately, watching her as she sipped her scalding drink from a thick cup and smiled at him through the tawny mist of her blown hair.

He had, with some difficulty, made arrangements for their being driven back in the butcher's Ford, at half-past five, when the butcher shop was closed. David did not dare risk the walk home in the early dark, and Gabrielle now began to feel through her delicious relaxation a certain muscle-ache and was willing to be reasonable. So that they had a full hour to employ, and they spent it leaning upon the little table, sharing hot toast and weak coffee, straightening the thick table-furnishing, setting sugar bowl and toothpick glass over the spots, talking—talking—talking as they had never talked before.

Gabrielle poured out her troubles like an exhausted child; her eyes glowed like stars in the gathering dusk, her cheeks deepened to an exquisite apricot-pink under their warm creamy colourlessness.

David watched her, listened, said little. But he began to realize that she was genuinely suffering and depressed and in the end a clean programme was planned, and David promised to put it into immediate execution.

Gabrielle liked Tom, but not as much as he thought she did. She wanted to get away, at once—to-morrow or day after to-morrow—to straighten out her thoughts and to see the whole tangle from a distance. Very good, said David, drawing a square on the tablecloth with the point of a fork. Aunt Flora should be told the whole story, and Gay should go in to Boston at once, to see—well, to see a dentist. She must develop a toothache, to-morrow morning, or as soon as the storm subsided. She could telegraph the nuns to-night, and be with them about this time to-morrow.

When he saw how her eyes danced and how impulsively she clasped her fingers together at the mere notion, David was able to form some idea of the strain she had been under.

"Oh, David—to see the streets and—and people, again! To feel that I needn't *face* Tom——"

"Meanwhile," David proceeded with his plan, "I'll get Tom to go off with me somewhere, just for a few weeks. Norfolk, maybe, or Palm Beach—it may clear up his mind, too. And perhaps I can explain to him that while you do like him, you don't feel quite ready to be any man's wife. I can tell him that the thought of it upsets you——"

"Ah, David, what an angel you are! But then what about Sylvia and Aunt Flora?"

"Well, they can follow you in to Boston. Sylvia spoke to me about either doing library work or teaching in some girls' school; they can be looking about for an apartment. But the main point is," ended David, "that you get out of it at *once*, before you make yourself sick."

"It seems so cowardly," said Gabrielle, fairly trembling in her eagerness and satisfaction.

"No, it's not cowardly. I suppose it's what all girls feel," David said, in a somewhat questioning voice, "before they get married——?"

"That's just it," Gay confessed, her cheeks suddenly scarlet. "I don't know what most girls feel, and I haven't any mother——"

She paused. But David, looking at her over his cigarette, merely flushed a little in his turn, and did not speak.

"But I know this," Gabrielle went on, feeling for words, and ranging knives and forks and spoons in orderly rows, very busily, as she spoke, "I know that what makes me feel so—so doubtful, about marrying Tom, isn't—isn't being afraid, David," she struggled on, her eyes pleading, and her cheeks childishly red. "It's—*not*—being afraid!"

Their eyes met across the sorry little board, and for a moment the strange look held and neither spoke.

"I have been playing a part with Tom," Gabrielle said, after a pause, "and I could go on playing it. I could marry him to-morrow, and—and still like him, and be kind to him! But, David," she said, in a whisper, "is that enough?"

"I don't know, dear," David said, with a dry mouth. "You mean, that it could be different," he added, presently, "that it *would* be different, if it were that other man—of whom you spoke to me one day?"

The girl only nodded in answer, her eyes fixed with a sort of fear and shame and courage upon his. If it were the other man! she thought—if it were David! And at the mere flying dream of what marriage to David would mean—going out into life with David—Gabrielle felt her heart swell until something like an actual pain suffocated her and her senses swam together.

He sat there, unconscious, kindly, everything that was good and clever, handsome and infinitely dear, and she dared not even stretch out her hand to lay it upon his. His black hair was blown into loose waves, his old rough coat hung open, his fine dark eyes and firm mouth expressed only sympathy and concern. She dared not think what love might do to them.

"I want—to be afraid when I am married," she said. "I want to feel that I am putting my life into somebody's keeping, going into a strange country—not just assuming new responsibilities—in the old!"

"I think I understand," David said. And feeling that further talk of this sort was utterly unsafe for him and likely to prove only more unsettling to her, he proposed that they walk to the Whittakers', a few blocks away, and see how the large and cheerful family was weathering the storm.

The Whittakers, mother, two unmarried daughters, two young sons, married daughter with husband and baby, were having a family tea that looked enchanting to Gabrielle and David, coming in out of the wind.

The big room was deliciously warm, and Mrs. Whittaker put Gay, who was a little shy, beside her and talked to her so charmingly that the girl's heart expanded like a flower in sunshine. Mrs. Whittaker had known Gay's poor little mother and both of Roger Fleming's wives; she said that by a curious coincidence she had had a letter that very day from Mary Rosecrans.

"But you don't remember her, of course," she said. "She was a lovely nurse—a Crowchester girl, but married now and living in Australia. Let me see—nineteen—Dicky's eighteen—she must have married when you were only a baby. But I had her when my Dicky here was born, and poor little Mrs. Roger Fleming had her for months and months at Wastewater. Now, Mr. Fleming, you're going to let me keep this child overnight? The girls will take good care of her."

"Oh, do!" said Sally and Harriet in one voice. And the Whittaker baby smiled up innocently into Gabrielle's face. "And why didn't you do this long ago, Gabrielle?" they reproached her. "You've been home almost a year."

Gabrielle, kissing the top of the baby's downy head, explained; David thought her more than ordinarily lovely in this group of youth and beauty. Harriet and Sally had been at boarding school, she reminded them, and Mrs. Whittaker had been staying with Anna and the new baby, and then Tom Fleming had come home——

"Ah, but now *do* do this again soon, you dear children!" their hostess said, when Gabrielle had pleaded that she really dared not stay, having run away for the walk in the wind as it was, and when the butcher's hooded delivery wagon was at the door. And Gabrielle went out, clinging to David's arm, into the creaking, banging, roaring darkness, with the motherly good-bye kiss warm upon her forehead.

The delight of this long afternoon of adventure and the prospect of escape to-morrow kept her laughing all the way home, and even when they got there, she seemed to carry something of the wholesome Whittaker fireside, something of the good out-of-doors with her into Wastewater.

But swiftly, relentlessly, the chilling atmosphere of repressions and fears shut down upon them all again; outside the night rioted madly, and the old house creaked and strained like a vessel at sea. Indoors lights seemed to make but a wavering impression on the gloom of the big rooms, doors burst open, casements shook with a noise like artillery fire, and voices seemed to have strange echoes and hollow booming notes.

Once some window far upstairs was blown in, and the maids went upstairs in a flight, exclaiming under their breath, and slamming a score of doors on their way. Chilly draughts penetrated everywhere, and the dining room had a strange earthy smell, like a vault.

The girls wore their heavy coats to dinner, and after dinner went up to Tom's study and built up the fire until the airtight stove roared and turned a clear pink. Tom lay on his couch; he had been oddly moody and silent to-night; Gabrielle played solitaire, talking as she played; Sylvia scribbled French verbs in the intervals of the conversation.

David and Aunt Flora had been with them until something after nine o'clock; then Flora had somewhat awkwardly and heavily asked him to come down with her to the sitting room; she wished to talk to him.

This was a common enough circumstance, for business matters were constantly arising for discussion. But her manner was strange to-night, Gabrielle thought, and the girl's heart beat quickly as they went away. Now David would tell her that she, Gabrielle, wanted to go into Boston for a few days—perhaps he was telling her now——

A quiet half-hour went by, and then Sylvia stretched herself lazily and admitted that she was already half asleep. Tom had been lying with half-shut eyes, but with a look so steadily fixed upon Gabrielle that the girl was heartily glad to suggest that they all go downstairs. There had been something sinister, something triumphant and yet menacing in that quiet, unchanging look. She had met it every time she looked up from her cards, and it had finally blotted everything but itself from her thoughts.

Tom rose obediently, and Sylvia folded his rug for him, and went about straightening the room. The girls were accustomed to perform small services for Tom, who really was not strong enough to be quite independent of them yet. All three went downstairs together, Gabrielle loitering for a few minutes in Sylvia's room, not so much because she had anything to say as because the nervousness and the vague apprehension, that possessed her like a fever, made her fear her own company.

When she turned back into the hall again Gabrielle was surprised to see Tom standing in his doorway.

"Did I leave my pipe upstairs?" he asked, in an odd voice.

"Oh, did you, Tom?" Gabrielle asked, eagerly, always glad to be useful to him; the more so as she found it more and more difficult to be affectionate. "No, let me! Let me!" she begged, taking the candle from his hand. "I'll not be two minutes!"

Again—she remembered afterward!—he was smiling his odd,

triumphant, yet threatening smile. But he said nothing as she took the lighted candle and started on the long way upstairs to the study.

Guarding the candle in the savage currents of air that leaked everywhere through windows and doors, Gabrielle had to move slowly, and in spite of herself the swooping darkness about her, the wild racket of the storm outside, and the shadows that wheeled and leaped before her frail little light made her suddenly afraid again. She was desperately afraid. David, Sylvia—all the human voices and hands, seemed worlds away.

Tom's study was two floors above Gabrielle's room, three above his own, and in a somewhat unused wing. The wind, in this part of the house, was singing in half-a-score of whining and shrieking voices together, and there was a thunderous sound, of something banging, booming, banging again with muffled blows, as if—Gabrielle thought—the house had gotten into the sea, or the sea into the house, and the waves were bursting over her.

Just as she reached for the handle of the study door her candle went out, and Gabrielle, with a pounding heart, groped in the warm blackness for the table and the matches and blessed light again! She was only a few minutes away from the protection and safety of the downstairs room, she told her heart—just a light and the half moment of finding the pipe again, and then the swift flight downstairs—anyhow, any fashion, to get downstairs——!

Her investigating hands found the brass box of matches, she struck one and held it with a shaking hand to her candle. There was no glow from the stove now, and the feeble light broke up inky masses of darkness. The square mansard windows strained as if any second they would burst in; a charge of howling winds swept by the window, swept on like a herd of bellowing buffaloes into the night.

Gabrielle, holding her light high the better to search the room for the pipe, and swallowing her fears resolutely, turned slowly about and stopped——

She thought that she screamed. But she made no sound. There was a man standing behind her, and smiling at her with an odd, sinister smile. But it was not that alone that froze her into a terror as cold as death, that held her motionless where she stood, like a woman of wood. It was that the man was Tom.

"Well, what's the matter?" Tom asked, slowly and easily. His voice restored Gabrielle to some part of her senses, and she managed a sickly smile in return.

"You frightened me!" Gabrielle answered, her heart still pumping violently with the shock, and with a sort of undefined uneasiness, bred of the dark night, and the howling wind, and her solitariness far up here in the lonely old house.

Tom had lighted the lamp.

"Sit down," he said. "I want to talk to you!"

"Oh, Tom—it's after ten!" Gabrielle said, fluttering.

"Well, what of it? Here——" He pushed an armchair for her, and Gabrielle sat down in it, and blew out her candle. Tom opened the stove, dropped wood and paper inside, and the wind in the chimney caught at it instantly, with a roar. "I wanted to talk to you," Tom added, "without Sylvia or any of the others around. They're always around!"

One of them would be welcome now, Gabrielle thought, in a sort of panic. For Tom's face looked stern and strange, and there was a rough sort of finality expressed in his manner that was infinitely disquieting.

She did not speak. She sat like a watchful, bright-eyed child, following his every word and every movement. Tom would not hurt her—Tom would not kill her—said her frightened heart.

"Here's what I want to know, Gabrielle," he began, abruptly, when he had taken a chair close to her own. "What's the idea? You know all about me—you can't keep up this stalling for ever, you know."

"Stalling——?" Gabrielle faltered.

"Bluffing—kidding—you know what I mean!" the man elucidated, shortly. "I'm getting kind of tired of it," he added, warming, "I'm getting *damned* tired of it! You know what I think about you, and you ought to know that I'm not the kind of man that lets anybody else walk off with my property. You're mine, ain't you—you're *mine*? Tell me that."

His manner had grown so alarming, so actually threatening, that Gabrielle drew back a little in her chair, and her great eyes were dilated with a sort of terror as she answered, placatingly:

"You—you know I like you, Tom!"

"Yes, and I've had about enough of that sort of thing!" Tom answered, harshly. "I've had enough of that kind of 'of course I like you—let me think about it!' You can make up your mind *now*. You're going to marry me, and soon, too. I'm going to tell them all to-morrow morning, and you and I'll go into Boston some day next week and get *married*. And then when you want to go off with some other man for the whole afternoon, and come back laughing and whispering, you can ask me about it first!"

"Why, Tom," Gabrielle said, with a frightened smile, "you're not jealous?"

"Yes, I am, I'm damn jealous!" he answered, roughly catching her wrist and drawing her to him without leaving his seat. "I want you. You've as good as said you'd marry me a hundred times! I've got money enough to give you everything in God's world you want. You can't go back now on all you said—you can't keep on bluffing and putting me off like a kid!"

"Tom, please——!" the girl stammered, on her feet and trying to free her hand. "You never did this before!"

He stood up, still holding tight to her wrist, and caught her in the grip of an iron arm.

"No," he said, in a low voice, "I never did this before! But there's no reason I shouldn't kiss my girl. What are you afraid of?"

His big left hand gripped her cheeks, and he turned her face up to his and kissed her violently, more than once—a dozen times. Gabrielle, smothered, frightened, and struggling, pushed at his breast with all the strength of her young arms.

The opposition seemed to enrage Tom, for he only held her the tighter, his superior height as well as strength giving him all the advantage.

"Tom——" the girl panted. "I shall call!"

"Call," he answered, easily and smiling. And the wild scream of the winds, whirling over the high roofs of Wastewater, seemed to echo the contemptuous note of angry laughter in his voice.

"No, but Tom—please—*please!*"

"Ah, well, that's better! Now you say please, do you? Now you're not quite so cold," Tom muttered, kissing her hair and forehead, and raising the two hands he had caught tightly in one, to kiss the fingertips. "Now you'll not be so cool, putting me off, asking for time, huh? Kiss me, Gay. You love me, don't you?"

She would be out of it all to-morrow, safe with the quiet nuns in Boston, Gabrielle reminded herself. If she could but get away now, down to lights and voices, into the peace of her own room, and to-morrow—away!

"Tom, I can't talk to you while you frighten me so!"

"Why, what are you afraid of?" he asked, very slightly releasing her, his black eyes seeming to devour her, and his breath in her face. "I'm not going to hurt you! I just wanted you to know that I'm tired of your holding me off, of having you tell me that 'of *course* you like me,' and all the rest of it. You're going to marry me next week, aren't you?" he asked, harshly.

Gabrielle held herself as far away from him as the iron grip about her shoulders permitted, and rested her hands perforce upon his shoulders.

"Tom, you will be ill," she began, pleadingly.

"Cut that stuff out!" he commanded, his face darkening. "You give me your word to marry me next week, and I'll let you go!"

The convent to-morrow. The safe bordered walks and walled gardens. The chapel, the refectory, the quiet footsteps and pleasant voices——

"Tom, don't be angry with me. Of course I will. Of course I will—if——"

"You'll not sneak to Aunt Flora, and say Tom scared it out of you, and get David to talk me off?"

The girl was silent during a second in which she sought words. But he saw the flicker of self-consciousness in her eyes, and instantly his fury returned again.

"Promise me, as God is your Judge. Swear it!" he said, in a low voice that shook with a passionate effort at control. "Swear it—or I swear I'll——"

The rest was lost. Gay was smothered in his arms again, her whole body bent backward so that she staggered in the struggle to keep her feet, her jaw caught in the grip of his hard fingers, and her lips stinging and burned and hurt under his kisses. The rich coil of her hair was loosened and fell in a web upon her shoulders, and through her choked throat and crushed mouth her voice came thickly:

"Tom! Tom—for God's sake—*David*!"

And suddenly, above the wild envelopment of the wind, she heard her name shouted in answer: "Gabrielle!"

The girl screamed hysterically as the door was flung open, and the lamplight swooped and flared in the gust from the hall, and David, white and shaking, came in.

Then there was a pause. Tom dropped his arms, and Gabrielle crossed to David, and, quite automatically and without moving his eyes from Tom, David put his arm about her. And Gabrielle laid one hand upon his shoulder, and hid her face wearily against his breast, and clung there, as he had seen a storm-blown gull cling to some chance-found shelter, without moving, without seeing, without sound.

Tom stood beside the table upon which he rested one big knotted hand. His hair was in disorder, his head hung forward menacingly, like the threatening jowl of a bulldog. He was the first to speak.

"Well, Dave, you can keep out of this," he said, in a slow

measured voice. "She's going to marry me. She promised me to-night—didn't you, Gabrielle? Tell him so—tell him you promised me. What's"—Tom's voice, under David's steady look, and opposed to the strange silence in the storm-bound room, and the strange and awful paleness of David's face, faltered slightly, and became less confident—"what's the trouble?" he said.

"Shall we talk about this to-morrow, Tom?" David said, in a constrained tone.

"No, by God, we'll talk about it now!" Tom answered. "I may be sick—or I may have been sick, for that's more like it! But you've no need to talk to me as if I were a baby!"

"David——" Gabrielle breathed, against his breast.

"I'll not leave you, dear," he answered, very low, his lips against the tawny hair. "Tom, old boy, shall we go downstairs? We're all nervous and upset to-night. I've got to talk to you."

"Tell him you are going to marry me, Gay!" Tom said, savagely, without altering his position or seeming to see David.

"No, Tom," David said, strangely and sadly,—"you can't—I'm sorry, Tom. But you two—you two——" he went on, stammering, and looking from Gay's face to the other man's with infinite pity and distress. "You can't marry her, Tom, now or ever. I've—I've got something to tell you that will make a difference."

"By God, you can't tell me anything that will make a difference!" Tom said, deep in his throat, still in the same position and without moving his eyes. "You keep your hands off her—keep out of my affairs!"

"David—don't be angry with him," Gabrielle pleaded. "Don't be angry with him! It's partly my fault—it's partly my fault!"

"Angry with him?" David echoed. "My dear Gay—Tom—you mustn't be angry with *me*. Aunt Flora just told me something, Tom. Gay's father was not the man named Charpentier—as we had all believed! Uncle Roger never knew it—but Gay is your half-sister, Tom—born in the year after you ran away, when he was hunting all over the world for you."

"What are you talking about?" Tom said, in a terrible voice. Gabrielle, her face ashen in the lamplight, was staring at David with dilated eyes. Now through her parted lips she breathed with utter horror:

"No—David, no——!"

"It's true," David said, simply. "There's a curse upon the place, I think, and upon us all! It has killed them—one after the other; it is killing Aunt Flora now. Gay—Tom, old fellow, we have to pay with the rest! You must believe it. You're brother and sister, Tom."

Then for a long time there was silence in the room.

"Who told you that?" Tom asked then, in a sharp, sneering voice that cut through the unbroken stillness and the surrounding tumult of the storm. And instantly he added, in a changed tone: "Look out for her, David—she's falling!"

Gabrielle indeed, with a long deep sob that ended with a sigh, had pitched against his shoulder. David caught her in his arms, her eyes were shut, and her whole body hung limp, her beautiful tawny hair falling free.

"Help me get her downstairs, Tom!" David said, everything else forgotten, brushing the silky, tawny tangle from her face and taking her in a firmer hold. "Open the door."

Tom slowly, and watching him as if he were under some enchantment, moved to obey. The lamp flared again, a blast of wind whined and sang about the windows, and the casement burst open with a wild shout of streaming air, extinguishing the light and careening loose papers noisily about in the darkness.

But Tom and David neither saw nor cared. The opened hall door had shown the lonely passage outside lighted with a sickly pinkish glow that flickered on the weather-stained walls and sent lurching shadows along the passage. Above the creaking and crashing of the hurricane and the howling of the gale and the sea in the dark night they could hear now a brisk crackling and the devouring sound of red lips of flame. The wind that instantly rushed upon them brought the acrid taste of smoke, and even in their first stupefied look, they saw a detached banner of fire blow loose, far down the long hallway toward the stairs, and twist on the wind a moment like a blown handkerchief, and lose itself in a thick rolling plume of approaching smoke.

Tom slammed the door shut behind them; they were in the hall.

"Fire!" he shouted. "By God, the old place is on fire!"

CHAPTER XVII

"SHE's all right—she opened her eyes a few minutes ago—she'll be all right——"

The voice was droning away close to her ear in the howling noise and blackness. Gabrielle made an effort to think and to move her head. But her senses all reeled together in a sort of vertigo, and her temples hammered as if they would split. She relapsed into blackness again.

David's voice, of course. She had fallen from a great height, she supposed, for she was lying in some bitterly cold place—out of doors—the sea never sounded so close inside.

Beyond and above the sound of the sea, breaking on the rocks, was a constant rushing of high winds and the creaking and dashing of bare branches. And there was another sound, of sucking and roaring, deep crashes—like the cascading of bricks.

"No, no, she's all right—she's coming round——" This was that droning voice, David's voice. Then a mutter of other voices, Hedda's saying something about china; John's, the gardener's voice, telling someone to "hoist it over there."

"I feel like Bill the Lizard!" Gabrielle thought, finding the idea very funny, and immediately beginning to cry. And she opened eyes brimming with tears and looked into David's anxious face, close above her own, against a background of red lights and shadows.

Dizziness overcame her, and she shut her eyes again, but not without a bewildered and weary smile that tore at the man's heart. And then there followed another period of utter darkness during which she could not quite tell if the roaring and crackling were inside or outside of her head.

Suddenly she remembered. They were in Tom's study, she and Tom and David, and David had come up to say——

And Gay instantly sat upright and looked at David with wild and frightened eyes. She wore the velvet gown in which she had dined, such endless ages ago, and about her, as she half lay in David's arms, a heavy blanket had been wrapped. David's face was grimed and sooty, and in the queer lurid light in the summer-house she could see that it was anxious and pale.

They were in the summer-house; that was it. But why should they be here upon this bitter wild night, and whence came the queer pinkish glow that was lighting the black garden and the bare trees in so unnatural a way? John and Trude were draping great curtains—were they the old library curtains?—against the latticed walls; outside, the closely set evergreen shrubs and the lee of the north wall combined to give the summer-house a sort of protection.

"Gabrielle—dearest——" David said. And she felt a hot tear on her face, and put up her finger to touch it wonderingly. "You're all right, dear!" he added, tenderly. And then, to someone in the gloomy confusion of old twisted benches and rickety rustic tables behind him, "She's all right, Sylvia. Tell Aunt Flora she's all right."

Gabrielle heard a thick, fretful murmur in answer, and asked, in a child's awed whisper:

"Is Aunt Flora sick?"

"Frightened," David said, in answer. "And you fainted, dear. Tom and I got you down by the kitchen stairway."

Recollection was beginning to come back rapidly now, and Gay frowned faintly with the pain of it as she said:

"Tom—you came up—I remember now. But David, was that true?"

"All true, dear. But don't think about it now!" David said. And Gabrielle closed her eyes for what seemed a long time again. The man her poor little mother had loved had been Roger Fleming! Roger was her father.

"Does Tom believe it?" the girl whispered, after a while.

"Oh, yes. He is very—very fine about it, Gay," David said. "There will be no arguing, no trouble for you, dear. Can you—can you—not worry about it?"

"But, David," she was more like herself every minute now, and spoke with a voice full of its own peculiar vitality, "what happened?"

"Fire, dear. Wastewater's going, Gabrielle! In an hour the old place will be gone!"

"Wastewater!" she echoed, in a whisper. And for the first time she turned her eyes toward the source of the glow. Three hundred yards away, and lighting up the whole black world upon the wild winter night, the old house was one roaring mass of flames.

"Tom?" the girl asked, instantly. "Did he—he was with us—did everyone——"

"Everyone is safe, dear! Some of the maids had gone in to Crow-chester when John took in his wife. The others are here. Sylvia was the coolest of all; she was asleep, but she had time to grab some clothes—got out easily! Aunt Flora was in the downstairs sitting room, where I had left her—she's here. I think the shock has been terrible, but she is safe. You fainted, seemed to come to just as we got you down here, and then fainted—or went off into a sort of swoon—again. But now you feel all right?"

"Perfectly! Even my head. But, David—I want to see Tom."

"Tom! He was with John and the girls, saving what they could, until it was too late. But he's here now. Tom!" David said, raising his voice. And immediately Tom, who had been with the group of maids in the doorway, watching the fire, turned and came toward them.

He was grimed and sooty, his black hair tossed about wildly, and he had a great overcoat on. Gabrielle saw the look on his handsome face, half desperate, half shamed, all questioning, and as he knelt before her, with a sudden impulse she opened her arms and laid her wet face against his own.

Tom tightened his own arms convulsedly about her, and for a long minute they clung together.

"Is it all right?" Gabrielle whispered. And Tom, gently putting the silky tangled web of her dishevelled hair back from her earnest face, answered:

"We got you out, huh?"

"Tom," she said, clinging to him, and looking into his face anxiously, "I'm so glad! I have never had anybody—of my own——"

"Are you?" he said, awkwardly, yet pleased, in a low, gruff tone, as she stopped. "You've got a brother now, huh?" he added, with a sort of clumsy lightness.

For answer, still resting her pale and soot-streaked cheek against his own, she tightened her arm about his neck, and he felt her breast move on a deep sigh, half of weariness, half of content.

And David saw his half-brother very reverently, very gently, kiss her upon her closed eyes.

"The wind's straight out of the northwest," Tom said then, in a significant tone to David, "the whole place is bound to go. Nice thing if we'd gotten 'em into John's house, like you suggested!"

"No, you were right about that," David conceded, as Gay, smiling bewilderedly, and still a little dizzy, got to her feet. "John tells me the barn roof has caught!"

"South wing, sir—everything. My God, she is doing it up in style now!" Walker, the chauffeur, said, from the group of watching maids and men in the summer-house doorway. All the night was lighted by the demoniacal glare, banners of flame were being blown and twisted like rags upon the shrieking winds.

"Keep this blanket about you, Gay, and over your head!" David commanded, as they joined the others. "Good-bye, Wastewater!" he added, under his breath. "Do you see that the library wing has collapsed already? You're looking straight across at the woods beyond! She's going like tinder."

"David, but surely that's the library wing, burning now—the highest point of all!"

"No, that's the very centre of the house. That's about where Uncle Roger's old rooms were. There—that's your corner, where that jet of fire blew out—that wall will go next!"

Gabrielle shuddered, and shivered with the cold.

"Mother seems—broken," Sylvia said, at Gay's shoulder. "She loved the old place!"

"There's going to be a change in the wind!" Tom muttered. "That river of sparks may be turned this way!"

"A change in the wind——?" Gabrielle echoed, incredulously. For to deduce any hint of a change from the furious gale that was blowing so strongly seemed miraculous to her. Even now the rush of air was so furious that they had almost to shout at times to be heard.

Somewhat sheltered in the black old shabby doorway of the long-unused summer-house, Gabrielle felt David's arm tight about her shoulders. Was he conscious of it? She did not know. But she was exquisitely aware of it, even under her vertigo, weariness, and excitement, and so reinforced, she might have endured a score of such wild nights.

They all stood in the shelter, exclaiming, and looking over each others' shoulders at the fearful conflagration that was sending great whirls and showers of sparks far up against the black winter sky. Flora alone made no move; she was rolled in what appeared to be a miscellaneously chosen half-dozen of blankets, a seventh rolled to pillow her head. She sat in the summer-house's one chair, an old wicker armchair, with her bare head dishevelled and dropped back, and her eyes closed in a leaden face that even in the hideous light of the fire looked deathlike.

"This night's work will kill her," Hedda whispered once, glancing over her shoulder at her mistress. And Trude solemnly nodded.

The flames of Wastewater swept southward, howling like fiends as they flung themselves up into the dark, crowded always from their places, as waves are crowded onward, by fresh roaring surges of fire. Where there had once been attic or mansard rooms in Wastewater there were now pits where pink flames burned under a play of dancing blue lights; at intervals of only a few minutes fresh portions of roofs and floors collapsed, and the maids would exclaim under their breath as the fresh grinding and sucking and devouring began.

"There won't be a wall left standing," Tom said. "And she's not been burning an hour!"

"Tom, it must be almost morning," Gabrielle whispered, too dazed with the night's events to believe herself yet awake.

In answer he twisted his wrist about; and in the pink light she saw the tiny face of his watch. Not yet one o'clock!

"What I can't understand," David said, "is why five hundred men aren't here from Keyport or Crowchester—of course there's a terrible tide, and that road through the dunes to Tinsall's may be under water. But you'd think a mob would be out here to watch the old place go!"

"You mean that they might have saved it, David?" Sylvia asked, shuddering with cold and nervousness as she wrapped herself in her blanket, and stood huddling at his side.

"Oh, no—nothing could do that!" he said. "Not even with all that water within a few feet," he added, with a shrug toward the sea. "That's the end of Wastewater!"

"David, we were all 'way upstairs. Did you and Tom get me down the stairs?" Gabrielle asked, presently.

"That's one of the things we'll talk about to-morrow," David said. But immediately he added quietly: "Tom saved us all. My instinct was to rush away from the flames. His, being a sailor, was to get through them. And if we had run away, I believe we would have been trapped. Hedda tells me the only stairway in the far wing, where I would have gone, has been locked for years. Tom got us back of the wind by crossing the upper hall, and we climbed over that strip of roof to the old sewing room, and broke the window, and after that it was easy, down the kitchen stairway."

"The fire was coming—where?"

"Straight up that main stairway, as if it were a furnace!"

"And did we cross—near it?"

David hesitated, and Tom, on Gabrielle's other side, said gruffly: "Not very."

Gabrielle shivered. And for a while they all watched the fire in silence.

"Luckily, John's wife and little girl and Daisy and Sarah, went in to Crowchester yesterday," David presently explained. "It seems that John saw it first; it started in the billiard-room wing. We think it may have been something the electricians did, or perhaps just rats and matches. John saw one of the windows all pink, from his room, but he thought probably some of us were down there, and actually went to bed. But after fifteen minutes or so he got up and looked out again——"

"My God, my heart turned to water!" John himself said, simply, as David paused. "The fire was bursting out of a dozen windows at once. She must have been burning since late afternoon, to get that start. I yelled for Frank, the Eyetalian, and Walker, and we all run to the house. Seemed to me we'd never rouse the girls!"

"We sleep," Hedda said, gravely.

"They ran up and waked Aunt Flora," David added, "and got her out here—she was still in the sitting room—and Sylvia had the presence of mind to grab a sheet full of clothes and things, the maids got out some china, and all the blankets that were in the store closet, and their own trunks—but there won't be much saved!" he finished, shaking his head. "Comfort to think that if there were five hundred men here we couldn't have saved it!"

And after a long silence broken only by exclamations of horror and concern, as the flames had their way, Hedda said again softly:

"This'll kill Mrs. Fleming, all right."

Sylvia had gone back into the summer-house and was leaning over her mother. They could hear Flora's feeble, hoarse murmurs in reply to the girl's tender inquiries. Gabrielle felt again that there would be no end to this fearful blackness, wind, noise, and confusion of body and soul.

An hour later there were shouts in the garden. A motor car rattled in, driven, already with a strange disregard for what had been the stately boundaries of Wastewater, straight over the ashy garden. It was the Keyport carpenter, with fifteen or twenty excited young men hanging on his car. The high tide had washed out a hundred feet of the road, he announced; "couple hundred people watching the fire from the other side, in spite of the wind!"

"Some fire!" said Harry Trueman. He had had to drive twelve miles out of his way to get here at all. He added cheerfully that he had thought he might find the whole family burned to cinders.

A stiff wind was still blowing, but its violence had enormously abated; the air was warmer every instant, and the fire, less than four hours after it had been discovered, had done its work, and had actually been blown out, against many a shattered remnant of black wall. Here and there it was still gnawing hungrily, sucking like a vicious and unsated animal among ruins that by its dying light the Flemings could barely recognize as the library, the old downstairs playroom, the office.

Now it was safe to move the women to what was left of John's house. The windmill, collapsing, had inundated the lower floor, and one side of the house had been caught by the flames. But on the south side a bedroom, dining room, and kitchen were intact, and Gabrielle and Sylvia found a lamp and turned down the bed where John's little Etta had slept for most of her fifteen years. Etta's innocent little trophies—Miss Alcott's books, pencil boxes, and hand-painted cups—were ranged neatly about. Flora, muttering, was lowered tenderly into the sheets, and the blankets and little blue comforter spread over her.

No further danger from fire; the worst was over. Rain was now sluicing as gently, as steadily and calmly over the wreckage as if the night of horror had been only a dream, as if Gabrielle might awaken in her comfortable big bed, as she had so often awakened, to look out upon a typical autumn sky and sea, a nameless little poor relation in Wastewater's splendid walls.

But now, wearied, confused, puzzled as she was, she knew that Wastewater itself had not disappeared from the earth more completely than that old Gabrielle. If she had not a name, a place in the world, she had a brother! And to Gabrielle this utter earthquake was like the presage of a more sunshiny and smiling morning than she had ever known.

Downstairs, in John's dining room, sacred hitherto to golden oak and tasselled plush, was heaped the incongruous salvage from Wastewater. Soup plates and cups filled with blackened water, chairs with sooty footprints upon the brocades, kitchen utensils and pots, books that had been useless and unread for sixty years and that were so much rubbish of paper, paste, and leather now, the shade of a lamp, standing alone, and another great lamp without its shade; just such miscellany as maids, chauffeur, and gardener had been able to snatch and carry away by the light of the fire itself.

Gabrielle and Tom worked valiantly at storing this mixed assortment at one side of the room; John lighted a coal fire in his own grate, and Hedda and Trude toiled kitchenward, extricating a coffee-pot from the crushed and saturated kitchen, and finding among Etta's neat stores all the necessities for a meal, which was served in the dining room at about four o'clock. Sylvia was now upstairs with her mother, and David called Gabrielle aside and with a grave face advised her to go up to her cousin.

"She gathered a good deal from Aunt Flora's muttering, Gay, and I've just been explaining things to her. Poor Sylvia! it's come like a thunderbolt to her. Suppose you go up and tell her we want her down here, that we're having some coffee?"

Gabrielle went up obediently. The lamp in young Etta's bedroom was shaded now, and Flora seemed asleep. Sylvia was sitting in the shadow, but Gabrielle saw that she had been weeping. She rose at once and followed Gabrielle into the little upper hall, and Gabrielle put her arm about her. Sylvia seemed confused and shaken; she said in a worried, quick tone:

"Mamma is very, very ill! David tells me he thought she was, even before she had the shock of the fire. I feel as if I were in a terrible dream—I can't believe what he tells me," added poor Sylvia, "I can't—I shall never believe that my mother could be—could be capable—my mother! whom I love so dearly——" She stopped.

"It doesn't mean that one can't love—one's mother," Gabrielle suggested, timidly. "You'll feel better when you've had some rest and some coffee. She did it to protect—Uncle Roger. We always knew she loved him."

"Oh, gracious—how little you understand—how little anybody understands!" Sylvia exclaimed, under her breath, in despair. "You tell me that I needn't stop loving her—and David tells me that it makes no real difference in my own life—as if I could!—as if I could go on living, and believing that my mother had been"—Sylvia's voice deepened—"had been living a *lie* all these years!" she finished, suffocating. "I tell you I simply couldn't bear it! I'm wrong, perhaps, it's all just pride, perhaps—but I never could look anybody in the face again, never hold up my head——"

"Sylvia, do come downstairs," Gay pleaded. "It isn't as bad as that, really it isn't!"

"Oh, what do you know, Gabrielle!" Sylvia exclaimed, impatiently. "You think being the child of a nobody, I suppose, is much the same as being Uncle Roger's own daughter?"

"I would rather have the name of Charpentier honourably, than any name as I have it," Gay answered, proudly and shortly.

"As you have it?" Sylvia echoed. "I don't believe you still understand," she added, bewilderedly, in a lower tone, and was still.

She let Gabrielle guide her downstairs and slipped into her place at the improvised table quietly, not looking up, nor tasting the solids, although she drank her hot coffee gratefully.

"David, could we possibly get Mamma in to a doctor—to a sanitarium?" she asked, presently, in a low voice.

"John and Walker have gone round the long way to Crowchester, for the doctor," David said, glad to talk. "The road's washed out, you know. They ought to be back in another hour, and then we can tell something."

"She looks—like death," Sylvia said, with suddenly trembling lips.

"I think it is only shock," David answered. Gabrielle, warmed and lulled by food and fire, had dropped her beautiful dishevelled head against the back of her chair; Tom had flung himself upon the little sofa and was already asleep. David replenished the fire, and he and Sylvia sat watching it, sometimes exchanging a few words, or sometimes going upstairs to look at the invalid, who seemed sleeping.

The doctor came and went at five without waking either Tom or Gabrielle; a cold dawn was over the world when the girl stirred under her heap of comforters and sat up blinking and rosy, wondering for a long stupefied minute where she was and why Tom should be stretched out sound asleep a few feet away. Margret had come out from Keyport, John's wife and daughter were lamenting and sympathizing in the disordered kitchen, and two or three score of sightseers were already picking their way about the ruins of what had been Wastewater.

Gay, going out with Tom, just as the winter sun rose dazzling and clear, and feeling strangely stiff and stupid, looked about her in blank amazement. Where the house had stood for more than a century was only a singed and hideous stretch of wreckage now, heaps of blackened bricks, tumbled masses of half-burned plaster and mortar. Twisted pipes glistened wet in rain, the whole smelled acridly, here and there some hidden heap of wood or paper smouldered sullenly.

The garden paths had been partly obliterated by fallen walls, trees were down, and ashes coated the leafless rose trees and the evergreens.

The sea was rolling gaily in the sunrise, emerald-green flecked cheerfully with white; gulls were dipping and arching, the fresh, clean, peaceful air was tainted acridly with the smell of wet burned ruins. The day was so crystal clear that Gabrielle could see the tiny figures of men going out under white sails at Keyport and at Crowchester.

When, between David and Tom, with her hair twisted up into a great coil, and one of John's coats buttoned about her, she walked slowly about the incredible desolation of the walls, the villagers drew back a little and eyed the family curiously.

"Pretty tough welcome home, Tom!" one of the younger men said, shyly but heartily sympathetic.

"Oh, that's all right!" Tom said, with a nod.

"Dead loss, hey?" asked an older man, interestedly, making a tut-tutting sound.

"Nope. Some insurance," Tom admitted. But the other merely shook his head, and made the same pitying, shocked sound again.

When they walked past what had been the sitting room Tom climbed over a mass of bricks and kicked free with his foot a segment of charred and soaked frame to which a tattered strip of canvas, stiff with paint, still clung.

"'Member this?" he asked.

David and Gabrielle looked at it, nodding. There were but a few useless inches of it left; but they could see it had been a painting. Still to be seen was a finely executed hand, a man's hand, laid upon the head of a beautiful greyhound.

"Uncle Roger," David said, gravely.

"My father," said Tom.

"And mine," Gabrielle added, softly, a warm young vital hand in David's, her beautiful eyes not raised from this tragic little last glimpse of the splendid and victorious Black Fleming of Waste-water.

CHAPTER XVIII

THE doctor returned with another doctor, in the course of the strange disorganized day, and Etta, murmuring with the other maids in the kitchen, sucked in a great sigh as she escorted them upstairs. Poor Mrs. Fleming would be a long time getting over this night's work! she and Hedda and Trude said, over and over again, while the professional men were in consultation. Sylvia, who had been lying down, went upstairs with them, Gabrielle waiting restlessly for their opinion.

Almost immediately after they had come down, however, David called her. She went out of the dining room to find him on the stair-way.

"Gay, dear, Aunt Flora wants to see you."

His tone frightened her.

"She's not very sick?"

"We hope not, dear. But they are not—satisfied. They give no hope. Sylvia's making her take some broth now. She wants to see you and me and Tom."

"But, David, we can get her in to Boston, can't we? Didn't Hedda say something about an ambulance this afternoon?"

"It's a question of whether the roads are passable. They are discussing that now."

A great awe fell upon Gabrielle as she went up to the crowded little bedroom. She could see nothing except Aunt Flora, lying straight in the girlish little bed with its paper and ribbon souvenirs tied to the white enamel bars; Aunt Flora looking sunken-cheeked and ghastly, and living only in her restless and tortured eyes.

"How do you feel now?" David said, cheerfully, sitting down beside the bed, and patting her hand. She did not smile. But she moved her eyes to his face and fixed them there.

Sylvia was at one side of the bed, David and Tom took chairs at the foot, and Gabrielle quite naturally sank to her knees beside Sylvia, so that the two girls' faces were close to Flora's.

It was afternoon now, a steely-clear winter afternoon at about four o'clock, and to Gabrielle's wearied senses no hour in the strange twenty-four since she and David had walked in the great wind to Crowchester seemed more strange or unreal than this one. Aunt Flora lying here, grizzled, dressed in one of the plain night-gowns of John's wife's and surrounded by little Etta's keepsakes; Tom serious and still, oddly dishevelled and disorderly from the long night and the day's broken rest; Sylvia pale, and with new and tragic deeps in her dark eyes; and David as always the balance wheel that seemed to keep them all steady.

Flora moved her solemn gaze to Gabrielle's face.

"I am very sick," she whispered.

"Oh, Aunt Flora, you'll feel so much better when you get into a comfortable hospital," Gabrielle said, gently, infinitely distressed.

"No," the sick woman said, shaking her head, "they'll not move me! David told you and Tom something yesterday," she added, wearily shutting her eyes and hardly moving her lips. "You should have known it long ago. You—and Tom, are angry at me?"

"Oh, Aunt Flora—no!"

"You are Roger Fleming's daughter, Gabrielle," Flora whispered, clutching her hand, and eyeing her anxiously.

"So David said," Gabrielle murmured, with a troubled glance at him. To talk in this childish, lifeless way, Aunt Flora must be very ill!

"You should have known it long ago," Flora repeated, beating gently on Gabrielle's hand. "It was the sin—the terrible sin of my life. But, David," she interrupted herself, appealing to him, "I did not mean to harm them!"

"I'm sure of it, Aunt Flora! But why worry yourself with it now? We are all safe, all well—couldn't it wait?" David urged, with infinite gentleness.

"No—no—no!" she exclaimed, raising herself to a sitting position and struggling almost as if they were constraining her physically. "I must talk now—and then I shall sleep! You must let me talk, and then I shall sleep! I want you all to understand.

"Did you ever know," she went on, seeming to feel her way for the right phrases, and sinking back into the pillows with shut eyes, "did you ever know how I happened to come first to Wastewater? My father was John Fleming, Roger Fleming's cousin—he was a dentist, in Brookline. We were very poor when I was a child, and the first days I remember were of a little Brookline flat, and my mother sewing at a sewing machine. My sister Lily was a delicate little baby then—Lily was six years younger than I. For days and days and days of rain I remember the sewing machine, and the crying of the baby, and my mother murmuring at the hall door to men who came about bills. In the spring I had to take the baby out, and sometimes the wind would chap both our faces, and we would sit crying in the park. It seems to me we were always cold—I don't believe children get such deep impressions of hot weather——"

"Dearest, do you want to talk now?" Sylvia asked, tenderly, as the harsh, deep voice paused.

Flora opened the eyes that had been slowly sinking shut, and widened them anxiously.

"Yes, I must talk," she answered. And she looked about the silent little group alarmedly, as if she feared that one of them might have slipped away. "When I was eight, and Lily two years old," she went on, "our father died. My mother was left miserably poor, and I heard enough talk then among her and her few friends to fear—as only a child can fear!—actual starvation.

"It was then that an uncle of whom we had scarcely heard came to see us. That was Tom Fleming, Roger's father. He had quarrelled with my father years before, and, as everything my father touched turned to loss, so everything that Tom Fleming went into prospered. It was a railroad venture that made his fortune finally, but everything—properties, bonds, stocks—went well with him!

"He came to my mother's poor little flat, and—ah, my God, my God!" whispered Flora, forgetting her audience, as she pressed a dark hand to her eyes, and speaking to herself. "What a day that was for me. He asked my mother to bring her little girls to his country house, to Wastewater, until she should get her bearings! He left money on the little red tablecloth in the dining room—my poor mother burst out crying, and tried to kiss his hand——

"A week later, on a summer afternoon, we got here. I had never seen the inside of a big house or the open expanse of the sea before, never been in a stable yard, where there were chickens and cats and horses. And we had half-a-dozen horses at Wastewater then, Uncle Tom's big Percherons, and riding horses.

"Why, I couldn't get enough of the stairs—I worked my way up and down them for days, singing to myself for pure rapture. It was all a fairy tale to me; the silver, the meals, the big rooms—what a wonderland it was!

"Uncle Tom was a widower with two sons, boys of thirteen and eleven—Roger and Will. They were out in the stable yards with some puppies when we got there, and Roger was not too big a boy to take a little girl cousin under his wing—he showed me the puppies, he let me name one of them 'Silver.'

"I have never seen any other puppies that were to me as—as

strangely important as those were," Flora went on, her eyes closed, her voice the mere essence of its usual self. "Nor such a lingering early summer afternoon as that was! It seemed to me my heart would burst with joy. To have supper in the pantry that was full of maids and sunshine, and such supplies of cake and butter and milk, and to sleep in a big smooth bed, in such a great room——

"All those early days were filled with anxiety for me. I was afraid any instant that we might be sent away. My mother told me long afterward that I cried myself almost sick with excitement when she told me that Uncle Tom had asked her to stay and take care of his house for him. I don't remember that, but I remember in my gratitude telling Roger that I hoped some day he would be out at sea in a wreck, and that I would save his life—and how he laughed at me.

"He was, I suppose, as handsome a boy as ever lived—it was not that. Surely I was too small a girl to know or care what real beauty was! But I loved him from the first instant I saw him.

"Not—I think now—as other children love, as other young girls love. There was no vanity in it—I can say that. There was no happiness, no prettiness. It was agony to me, almost from that first June afternoon.

"He seemed to me to be in a class all by himself. Whether I liked it or not—and it was years before I realized it fully—I had to keep him there! His least word was important, his kindness made me tremble all over, and if ever Roger were cross with me, I used to be actually sick with grief, and my mother would ask him to come up to my room and let me sob wildly in his arms and beg him to forgive me.

"I never got any pleasure out of it, God knows. It was constant pain. If he smiled at any one else, I was wretched. No matter what he did, his laugh, his voice with his horse, his use of his hands—and he had beautiful hands!—was full of magic for me. I used to pray—to *pray* that he would not always seem so wonderful to me, that I would see him in ordinary human daylight. I never did. He was my whole world.

"So the years went by, and Uncle Tom died, and Roger was the heir. Roger was twenty-five then, tall and straight, and so clever that he could do anything! He rode and he sang, he danced and shot better than any of his friends. Women were already beginning—ah, how women loved him!

"Will, his brother, had been wild from his very boyhood—from his fifteenth year. He drank heavily, gambled; he and his father had been enemies for a long time. Uncle Tom had advanced money

179

to Will, great sums of it, and Will had gambled it away. He left Will a comfortable fortune, he left Roger Wastewater and the rest of his money. And Roger was—everything. He had a manner, a sweetness—I don't know, a way of seeming interested—seeming absorbed in what you were telling him.

"And he was witty, too. What parties I can remember here, when they would all be laughing at him—crying with laughter——

"I was twenty when Uncle Tom died. My mother went on keeping house for Roger and Will, and perhaps she thought sometimes of what I prayed and prayed might come to pass—that Roger Fleming and I might be man and wife, and Wastewater her home for ever!

"For years I had to see him depart for those long visits of his in Boston, when he was—ah, yes, it wasn't only my imagination!—when he was the idol of them all—fêted and followed and imitated by the very best of them. I had to say good-bye to him when he started off to Europe with beautiful girls in the party—money, youth, lovely clothes, romantic settings—all against me!

"Presently he was thirty, and I was twenty-five—twenty-six—twenty-seven—— And then, suddenly, he seemed for the first time to see me. I didn't dare believe it at first.

"I didn't dare believe it. He would follow me down to the shore and sit there with Lily and me—he would come back unexpectedly from Boston or New York—I would hear his voice, as I hear it now: 'Flo! Where's Flo?'

"Ah, what days those were! They seemed all rose-colour. I've come to hate the memory of them now—but they were Heaven then! Sometimes now I find myself obliged to go over them, day after day, and hour after hour—day after day and hour after hour of a fool's Paradise——

"One day he said to me—one night rather, when there was gray moonlight over the garden, and he and I were walking up and down, and poor Lily, inside at the piano, was singing—'Flo, why is it that I have grown to prefer puttering about this old place with you and Lil to any other thing in the world?'

"'Perhaps because you like me, Roger,' I said. I've been ready to bite my tongue out for it a thousand times in these thirty years! But it bought me a few more hours of insanity then. He caught me in his arms and laughed as he kissed me.

"'Why, that's the way of it, is it?' he said. 'How long has this been going on, eh?'

"'Always,' I told him. 'Poor little Flo,' he said, 'with all you know of me, is it like that?'

"'Like that,' I said, and he kissed me again. 'Well,' he said, 'we will have to see about this!'

"That was all. Presently I ran into the house with my heart simply singing, and all that summer night I lay awake laughing and crying for joy. And the next morning I hardly dared raise my eyes to him.

"It was that next day that your mother came to Wastewater, David. It was the very next day——"

Flora had been talking with her eyes shut. Now she opened them, almost as if she were surprised to see the circle of attentive and serious young faces. Her hand beat the coverlid restlessly.

"Your mother was about thirty, and a widow," she said. "She had been widowed a few months before your birth, and you were only three or four weeks old. She was a beautiful woman, with reddish thick hair, all swathed in crêpe, and with the trailing dresses of the tiny baby in her arms. Her father was an Argentine planter, and she was taking you—David—back to Rosario, where she had sisters and cousins. But for some reason the boat was a month delayed—a strike, perhaps, the service was very uneven then—and she had written my mother asking if she might come for a few days to Wastewater. Families did more of that sort of thing then. Her husband had been a Fleming, and I remember that he had once spent a vacation with us here, when he was a little boy—David Fleming. She told me a hundred times afterward that she had written my mother only because she was so lonely and sad in the big city—she hardly expected an answer. She knew that Tom Fleming was dead, she hardly knew anything about Roger and Will.

"So she came here, not six months a widow, and from the instant she got here Roger Fleming was a changed being. I never saw a man so instantly—possessed. That very first night he was asking me: 'Isn't she beautiful, Flo? Isn't she wonderful?' He hung about her—I don't think he ever thought of me again, or of anything but Janet. Seven weeks later they were married.

"She was beautiful," Flora went on, after a dead silence in which none of the young persons seemed to find the right word, and in which her hand beat steadily on the bed, and her eyes were shut. "She went with him to Boston, Washington, everywhere! And ten months later she gave him a son—Tom."

She looked at Tom strangely, closed her eyes again.

"My mother, all this while," Flora resumed, "had been like a sort of housekeeper. She was a little, wiry woman, very gray, as poor Lily was, at the end. Two years after Roger and Janet were married my mother died, and then Lily and I felt keenly what our exact position here was—poor relations in a rich man's house.

"Roger always was generous to us, he was the soul of generosity, and he was prospering as steadily as his father had. And Janet was kind, too. She and Roger sometimes went away for weeks and left the two little boys with us, and I remember more than once Roger telling me that it was only my influence that kept his brother Will straight at all.

"Will was like many a young man in those times. He would have a position for a while, give it up for different reasons, drink and gamble and idle for a while, and be persuaded into another position again. It wasn't considered disgraceful then. He was a sweet, good-natured sort of fellow—he would spend weeks here at Wastewater, perfectly willing to idle about with Lily and Janet and me, and the babies—for David was hardly more!—and to have a little pocket money from Roger. And then he would go over to Keyport or Crow-chester and be there whole days—drinking and playing poker——"

Sylvia drew a quick, sharp breath.

"You mustn't judge your father too harshly," Flora whispered, moving her troubled eyes to her daughter's face. "Nowadays it sounds far worse than it did then. Almost every family had such a son, and frequently you would hear even mothers laughing as they said that it was time for Dick or Jack to marry and settle down.

"Afterward, Will would be two or three days sick in bed," the droning, weary voice presently resumed, "and Roger would talk to him so kindly, begging him to pull himself together and get a new start. And then Roger would find him a new position, and Will would come down to dinner, rested and shaved and well dressed and in high spirits, telling us all how rich he was going to be!

"So I tried to make myself indispensable, and I hoped and hoped that Lily would marry—marry Will or anybody, as a sort of justification for my remaining single. I looked out for you boys' wardrobes, mothered Will, managed their parties—managed the servants.

"Your mother, Janet, went to the opera with your father one night," she added, opening her eyes to look at David and Tom, "and a day or two later he telegraphed me from New York that, as she was not well, he would keep her there until it was safe to bring her home. That was a snowy Sunday afternoon. I remember that Will and Lily and I played games with you little fellows, put you to bed ourselves—it was almost as if we knew that you were not to see your mother again.

"The days went by: you went back to school——and I knew—I

knew all the time that it was the end! Ten days later your Mother died, and the day after her funeral Roger went away—where, I never knew. He was gone for weeks, came home, would burst out into bitter crying at the table, walk up and down the garden like a madman, and be off again.

"One day, about six or seven weeks after Janet's death, he said to me, in a dark, moody sort of tone: 'Flo, how long am I to wear mourning—outside? Inside,' he said, passionately, 'I shall mourn her all my life!'

"'A year,' I told him.

"It was a dark, misty day, I remember, with the garden full of thick cold fog, and lights burning at the lunch table. He and I had come out and were walking along the cliff road in the mist. We could hear the buoys ringing—ringing away toward Keyport.

"'Flo,' he said, 'when that time is up, will you forgive me and marry me? You and I understand each other. I want to be anchored. I want to be done with the world and make this my world!' And he looked back toward the garden and the house.

"'Gladly, Roger!' I said. And for a long while we did not speak again. Then he said to me, 'Will you tell Lily and the boys and Will that it is to be that way?' and I said yes. You remember, David?"

"Yes, I remember your telling us that you were to be married to him," David's voice said, strangely vital against that other monotonous voice.

"Sometimes—but not often!—we would talk of it quietly," Flora resumed. "Not that I was ever happy about it. But I told myself I would be! I told myself that it should—it *must*—mean happiness to us both.

"Janet died in January. This was—perhaps—March.

"A few days later, in April, a Mrs. Kent, whom Roger had admired immensely as a beautiful girl when he was hardly more than a boy—when he was, in fact, in college—came here with her daughter for a visit. I don't think the mother was more than thirty-seven or -eight; she had been a great belle and had married at eighteen. She was plump and pretty, covered with jewels, full of life, and had left her husband and little boy in Canada to bring this child from a school in Baltimore. She had—just this hair," Flora said, laying her dark thin hand upon Gabrielle's tawny rich masses as the girl knelt beside her.

"The girl Cecily was seventeen, dark, and pale-faced. She looked like a child—she had her hair in a braid.

"There were other old friends in the party, a group of them had come down from Boston to see Roger Fleming, and we were very gay. I don't know that I ever heard greater laughing or chattering here, or that we ever served more formal meals—I had my hands full. Lily saw more of little Cecily Kent than I did, and she told me one day—not that it interested me particularly then!—that the girl had been attending a convent in Montreal and longed to be a nun, and that her mother had said that she would rather see her dead.

"They were only here a short week—it was spring, and there were walks and picnics, and bridge and music and billiards—the time flew by. And it was on the afternoon when the Kents were going, their baggage in the hall, and when the other guests had gone, that Cecily Kent burst out crying, and Roger put his arm about her.

"The moment I saw that my heart turned to water. That moment," Flora said, with sudden bitter violence, raising herself upon her elbow, "all my hopes died, all my trust in him! It was my curse that I could not stop loving him as well——!"

The cold winter sunset, streaming through the bare woods beyond the stable yard, shone red upon the cheap cheerful paper of the walls, and struck Flora's grizzled hair with a tinge of blood, and shadowed clearly behind her the hand she raised.

"They had already been man and wife forty-eight hours," she said. "I think Roger Fleming felt remorse for the first time in his life when he saw the mother's face. Perhaps life had always been too easy for him, perhaps it had really never occurred to him that a few months a widower, and with his two little sons, and with his forty years, he might not be thought an ideal match for a dreamy girl of seventeen. He had always been so courted—so wanted.

"At first Mrs. Kent talked of annulling the marriage—she was more like a woman suddenly smitten with insanity than any one I ever saw before or since. She grasped the girl by the arm, and her eyes blazed, and her face was ashen. 'No,' she said, 'you shall not have her! She's hardly more than a baby—she knows nothing of life!'

"'Mamma,' Cecily said, crying and clinging to her, 'we were married two days ago. I am his wife.'

"I remember the mother looking at her, and the terrible silence there was in the hall. Lily began to whimper, beside me, and I caught her by the wrist. There were servants staring from the dining-room doorway.

"'You—Sissy?' Mrs. Kent said, in a whisper. Cecily went down on her knees, sobbing—almost screaming—like a child, and caught her mother about her knees.

"'Cecily,' Roger said, trying to raise her, 'you are mine now. Your mother cannot hurt you. You are my wife!'

"'Oh, let me go with my mother!' she sobbed. 'I hate you!'

"'She is—in fact—your wife?' Mrs. Kent said, looking over Cecily's head at him.

"Roger nodded. 'Then you must stay with your husband, my child,' Mrs. Kent said, very gravely. 'And may God punish you through your children, Roger Fleming,' she said, 'for what you have done to mine. Go tear the buds from those rose trees,' she said, pointing to the garden, 'go strip the new green fruit from your trees—and you will harvest what you must harvest now! Your little boys there, playing in the drive, are better fitted for life than she is!' And she turned to Moses, the coloured butler we had then. 'Moses, put my bags in the carriage,' she said.

"Nobody spoke as she went away. Cecily lay on the floor, moaning, Roger on one knee beside her, talking naturally and kindly. She never saw her mother, or her father, or her brother again. I heard long afterward that the pretty, cheerful mother had died and the father married again. They—they would be your people, Gabrielle. You could easily trace them.

"Cecily had been three days a wife, but she had lost her husband then! She never knew it—but I did, and I—God forgive me, I was glad. When she clung to her mother and screamed that she hated him, a look came into Roger Fleming's face that only I could understand. It was as if she had said, 'I am seventeen and he is forty! I knew nothing—he knew everything. My only loves were a daughter's love—a sister's love. He demanded more of me, and—if I had it!—I would loathe myself for giving it! He has robbed me of my mother, and my father, and my body, and my soul!'

"She cried all that night—would not come downstairs, or eat, or look at him, or talk to him. She cried for many days, and Roger used all his patience and all his kindness trying to console her. But he never gave her love again—he never had it to give, after that day! She had cut him to the very heart, and the Flemings are all proud, and none of them ever prouder than he!

"After a while she began to slip about the house like a shadow; she had never been pretty—except for her eyes that were like Gabrielle's, here—and she grew so thin and so white that she seemed all eyes. She would have no company, no entertaining, she seemed even to dread talking to Roger, and was fondest of you children and poor Lily. It was never any definite illness at first, just the doctor for one pain or another, and Roger taking her in for consultations and advice. They all gave the same advice, she needed amusement and relief from mental strain. But that was one thing he couldn't buy her! She used to lie out there in the garden telling Lily about her mother and father——"

Flora's voice stopped abruptly, with the effect of an interruption.

"I hated her," she said, simply, after a moment, and was still.

"Ah, yes, I did, David!" she added, suddenly, her eyes always closed, and as if David had protested. "I hated her. I managed her house, I answered the inquiries of anybody who came to call, I talked about her with Roger when he was anxious—and I hated her.

"She made him—miserable. She was a mixture of a child and a nun. She hated life, hated marriage. Lily and I were ready enough for it, watching our friends marry, and be widowed, and marry again! But this girl loathed her wifehood, her position, her husband—and her husband was Roger Fleming! He couldn't kiss her but what she would shut those dark, sad eyes of hers and offer her cheek like a child!"

"I remember her, shutting her eyes and turning her face away when we would kiss her," Tom said, clearing his throat.

"Whether she actually wrote to her mother asking for a reconciliation or not, I don't know," Flora resumed. "Roger had forbidden her to 'truckle,' as he called it; he felt that she must wait for advances from her mother. They never quarrelled about it, but I heard her say sometimes, 'I wish my mother would walk in!' and heard Roger answer her, not unkindly, but half-jokingly: 'Not into my house!'

"One day, when they had been married a few months, he was talking to me about his brother Will. 'Why don't you marry Will, Flo?' he said to me, with a sort of laugh. 'Good enough for the poor relation?' I said, trying to laugh back. But I was bitter, then—life was utterly hateful to me. 'Why, how you can remember!' he said, with a look that told me that he knew that he himself, and that old unhappy love of mine for him, was keeping me dark and angry and fuming about Wastewater for the best years of my life!

"'I may marry Will,' I said, trembling all over. And a few months later I did, although the idea had never come into my mind until that day. Not that I didn't love your father, Sylvia; I did. Everyone loved poor Will, and he had loved me a long, long time. Will and I were married, and Roger gave his brother a handsome check—which Will put into a patent for a bed-couch——

"Not that it mattered! Not that it mattered!" Flora's tired voice said, drearily, and was silent.

"Part of the time we lived at Wastewater," she resumed, "and sometimes, when Will was trying one of his new jobs, we had an apartment in Boston. Lily was sometimes with us, and sometimes she and Cecily and Roger went on short trips—they went to Bermuda one spring, I remember—Cecily was having one of her better times.

"Then Roger would come to me, distressed; Cecily was having those hateful pains again. She would come in to a Boston hospital for an operation, and I would go to see her every day, and bring her and her nurses back to Wastewater, and stay for a while, until she felt stronger.

"Sylvia was born in Boston, but a few weeks later we came to Wastewater, and both Roger and his wife grew so fond of her that I had an excuse for almost never leaving, although I kept my little Boston flat. Will was in the West for almost two years, working in Portland, and Oakland, and Los Angeles, and sometimes we would talk as if the baby and I might join him there. But as Cecily grew no stronger, and poor little Lily began to show signs of a sort of well—they called it 'passive melancholia,' and as the baby grew to be everybody's plaything——"

She opened her sunken eyes and fixed them with the shadow of a dark smile upon Sylvia's stricken and acutely attentive face.

"Mamma——" Sylvia breathed, bowing her dark head over her mother's hand.

"Poor little Silver, as Roger used to call you!" Flora said, tenderly. "I did it for you, dear, or at least I meant it for you. But it was never deliberate—it was all an accident."

She sank into quiet, and almost immediately breathed as if she were deeply asleep. Sylvia, not changing her position by a hair's breadth, signalled to the others a question as to the propriety of their slipping away. But no one had stirred when Flora quite simply opened her eyes, and said in a relieved tone:

"I want you to know everything. You don't blame me too much, Sylvia? Have I told you"—she added, anxious and alarmed—"did I tell you about Gabrielle?"

"Mamma, darling—to-morrow——?"

"No, no," Flora said, feverishly, "to-day! I had told you of my marrying—yes, and that poor little Lily seemed so upset.

"She had always been a forlorn, sentimental little thing, Lily. There had been different admirers, and she always took them seriously, weeping and questioning herself and her motives until my mother and I used to want to shake her. But after my mother's death, and your mother's death, David, and when you boys went off to

187

school, she became gently melancholy—yet not always sad, either, but wandering a little, and strange.

"There was a handsome, good-for-nothing sort of fellow hanging about at Tinsalls in Keyport then. Charpentier his name was—he was an agent for something, if he was anything. He and Lily used to walk along the cliff road, and sometimes she would cry and tell Cecily that he was as fine a gentleman as any man she knew, only unfortunate—that sort of thing.

"I didn't like it, but I dreaded telling Roger, for he was so quickly roused to anger, and I thought he might horsewhip the man and drive Lily clean out of her senses.

"Well, one day, when Sylvia was almost three, and Will had been in the West for six months or so, and when Cecily was all upset and lying on the couch like a little waxen ghost, Margret Nolan came to me—this same Margret we have now; she was an old servant here even then—and shaking all over and crying—poor Margret!—she told me that she was 'worried' about Miss Lily.

"'If that ruffian Charpentier has taken advantage of her, poor little wandering-witted thing that she is, I think they'll hang him!' she said.

"I was sick with the shame and the fright of it. I knew Roger would go after any man that touched one of his household with a revolver. It was all terrifying to me, but I told Margret—whom poor Lily had taken into her confidence—to go after the man Charpentier, find out if he could marry Lily, and keep the whole thing absolutely secret. It meant banishment for Lily from Cecily's presence, I knew that, for Cecily had a horror of such things—had a horror even of little babies and their needs—used to shut her eyes with a sort of sickness if I nursed Sylvia, or discussed one of her little illnesses in her room. Such a thing as this would have revolted her!

"Margret found out that Charpentier had disappeared, and all our efforts to get hold of him, then or since, were useless. He had no ties, no responsibilities, nobody cared whether he lived or died. He simply went away.

"So a few weeks went by, and I was sick with anxiety and shame. Lily—I used to marvel at it—was perfectly serene and quiet. She was so simple, poor soul!—that she would go in to the village and buy pink baby-ribbons—God alone knows how many hints she gave or whom she told!

"Finally, I planned to take her to my apartment in Boston, live quietly there with the baby—that is, my Sylvia, and perhaps one other servant, and tell Roger and Cecily that Lily wanted to study art—or music. Afterward, we could place her poor baby in some good institution, and then, maybe, I could tell Roger.

"That was August—late July and August. And that was the August that Tom ran away from school."

She opened her eyes, looked about the circle.

"We didn't hear of it until three days later," Flora went on, presently, addressing herself now to Tom. "For that master you had was positive that he would find you. After three days he telegraphed Roger: 'Is your son with you? Missing since Monday morning.'

"Roger, poor fellow, was proud at first. His son, fourteen years old, had run away to sea—the young monkey! 'He ought to be thrashed for this,' he would say, chuckling. He notified the police and went down to New York that week, getting the whole machinery in motion. 'You'll not thrash him,' I used to say. 'You'll give him a new bicycle—that'll be your thrashing!'"

"Proud, hey?" Tom interrupted the narrative, with a grin.

"Oh, yes—just at first. But after a few weeks—perhaps not so long, he began to speak more seriously. 'He couldn't have given us all the slip—he isn't more than a child,' he would say, as he came and went."

"I told them I was fifteen," Tom contributed. "All I did was sign up with the whaling fleet!—I'd thought it all out. The Saturday before, on a school hike, I shipped a bundle to New York harbour. There were some clothes in it that I didn't want—it was all a blind. And in my note to Dad I said that I had seen the Panama fruit boats going out, and they made me sick to get to sea."

"We found the bundle, and we searched the fruit boats, but we never got trace of you," Flora said.

"I was an ass, and I got it pretty well bumped out of me," Tom said, musingly. "A lot they cared who I was, on old Jensen's *Valkyr*. A fellow named Kelly went overboard that first run, and I went into Montreal three months later, with Kit Kelly's papers. Kelly and I stuck together until he got married; everyone always called me Kit. I never took any special trouble then to hide myself.—I always thought I'd come home, my next shore leave."

"Roger spent the rest of his life hunting you," Flora said. "He was never at home for more than a few weeks, or a few days, at a time, after that, and we all knew Cecily was happier when he was away. She had been much better that spring; he and she had gone to Old Point Comfort, and she had seemed much more human, somehow. But this autumn she was wretched, sad and worried about herself, and she had begun to say again, even to him, what she had often said to Lily and me: 'My marriage was a sin. All marriage is not wrong. But God intended me for a life of prayer and holiness, and what have I accomplished by disobeying the guidance of my own conscience?'

"This sort of thing made Roger furious, and I could see it, if she could not. 'We'd have a fine world, if you had your way, Sis,' he said to her once. 'Where would the younger generation come from?'

"'Oh, Roger, don't!' she would say. He would look at her, look at me, shrug, and smile. But presently I would see into what impatient lines his face would fall. 'It would have been a calamity for her to have a child!' he said to me one day. 'We would surely have had two children on our hands then!' Once he had told me, bitterly and resentfully, that her hasty and ill-considered marriage was killing her. 'She was seventeen in years when we were married,' he said. 'But I can understand her mother's fury now. She was about nine years old where life was concerned—a mystic, a child saint—torturing herself with scruples and with half-assimilated scraps of theology and mysticism!'

"That was the situation here at Wastewater that September, when Roger had word from the police at Guam that a boy who might have been Tom was there. As a matter of fact, this was that first 'false Tom,' who had them all deceived for so long. Roger went off to San Francisco, possibly to sail—as indeed he did finally sail—for the Orient. Will, my husband, had been away almost a year. David here was in boarding school.

"Left alone with Cecily and Lily, I did not dare risk Lily's baby being born in Wastewater. It would have started any amount of talk, and although poor Lily was not responsible, and although Margret had been spreading hints as to Lily's having secretly married this Charpentier, it seemed wiser not to have the whole thing here. Lily went in to my Boston apartment, and I got her a good practical nurse, and her baby was born months too soon—and died within a few minutes!"

"Died!" said more than one of the young voices.

"Died. Indeed, it never breathed at all. Lily was very ill, and went—as is not uncommon in such cases—into a sort of low fever, like the old brain fever, and she was near death for a long, long time.

"I lived with her, and the nurse, and a good servant named Carrie, in the Boston apartment, for Cecily had grown worse by that time, and the Crowchester doctor had quite frankly diagnosed her trouble as a tumour. We had heard that word before many times, but Roger never would believe it. Cecily believed it though, and she was furious at the Crowchester man because he would not operate in her husband's absence. So we had dismissed the Crowchester doctor—always a hard thing to do—and Cecily told him frankly that she wanted to come in to Boston and stay at a hospital for observation.

"She was at St. John's, only a few blocks from my apartment, and I went to see her every morning before luncheon and every late afternoon. She seemed more cheerful in the hospital, and the doctors were hopeful that a few weeks of it would make a new woman of her.

"One day, about a week after Lily's poor little baby had come and gone, the old doctor in whom Cecily specially trusted, the man who had her in charge, walked down the hospital steps and into the park with me, and we had a long talk, sitting on a park bench. He told me then—and you may imagine what I felt when I heard it!—that there was every probability that young Mrs. Roger Fleming was about to become a mother.

"For a while I was stupefied. I asked him to have a consultation. He said no, that was not necessary now, and might distress her. She had, he gathered from hints to the nurse,—she had a certain curious dislike for the idea of motherhood.

"'Dislike, Doctor!' I said. 'I believe it would kill her, if she did not kill herself!'

"And I tried to give him some idea of her character, what a strange half child, half mystic she was. He listened to me very gravely. It was important, he said, not to shock her.

"That was the first time I ever heard of shock as an actual danger to a sick person. I remember he explained it carefully. Cecily did not have the vitality of a humming-bird, he said. If we could get hold of the husband——

"I had to go on. I explained that her husband was much older, was, in fact, twenty-three or -four years older, and that—in the true sense—she did not love him. And I said that I was sure that if she were to have a baby, her love for it would come with the child.

"I said all the usual things, and he agreed with me. He told me the circumstance of the false diagnosis was unusual, but it had happened before—happened in his practice before. There was of course a possibility now that he was mistaken, that it was what the other doctors had always supposed. And there was every probability that the baby would not live, under the curious circumstances. But it seemed cruel not to give young Mrs. Fleming this hope.

"'It would be no hope to her!' I said. 'Whatever the child, if it lived, might come to mean to her, this prospect would make her absolutely ill.'

"We agreed that for a while, therefore, nothing must be said about it. But it was only ten days later that they took Cecily up to the surgery, and her baby, two months too soon, was born. She was dying, they thought that night, and there seemed every probability that the baby would die, too. A nice little nurse there told me that she wanted to give the child lay-baptism, and I made no objection. She asked what name, and I said, 'Mary.' It was the first name I thought of. 'I'll name her that and my name,' she said. 'I'll call her Mary Gabrielle!'"

"Me!" said Gabrielle Fleming, in a sharp whisper that echoed like a pistol shot in the room. Her dilated eyes moved to David's face.

"I told you last night, Gay," David said, gently.

"You told me—yes, but I thought my mother—I thought Lily—I only thought that she had loved Uncle Roger, instead of the man Charpentier!" the girl stammered. "I—I am their child——" she whispered.

She got to her feet, her eyes upon the distance, her mouth working, and walked bewilderedly to the door.

"Mamma!" Sylvia said, sharply, as Flora moaned and seemed to contract into something smaller than her already shrunken self as she sank deep into the white pillow. "Tom, give me that medicine," Sylvia commanded, in a frightened, low tone.

"Bring her back, David!" Flora said, struggling to raise herself and following Gabrielle with her eyes. "She must hear."

"Gay," David said, at the girl's elbow. She gave him a dazed look devoid of any expression whatsoever. "Aunt Flora wants us all to listen," the man said.

Without protest she came back to her place at the bedside.

The sunset was dying from the walls now, and a dull wintry chill was falling through the cold dark afternoon air. Flora looked fixedly at Gabrielle, who, pale and tense, with a bitten lower lip and starsapphire eyes widened with excitement and pain, never moved her gaze from her face.

"Cecily was so ill," said Flora, after a moment, "that for two or three days they feared for her life. I got a good nurse, and stayed at the hospital myself, and sent the tiny new baby to my apartment, when she was about nine days old, trying all the time to get in touch with Roger in San Francisco. He had sailed then, for Guam, but we did not know that until weeks later, when the telegrams all came back. But there was no attempt at secrecy."

"The old doctor told me that he had tried kindly and gently to inform young Mrs. Fleming of the birth of a child—that indeed she had some hazy recollections of the crisis of her illness, before the anæsthetic, but that she had given no sign of understanding him.

"I rented the furnished apartment next to mine and brought her there; she looked dying then, as she was—she lay perfectly passive and motionless all day, sometimes crying, sometimes reading, only taking a little tea, or a little soup.

"One day I came home, and she had put on a wrapper and come into Lily's room. Lily was better and was sitting up, and I had begun to feel as one does feel in such emergencies that I might weather this time—strange and terrible as it was. Sylvia was on the floor with a doll, and the nurse had brought the new baby in, in her basket, to get the sunshine in the window there.

"Cecily was crying—crying hysterically—but even that much emotion seemed to me a good sign. Lily was lying on the bed, and Cecily kneeling beside her with her face buried against her knees.

"I had been utterly dissatisfied with Cecily's nurse, who was a careless, neglectful creature, and I was furious to see that she had let her patient get out of bed at all.

"'Cecily!' I said. 'You *must* not—excitement like this will be dangerous to you!'

"Lily looked at me with that bright, childish smile she had had since her illness. 'Cecily has been looking at my baby, Flo,' she said, happily. 'Isn't it a sweet baby, Flo? It couldn't be wrong to have a sweet baby like that, could it?'

"The servant, Carrie, looked at me significantly. And I saw that salvation for Cecily might lie here. Cecily had been looking into my eyes. Now she buried her face again and burst out, in a sort of whisper:

"'Oh, my God, I thank Thee! Oh, my God, how good Thou art! Oh, I am so grateful—I am so humbly grateful!'

"We got her back to bed, and when we were alone she said to me: 'Flora, I must tell you something. I can tell you now, for I am going to die, and God has forgiven me! I could not give life to any other soul, Flora, and I could not die knowing that my sins would be visited on a poor little baby! No, no—I could not bear that.

"'They told me, the doctor told me at the hospital—or I dreamed it, on that terrible night of the operation', she said. 'Flora, did you know that I thought I had a child that night? No, or they told me I did——' she said, beginning to be frightened again.

"'Don't bother your head about it now, Cecily,' I said. 'Just get

193

well, so that when Roger comes back——'

"She shuddered at Roger's name, and began to get excited.

"'I will be dead before that, and God will have forgiven me, Flora,' she said. 'Ah, you don't think I was a sinner, but I was! Before I ever took my marriage vow, I had taken another, when I was only fourteen years old! Another girl and I at the convent had taken a solemn oath to God that we would never marry!'"

"Poor child!" breathed Gabrielle's pale lips, involuntarily.

"Poor child," Flora echoed, without opening her eyes. Her voice was so weak that David held water to her mouth, and she drank with difficulty. "Poor little Cecily! She said that when she had first come to Wastewater she had no thought of lovers or love in her mind. That she had been bewildered and astonished at the emotion Roger had almost at once roused in her, but that she had never thought of it as love. That all her thoughts and senses had been in a wild confusion, culminating on the day that he and she drove in to Minford, beyond Tinsalls, quite simply, and that Roger, who knew the Justice there, got a special license and they were married.

"That night she went quite simply away from her mother's room, expecting to be questioned in the morning. But her mother did not miss her; Cecily was quietly dressing when her mother awakened the next day. She said she remembered her vow that day. And when she came to this part, I thought she was going to die. She said quite seriously that she had had not one single happy moment since, and I suppose when Roger laughed at her scruples—as he did laugh—he broke her heart.

"I told her that no minor child could take a valid vow of that sort, and that indeed her very marriage might be questioned, since her age had been given as nineteen. No use! She believed me only enough to say that no irregularity in her license could possibly make her child more accursed than she would feel a child of hers to be.

"'But I understand now—I never had a child—it's Lily's child!' she said, over and over again, with so much deep thankfulness that I could only be thankful, too. 'Lily told me all about it,' she said, so humbly and tenderly, 'and she is no worse a sinner than I—less, perhaps, for she loved and I did not!'

"I dismissed the nurse that afternoon, as it chanced, and sent for a nurse we had had from Crowchester, Hannah Rosecrans, a fine girl. She came the next day, and I told her, naturally, the whole truth, but that both my poor Lily and Mrs. Fleming must be treated with the utmost consideration until Mr. Fleming came home.

"Cecily was now all anxiety to get back to Wastewater. She said that she never wanted to see again the cruel old doctor who had frightened her so. I explained the situation to him, and presently we all came back to Wastewater, leaving Carrie behind us simply because she did not want to come.

"Hannah Rosecrans was engaged to be married, she was with us only a few weeks, and then went to Australia, where her husband has become well-to-do. She idolized the baby, and loved Lily, too, but I suppose, servant-fashion, she gave the other servants to believe that there was something amiss. Anyway, it was always 'Miss Lily's baby,' from the very first. Lily had told Margret about her troubles months before, and I was never in any doubt what Margret thought.

"As for Cecily, she seemed to think it settled. Our Crowchester doctor was recalled, but there was nothing he could do except keep her quiet. She was sinking very fast; she died when Gabrielle was only seven or eight weeks old.

"Roger got home too late—the day before the funeral—but even then I thought that any accident might show him the truth. I told myself that in all this confusion it would only sadden him more. I—I don't know now what I thought, or why I did what I did! But Lily and the baby and Margret had their own suite of rooms, and Roger naturally paid little attention to them—in his grief for his wife. He saw the baby, took it for granted she was Lily's. And I told myself that sometime I would of course tell him the whole story, or somebody would. He would meet the old doctor who had attended Cecily, or the doctor who had attended Lily, in Boston. Or he might run across Carrie, or Hannah Rosecrans——

"Cecily was buried here where we buried Lily only last spring. Roger went off on his searches, came home—gray-headed and so changed!—went off again. And I never told him.

"I had begun it to protect Cecily, to comfort Lily—I never had planned it; it all seemed to come about of itself, and for the first six years of her life Gabrielle called Lily 'Mamma.' Then Lily became very bad, and we put her in a sanitarium, and she never knew. And then Will Fleming, my husband, died, and I thought——

"Fool that I was," Flora added, after a pause, with infinite fatigue and a sort of self-contempt in her voice, "I cared for Roger even then—I cared for him even then. I was widowed, and he twice a widower. He loved my child, but he loved Gabrielle as well. I could not—I could not put Cecily Fleming's child ahead of mine. Roger needed me, he turned to me for everything. I could not see his little girl—placed ahead of me—pushing me out of his life——

"I couldn't!" she said more loudly, choking. "I had given my life to him—my whole life! He had trampled me under his feet. Gabrielle was fair—she was like Cecily's mother—she was a beautiful baby. I knew he would give his whole heart to her, live for her——

"One day he said that he was going to change his will, make a generous provision for Lily's poor little girl, and I was glad. It wasn't money that mattered—to me. I would have starved for him. He said that in case his boy never came back, the little girls should share and share alike, like sisters, and I was glad. There was never any plan in what I did—I used to think that any hour might change it, any chance word! I knew that Roger had written a will in Janet's day, when Tom was a baby, and when he might have had half-a-dozen other children, but after this talk he had a good many interviews with his lawyer, and I supposed that he had done what he said.

"He was not here very much; I came to believe that he hated the old place, and me, and Lily, and everything that reminded him that he had once been young and free with the world at his feet. I used to think that even if he had found Tom, he would have gone on wandering. But at last, when he came home, it was to die. He died—you remember, David, quite quietly and without pain, one summer day—he had been warned of his heart. He was packing to go off to Panama, a doctor there had written that there was a young fellow just answering Tom's description—with—with whatever it is when a man loses all memory—amnesia——

"A few days later we read the will. You remember, David, on such a hot morning, in the library? Sylvia and Gabrielle were playing outside on the terrace where the hydrangeas are; old Judge Baron had come down from the city.

"We read the will, and I knew then what I had done. Gabrielle was not mentioned. Gabrielle was not mentioned! The will stood as it had stood when he wrote it, when Tom was a baby. Everything, everything to his child, or children. And there was a codicil, dated about the time of his last return home, giving everything, everything, to Sylvia, in case Tom did not come back!

"My God, my God——" Flora whispered, under her breath, and lay still.

"I had wanted it all my life, and now I had it," she said, after a while, in a voice that was weakening, weakening from moment to moment, and yet full of passion and fire still. "I had it all. Judge Baron went away, David went away, I was alone with Sylvia and little Gabrielle, and Wastewater was mine. I remember, in the first long warm afternoon, that I walked slowly through it, from room to room, and thought that I had survived them all—Uncle Tom, Roger, Janet, Cecily, Will—all, all the Black Flemings gone except me! I had only to keep silent, and my child would be rich.

"I think that's all," she added, opening her sunken dark eyes and fixing them steadily upon David's face. "That explains it all, doesn't it? I have lived in fear. I knew the old doctor was dead, but I used to lie in the nights imagining that he had happened to tell some-one—someone who was drawing nearer and nearer to my life every moment. Hannah Rosecrans, the Carrie we had in Boston, the doctor Lily had, whose very name I can't remember—they all knew! Any day might have brought them back to me with their questions.

"I used to imagine that I might go to jail! But I never was any-thing else but in jail all my life long!"

CHAPTER XIX

SHE stopped. And after a long minute of silence the young persons looked at each other. Tom had been sitting throughout in a low chair with his hands locked; now he merely grinned nervously and shrugged. David's face was stern and grave; he had folded his arms and had been staring ahead of him with a faint frown. Now his eyes moved about the circle and returned to space. Sylvia's vivid dark face with its white, white skin was drained of colour, her eyes looked tortured, and she was breathing fast. As she knelt beside the bed, she half supported her mother upon her arm, her anxious and stricken face close to the leaden, ghastly face upon the pillow.

Gabrielle had been kneeling, too, as she listened. But at the end she rose and walked to the little window.

Outside, in the winter dusk, lay the soaked, blackened ruins of the old stables, those clean big airy stables that Gabrielle had so loved as a little girl. Nearer, against the angle of the house, lay the wreck of the windmill, the great rusty hoops and singed wood piled almost as high as the window. Beyond all were the bare winter woods, looking desolate and forlorn in the cool gray light, and on the right brimmed and lowered the steely surface of a cold and unfriendly sea.

As Gabrielle stood there, her weary heart and mind whirled hither and thither by a hundred conflicting thoughts, in a very storm of pity and pain, the island lights suddenly pricked through the dove-gray of the gloom and flashed their pinkish radiance against the gaining and prevailing shadows. The girl's thoughts travelled to them idly—she thought of little ships cutting their way through the trackless waters, and dark-faced, rough men twisting the spokes of the little wheels and peering out across the waves to find that steadily pulsating flash.

Somebody had lighted a light in the room behind her; she saw her own reflection, slender, aureoled, against the dark night. David touched her arm.

A sudden bitter need of tears possessed her, and her breast swelled. But she only raised heavy eyes to his questioningly, and bit her lip to steady it.

"Aunt Flora wants to speak to you, Gay." The girl could tell by David's tone that he had said it before. He gently turned her toward the bed.

She looked bewilderedly at Tom, who was busy at the lamp, and at Sylvia, who stood at the foot of the bed. Like a person in a dream she went slowly toward Flora, and knelt down beside her.

Flora reached out hard and anxious fingers and gripped the girl's hand.

"I told David this yesterday—he told you and Tom—he was to tell you—when the fire came——" Flora whispered.

"He did tell us." Gabrielle's beautiful voice sounded childish and husky in contrast to the other weak voice. "But I thought—I thought that—my mother—Lily was still my mother, and that Uncle Roger was my father—that I had no right to call him father. It seems"—her lips shook again—"it seems that I might have had—a father——" she faltered. Her voice thickened and stopped. She raised her eyes appealingly, almost apologetically to David, who was watching closely. "I never—had—any one," she said, with suddenly brimming eyes.

Flora spoke, and immediately afterward, in a strange muse that was not hearing, Gabrielle heard Sylvia give a sort of cry, and then David leaned over her and said tenderly:

"Gay—she is very ill, dear. If you can——?"

"If I can—what—David?" she repeated, confused, her beautiful eyes wide and anxious.

"She wants you to forgive her, Gabrielle," David answered.

Gabrielle still appeared bewildered; she looked from one face to another.

"Yes, I will, of course I will," she said, quickly and simply.

"Then tell her so, Gabrielle."

Gabrielle bent her gaze upon her aunt's sunken face, a blot against the white pillows, and Flora fixed upon her the tragic look of her darkening eyes.

"I am sorry, Aunt Flora," Gabrielle stammered, in tears. "I know—I know how hard it must have been for you. I am so sorry."

"You will forgive me, Gabrielle?" Flora whispered, feverishly. "In all the years to come you will not hate me? You have grown to be a lovely woman—I did not harm you. I might have harmed you—but it was Sylvia, in the end, who paid for what I did."

"I will never hate you," Gabrielle said, slowly and steadily, like a child repeating a lesson.

"It was because I loved him so," said Flora's drawn, dark mouth, in a whisper. She sank back, seemed to be sinking away from earth and the things of earth altogether. "God bless you, Gabrielle, you have made it easy for me to die," she added, in the mere breath of a voice.

"I'm—so—sorry!" Gay said, with a great sob. And she buried her face against the coverlet and burst into crying. "I'm so sorry that he was unkind to you—and that you could not forgive him and forgive me!" she sobbed. "We might have been—we might all have been so happy!"

"We might have been so happy," Flora's lips repeated. No other muscle of her bloodless face and shut eyes moved. "God bless you, Gabrielle," she whispered again, as Gabrielle, drawn away by David's hand, stopped to lay a wet cheek against hers and kiss her in farewell.

The girl, halfway to the door, and hardly conscious of what she was doing, suddenly wrenched herself free and went back to the bed. She fell on her knees, and catching the languid dark hand, put it to her lips.

"Aunt Flora, indeed I forgive you!" she said, weeping, "from my heart. I am so sorry you were so unhappy—that they all hurt you and failed you so! Dear Aunt Flora——"

Sylvia was on her knees on the other side, and crying as bitterly as Gabrielle, when David led the younger girl away. He and Margret established her upon a downstairs sofa, with cushions and covers before the fire, and she lay there in a dreamy state, not talking, hardly thinking, as the strange panorama of the last twenty-four hours wheeled through her weary head. She saw Flora only once again, and that was at the end, at seven o'clock.

At ten Tom drove them to Crowchester and they boarded the Boston train; Sylvia veiled and clinging tightly to Tom's arm, Gabrielle and old Margret guiding them through the interested, warm train to the privacy of their drawing room.

Gabrielle's last look at Wastewater had shown her only bare trees, blackened masses of ruins darker than the prevailing dark, open levels where the stately walls had been. A cold moon had been shining brightly upon the sea, had thrown the shadows of leafless bushes in a lacework across the bare brown space of the lawn, and against the steady rush and retreat of the short waves she had heard the tumbling cascading sound of some bit of wall collapsing upon the general collapse. Toward the distant west wall, beyond the woods, the changed perspective had left a long vista free, and Gabrielle could see the white gravestones in the moonlight.

Graves and ruins, ashes and bare branches, and beside them the unchanged, restless sea, and above them the unfeeling moonlight. The child of Wastewater looked back with a great gravity, a great solemnity in her heart. There had been laughter here, music and voices. Wastewater had had a housewarming, more than a hundred years before, when beautiful women, in the capes and high-waisted gowns of the Empire days, had been driven in jingling great coaches all the way from Boston City to dance and rejoice with the young master of the mansion.

There had been a first Roger, in the buff and blue of the Revolution, Colonel Fleming, as black and as handsome as any of them, and there had been his son Tom, the good-hearted Tom who had come all the way to Brookline to find a cousin's disconsolate little widow, with her sewing machine, and her girl babies, and offer them a home.

And there had been Tom's son Roger, handsomest and most dashing of them all—David's young mother, who was to win his heart, and that shadowy little Cecily, who must now be "mother" in Gabrielle's thoughts.

Aunt Flora always watching jealously; Aunt Lily tearful and singing her romantic little songs; gallant little Tom reading his sea stories on the old nursery window-sill; dark little proud Sylvia with her glossy curls; baby Gay herself, wistful and alone; they all seemed to pass before the girl's eyes in a long and haunting procession, crying as they went that they had always failed, even here, in all this wealth and beauty, to find happiness and peace!

"I will be happy," Gabrielle had sworn to herself solemnly, frightened at the history of the place. "I will try never to be proud or jealous or cruel. We are Flemings, we four—and I as much a Fleming as any one of them now, and we must not make their mistakes! God helping us," she thought, remembering the little nun who had years ago read the Sermon on the Mount to a class of inattentive little girls so many times, "we will all be good, and meek, and merciful, and some day—years and years from now—we will come back to Wastewater again and rebuild it.

"Good-bye, Wastewater!" she had whispered, leaning back to look through the glass window of the motor car. And from beyond the ruins, the ashes, the bare garden, and the moonlit sea, the island lights had flashed her an answer.

CHAPTER XX

IT was more than a long year later that David Fleming, driving the car that Sylvia had ordered with such happy confidence before that long-awaited twenty-first birthday, left Crowchester, and followed the familiar road along the cliffs.

The spring was early, and the sweetness of it was already in the air; there were patches of emerald grass in sheltered places, and all the rich warm milky odours of turned earth and fruit blossoms, new leaves and the first hardy lilacs. Babies in sheltered coaches were airing along the little streets of Keyport, and if the restless little breezes and the sunless shadows were chilly, in the sunlight there was a delicious warmth.

The familiar dips and turns of the road were all like so many welcoming faces to David, and when he reached the boundaries of Wastewater he might almost have fancied, for a moment, that the old order of things had remained unchanged, that back of that barrier of great trees, now trembling into tiny dots of palest green, he might indeed find the grim dark building, the shuttered windows, the dank unhealthy shrubs and paths that had been the first home of his recollection.

The brick walls and the iron gates, more deeply bedded than ever in fallen leaves and mould, were unchanged, but the road between them, so many years unused, had been somewhat cut by wheels, and had been churned into mud. It stood open, but David left his car outside, got out and turned his back to the land for a moment, standing staring out to sea, as he had done upon that autumn day more than two years ago, that dreary, dark October day when Gabrielle had first come home.

He remembered, as his eyes idly followed the scrambling path down between the rocks and the bare mallow bushes to the shore, the muggy smells that had always assaulted his nostrils when the big side door of Wastewater had been opened, the smell of distant soup bones, dust, horsehair furniture, decaying wood, stifling coal fires that smoked. He remembered his aunt, rigid and stern, before the fire, her apprehensive, nervous eyes always moving behind him when he entered the room, and searching there for some menace always feared and never realized. He remembered the lamps, the antimacassars, the booming voices of the maids in the gloomy halls.

And then Gabrielle, in her velvet gown, with her big, starry eyes. Gabrielle, so young and so alone, met by such staggering blows, such bitter truths. Gabrielle watching Sylvia's youth and happy fortune so wistfully, bearing her own sorrows and burdens with her own inimitable childish courage and dignity.

What a time—what a time! the man mused, his breast rising on a great sigh, as he shook his head slowly. Sylvia's majority, and then Tom's return, Aunt Flora's stupefying revelation as to Gay's parentage, and then the last scene—or almost the last—when he had gone upstairs to tell them—Gabrielle and Tom, that they were brother and sister, and the great wind and the fire had trapped them there.

So that had been the end of Wastewater, with these four young persons, all Flemings, flying for their lives through the night, and Aunt Flora, who had spent all her life there, killed by the falling of all her moral and material walls in one terrible crash. She had lain for almost twenty-four hours in John's dismantled house, without pain of body, and in a lulled state even of mind, but she had been dying none the less. David had reviewed a hundred times the dark and forbidding afternoon, the ugly red of the sunset, as it shone upon the walls, and the memory of Aunt Flora's sunken face against the pillows, the memory of her monotonous, weary voice.

The last of her generation, that stormy and ill-governed generation whose passions and weaknesses had filled the whole house with tragedies for so many years, she had died very quietly, quite as if going to sleep, before the ashes of the old place had been cold. Sylvia, beautiful, twenty-one, her own life as truly in ruins and ashes about her, had been kneeling beside her mother at the end, the doctor standing gravely near, and David himself watching them all with that strange quality of responsibility that seemed to be his destiny where each and every one of them was concerned.

Afterward, Tom had taken the girls in to Boston, where Sylvia, ill from shock and sorrow, had been left in the care of Gabrielle and a nurse, while Tom and David came back to Wastewater for the funeral.

David, reaching this point, turned back and looked across the old garden, to find the glint of headstones far up the northwest corner of the estate, beyond the woods, and under a fountain of delicate blue-green willow-whips.

Much of the garden was left after only one season's neglect, he mused, and could be reclaimed. There were healthy-looking roses, and the splendid hedge of lilacs was already bursting from hard brown buds into white and lavender plumes. The conifers looked clean and fresh in their new tips, even the maples and elms were magnificent as ever.

An odd new look of something like pioneer roughness had been given the place, however, by the raw wood-piles. Gay's one stipulation, David smiled to remember, in one of the few allusions she had made to the subject, had been in reference to the heavy evergreen shrubbery close to the house. Mightn't—she had put it so, although all this land was hers now—mightn't a lot of those ugly old pines and cypresses come down?

Down they had accordingly come, to be chopped and piled into substantial stacks against some coming winter. Also stacked and piled were the bricks that had been Wastewater, the thousands and hundreds of thousands of bricks, that had been scraped and aligned into long solid blocks.

Some day, David mused, there would be a home here again. But when, the young persons most concerned had not yet definitely stated. He sighed as he thought of them, and smiled above the sigh.

A start had been made, at least. There was a handsome building already standing; a long low barn of friendly warm clinkered brick, with the wide new doors of a garage at one end, and at the other, across an arch, beyond which cows and horses might be fenced some day, was a homely, comfortable cottage, of the type that faces a thousand English lanes, steep roof cut by white-curtained dormers, latticed deep windows against which vines were already trained, and a hooded doorway with a brass knocker.

An Airedale, whirling about the corner of the building with a wild flourish, leaped upon David in welcome, and immediately curled himself rapturously in the short film of the grass, with all four feet in the air, writhing in puppy ecstasies.

"Here, here, Ben!" David said, laughing. "Grow up! It's ridiculous to see a dog of your age acting that way!"

But he was rubbing and tousling the rough head affectionately, none the less, as he called, "Etta! John!"

In answer Etta, John's wife, appeared with an undisturbed smile. For the months of building last fall, and again this spring, Mr. David had been living in his little Keyport farmhouse and might be expected here at almost any minute to inspect and approve. Etta herself had watched so much of the re-building with secret contempt. It seemed odd, when one could afford a nice square plastered house, and a corrugated iron barn, to waste twice as much money on what John considered "monkey shines." But Miss Gabrielle and Miss Sylvia and Mr. Tom had all been away for more than a year now, in California and Mexico and Panama, and now it was Central America, and dear knows what it'd be next, and consequently Mr. David and his friend Mr. Rucker had had it all their own way.

Etta had no objection to Mr. Rucker, who was always so kind and polite, and funny, too, if you always understood just what he meant, but she could not understand why he should drag in talk about Swedish farmhouses and Oxford.

"I don't know anything about Oxford," Etta had more than once commented to her husband, "but I do know that the Swedes all get here as fast as they can, and why any one'd want to bring their clumsy-looking old barns after them beats me! Mr. Rucker was showing me the pitchers in a book; 'It looks like something a child would make with blocks, if you'd ask me!' I told him."

"I hope when they build a house it's going to look decent," John might answer, uneasily. "I don't know what better they'd want than three stories with plenty of bay windows and porches. I seen one pitcher Mr. David had in a book with all the roofs kinder sloping down into the garden, and the windows all different sizes and levels. Mr. Rucker says he has some old leaded windows from a barroom—that's what he said—for the liberry. I had Davis, over to the Lumber Company, send him a catalogue, and mark all the new doors and windows with a blue pencil, but I don't know if he got it."

To-day David gave Etta an opportunity for criticism when he said cheerfully, as she somewhat reluctantly accompanied him about the place:

"How's the house, Etta—comfortable?"

"Oh, we're quite comfortable, thank you," Etta answered, primly, in a faintly complaining tone, "and John's got the Eyetalians engaged to start the side garden anyway before the folks get back. But here's the thing that I'll never get through my head," Etta added, with the readiness of an already well-aired grievance, as she looked up at the wide archway and its casement windows above; "it don't seem sensible to have that arch, or gate, or whatever you call it, making the barn and the house into one. As far as needing the room goes, we'll never need it, for John would no more think of going through that way for the hay than flying over the moon. I was thinking it would look handsomer to have the barn separate—and while the men are right here, and before Miss Gabrielle gets home to look at the plans for a house, and dear knows when that will be now!—why, they could tear out that arch real easy, and smooth the brick up so that it'd never show—and it does seem as if it'd be more Christian—more like the way other places look—places like the Smiths', over to Tinsalls, that have millions of dollars, but their house looks so neat and square——"

"Ah, they've got the stable foundations started," David said, in satisfaction, paying no attention to Etta's remarks.

"Oh, yes, sir, they got the cement in day before yesterday," Etta, diverted, answered, in the same placid whine.

"That's fine," David said, nodding to the various workmen as he walked about. "Room for four cows and about that many horses, and some day we'll put a chicken run on that end."

"Do they say when they'll be coming back, sir?" Etta asked.

"Any time this summer, I suppose," David said. "Mr. Tom is quite himself again—too well, in fact, Miss Sylvia wrote. I think she and Miss Gabrielle would have been glad to come straight home from San Francisco, but Mr. Tom saw the masts of ships again, and that was enough. He wired they wanted me to go around the world with them, but eventually they seemed to have compromised on Panama. I've not had letters yet, but in a telegram a few days ago—I told you that?—there was some talk of Central America."

"Dear me," said Etta, who always made this remark in any pause, "haven't there been changes? That grand old house—John says it'd cost a million dollars to rebuild it now—it does seem such a pity it had to burn down!"

"The insurance," David said, consolingly, "will more than build a much prettier and more homelike Wastewater."

"Oh, I don't know," Etta said, with the relished pessimism of an old servant. "I was wondering if Mr. Rucker had seen them pretty plastered houses over to the Crowchester Manor Estates?" she asked, adroitly.

David did not answer. He looked at the mud-spattered and torn blue-print that was anchored from the coquettish spring breezes upon a plank with two brick-bats, murmured to the contractor, suggested, approved.

It was easy for his thoughts to find Gabrielle at Wastewater, for they were almost all of her in these days, and it was here that she had spent her life, except her school years. David had no recollection of her in any other setting. To-day, as always, she seemed to be beside him, walking through the strangely altered spring garden, talking with him of the changes to be.

She had borne herself, he had thought, with his affectionate quiet pride in her carrying as ever an undercurrent of pain—she had borne herself in the trying time of readjustments and changes better than all of them. There was a native dignity, a fineness about her, that made it possible for her apparently to forget herself entirely.

As he remembered her, in the few weeks that had intervened between her departure with Tom and Sylvia for the West, in old Margret's care, it was difficult to recall any special demonstration of her own feelings at all. Sylvia had been actually if not seriously ill, Tom had suffered a dangerous relapse after the strain and exposure of the night, but Gay had been just her usual self. David had had a thousand cares: first to establish them temporarily in a comfortable hotel, then to commence the endless business of placing Gabrielle in her rightful position, with all it involved in the matter of taxes, transfers, legal delays of every sort.

He had written to the far-away Hannah Rosecrans in Australia, and had had a prompt and satisfactory reply. Hannah was Mrs. Tarwood, now, with children of her own. She gladly and unsuspiciously supplied a hundred details: the Fleming baby's first nurse's name at the big hospital, the name of a young doctor who had more than once come to see little Gabrielle in her first delicate weeks of life. Through these and Flora's other clues David established the matter legally beyond all doubt, and Tom simplified the question of property division by being eager to reserve about only one fifth of his father's estate for himself, giving his half-sister everything else. Wastewater, the jewels, this piece of property, that other, this stock and those bonds, everything, in short, about which division might have presented the slightest difficulty, Tom would have impatiently discarded in her favour. He was going to die anyway, he would remind them.

Beyond all this, David had Sylvia's inheritance to handle. Flora had left a will, but it was superseded by an urgent note to her daughter, written at the time when Sylvia was supposed heiress to the whole Fleming fortune, begging her to make over her own money to Gabrielle.

Sylvia, hysterical and sensitive and unreasonable, had still persisted that this must be done; Gay—she protested in floods of shamed tears—had been wronged long enough! No, it must be all, all Gay's, and she, Sylvia, would go forth into the world penniless, and make her own way—she would be happier so.

It had been Gay, patient and serious, in her new black, who had talked her into a healthier frame of mind. Gay had sat beside her cousin's bed, smiling, talking occasionally, interesting Sylvia in the various phases of the business as they had come up, had managed both invalids and the whole comfortable suite, and had joined David, to affix a signature or witness a deed, as quietly as if this earthquake had touched her personally not at all.

Most admirable, he thought, had been her attitude with Tom. From the strange, disorganized winter day of Aunt Flora's death, Gay had been quite simply, affectionately, and appreciatively Tom's little sister. There had been no scenes, no hysteria, no superfluous words; David did not even suppose that the sister and brother had discussed the subject. Immediately, and with a youthful and almost childish grace that David, remembering, would recall with suddenly blinking eyes, she had adopted big, clumsy, unpolished Tom. In three days, quite without awkwardness, if with a sometimes slightly heightened colour, he had heard her speak of "my brother" to doctors, nurses, waiters in the hotel.

She had carried Tom, he realized now, by storm, by the sheer force of her own extraordinary personality. If Tom had ever been in any doubt as to the fashion of recommencing their friendship along these wholly altered lines, Gabrielle had instantly dispelled it.

More, she had given Tom as a brother ten times the visible affection and confidence that she had been willing to give him in any other relationship. Gabrielle had been afraid to be too friendly before. Now she was free to laugh with him, to spoil him, to tease him, to sit on the edge of his bed and hold his big, hard hand while she recounted to him her daily adventures.

And Tom had proved quite unconsciously, by his pathetically eager and proud acceptance of this new state of affairs, that it was her companionship, her sympathy he had wanted. He had wanted to be a little needed, a little admired, to be of some consequence to David, to the admirable Sylvia, and lastly, to inconsiderable and neglected little Gabrielle.

He had seized upon his half-brotherhood with her as he had never developed exactly the same relationship with David. Indeed, so consummately wise had been this child's—for David thought of her as scarcely more than a child—this child's handling of the situation, that within a week of the change Tom's tone had actually taken on the half-proud, half-chiding note of an adoring elder brother, and David had seen in his eyes the pleased recognition of the fact that at least no one else was, or could be, Gabrielle's "family" but himself.

Tom's condition appearing to be supremely unsatisfactory, there had immediately been talk of southern California or Florida for the winter. For Sylvia, who was strangely shaken, quiet, and unlike herself even when physically well again, it seemed a wise solution, too.

Gabrielle was of course to accompany her brother, and David must follow as soon as all their complicated affairs permitted.

Saying good-bye to the little black-clad group, when he had escorted them as far as Chicago, David had returned somewhat sadly to his duties as doubly, trebly an executor, his canvases, and the lonely painting of the first snows. And after that the months had somehow slipped by in a very chain of delays and complications: upon the only occasion when David had actually been packed and ready to start for the West, a telegram from his closest friend, Jim Rucker, or rather from Jim's wife, in Canada, relative to an accident, illness, and the need of his help, had taken him far up into the Winnipeg woods instead.

Had the three Flemings been in La Crescenta, high and dry above ocean and the valleys of southern California, where they had at first quite established themselves, with a piano and a garden and a telephone, David might have joined them during the second summer. But by this time Tom was entirely well again, perfectly able to live in the East, winter and summer if he liked, "but catch me doing it," wrote Tom, in his large sprawling hand, and the travellers had gone into Mexico.

"Do for Heaven's sake be careful, Gay," David had written anxiously. "You appear to be the brains of the expedition. You may get into hot water down there!"

"Sylvia, on the contrary, is the brains of the expedition, as you so elegantly phrase it," Gabrielle had answered, cheerfully, "and as to getting into trouble—no such luck!"

Then they were in San Francisco again, and David, with a muffled hammering going on steadily in his heart when he thought of seeing Gay again, had been expectant of a wire saying that any day might find them turning eastward. But no, for Tom had caught sight of all the huddled masts in the San Francisco harbour, the mysterious thrilling hulls that say "Marseilles" and "Sydney" and "Rio de Janeiro," and he had been all for Australia—all for South America—had compromised finally upon Panama.

That was two months ago. Now, perhaps still feeling that the late New England spring would be chilly, they were apparently off for Guatemala and Honduras.

David could school his heart the better to patience because he had no hope. No hope even in her obscure little friendless days really of winning Gabrielle, and less hope now. His attitude toward all women, as he himself sometimes vaguely sensed, was one of an awed simplicity; they seemed miraculous to David, they interested him strangely and deeply, as beings whose lightest word had a mysterious significance.

If he had once loved Sylvia dearly, loyally, admiringly—and he knew that for almost all her life he had—then what he felt toward Gabrielle was entirely different. There was no peace in it, no sanity, no pleasure. It burned, an uncomfortable and incessant pain, behind every other thought; it penetrated into every tiniest event and act of his life.

The mail to David, nowadays, meant either nothing or everything. Usually it was nothing. Once a month perhaps it glowed and sparkled with one of those disreputable and miscellaneous little envelopes that Gabrielle affected: sometimes a hotel sheet, sometimes a lined shiny page torn from an account book, but always exquisite to David because of the fine square crowded writing and the delicious freedom and cleverness of the phrases.

For two or three days a letter would make him exquisitely happy. He always put off the work of answering for a fortnight if possible—but sometimes he could not wait so long—to savour more fully the privilege he felt it to be, and to lessen the interval before the next letter from her.

When his answer had gone there was always a time of blankness. David would walk past the Keyport post office, go back, ask casually if there were letters—no matter. But when something approaching a fortnight passed, he would find himself thinking of nothing else but that precious little sheet; find himself declining invitations to Boston or New York for fear of missing it for an unnecessary few days, find himself wiring Rucker in the latter place, "If letters for me, please forward."

For the rest, when Sylvia wrote with charming regularity every week Gabrielle was, of course, always mentioned, and almost always in a way that gave David more pain than pleasure.

The doctor, Sylvia might write, for example, "of course madly in love with Gay," had said this or that about Tom's staying where he was. Or, "our fellow traveller, whose son is the nice Yale boy, has taken a great fancy to my humble self, perhaps in self-defence, as the boy can see nothing but Gabrielle." Gabrielle "got a blue hat and a dark blue suit in San Francisco, and looked stunning." Gabrielle wanted to add a line. And there, added, would be the precious line: "Love; I am writing."

What David suffered during these crowded months that were yet so empty without, only David knew. He knew now that whatever his feeling was, it was the only emotion of any importance that he had ever known in his life. The departure for the war front, five years before, somewhat reminded him of it, but, after all, those feelings had been faint and vague compared to these. Buying his uniforms, equipping his bag, cutting every tie with the old life, facing the utterly unknown in the new, David remembered feeling some such utter obsession and excitement as he felt now.

But, after the thrilling commencement, that military life had faded into the stupidity of mismanaged training for what he had felt to be an ill-conceived purpose. David could only remember it now as a boy's blind exultation and enthusiasm.

This other thing was the realest in the world—the devouring need of a man for the one woman, the beautiful, inaccessible, wonderful woman who could never again, lost or won, be put out of his life. David was perhaps not so much humble as unanalytical; he never had felt himself a particularly desirable husband, although at one time, studying Sylvia's future prospects with his characteristic interest and concern, he had been obliged to recognize the fact that her marriage to him would be an extremely suitable thing.

Now he felt that nothing about him was suitable or desirable. No woman could possibly contemplate marriage with him with any enthusiasm; least of all this beautiful woman of twenty, whose wealth was the smallest of her advantages. David was not a particularly successful painter, past thirty, leading the quietest and least thrilling of lives. It was a part of the conscientiousness that these brilliant Flemings and their exactions had bred in him, that he felt himself in honour bound now not to complicate Gabrielle's problems by any hint of his own personal hopes or fears. She needed him too much, in the management of her own and Tom's business, for that. Self-consciousness between them would have been a fresh trial for her, just emerging from too many changes and sorrows.

Wastewater was all hers now, for Tom did not care to live there, even if it had been the wisest thing in the world for him to do. He had deeded it all to her, and she and Rucker had held a casual correspondence regarding the new barns and John's house, and the prospect of a new Wastewater. It must be "rambly and irregular," Gabrielle had stipulated, "perhaps a little like one of those French farmhouses of creamy white brick with the red roofs." It must have "one long nice room, with an open fireplace at the end, where supper or breakfast could be brought in if it was snowing." And she "would love a hall with glass doors and fanlights at the front and back, so that when you stood at the front door on a hot summer day you could see wallflowers and gillies and things all growing in the back garden, right straight through the house."

Rucker, who did a good deal of this sort of thing, had been immensely interested; indeed, he and his wife and the tiny baby were established at Keyport with David now, so that his summer holidays and week-ends might be spent in the neighbourhood. He had submitted certain plans to Gabrielle in Los Angeles, and Gabrielle had wired her approval from Mexico City; now they were to commence building, but with some agitation on the part of Rucker, who made worried references to "moving the hollies," and "saving those copper beeches and maples on the north front."

"Mr. Rucker got those red tiles, John," David said to-day to the foreman, "and they come fourteen inches square. So just give me an idea in a day or two how large that terrace is."

"There's Mr. Rucker now," Etta said, disconsolately, as a Ford came in the service gate, and turned toward the barns. "No, it isn't," she added, peering.

They all looked in that direction as the car stopped, and a young woman jumped out, and dismissed it, and came toward them.

CHAPTER XXI

SHE was tall, and wearing a dark blue suit under a belted brown coat, a loose rich sable-skin about her shoulders. A blue hat, bright with cornflowers was pressed down over her sunny hair.

David's heart gave a great plunge, raced, stopped short, and began to plunge again. It was really Gabrielle.

But she was so beautiful, she was so graceful and swift and young and radiant, as she came toward them, that David was incapable of speech, bereft of all emotion except the overpowering realization of what she meant to him.

The day became incredibly glorious, became spring indeed, when she put both her warm hands in his, and held him at arm's-length, and looked at him, and then at the reconstruction, and the young green about her, with a great sigh of relief and joy that was half a sob.

Perhaps her own emotions were also unexpectedly overwhelming, for even while she laughed and greeted Etta and John and the dog with quite her usual gaiety, David noticed an occasional break in her eager voice and a film of tears in her shining eyes.

"Oh, David—Wastewater again!" she said. "If you knew—if you knew how hungry I've been for the old place! Oh, David—what a wonderful barn—but isn't it *delicious*—and that's your house, Etta, and it looks so comfortable—like a little English inn—and the arch—David, it's all so wonderful! Oh, do tell me everything, everyone! I'm so glad to get home——"

He had known that he loved her, but David had never dreamed that he could love her like this. To see her take off the heavy brown coat and consign it and the fur to Etta, and to have her straighten her little white frills at throat and wrists of the trim little dark blue suit, in just her old, busy way, and to have her fairly dance along at his side, excitedly inspecting all that had happened and that was to happen, was to be transported—for David—straight into a country of no laws and no precedents. Gay, sweet and blue-eyed and husky of voice; Gay, slender and eager and responsive; Gay, home again.

"But let me tell Etta and John my news before we leave them," she had said, in the first rush of greetings. "Who do you think has just gotten married?"

"Not you, Miss Gabrielle, although goodness knows you look happy enough for anything," Etta had said, cheered in spite of her determined efforts to resist.

"Not I—do you hear her, David! No, I'm to be next," Gabrielle had answered, with a gaiety that stabbed David to the heart. "No, but Miss Sylvia and Mr. Tom were married a month ago, before we ever left San Francisco," she added, joyously.

"Good grief!" Etta said, in a hushed voice. David only fixed astonished and suddenly enlightened eyes upon the girl's face.

"Married in San Francisco," Gabrielle repeated, nodding triumphantly. "You're not one bit more surprised than I am! Well, yes, for I did suspect it," she added, more moderately. "I knew that they were falling in love with each other, of course. But I never dreamed that they had *done* it until we were three days out! Then Sylvia wouldn't let me wireless, because she said everybody on the boat would know. So we went on to Panama, and then she and Tom wanted to go on farther, and Margret and I wanted to come home—and here I am!"

Etta was by this time sufficiently recovered from her stupefaction to ask for further details, and David, watching Gabrielle as she half laughingly and half seriously gave them, had time to appreciate how the girl had grown to womanhood in this time of absence. With a sort of negligent readiness, and yet with a certain dignity, too, she satisfied the eager questions of the older man and woman, all the while reserving, he could see, the more intimate narrative for his ears alone.

They were not to be alone immediately, however, for Etta and John accompanied them through the barns, Etta harping plaintively upon the quality of the buildings now in course of erection in the Crowchester Manor Estates.

"But you won't want a big house here, all by yourself. Them Crowchester houses are handsomer than any Mr. Rucker ever showed me," Etta said.

"I had breakfast with Mrs. Rucker. Isn't she always the nicest person?" Gabrielle was thereby reminded to tell him. "And what a ducky baby. We got in to New York yesterday morning, you know, and came up on the night train. I went straight to your Keyport house, hoping to find you, but you'd just gone. I left all my things there, and of course I'm to stay there to-night."

"You won't be going away again, Miss Gabrielle?" John asked.

"Why, that depends——" She looked at David in a little confusion, looked back into the sweet open spaces of the barn. "I may go to England——" she began.

"Looks like you might be surprising us, too, one of these days!" Etta said, shrewd and curious.

David glanced quickly at the girl; she was walking beside Etta.

"You wouldn't want me to be an old maid, Etta?" she asked, once more with that new, poised manner.

"No, ma'am!" Etta said, positively. "We certainly need some new life about the place. I's saying to John a few days ago I hope both the girls'd get married."

"Well," Gabrielle said, with a somewhat dreamy expression in her blue eyes, "then let's hope we will." And David, although she immediately changed the subject by speaking of the kitchen yard of the new house, was certain that he saw the colour creep up under her clear skin, and the hint of a mysterious smile.

"Don't shock us with too many surprises in one morning, Gabrielle," he warned her, trying to smile naturally.

"Ah, no, I shall save something and let things appear by degrees!" she answered, cheerfully. "Brick wall here, David?"

"Brick wall here, joining the stable wall in a long line, with the poplars back of it," he agreed, with a suddenly cold, heavy heart. "Jim has managed to save the poplars, you see. And all the kitchen matters will be reached through a little round-topped gate in the wall about here."

"And the dining-room windows looking out here where all the lilacs are?"

"With a sort of portico—an open court, tiled, here on the north front—where it will be cool in the afternoons."

"David, it's so much more wonderful than I dreamed it would be! Imagine a new Wastewater, all sunshine and happiness, instead of that terrible old barrack full of jealousy and secrets and plots! Isn't it like a fairy tale? To think that life can be so sweet——"

"Gay, there's no sweetness that you don't deserve," David said, suddenly, as they followed the others. "After that defrauded childhood, and all the shocks and sorrows you had when you first came home two years ago, nothing could be too much!"

"I feel now," the girl answered, seriously, "as if, on that last night of fire and horror and bewilderment, the whole dreadful thing had been burned out—cauterized, made clean once and for all, and that now we start with a new order!"

"I don't know as there's a prettier place anywhere than Browns'," said Etta's mildly complaining voice. "If she has one window she has a hundred——"

"Etta!" Gabrielle said, briskly, paying no attention, "have you some chops? Mr. David and I are going to have our lunch down on the shore. And will you make us some coffee, Etta, and give us matches and butter and all the rest of it? It's half-past eleven now, and we'll want to start about one.—Now, show me everything, David, and tell me ten thousand things about everything!"

"John, have you those blue-prints?" David, out of whose sky the sun had dropped leaving everything dark and gray, asked the foreman.

"The plans for the house that looks sorter slumped down, with the roof two stories deep?" John asked, as one anxious to coöperate intelligently.

"Certainly! The only ones we have," David answered, impatiently. Gabrielle bent suddenly down over the dog, but when she and David were strolling away through the perfumed warmth and the sweet young green of the garden, she asked, with her old wide-eyed, delighted smile:

"John and Etta don't approve of Mr. Rucker's plans?"

But David's heart was too sick for laughter.

"You really may be following Sylvia's example one of these days, Gabrielle?"

Instantly the clear warm skin was flooded with colour and an oddly troubled look came into her beautiful eyes.

"Well, I suppose so——"

David spoke smilingly, but with rather a dry mouth.

"You got over—you forgot—the man of whom you told me more than two years ago?"

"No," she answered, briefly.

"You mean that you have seen him again?"

"Oh, yes!"

"Ah," David said, blindly trying to say something that should avert her too-close scrutiny, "I see."

He felt his heart leaden. It was with sort of physical difficulty that he guided her through the new Wastewater that was yet in so many ways the old.

So much was his anyway, he told himself. This day of her dear companionship, this luncheon on the rocks, this monopoly of her husky and wonderful voice, her earnest, quick glances, her laughter, were his for a little while. Even over the utter desolation of his spirit, he was won to an exquisite and yet agonizing happiness by this nearness of all her sweetness and charm again.

First, she must see the plans. They sat down upon a pile of clear lumber in the trembling green shade of overhanging maple branches, and pegged the fluttering blue sheets with bits of rock, and bent over them.

And now, as she eagerly identified the placing of casement windows and bricked terraces, she was so close that David got the actual flowery fragrance of her, and her warm, satin-smooth hand occasionally touched his. She had laid aside her big coat, and looked a little less impressive in the plain little suit and delicate white frills, and somehow all the more her own wonderful self, the eager, busy, interested little Gay of years ago.

"David, see here, dear——" She added the little word so unconsciously, he thought, with a pang! "See here, dear, these two rooms upstairs will be almost empty—this with a north light, in case my smart cousin should want to do some painting."

"Do you mean that you and Tom and Sylvia really plan to make your home here?" David asked.

"As for Tom, I can't say—he and Sylvia will surely spend their summers here. But this will always be home, headquarters, for me," Gay said. And she laid her beautiful hand upon the blue-prints almost with a caress. "My little house!" she said, lovingly, "with its chimney seats and casement windows—and we must have roses and hollyhocks jammed up against them in summer, and with its darling white woodwork and pink and blue papers, and with its little breakfast room looking over the sea——"

"Not so little," David warned her, "you will have a dozen rooms, you know, besides the servants' quarters in that high roof that John dislikes so heartily."

"Little beside all those high brick walls and wings and windows of the old Wastewater," she countered. "Poor unhappy Wastewater!" she said more than once, as they walked slowly about, in the increasing warmth of the day. "*Sic semper tyrannis!*" And she touched the neatly ranked bricks with a gentle hand. "We could build ten houses, couldn't we?"

"You will have enough bricks there to do everything you ever want to—walls, bath-houses, paths, new buildings," David assured her.

Gabrielle had picked a plume of purple lilac; she slowly twirled it and sniffed it as they walked. The late morning was so still that they could hear an occasional distant cock-crow. Silence, fragrance, and the sweetness of expanding life lay upon the world like a spell.

"Do you see that angle of land there," the girl asked, presently, when with their lunch basket they were going toward the shore, "there, just beyond the spit, with its own little curve of bay? That never seemed quite to belong to the rest of the place."

"You could sell it," David suggested, catching her firm hand in his as she cautiously followed him down the rocky path.

"Oh, no! I don't mean that. But you see what a cunning little homestead it would make all by itself," Gabrielle said, making her way to their old favourite spot and beginning the preparations for a little driftwood fire. "It has good trees, and that line of silver birches, and it has dogwoods. I was wondering if Tom and Sylvia wouldn't like a house there all their own—no responsibility, a place they could shut up and leave when they wanted to wander."

"Then they are not going to live with her," David thought, with his heart sinking again.

She had been talking about them in a desultory fashion all morning, but when the coffee was boiling, and the buns toasted, and the chops dripping and sizzling, she settled herself back comfortably against the rocks, and gave him the story consecutively.

"Sylvia is a changed person in lots of ways," said Gay, with relish. "And in other ways she is exactly what she always was and always will be. She has the—you take cream, David?—she has the family pride. Only it takes a rather nice form with her, the form of self-respect. Sylvia must—she simply *must* respect herself. And after poor Aunt Flora died, what with having lost her fortune and then having to bear what she considered—and what really was!—a terrible blow to her pride, poor Sylvia really suffered terribly. She kept trying to analyse how she felt, and convince me about it, and I know that's what made her ill. She couldn't quite get used to not being—what shall I call it?—admirable, superb, superior—that was always my old word for her.

"She talked about college courses, and I think she must have written the Dean about it, but perhaps she wasn't much encouraged. After all, Sylvia's only twenty-two, and perhaps professors have to be a little older.

"So we drifted down to southern California, Sylvia in mourning, of course, and not taking any interest in anything, and Tom worse. But when we got to La Crescenta suddenly we all felt better. Tom began to eat and sleep; Sylvia and I took long walks; we even went in to Los Angeles to concerts.

"And in no time she found that she could still be—superior, with Tom. He began to admire her tremendously—he thought she knew everything! But never in my life have I seen Sylvia so—well, so gentle with anybody as she was with Tom! She began to make much of what *he* knew—regularly draw him out; he speaks very good Spanish you know, and you can use Spanish a good deal there. Sylvia talked to him about boats, navigation, places he had been and we hadn't, and all the time"—and Gabrielle's eyes danced—"all the time it was just as if she was afraid of breaking the spell she had put on herself—if you know what I mean, David?"

"I think I do."

"Meanwhile," the girl resumed, with keen enjoyment, "Tom was changing, too. He's gotten—*finer*, in a funny sort of way. His voice has grown finer, and he—he just stares at Sylvia whatever she does, and smiles at whatever she says, and he is like a lion on a string!"

Her joyous laugh was infectious, and David laughed in spite of himself.

"About—this is April. About Christmas time," Gay resumed, "I began to notice it. Tom was funny and humble and quiet with Sylvia, and Sylvia was bent upon making much of Tom; she'd quote him—I don't know whether I can convey this to you—but she'd say to me so seriously, 'Tom says the rain isn't over. Tom doesn't like Doctor Madison; he thinks his manner with us is a little too assured', that sort of thing," Gabrielle explained, frowning faintly despite her smile, in her eagerness to make him understand her.

"Well, we went to San Francisco, and there I really did have the best time I ever had in my life!" Gabrielle said. "The Montallen girls were there, with their brother, and we had some wonderful parties—we went through Chinatown, and out to the beach, and up the mountain, and everywhere. And I suppose I hadn't been noticing Sylvia very closely, because, after the Montallens left——"

"Oh, they left, did they?" David, interested in the brother, asked.

"Yes, they came straight home. It's the Montallens," Gabrielle said, parenthetically, "that want me to go abroad with them in June."

"I see. Will the brother go?"

"Oh, I think so."

"I see. But go on—about Sylvia."

"Well, when they left Sylvia suddenly seemed so odd. She cried a good deal, and she was quite cranky—not a bit like herself. By this time we were all getting ready for the Panama trip. Margret thought that perhaps it was young Bart Montallen, who is a perfectly stunning fellow—in diplomacy——" Gabrielle elaborated.

"I remember him," David said, briefly.

"But one day Sylvia broke down and cried for an hour," Gabrielle said. "It was the day before we sailed, and we were at the

Fairmont. It almost drove me wild—it had been a real responsibility, anyway," the girl interrupted herself to remind him. "When we left here I was worried sick about Tom, we were all blue and dazed—and really I'd had it all on my mind until I got a little nervous.

"I coaxed Sylvia and petted her, and finally she told me that he had asked her to marry him—and there I made my first mistake," Gay added, widening her eyes so innocently at David that he laughed aloud. "I said—trying to be sympathetic, you know—'And of course, you wouldn't!' and she got rather red and looked straight at me and said, 'Why shouldn't I?' I said, rather feebly, 'Well, I didn't know you cared about him,' and she said, 'I don't. But I consider him in every way one of the finest men I ever knew!' Of course I said I did, too.

"Then she began to cry again, and said that she was entirely alone in the world—all that," Gay resumed, "and she said that any woman would be proud to marry Tom, but that she was afraid everyone would think she was influenced by the thought of his money."

"And what did you say to that?" David asked, diverted.

Gabrielle gave him her gravely wise look, and the beautiful face, flushed with the warmth of the day and shaded by the blue hat, was so near that David lost the thread of her words for a few seconds, in sheer marvelling at her beauty.

"I said I did not think that that should be a consideration," she answered. "I said that no one had thought that of *you*, when you were engaged to her," she added, after a moment, and with a sudden smile.

David, who was leaning back against a rock and had his arms folded, flushed a little in his turn.

"I don't think that was ever, really, an engagement," he offered.

And remembering suddenly that he had terminated what had been a rather definite understanding with Sylvia, simply that he might offer Gabrielle his name and his protection, he had an instant of being hardly able to believe himself the same man.

"So then we all left the next morning. That was fun!" the girl went on. "The ship was delightful, and nobody was sick, and it was a January day as warm and green as June—and Tom was just wild with high spirits; I never saw him so gay! And well he might be, for he and Sylvia had been married that morning.

"Sylvia, on the other hand, acted very queerly; cried a good deal—stuck close to me and seemed cross. Once when I asked her if it was Tom that was worrying her, she said savagely 'No,' that she wished she had never seen Tom Fleming, and that he had wrecked her happiness for life. And she went back to Aunt Flora's old talk,"

220

Gabrielle added, seriously, "about the curse on the Flemings, and all that.

"She would hardly speak to Tom—and I can tell you, David," the girl interrupted herself again to say, "I didn't anticipate a particularly pleasant trip to Panama. Tom seemed queer, too, and Margret told me that she thought the whole thing was a mistake.

"I remembered afterward that Sylvia talked a good deal about the annulment of marriages on those first few days. She kept telling me that for a woman an annulment had no value, because any 'honourable' woman would feel herself just as much bound after it as before, but it would at least set the man free. That was two days after we sailed, and it was that very night that I was playing cribbage with the old captain—who was a perfect old Scottish darling!—and afterward went up on the bridge with him. And when I was slipping down to my room, knowing that Margret would be out of her senses with anxiety, and Sylvia hunting for me perhaps, I passed a man and a woman at the rail.

"It was midnight, and there was no moon, but as I went by I heard the man's voice, and it was Tom's. And then I saw that the woman was Sylvia, and that she was crying. Tom was sort of growling—you know how he talks when he is a little angry and a little ill at ease—and I heard Sylvia say the word 'annulment.' 'I can't stand it, Tom, it was all a silly mistake!' she said. 'You can't talk like that, Sylvia,' Tom said, in a sort of shocked voice.

"Suddenly the whole thing came to me," Gabrielle said, with all a child's wondering, delighted stare fixed upon David, "and I went straight up to them and put my arm about them from behind and said, 'Tell me about it, I *know* you're married!'

"Of course, I was delighted—much more so than you can believe—I didn't have to pretend *that*! Because I had had a sort of fear that once they both got back to their natural surroundings Sylvia would get proud and collegy—you know what I mean?—again," the girl went on, "and that Tom would begin to feel awkward and nothing would come of their affair. So I made a great fuss—cried, really, I was so excited! And just then Margret came along the deck, afraid I'd gone overboard or something, and we told her—and *she* laughed and cried. And Sylvia began to seem more normal, especially when we went to our cabin, and I said what a dear old fellow Tom was, and how he adored her. She began to smile—the way she does, you know, when she really doesn't want to smile—and began to talk pityingly about a very pretty English girl on board who had taken an immense fancy to him.

"Well, after *that*," and Gay's laugh was delicious to hear, "you should have seen Sylvia! She—*glowed*! I never saw her so handsome, and so happy, and so—well, you know her!—so superb. She was *all* the proud wife. Everything Tom did was mysteriously perfect, and everything he said she listened to with as much attention as if it were his dying words. She quoted him, she fenced herself off with him with rugs and deck chairs and books, and read to him; they walked round and round the deck together.

"It seems as if Sylvia must be a little superior on some count or other to be happy!" Gay commented, affectionately and amusedly. "Now she's infinitely happy. She is Mrs. Tom Fleming, and she has a handsome, rich husband who adores her, and presently they'll have the most superior children—and believe me," the girl finished, laughing, "Sylvia will feel that just what those children do is the astonishing thing; if any other child is taller, she'll say it is weedy and has outgrown its strength, and if any child is smarter she'll say it is unpleasantly precocious!"

"So you got to Panama——?" David prompted after a silence devoted to smiling musing, and the warmth and sweetness of the day, and the delicate silver whisper of the sea among the rocks.

"So we got to Panama, and by this time Mr. and Mrs. Tom Fleming only wanted to be left alone," Gay resumed, raising her blue eyes to smile at him. "So there were great debates. They didn't want to wire you, because such a wire is very apt to be noticed, and they didn't quite want to come home; in fact, they planned this Southern trip as a sort of supplementary honeymoon. So, as there was a charming navy woman, a Mrs. Stephens, coming all the way up, I was delighted to put myself and Margret in her care. And that's all."

She had packed the remains of their meal into the little basket in the old quick, capable way that David so well remembered, and now she descended to a certain little pool among the rocks, and washed her hands, pushing the frills of her cuffs back from her slender wrists as she did so, and waving her hands in the air to dry them.

"You've told me everything—except your own affair, Gabrielle," David presently prompted, when they were making their way up the cliff path to the garden.

"My—my own affair?" Perhaps she had not understood, for although she turned scarlet suddenly, she made no further admission.

"There is—somebody, you told me once?" David prompted her.

"Oh, yes!" She dismissed it with a shrug. "*That*," she said, with a thoughtful note in her voice.

She added no more at the time. The enchanted hours of the day moved to three o'clock. But when David, knowing her to be tired from the long trip and probably confused with all the changes and impressions, suggested their return to Keyport, she showed a reluctance as definite as his own.

She had given him, on this spring day of lingering lights and soft fragrance, such a revelation of her own sweetness, her own personality, as made all his other recollections of her seem pale and dim. Every turn of her head, every movement, every direct look from her star-sapphire eyes, had deepened the old impression that there was nobody quite like her in the world.

Nobody so gracious, so quietly joyous, nobody else at once so youthful and so wise. A hundred times, by some quality of being simply and eagerly happy just in the springtime, and the garden, and his company, she reminded him of the long-ago little girl Gabrielle, and yet, at twenty, David thought her already a woman.

They talked of the old Wastewater, as they planned and went to and fro busied with problems of the proportions and the placing of the new. Of the family, with its passions and hates, its jealousies and weaknesses.

"The new house," Gabrielle said, whimsically, "will stand as much for the new order as the old one did for the stupidities and affectations of the old. It's all to be simple, no affectations, no great big gloomy basement regions for the servants—they'll have their section as comfortable, as sunshiny as the other. There'll be open fires instead of the old hideous grates, and rugs and clean floors instead of the old dirty, hard-and-fast carpets, and bathrooms full of tiles and sunshine, and sleeping porches instead of all that horrible rep curtaining—and there'll be——"

Her voice lowered. "There'll be people loving each other," she said. "After all, isn't that the answer to the whole problem? Women being loyal and generous, instead of jealous and watching all the time, men thinking of other people's happiness, instead of having themselves painted in picturesque attitudes."

She finished laughing, but her face was presently serious again. They were idly wandering through the ruins of the garden now, Gabrielle a little flushed and tumbled from the efforts of raising a bent rose bush, or straightening, with a little air of anxiety and concentration that David thought somehow touchingly mother-like, a sheaf of timidly budded whips that would some day be sweet with white syringa bloom.

She stopped at the old sundial and cleared the fallen packed damp leaves from its face with a stick, and busied herself so earnestly about it that David thought her more like an adorable child, and more like a responsible little housewife, than ever. He thought of the wife she would make some man some day, and felt suddenly that he must get away—out of the country—anywhere!—before that time came.

"You can't tell me your plans yet, Gabrielle dear?" he said, with a rather dry throat, when they were beside the dial.

The girl's colour deepened a little under the creamy skin, and for a moment she did not answer. Then she said with a look straight into his eyes:

"I could tell you—as far as they have gone."

"Not unless you want to," David answered, from the other side of the dial, which he gripped with fingers that were suddenly shaking.

"The man of whom I spoke to you, so long ago," Gabrielle said, presently, "I saw again—this spring."

"I see," David said, with a nod, as she paused. "He did not marry the other woman, then?"

"What other woman?" the girl demanded, amazed.

"I thought you said that he had cared for another woman?"

"Ah——? Ah, yes, so he had. No, he didn't marry her. He is—quite free," said Gabrielle, working busily.

"You're very sure you care for him, dear?" David said, already relegated, in his own mind, to the sphere of the advisory, loving older brother.

"Yes," she said, with another upraised look. "I am sure. I have never felt for anybody else what I do for him, and I know now I never shall. When I first saw him—more than two years ago——"

"You saw him first then?"

"Well, I had seen him as a child. But after I got home from Paris I saw him again," the girl offered, lucidly.

"I see." She was so radiant, she was so wonderful! If he should be some utter good-for-naught, David thought——

"Then I did not see him, except occasionally," Gabrielle resumed. "And when I did not see him, then I knew that logically, actually, he was everything I could love; a gentleman, kind, wise, admirable in every way."

"Rich?" David asked, in a silence, and with a faint frown.

"No. Not—exactly poor, either."

"But does he know that you are rich, Gabrielle?"

"I don't think it makes any difference to him," the girl said, thoughtfully, after a moment.

"I don't suppose, of course, that it would!" David agreed, immediately.

"No. So that when I was away from him, I had time to think it out logically and dispassionately, and I knew he was—the one," the girl resumed, "and when I saw him—whenever we were together, although I couldn't think logically, or indeed think at all," she said, laughing, and flushed, and meeting his eyes with a sort of defiant courage, "I knew, from the way I felt, that there never could be, and never would be, any one else!"

"I see, of course," David said, slowly.

"Both ways," Gabrielle went on, smiling a little anxiously, "I feel safe. When I'm not with him I can reason about it, I can look forward to all the years, thinking of myself as older, as the mother of children," the girl went on seriously, her voice lowered to the essence of itself, her eyes upon the softly heaving and shining sea, "thinking of the books, the tramps, the friendships we will share. There is no moment of life that he will not make wonderful to me, poverty, change, sorrow, travel—everything," she finished, looking up smiling, yet with the glitter of tears in her beautiful eyes.

"I——" David cleared his throat—"I am so glad you can tell me, Gay," he said, a little gruffly.

"I love to tell you!" the girl said, with an illuminated look.

"It—is settled, Gabrielle?"

"No. Not exactly. That is——" She coloured violently, laughed, and grew suddenly pale. "No, it's not settled," she answered, confusedly.

"You can't tell me anything more?" David asked, after a pause.

"Not—now, very well. At least, I think I can soon," Gay said, laughing and flushed, yet oddly near, he could see, to tears, too. "I know that he—cares for me," she added, after another brief silence.

"He has told you?"

"Well, no. Or yes, he has, too—in a way. But all that——" she broke off, appealingly.

"Yes, I know," David reassured her. "You shall tell me when you're ready."

"David, I suppose we should be going back," the girl said, reluctantly. But she did not change her comfortable position, resting against the dial, and looking alternately at its blackened old stone surface and across the shining sea.

"Presently. I hate to end—to-day," David answered, simply.

"So do I. Hasn't it been a wonderful day? Doesn't it seem like the beginning of heavenly times?"

225

"One of the happiest of my life," David said, trying to lighten the words with his old friendly smile, and failing.

Gabrielle was silent, and in the stillness all the sweet sounds of a spring afternoon made themselves heard: the lisp of the sea, the chirp of little birds flying low in short curving flights among the budding shrubs, a banging door in the farmhouse and the distant sound of voices as the workmen put up their tools and started their motor engines.

The sun was sending long slanting rays down across the torn earth, and the old garden, and the piled bricks. John's and Etta's house, joined by the simple curve of the arch to the long, low roofs of the barn, looked everything that was homelike and comfortable in the sinking glow.

"I see summer suppers here, in the court," Gabrielle said, presently, in a low voice, as if half to herself. "Guest rooms all fresh and airy, Sylvia's children, and my children, drawing others here for picnics on the shore, white dresses, and the harvest moon coming up there across the sea, as we have seen it rise so many hundreds of times! I don't know which will be most wonderful, David: the long summers with the hollyhocks and the twilights, or the winters with big fires and snow and company coming in, all cold and laughing.

"I do think of going abroad," she added, as for sheer pain David was silent. "But I find myself thinking most often of getting home again, with all the trunks and excitement, to settle again in Waste-water!"

"You really are going abroad, Gabrielle?" David asked. And to himself he added, "Honeymoon."

"Why, I don't know. To-night I don't feel as if I ever wanted to go outside these gates again; I feel as if I wanted to stay right here, watching them put every brick into place! But—*you* would like to go abroad again some day, wouldn't you, David?"

"Oh, I? Yes, but that's different," the man answered, bringing himself into the conversation with a little self-consciousness. "Yes," David said, slowly, frowning into space with narrowed eyes, "I think I may go, one of these days. I would like to do some painting in Florence."

Another silence, so exquisitely painful, so poignantly sweet, that David felt he might stand so for ever, watching her, leaning in all her beauty and her fragrant youth against the grim old dial, looking sometimes at him, and sometimes off to sea, with her glorious and thoughtful eyes.

"David, I got your message," she said, suddenly, in a voice oddly

226

compounded of amusement and daring and a sort of fear.

"I'm glad," David answered, mechanically. And then, rousing himself, he added in surprise, "What message?"

"On the little draught of the house plans," Gabrielle answered, serenely.

"Which plans were those, dear? The ones Jim sent to San Francisco?"

"He sent them to San Francisco too late, but they sent them on and we got them in Panama."

"Did I send a message with them?" David asked, not remembering it.

"Scribbled on the margin of one of them," Gabrielle nodded.

"A message—to *you*?" David said, in surprise.

"Well, I read it so." The girl fell silent, and a robin with a warmly stained breast, and a cocked head, hopped nearer and nearer to them.

"I don't remember," David admitted, after thought. It was obvious that she wanted him to remember it, but, stupidly enough, he seemed to have no recollection of it whatever.

"I think it must really have been to Jim Rucker," Gabrielle added, innocently. "It began 'Dear Jim.'"

The blood came to David's face and he laughed confusedly.

"I—did I scribble something to Jim on the margin? I remember that we sent the plans back and forth a good deal," he said, in a sort of helpless appeal.

"I'll show it to you," Gabrielle answered, suddenly. She put her hand into her pocket and brought out a curled slip of paper that had been cut from the stiff oiled sheet of an architect's plans. "Here, David," she invited him. "Read it with me."

And she flattened it upon the old dial and glanced at him over her shoulder.

David, hardly knowing what he did, let his eyes fall upon the pencilled words. He read:

DEAR JIM:

No letter, but a message about her in one from
Sylvia. Tell Mary I'm sorry I cut her dinner party!

It was signed with David's own square, firm, unmistakable "D."

"When I read that," said Gabrielle, looking up with her face close to his, as he leaned at her shoulder, "I knew that the man I loved, loved me. And after that I couldn't get home fast enough."

"Gabrielle," David said, trembling, and now she was in his arms. "Is it really so, dear? Dearest and loveliest of women, do you mean what you say?—Do you know what you are doing? I'm not the brilliant sort of man that you might marry, dear—I'll never be rich, perhaps I'll never be successful——"

"Ah, David," the girl answered, facing him now, with both hands upon his shoulders, as he held her with his arms lightly linked about her, "do let's not have any more misunderstandings and silences and half-said things at Wastewater? Tell me that you love me——"

* * * *

There was a milky spring twilight in the old garden now; the sea had mysteriously blended itself with the sky, and a mild great moon was rising before the last of the sun's radiance had fairly faded from the west. As the enervating warmth of the day died, delicious odours began to creep abroad in the dusk, and the plum tree that had burst prematurely into bloom shone like a great pale bouquet against the gathering shadows.

There were smells of grass and earth, the sweet breathing of a world wearied after the unwonted hours of sunshine; there was the clean smell of new paint from the regions back of the farmhouse and barn. The birds were still now, and the very sea seemed hushed.

And to both David and Gabrielle, as they dreamed of the days to come, the golden days of responsibilities and joys unthinkable now, it seemed that no hour would eclipse this hour, when they two, children of the old place, found love among its ruins, and planned there for a better future.

All the terrors, all the whispers, voices, fears, and hates, all the secrets and conspiracies that had shadowed Wastewater in its old and arrogant days were gone. Roger with his vanity and arrogance was gone, Lily with her tears, Cecily frightened and saddened in her youth, Flora with her dark repressions and thwarted love.

The old Sylvia was gone, too, and in her academically complacent place was the much more human Mrs. Tom Fleming. And David was gone; never again would he be only the dreamy, detached painter, the amused older brother and audience for the younger folk, the philosopher who looked at love dispassionately. David was a man, now, and the thought of having this woman for his wife, the thought of the future, when they two would make a home together, for ever and for ever, as long as life should last, made him feel as shaken, as awkward, as humble and ignorant as the boy he had never really been.

All gone. But there remained, steadfast, gray-eyed, sometimes all a mother, sometimes all a child, always simple, direct, loving, anxious for peace and harmony, this tawny-headed waif who had drifted in among the black Flemings so mysteriously, who had flourished upon neglect and injustice, who had borne sorrow and shame courageously and unfalteringly, and who was now, of them all, left to be mistress here, to begin the new history and the new line.

"David, we will go to Florence together, in the fall, if we can tear ourselves away from our new house, and you shall copy little Dizianis and Guardis!"

"Ah, Gabrielle, don't, my dear. I can't—I can't believe it. It seems too much."

"But we'll come back for a housewarming at Christmas time, David, and not miss one instant of the spring!"

"Yes, my darling," David said.

"And we'll have days in the city, David, buying towels and muffin rings," the girl said, rejoicingly. "And then you'll have an exhibition in April, and won't you be proud of your nice furry wife, walking about among the pictures and listening to what people say!"

"I can hardly be prouder of her than I have always been, Gay."

Silence. Her right hand was upon his shoulder, and his arm was strong and warm about her. David had only to bend his head to kiss the crown of her tawny, uncovered hair; the whole gracious, fragrant woman was in his arms. Their left hands, clasped, rested upon the dial.

So resting, they obscured the blackened old face that had serenely marked the hours under thin Scotch suns, under more than a hundred passionate years of the hotter suns of the New World. They hid the old legend:

Turn, Flemynge, spin agayne,
The crossit line's the kenter skein.